# THE
# ALBORAN
# CODEX

## JC RYAN

# THE
# ALBORAN
# CODEX

JC RYAN

YUCI
BOOKS

## By JC Ryan

Carter Devereux Mystery Thriller Series

*Nothing New Under The Sun*
*The Wolves Of Freydis*
*The Alboran Codex*
*The Nabatean Secret*
*The Labyrinth of Minos*

Vinci Books

vinci-books.com

Published by Vinci Books Ltd in 2025

1

Copyright © JC Ryan 2016

The author has asserted their moral right to be identified as the author of this work in accordance with the Copyright, Designs and Patents Act 1988. This work is a work of fiction. Names, characters, places and incidents are the product of the author's imagination or are used fictitiously. Any resemblance to actual persons, living or dead, places and incidents is entirely coincidental.

All rights reserved. No part of this publication may be copied, reproduced, distributed, stored in any retrieval system, or transmitted in any form or by any means, including photocopying, recording, or other electronic or mechanical methods, nor used as a source for any form of machine learning including AI datasets, without the prior written permission of the publisher.

The publisher and the author have made every effort to obtain permissions for any third party material used in this book and to comply with copyright law. Any queries in this respect should be brought to the attention of the publisher and any omissions will be corrected in future editions.

A CIP catalogue record for this book is available from the British Library.

Paperback ISBN: 9781036703295

Printed and bound in Great Britain by Clays Ltd, Elcograf S.p.A.

# Prologue

## 1897 BC—Twelve mighty princes

It was a time to celebrate. Today was Isaac's weaning, her firstborn's second birthday. He had survived the fragile stage of infancy and could now eat solid food rather than being breastfed. He would live a long and healthy life. But Sarah was quiet. She heard the music, saw the people eating, drinking, and laughing, but her insides were steaming — and had been for a long time.

*Oh, how I rue the day I gave that slave woman to Abraham to produce an offspring for him. I was seventy-five and Abraham was eighty-five — how was I to know it was even possible to bear my own child at ninety? And now look at this. My slave is insolent, and her son thinks he is the heir. It must be Hagar who's putting him up to that.*

She was startled out of her reverie by Isaac's wailing. Ishmael was dancing around the little boy, mocking and scaring him with a knife. *This is the final straw. This slave woman and her son must go. Now! Both of them. I've had enough of their impudence.*

She moved to pick up the terrified Isaac and place him on her hip, then turned and shouted at Ishmael, "You are fourteen years old. You should know better than to scare a little two-year-old. Leave Isaac alone. I never want to see you near him again! *Ever*."

Isaac's jeering smile disappeared from his face. He turned and with sagging shoulders walked away to find Hagar.

"This has to end today," Sarah said to herself. "God told Abraham to change my name from Sarai to Sarah? Abraham told me God said, *'As for Sarai your wife, you are no longer to call her Sarai; her name will be Sarah. I will bless her and she will give you a son by her. I will bless her; she will be the mother of nations; kings of peoples will come from her.'"* (Genesis 17:15-16)

Abraham saw the thundercloud on Sarah's face where she stood with Isaac on her hip. He excused himself from the men and walked over to her. "Sarah, what is wrong? This is a time to be happy and to be celebrating. Why the anger on your face?"

"When we were living at the well of Beer-lahai-roi, Hagar absconded, but then she came back. I don't know why she came back, but it would have been better if she had just stayed away. She is trouble and nothing but since she gave you that child," Sarah said.

"You know why she came back, Sarah. God told her to do so. She went away because you were treating her harshly."

Sarah's eyes were blistering when she answered, "Yes, that may be so, but look at it now. She despises me, and Ishmael is incessantly insulting and scaring Isaac. I've had enough," Sarah hissed. "Get rid of that slave woman and her son, for that woman's son will never share in the inheritance with my son Isaac." (Genesis 21:10)

"Sarah! I can never do that. Ishmael is my son. I can't send them away."

"God's promise was made to Isaac, not to Ishmael. Isaac is your only heir, not that slave's son," she snapped.

Abraham knew better than to argue with Sarah. Once she made up her mind, she became an immovable force. "Let's discuss this later," he said and turned away.

Later that afternoon, when the festivities were over and the guests had left, Abraham took a long stroll into the field. He had no idea what to do. Ishmael was his son, his own blood. How could he send him away? He climbed up a hill and watched the sun sinking below the horizon in the west. The desert was silent; it was as if everything in nature stopped and went quiet to watch as the sun slowly disappeared.

Then he heard the voice of God. *"Do not be so distressed about the boy and your slave woman. Listen to whatever Sarah tells you, because it is through Isaac that your offspring will be reckoned. I will make the son of the slave into a nation also because he is your offspring."* (Genesis 21:12)

It was dark when Abraham returned and began preparing. Early the next morning, he called Hagar and Ishmael to his tent.

It was with sadness he said, "Hagar, God spoke to me about you and Ishmael, and you can no longer live with us. You and Ishmael must go away from here and find another place to live."

Hagar was shaken. "How can you do this, Abraham? This is our son. He is *your* firstborn. How can you just cut us off from you? What will become of us? How can you throw your own blood away?"

"Hagar, I have asked God to bless Ishmael and He said to me, '*And as for Ishmael, I have heard you: I will surely bless him;*

*I will make him fruitful and will greatly increase his numbers. He will be the father of twelve mighty princes, and I will make him into a great nation.'"* (Genesis 17:20)

Hagar had tears in her eyes as she looked at Abraham, but she knew this was how it was to be. Nothing would change his mind.

In silence, Abraham took the skin-bags with food and water and set them on her shoulders. He looked to Ishmael and handed him a small wooden box wrapped in skin. "Ishmael, keep this with you always. It contains God's promise to you."

Abraham wiped the tears from his eyes, took a step back, and said, "He who has protected and blessed me will bless and protect you."

Hagar and Ishmael went away into the Desert of Beersheba. They wandered without direction with nowhere to go, and finally the water in the skin-bag was gone. Hagar had squeezed the last few drops onto Ishmael's cracked lips. "My son and I will die in this wilderness."

She was weak and parched when she placed Ishmael in the shade of a bush, walked a bowshot away, sat down, and moaned softly. "I cannot watch the boy die."

*"What is the matter, Hagar?"* (Genesis 21:17)

The voice startled her. "Am I hallucinating?" she whispered to herself.

But then the voice was there again. *"Do not be afraid; God has heard the boy crying as he lies there. Lift the boy up and take him by the hand, for I will make him into a great nation."* (Genesis 21:17)

And then the voice was gone and the desert silence returned.

She was bewildered. *What… who was that?*

Her head cleared as she took a deep breath. Looking

around, she saw what seemed like the rim of a well. *That was not there before. Or was it? Why haven't I seen it?*

She stood and walked to it — it *was* a well. And there was water in it! Then she remembered Abraham's parting words to her and Ishmael.

*"It must have been the angel of God who spoke to me just now,"* she thought.

She cupped her hands and drank, then filled the skin-bag and ran back to her son. Propping his head, she helped him drink. His whimpering stopped, and he looked around.

Hagar spoke softly to Ishmael. "My son, your name means '*God will hear*' and today God has heard me. I am the daughter of the Pharaoh of Egypt. You, Ishmael, are a prince; you are of noble descent. I will get you a wife from the house of the Pharaoh, and you are going to be the father of a great nation. It will be as God has promised to your father, Abraham; twelve mighty princes will you beget."

## 1774 BC—He was gathered to his people

Ishmael's hair and beard were white as snow, his eyes were hazy, his hands were shaking, and his skin bore witness of 137 years' of desert life. His breathing was labored when he spoke to his wife.

"Aisha, my days have been numbered; my time to be gathered to my father, Abraham, and my ancestors has come. You must send a message to my children to come to me without delay." Aisha nodded and left to summon the messengers.

A few days before the full moon, Ishmael's twelve sons, Nebajoth, Hadad, Dumah, Adbeel, Mibsam, Tema, Naphish, Mishma, Jetur, Massa, Kedar, Kedemah, and his daughter, Basemath, also known as Mahalath, who was married to Esau, the son of Isaac, stood around his bed. They were sad. It was obvious that their father had reached the end of his days. (Genesis 25:12-16)

Ishmael's voice was soft and gruff as he spoke.

"My days on the earth have come to an end. God had blessed me as He had promised my father Abraham, your grandfather. God has given me twelve mighty princes and a beautiful princess, Basemath.

"God made His promise to your grandmother, Hagar, before I was born. It was by a fountain of water in the wilderness, on the way to Shur, when God's angel said to her:

*"I will multiply thy seed exceedingly, that it shall not be numbered for multitude. Behold, thou art with child, and shalt bear a son, and shalt call his name Ishmael; because the LORD hath heard thy affliction.* (Genesis 16:10)

*"And he will be a wild man; his hand will be against every man, and every man's hand against him; and he shall dwell in the presence of all his brethren."* (Genesis 16:12)

Ishmael took a deep breath, a sip of water, and continued, "And that is how it was. I am Ishmael - '*God will hear*'- and I have been a wild man. Everyone was against me, and I was against everyone. But despite my wild nature, God has kept His promise and blessed me.

"I was a boy of fourteen when my mother and I arrived in the Desert of Paran. We had nothing, only water and a little food. I am now 137 years old, and my twelve sons are ruling my kingdom from Havilah to Shur." (from Assyria to the border of Egypt)

He lay back on his bed and closed his eyes. His children stared at the old patriarch, the strong man, the archer, the man who knew the desert, the warrior, and the conqueror;

the man who formed them and set them in their ways. What was it going to be like without him?

Slowly Ishmael opened his eyes again. "You must all now go outside and wait there. I will call you in one by one so I can give you my blessing, starting with Nebajoth. Then when I die, you must bury me next to my mother, Hagar, in Makkah."

All of them except Nebajoth bowed and left.

"Come closer, Nebajoth," Ishmael whispered.

Nebajoth went to his father's bed and knelt. Ishmael placed his right hand on Nebajoth's head and said, "Nebajoth, you are my firstborn, the sign of the strength of my youth, shining in honor, outrivaling in power.

"Your grandmother was a princess from the house of the Pharaoh. You are a Prince, and you will be nobody's slave.

"You will draw water from the desert, trade from the east to the west, and you will become the father of a great nation."

Nebajoth had to lean in close to his father to hear his faltering voice.

Ishmael continued, "Under the bed is a small box wrapped in skin, given to me by my father, Abraham. It is now yours. Keep it with you always. You and your offspring are the heirs of the promise in that box."

Tears were streaming down Nebajoth's face when he left Ishmael's tent.

One by one, the rest of his children entered and received their father's blessing.

*"Ishmael lived a hundred and thirty-seven years. He breathed his last and died, and he was gathered to his people. His descendants settled in the area from Havilah to Shur, near the eastern border of*

*Egypt, as you go toward Ashur. And they lived in hostility toward all the tribes related to them."* (Genesis 25: 17-18)

## Modern-day Paris, France

It was 11:05 when the electronic double doors slid apart. A woman stepped into the opulent chamber ten stories below the house located on the bank of the River Seine in the 3rd *Arrondissement* (district) of Paris. She wore no jewelry — her white dress trimmed in gold was more than enough to strike a stately figure — the epitome of elegance.

As she made her way to the round table in the middle of the room, everyone admired her athletic body and unflawed features. No one knew how old she was, and no one would ask, but she didn't look a day older than forty. Graziella Marie Nabati's life, filled with the privileges of money, not only granted her an extended middle age, it also gave her the best possible education and a healthy lifestyle. It was not arrogance that she radiated, it was confidence — the absolute conviction that the world around her had been organized exactly the way she wanted it. It bestowed on her a graceful *sang-froid* that made her peers pale by comparison. Her dark-brown eyes were sharp and piercing, and her dark hair was cut in a voguish bob that dropped to her strong jawline.

She was beautiful — very beautiful — in the same way an iceberg is beautiful, and equally forbidding.

When she arrived, the eleven people already seated at the enormous round oak table in the middle of the chamber all stood, bowed to her, and in chorus said, "Behold the daughter of Hagar of whom God said, *'I will multiply thy seed exceedingly, that it shall not be numbered for multitude.'* The mother of Ishmael of whom God said, *'I will make him into a great nation.'"*

Graziella bowed in acknowledgment and took her seat. Everyone followed suit. Her smile was as cold as it was seductive.

In the center of the table was a small gold monument, about ten inches high —a miniature roundtable with three gold swords as legs. Atop rested a small wooden chest roughly the size of a modern-day shoebox.

The chamber was circular, about ten yards in diameter. The four pillars looking as if they held the ceiling up were covered with inscribed gold plates. The floor was covered with a made-to-specifications Isfahan rug, the elite of Persian carpets, with silk foundations and silk inlaid kourk wool pile, displaying a Garden of Paradise pattern in the center. The paintings on the walls continued the Garden of Paradise theme of the floor rug with a lavish display of water features — canals, ponds, fountains, and waterfalls. There was a particularly striking painting of a bottlenose dolphin surrounded by other marine mammals of the Cetacean order, including porpoises, whales, and dolphins.

The chamber below Graziella's house was part of *les carrières* de Paris, better known as the Paris Catacombs — also at times referred to as "The World's Largest Grave" because of the more than six million bodies that have been buried there over the ages.

The catacombs were created when rich limestone deposits were discovered below the Left Bank many centuries ago, and the limestone was excavated and used to build the city. In some places, the diggers delved up to ten stories underground, etching out massive cavities and tangled tunnels spreading over more than two hundred miles.

In ancient times, these quarries were on the outskirts of the city. But over time, as the city of Paris expanded, it eventually covered the top of the old labyrinth, until almost half of the modern-day metropolis was located above the mines.

During the eighteenth century, when Parisians had a problem with overcrowded cemeteries, the authorities ordered all city graveyards be dug up and the skeletons dumped in the underground tunnels. Millions of skeletons were moved, broken up, and stacked there like firewood.

In 1788, after the riots in the *Place de Grève*, the *Hôtel de Brienne*, and *Rue Meslée*, the bodies of those dead were also dumped in the catacombs. In 1871, *communards*, members of the Paris Commune, killed a group of monarchists there. The French Resistance used the tunnel system during World War II. The Nazis established an underground bunker below *Lycée Montaigne*.

In 2004, police found a movie theater in one of the caverns. It was fully equipped with a huge viewing screen and seating for an audience. There was projection equipment, film reels, a fully stocked bar, and a restaurant with tables and chairs to cater to the attending people. Who was responsible for it and how it was powered remains a mystery.

To this day, large parts of the elaborate labyrinth remain unexplored, unmapped, and mysterious.

# Chapter One

## JUDICIAL PROCESSES

### Saudi Justice

The Minister of Interior of Saudi Arabia's stomach roiled as he listened to the voice of the Director of the Mabahith.

"Yes, Minister, that's correct. American Special Forces raided the compound of the Institute of Scientific Research and Development in Mecca two hours ago."

"Where precisely in Mecca did this happen?"

"It is on the south side of Mecca, sir. About six miles from the city center in the mountains of Jabal Thawr."

The Minister sighed. The Mabahith, the Arabic word for intelligence, also known as the General Investigation Directorate, was the secret police agency of the Ministry of Interior in Saudi Arabia — his responsibility. And they were responsible for domestic security and counter-intelligence.

"Make sure you keep me posted as more information comes to hand," the Minister said as he put the phone down.

The Minister was tense — although this attack came

from a foreign power and, therefore, was not his bailiwick, he still couldn't shake the uneasy sensation that one way or another this was going to land in his lap. He got out of bed, dressed, and as best he could, tried to prepare himself for a long, arduous day.

It was a few minutes past eight a.m. when the Minister bowed before King al Saud.

Ex officio, the Minister, was in regular consultation with the King, and he knew the monarch's moods and mannerisms. The King was a man with unadulterated natural authority — the sort of man who could shout a person, even a group of people, down with a whisper.

One look at the King, and the Minister had no reservations — the King was in a foul mood.

It did not escape the Minister that the King didn't invite him to sit down as he usually did. Neither did he address him by his name or title as he usually did.

"I received a very perturbing telephone call from the President of the United States a short while ago," he started.

The Minister felt his blood run cold as the King relayed the information he received from the President and the Secretary of State of the United States of America.

The Mabahith's mandate was to deal with domestic security and counter-intelligence. For that reason, this was information the Minister was supposed to bring to the King, not the other way around. In fact, the Minister was expected to have already dealt with it by the time he spoke to the King.

At the end of the disquieting chronicle, the King looked at the Minister with lifeless eyes and whispered only one question: "Why did I have to learn about this from the President of the United States and not from you as the Minister in charge of the Mabahith?"

The Minister knew he was as good as dead if he showed any hesitation. If he tried any excuse, he would not exit the palace alive. In ancient times, this would have been the moment to fall on his knees in front of the King, begging for his life.

He swallowed. "Your Majesty, I have no excuse. I beseech your mercy and your forgiveness. I am dumbfounded as to how this abhorrent plot could have been going on without the Mabahith's knowledge. Your Majesty, all I can ask is that your divine authority will grant me the opportunity to deal with this wickedness at once."

The King half-lifted his index finger and said, "I want progress reports three times a day."

The Minister jumped up, bowed, and left in haste. He was on his cell phone by the time the door closed behind him. He already knew his political career had ended a moment ago. What was at stake now was his life.

Within three hours, the Minister was pleased to inform the King that the three primary malefactors, Xavier Algosaibi, Ibrahimi El Fadl, Deputy Director of the General Intelligence Presidency, and Daiyan Nasser, Director of the Institute of Scientific Research and Development, were in custody, and interrogations were in progress.

Over the next few days, several things worked in the Minister's favor to get to the root of this evil cabal quickly.

First, the Mabahith — a law unto itself — ran its own prisons, its agents operated with impunity. Enhanced interrogation techniques, including waterboarding, denailing, flagellation, beatings, sleep deprivation, starvation, and the old favorite, electrocution, were standard operating procedures.

Second was the fact that judicial proceedings in Saudi Arabia were conducted in secret. Witnesses, lawyers, juries, and evidence was a waste of time in a legal system dependent almost exclusively upon signed confessions obtained by the police.

In the event where an accused appeared before a judge and repudiated the signed confession, the judge would refer the matter back to the police for further investigation. Rumor had it no one had ever gone before a judge for a second time to revoke their declaration of guilt — a testimony to the efficiency of the Mabahith and their enhanced interrogation techniques.

All of this ensured a swift judicial process.

Xavier Algosaibi, Ibrahimi El Fadl, and Daiyan Nasser's judicial process commenced at eight thirty a.m. on the morning of the Wolves of Freydís' raid on the Institute of Scientific Research and Development.

Algosaibi had been weighing his options since two a.m., when he received the telephone call from Ibrahimi El Fadl. In his younger days, Algosaibi was the deputy director of the General Intelligence Presidency, where he had often worked closely with the Mabahith; he understood their modus operandi. So, when the news about the raid on the ISRD reached him, he had a few options — run and hide, suicide, or surrender.

The Koran strictly forbade suicide, and he was still convinced he was doing the work of Allah — therefore suicide was out.

Run and hide? *I am an old man. Where can I go? I know how the King and the House of Saud operate — there is no place on the planet where they cannot reach me. The price on my head would lure the world's assassins, bounty hunters, and opportunists. They would hunt me down like a dog, and if I am lucky, kill me. If I am not that lucky, they will bring me back here.*

First, he called his two children — his son, Mayon, and his daughter, Aisha — and while he was waiting for them, he made a few more phone calls to different contacts and friends to make final arrangements. Xavier Algosaibi was a prominent and revered member of the Wahhabi sect; he had many very loyal, affluent, and influential friends amongst them. Many of them owed him favors, and he was now calling in some of those. It was three a.m. when his children arrived at his house. He took them to his study, and for the next four and a half hours, he imparted to them their almost six thousand-year-old family history. The two of them left at seven-thirty a.m.

When Hamza Kouri, the Director of Mabahith, and his agents, dressed in their notorious white tunics with red-and-white checkered headdresses, turned up at Algosaibi's house shortly after nine a.m. and showed their identity cards to his security guards, he was already waiting for them.

"Hamza, I have been expecting you and your men," Algosaibi said.

If Hamza Kouri was surprised by the almost cordial reception, he didn't show it. "Mr. Algosaibi, I assume then you know why we are here?"

"Yes, I know," Algosaibi replied. "And I am ready to go with you. Insha-Allah, this will all be over soon."

"I appreciate your cooperation, Mr. Algosaibi." Hamza nodded to his men. Three of them came forward and placed handcuffs on the old man's wrists, which he had already extended to them. He didn't argue or resist. In fact, he didn't say much further. There was going to be plenty of time for him to talk — he understood the Saudi justice system. He didn't attempt to hide or destroy any evidence.

That would only prolong the process. No, he gave his full cooperation and dutifully handed the agents everything they would need for their investigation.

Ibrahimi El Fadl was the incumbent deputy director of the General Intelligence Presidency and was among the first to hear the news of the raid on the ISRD. He'd passed it on to his benefactor and counselor, Xavier Algosaibi, shortly after two a.m.

El Fadl also had a few hours to weigh his options. Like Algosaibi, El Fadl had no misconceptions about his future — short and long-term. He also had three options — run and hide, surrender, or suicide.

When the Mabahith agents opened his office door, he pulled the trigger. The agents were just in time to see his brains bespatter the wall behind his chair. It is possible the 9mm bullet that went through his brain at the time could have prevented the answer to the question *How did it happen?*

Daiyan Nasser was in the hospital when the agents turned up. They ordered his family members out of the room, unceremoniously pulled him out of his bed, handcuffed him, and dragged him away.

Nasser was a scientist; he didn't understand the intricacies of the Saudi judicial system as well as his fellow perpetrators did. He had no political affiliations or ambitions. As far as he was concerned, he'd been hired to do a job, and he'd done it. He was a victim, not a criminal; therefore, he had nothing to fear.

What Nasser didn't know, and was about to find out, was the power of persuasion wielded by a heavy-duty truck battery fitted with a few lengths of electric wire, ending in alligator clamps clipped onto the genitals and nipples.

Getting signed confessions from Algosaibi and Nasser about their guilt was a walk in the park for the experienced

Mabahith interrogators. What took a bit more time was to extract all the information about their co-conspirators and their plans.

The Minister, wanting to make absolutely sure this was a comprehensive inquiry, gave orders that all family and friends of the accused be included in the Mabahith's investigation.

Xavier Algosaibi's purpose-built laptop, which he trusted to be absolutely one hundred percent secure, was saturated with the most intimate and elaborate material about the Foundation of the Real Princes of Saud. This proved to be the most valuable source of information. The heavy-duty truck batteries with alligator clamps helped to double-check specifics, refresh memories, and corroborate all the facts.

By nightfall of the first day, all five members of the Foundation of the Real Princes of Saud with all their family members and friends, numbering more than four hundred, were in custody.

The only two family members at-large were Algosaibi's son and daughter, Mayon and Aisha. Hamza Kouri had already ordered an unprecedented massive manhunt to find them and assured the Minister their apprehension was imminent.

## USA Justice

While Saudi Arabia had its own brand of justice, the American justice system, where the primary rule was the presumption of innocence, operated very differently. Presumption of innocence meant a person was assumed to be innocent until proven guilty. The prosecution had the burden of proof. In other words, the accused was not required to prove his or her innocence. Instead, it was the job of the prosecution to prove his or her guilt.

Furthermore, the American interpretation of the dictum "justice must be seen to be done" guaranteed the entire judicial process was conducted in public. The accused's right to legal representation, as well as independent, unbiased, and uncoerced evidence was a fundamental part of the process. If at any time during the trial process it was discovered that the accused was intimidated into making an incriminating confession, it would almost certainly guarantee the accused's acquittal. Therefore, signed confessions of guilt were not as common in the American judicial system as in Saudi Arabia. And heavy-duty truck batteries fitted with alligator clamps — never.

The American legal process was designed to protect the individual's right to freedom. It was open to public scrutiny, and although it was thorough and fair, most of the time it was a very slow process.

Similar to the situation in Saudi Arabia, on the American side of the investigations, there were also three prime suspects. They were Dwayne Miller, CEO of Competitive Response Solutions, Nate Gordon, one of the directors of Competitive Response Solutions, and George Robertson, the incumbent Vice President of the United States.

In compliance with the laws of the United States, Gordon and Miller were brought before a judge within 48 hours of their arrest, which happened a few days after the President had authorized Operation Freydís to extract Mackenzie and Liam from the facility in Saudi Arabia. The accused were duly informed of the pending legal charges, their right to retain counsel, and that they would be remanded in custody, which meant bail would be denied. They were not required to plead at the first appearance so they would have the opportunity to seek legal counsel and prepare their defense.

In the months leading up to his arrest, Dwayne Miller had become disgruntled with his job as CEO of Competitive Response Solutions. He had made up his mind to abandon his position, not resign. He couldn't. The reason being that his resignation would not be accepted because of his firsthand knowledge of the nature of CRS's activities. It was an until-death-do-us-part, or more accurately, an only-over-your-dead-body situation.

Miller had been looking for a way out of this quagmire, and although his arrest was not exactly how he would have wanted to get out of it, it was still better than being assassinated.

Therefore, Dwayne Miller offered his full cooperation to the investigators and prosecutors. In exchange for his cooperation and testimony against the directors of CRS, he hoped to, first, stay alive. And second, he hoped to get away with a lighter sentence than anyone else.

Miller's cooperation ensured the speedy arrest and arraignment of the remaining CRS directors as well as many officials of CRS client organizations and other businesses that had provided services to CRS in the past.

As the senior director and founding member of CRS, Nate Gordon didn't have as many options as Dwayne Miller. He, Gordon, was right at the top of the pyramid of perpetrators, one of those who would have to face the consequences.

Miller's statements and the information collected from the CRS servers produced evidence against Gordon so overwhelming the prosecutors had absolutely no incentive to plea-bargain with him.

At first, he thought he could get away scot-free because

of his illegal abduction, interrogation, and the bullet through the knee to make him talk. But those ideas were short-lived when his lawyer advised him that although the maltreatment certainly entitled him to take legal action against his abductors, it would have no impact on the treason or any other charges against him. The prosecution's case was based on Miller's evidence and information retrieved from the CRS servers, not on anything he told Sean Walker or James Rhodes while under duress.

He was placed on twenty-four seven suicide watch. He could not escape, and… well, there were no other options. All he could do was admit Sean Walker was right when he said, *"Gordon, sooner or later in life, we all sit down to a banquet of consequences."*

## Chapter Two

### THE VICE PRESIDENT'S WAY OUT

The Vice President, George Robertson, was not arraigned with Gordon, Miller, or any of the other suspects for two reasons. One, he was "in a coma" due to a "debilitating stroke". Two, because of a stipulation in the Constitution, which reads as follows: *"The President, Vice President and all civil Officers of the United States, shall be removed from Office on Impeachment for, and Conviction of, Treason, Bribery, or other high Crimes and Misdemeanors'"*

That clause meant only the House of Representatives had the power to impeach the Vice President, and the Senate had to convict him, and only then could he be arrested and punished.

This latitude for *"the President, Vice President and all civil Officers"* built into the Constitution afforded Robertson much more time to ruminate about his options than the other accused had.

Even so, it was debatable whether Robertson had a good understanding of the gravity of his situation.

For the past five and a half years, Vice President Robertson had been living in a surreal world where there had never been one single moment when he had been alone. At any given point in time during those five and a half years, at least twenty-five people knew where he was, although they didn't always know what he was doing. Always being surrounded by officials, media, and guards — constant movement, ideas, action, planning, scheming — by God, he loved every moment of it. And he would love it even more if he became President.

Whenever asked, and very often even when not asked, why he wanted to be President, he responded with the tried and tested platitudes — *love for our country, service to the American people, a better future for all of us and the generations to follow.*

Of course, that worked. That's what people wanted to hear, and that was part of the reason he was so far ahead in the polls. But that was a lot of horse manure; he didn't believe one word of what he told the people.

The truth?

*Well, if the President was the most powerful man in the world, then surely, I must be the second most powerful man in the world. And I reached this position without getting one single vote. I was asked. No, actually, they begged me, no doubt because of my extraordinary intelligence and exceptional leadership abilities, to take up the position.*

It was undeniable; he was destined to ascend to the command of the most powerful nation on the face of the earth.

He had never doubted it was his destiny to be President; *I was born to it; I was carved out for it. And by the way, when in history was it ever possible to become a deity bloodlessly?*

The secret service agents guarding the Vice President at the undisclosed clinic struggled to fathom his tempestuous moods and bad behavior. Although none of them uttered the words, all of them were perturbed by the fact that a man such as George Robertson could become Vice President, and none could imagine he could *ever* become President.

Maybe it was because he was "appointed" — not elected.

In his room at the clinic, there were days when Robertson was crying, some days he was quiet and looked depressed, still other days he was screaming and swearing, and some days he was making speeches.

The Vice President would watch his former opponents in the Presidential race on TV addressing the crowds, and then he would turn the sound off and make his own speech to the voters who were soon going to slingshot him into power.

The secret service agents just shook their heads every day in disbelief, the TV turned off at the end of the talk show featuring four women sharing their varying views on the world so the Vice President could have his turn delivering his campaign debate speech to the "crowd" – the crowd being them and the health care aides attending him, who faithfully stood at attention through the entirety of the ramblings and would clap at the conclusion to soothe the Vice President's ego.

He almost never slept — the campaign trail was hard work.

Was the Vice President delusional?

Absolutely.

Could the Vice President escape the inevitable consequences of his evil deeds with an insanity plea?

Maybe.

His condition was critical, and it was imperative that he did not receive any visitors, not even his family — doctors' orders. However, there was no prohibition on receiving flowers and presents.

The Vice President was curious to see what was in the little box wrapped in red gift paper, which arrived with a bunch of flowers. When the door closed behind the Secret Service agent who brought the items in and placed them on the small table, he got up from his bed and walked to the table.

Squinting at the contents of the little box — a 9mm SIG Sauer P938 pistol.

He frowned at it for a while, then took it out of the box. There was no magazine. He was perplexed. *A gun without bullets?* He opened the breech slightly and saw there was one round in the chamber.

"Oh, now I know what to do with this," he muttered. He placed the front end into his mouth and pulled the trigger.

For Vice President George Robertson, the judicial process ended abruptly on the eleventh day after he suffered a stroke at the White House.

For the rest of the accused, the judicial process would stretch out over years, and for those who would receive the death penalty, the process would end only after a decade or more.

---

The news about the Vice President's demise was given to them the night when Carter and his family, accompanied by Liu and the rest of the rescue team, arrived back in America. There was no jubilation amongst the group when they heard the news. On the contrary, it caused a somber mood.

The senseless death of so many people over the past ten months was no cause for celebration.

Carter was surprised to discover he didn't care about George Robertson's death and that his apathy was actually a relief. In the final instance, Robertson's death amended nothing. It didn't restore life nor did it heal injuries — physical or psychological.

## Chapter Three

### MAYON AND AISHA'S WAY OUT

With their father's parting words, *"May Allah go with you and bless you in every undertaking,"* still ringing in their ears, Mayon and Aisha were quiet as they headed south out of Riyadh. Aisha had donned her full-face *niqab* and stuffed some clothes under her long black dress over her tummy, making her look more than a little pregnant. Mayon had put on dark sunglasses and a black and white *kufya*, held in place with a camel hair circlet — the `iqal* — covering his head and most of the lower parts of his face.

They had left an hour and a half before the Mabahith agents arrived at Xavier Algosaibi's house. They were frazzled to the verge of panic. They'd had no idea about their father's surreptitious life, neither did they have the profound knowledge about their ancestry, until a few hours ago. Illustrious as their lineage might be, they knew it was not going to avert their heads being separated from their bodies with their father's. Although they had lived much of their lives in Europe, both graduating from the prestigious Pierre and Marie Curie University, Paris, they understood the Saudi justice system all too well. Being the progeny of the architect of the plot to overthrow King al Saud's empire carried the death penalty.

They'd tried to persuade their father to take flight with them, but he was resolute in his decision. He was going to face the music, and his children had to get away to continue the noble lineage. He always had contingency plans in place, and this time was no exception as he opened his safe, took out two envelopes, and handed one to each of his children. They contained fake passports and $250,000 US dollars in cash for each of them.

Mayon and Aisha had opened the envelopes and stared at the contents in silence. Nothing had to be said — it was clear what had to be done.

Next, Xavier had taken a miniature portable hard drive, the size of a box of matches, out of the safe. "This contains your promise. This is my blessing to the two of you," he said in a melancholic tone. "On it is the latest backup of my laptop and a lot of other information I never kept on the laptop. Information about my businesses, contacts, plans, family history, and a lot more. With this in your hands, you can start a new life and become very successful. Keep it with you always, and use it wisely."

Mayon and Aisha gaped at him, nodding slowly. No doubt this was the worst day of their lives. At first, they were besieged by the realization that their lives of extravagance and privilege had come to an end. Then came the awareness of the reality awaiting them if they didn't get out of Saudi Arabia immediately — run and hide — fugitives for the rest of their lives.

Mayon was thirty-two, and apart from the science degree from the Pierre and Marie Curie University, he held a master of business administration (MBA) from Heriot-

Watt University in Edinburgh. He was married but childless because his wife was infertile. For years, his father had been putting pressure on him to get a second wife, as was allowed by Sharia law, but Mayon's many years in a Western European society convinced him of the sensibility of monogamous marriage.

There was no time for him to collect his wife to join them in the escape. His father's contingency plans did not include his barren daughter-in-law. All that Mayon could hope for was that the authorities' hunger for vengeance against his father would not extend to his wife. He could not even warn her; neither would he be able to contact her in any manner, ever. When he left their house earlier, it was the last time he would see her.

Aisha didn't have many family matters to worry about. She was thirty, not married. Unusual for an Arab woman at that age, but maybe not for an Arab woman with a Ph.D. in quantum physics from one of the top six universities in Europe. She was dedicated to her work on quantum computing. Men were not on her mind; besides, homosexuality was a capital offence in the Kingdom of Saudi Arabia.

Their father had one more item to take out from the safe. It looked like a credit card, except it had no logos, names, or engravings on it. "This card holds the digital numbers to three of my secret bank accounts in Zürich. Those accounts can only be accessed by the bearer of this card. I have been putting money into those accounts for years. No one else, except, of course, my banker, you, and I, know about the accounts. There is twenty million US dollars in the accounts. If you so choose, the two of you can live comfortably off that for the rest of your lives without having to lift a finger."

Mayon swallowed hard to get the dry lump out of his

throat. Aisha was sobbing. They had so many questions and thoughts, so much to talk about, but no time.

Xavier was beginning to get more and more nervous. "You have to get ready to leave now. We can't wait any longer."

They got up and hugged their father.

When they took a step back and looked at each other, all of them had tears in their eyes. Xavier said, "Listen carefully now. Here is the map of where you have to go from here . . ." For the next ten minutes, he gave them detailed instructions about the escape plan, then handed them a suitcase with a variety of outfits, disguises, and a makeup kit, before he literally pushed them out of his study and down the hallways and stairs to the basement where Mayon's car was parked.

Mayon and his father quickly clipped new registration plates on the car, and Mayon got in on the driver's side. In the Kingdom of Saudi Arabia, women were not allowed to drive.

---

It was about thirty miles to the estate of their father's friend, Rashid Ajmal Kasab, who had a four-seat, twin-engine airplane and his trusted pilot ready to fly them to Salwa, a small town on the Gulf of Persia on the border with Qatar.

When they arrived on the Kasab estate, they parked their car out of sight in one of the sheds on the property. Kasab would take care of the destruction of the car later. He was waiting for them inside the shed. Mayon and Aisha got out, retrieved everything they would take with them from the car, and greeted Kasab as he approached them. Mayon quickly dressed up as a woman, donning a long black *abaya*, full-face *niqab*, and a walking stick. They got into Kasab's car, and he drove them out to his private airstrip where the plane was waiting. The pilot was told that the two women, his passengers, were a mother and daughter going to the funeral of a close relative. Lucky for them, in the Kingdom of Saudi Arabia, men were not allowed to talk to women unless their husband, father, or older brother accompanied them — it was a very quiet flight.

Salwa was only 240 miles east of Riyadh, less than two hours flying from Kasab's estate. When the plane landed at Salwa, another friend of their father, Nidal Deobandi, the head of the border control post, was waiting for them and took them to his house, about ten miles outside of town, where they would hide for the rest of the day. By the time their plane landed at Salwa, their father was already in Mabahith custody.

When darkness fell that night, Mayon and Aisha were taken down to the beach, just a few hundred yards from the house. There a small, twin-engine fishing boat picked them up and carried them to a secluded spot on the beach ten miles away, just outside As Salwa in Qatar. Deobandi had stamped their passports to show them leaving Saudi Arabia. Closer inspection of their passports would have revealed that they were Faisal Shazad and his wife, Farhat. The many stamps in their passports were testimony to their globetrotting habits.

The fishing boat arrived on the Qatar beach, dropped them off, and turned back immediately after they went ashore. The two of them stood on Qatar soil, and for both it felt as if they could take their first breath since the ill-fated call from their father at two a.m. that morning. However, for the first time in their lives, they also felt deserted, without sponsorship, orphaned. There was no one on the beach to welcome them and take care of them. No one to take orders from them. They had to wait — a displeasure they would have to get used to. The days of a crowd of obedient subordinates, always ready to please them at the snap of a finger, were over.

Aisha turned to her brother, trying to hide her fear and the feeling of helplessness as best she could. "Mayon, I was so scared we would never get here. Allah has indeed been merciful to us."

Mayon put his arms around her and hugged her. "It is not over yet, Aisha. We must remain vigilant, and to be honest with you, I think that is going to be required for the rest of our lives. But so far we have done well."

Aisha stared at her brother and slowly nodded. "Yes, those thoughts have been on my mind since we left Riyadh this morning."

Just then, Mayon caught a glimpse of a beam of flashlight about a hundred yards away from where they were hiding behind a small sand dune. "Shhh," Mayon whispered as he moved lower down the dune to get out of sight of the visitor. "Someone is coming this way."

After a while, he peeked over the crest of the dune again and waited. He saw it again. The light was pointed in their direction. It went on and off in four short bursts, a long pause, and then two more on and off flashes.

Mayon turned to Aisha. "Hand me the flashlight. It's our contact. I need to answer the signal." He crawled back to the top, switched the flashlight on and off three times in short succession, counted to ten, and did it again with two short flashes.

The visitor's flashlight came on and remained on as Mayon and Aisha approached.

From As Salwa to Doha, the capital of Qatar, was about 450 miles, a distance that could easily be covered in seven to eight hours by car. However, traveling only at night to attract as little as possible attention to themselves, it took them two days to reach Doha, from where they took a late-night flight to arrive in Istanbul four days after they had left Riyadh.

After clearing customs at Istanbul Atatürk Airport, they both sighed a deep breath of relief. They still had a long way to go, but now they both felt a lot safer than they had at any time during the past four days.

## Chapter Four

### THE COUNCIL OF THE COVENANT OF NABATEA

Graziella Marie Nabati and her son, Mathieu Nabati, were busy doing research in the secret library ten levels below her house on the bank of the Seine River in the third district of Paris. The library was adjacent to the chamber in which the twelve members of the Council of the Covenant of Nabatea conducted their meetings.

She had a wry little smile playing on her strikingly beautiful face as she read the article about Confucius's lineage. "You keep on believing that," she whispered. "It suits us just fine as long as you keep on believing and publishing that."

"Did you say something, *maman*?" Mathieu asked.

Mathieu Nabati was forty-five years old and lived in Zürich, Switzerland, where he was the owner-manager of a small boutique private bank, catering to by-invitation-only clients from around the world. He cut a striking figure — six foot one, slim, well-turned legs like a fencer, square shoulders, ramrod straight back, and deep-set, coffee-colored eyes. His curling, lush, black hair shone in the light, with a few attractive speckles of gray here and there on the sides.

Graziella was proud of her son — no doubt about that. She had been grooming him to step into her place as the chairperson of the Council of the Covenant of Nabatea. And he did not disappoint her — Mathieu held doctorates in computer science and economics, he was married and produced three children, two boys and a girl. He was a brilliant businessman and a natural leader.

"I'm looking at this family tree," she replied. "The Guinness Book of World Records states that the longest *known* family tree spans more than eighty generations — more than two thousand years — calculated at twenty-five years per generation.

"This so-called 'world record' lineage belongs to the illustrious Chinese philosopher, thinker, and educator, Confucius, who lived between 551 and 479 BC, a descendant of King Tang, who died in 1646 BC.

"In September 2009, the 2,560th anniversary of the birth of Confucius, the Confucius Genealogy Compilation Committee released an updated version of his ancestral tree, showing that there were more than one-point-three million living descendants of this revered man scattered around the world."

"But I guess the operative word there is *known*." She smiled as she looked up at her son.

Mathieu chuckled. "Well, I am sure we won't make them wiser by presenting our 6,100-year-old, 245-generation lineage."

Graziella nodded. "Definitely not."

They both went quiet again, continuing their research — determining a legitimate successor to fill the void on the Council of the Covenant of Nabatea left by Xavier Algosaibi's untimely demise required meticulousness. The selection of council members was based on more than just their bloodline — education, personality, achievements, influence, contacts, and wealth were all factors that had to be considered.

The oldest *known* noble lineage in the world was said to be that of the House of Ficquelmont, who could list their members since the ninth century AD. Over centuries, they have spread across Europe as the Duchy from which came the Habsburgs and many other prominent noble families of the Holy Roman Empire, Lorraine, Austria and Hungary, France, Russia, the Netherlands, and Belgium.

However, those family lines paled in comparison to that of the Nabateans, who could trace theirs back not only to their original patriarch, Nebajoth, the oldest son of Ishmael, but right back to Adam, more than 6,100 years ago.

"Algosaibi made a fatuous mistake when he strayed from the legacy of Nebajoth and tried to fulfill the sacred prophecy before its time has arrived," Graziella said with no little acrimony in her voice.

Mathieu looked up from the computer screen to his mother across the table from him. "That's so true. It perplexes me to see how some of our bloodlines become impatient, ignore the promise, and become power-hungry warmongers and land-grabbers."

Graziella nodded. "It is indeed troublesome that every now and then someone like Algosaibi takes a seat on the council — someone who just can't wait for the fullness of time to arrive."

Mathieu shrugged. "Maybe it's the results of the battle inside all of humanity. That between evil and good; the war of the seven deadly sins — pride, greed, lust, envy, gluttony, wrath, and sloth — versus the seven virtues — prudence, justice, temperance, courage, faith, hope, and charity."

His mother smiled. "That could be part of it, Mathieu.

But I don't need to remind you that the Nabateans don't claim to be the embodiment of the seven virtues. Our sanction is expressed in the blessing of Ishmael to Nebajoth — to *'draw water from the desert, trade from the east to the west, and be a great nation'* in that order.

"The Nabateans are the secret Turkomens or Gypsies of history — we have no territory, yet we have our own culture and history. We set up our 'tents' in the cities of others, and we draw 'water' from their land, but we have no cities of our own. We trade, yet have no trade agreements with any government. We move invisibly in the shadows of established civilization. The time to become a great nation, the fulfillment of the last part of that promise, is upon us."

He grinned. "Couldn't have said it better myself, *maman*."

A long silence followed before Graziella spoke again. "There is something that has been bothering me since I got the news about Algosaibi's arrest."

"What is that?"

"His children," she said.

"I have never met them. Have you?"

"Yes, on two occasions. The oldest is Mayon, named for the first born of our patriarch, Nebajoth, and Aisha, named for the wife of Ishmael, and as you know, Aisha was also the name of the wife of the Prophet Mohammed, many centuries later."

Mathieu was listening attentively.

"Our sources in Saudi Arabia say that Mayon and Aisha were neither arrested by the Mabahith nor by any other law enforcement or security organization. Despite a massive manhunt, there is still no sign of them — it's been ten days since Xavier's apprehension."

"Could they have been killed without the knowledge of your sources?"

Graziella shook her head passionately. "No, Mathieu, that's not a possibility. Our sources sit next to King al Saud and all his Ministers; some of them *are* the Ministers. No, definitely not. If Mayon and Aisha were dead, I can assure you I would've known about it.

"They have escaped, and I am sure they will turn up in Paris sooner or later. This is where they have studied and lived for many years. They know the place. I think this is where they will feel safe. They are part of the bloodline and therefore deserving of our protection."

"What is the problem then? I get the feeling it's not only their safe passage to Paris that's troubling you."

"You are the only one of the children and spouses of the council members who has been authorized by the council to receive the knowledge of our existence and activities. It has been a centuries-old tradition and safeguard to nominate and educate the shadow leader of the council in advance, to ensure continuity in the event of the death or incapacitation of the incumbent leader. That is the only exception that has ever been allowed.

"Through the ages, we achieved success only because the numbers of the council were restricted to twelve, and the oath, under penalty of death, everyone took to keep our existence a secret from everyone else, including family. We would have attained absolutely nothing if we didn't do it in secret.

"You can read our chronicles; they are all available here in this library. And you will see that whenever someone failed to abide by their oath were the times when the Nabateans got into trouble. Breaches of our secrecy by defiant councilors have brought us to the brink of disaster on more than one occasion in the past. Someone breaching our secrecy is always the council's biggest risk."

"Do you have reason to believe that Algosaibi reneged on his oath of secrecy?"

"Nothing specific, just intuition, because I am mindful of the fact that he must have been under tremendous stress when his plot was uncovered — people can do very strange things in the heat of the moment. Moreover, Algosaibi was rebellious by nature — he didn't want to heed the council's advice to cease and desist with his foolhardy plans."

Mathieu nodded. "We must find out where they are and what they know — as a matter of extreme urgency."

Graziella slowly nodded as she stared at the unique and priceless, handmade Persian tapestry on the wall. She would not hesitate to issue a termination order if required — she had done it in the past and would do it again. "Since the beginning, our society has been structured along bloodlines. But as we know, every so often bloodlines have to be protected with bloodstained lines."

## Chapter Five

### ONE BATTLE IN THE WAR

President Grant had summoned the Directors of the CIA and A-Echelon, William "Bill" Griffin and James Rhodes, to the White House for a top-secret meeting. He had also requested that Irene O'Connell, the Deputy Director of A-Echelon, be present at the meeting.

On arrival at the White House and clearing all security checkpoints, the three of them were escorted by one of the President's Secret Service agents to the Executive Residence, where the President was waiting for them to join him for breakfast.

When they entered the room, the President put down the morning paper he was reading and stood.

"Good morning. My breakfasts are usually such solitary affairs, it's great to know this one won't be so lonely." He smiled and shook hands with everyone.

"You're welcome, Sam. I'm sure none of us would ever object to help make your breakfasts a more companionable event." Bill laughed.

The President's full name was Samuel Houston Grant,

and he and Bill had been friends since college. Bill was one of very few people who called him Sam. For James and Irene, it was Mr. President.

The President asked them to take their seats, and the chef approached to take their orders.

"Have any of you had contact with the Devereuxs and Liu Cheun lately?" the President asked when the chef left.

Irene nodded. "Yes, Mr. President, I spoke with both Mackenzie and Liu yesterday."

"How are they doing? I often think of the hell those people went through."

"They are all doing well, sir. That place of the Devereuxs' out in the wild is the ideal environment for rehabilitation of mind, body and soul. As for Liu, she is also doing very well, thanks to the caring attentions of Dylan Mulligan." Irene smiled.

"Dylan Mulligan. Sean Walker's second-in-command? Is he not the guy who carried Liu out of her room and up the stairs during the rescue?" the President inquired.

"Yes, sir, that's correct."

"From your smile, I deduce there is a bit more than platonic friendship going there?"

Irene laughed. "Yes, sir, indeed, but the only ones who can't see it yet are Dylan and Liu."

"It will happen, just give it time." The President laughed.

They made small talk until their food was served and the wait staff disappeared before the President got to the purpose of the meeting.

"I take it you've all been ruminating on the events of the past ten to twelve months leading up to the rescue mission in Saudi Arabia and, of course, the inevitable reverberations?"

# The Alboran Codex

The three of them nodded in unison. "Yes, in fact, we," Bill pointed to himself, James, and Irene, "have been very busy mapping out this global labyrinth of deceit, and I can tell you it's going to take a lot more time to get the full picture — if ever."

The President was shaking his head. "You know, it's still bloodcurdling to think about this whole mess, and it's as you alluded to earlier, Bill. We haven't seen all the heads of the Lernean Hydra yet."

"Well, for now, on the national security front, all we can do is to keep on digging until we get to the bottom of it," Bill responded. "So far, we are getting excellent cooperation from the Saudis and other security agencies across the world. As for the political front, that is your turf, Sam."

"I wish I could just wash my hands and leave it to my successors to deal with, but I can't. The political fallout has not even begun. I doubt any of us can imagine what will happen in the next few weeks when the media finds out about George Robertson's role in all of this."

"It's going to be ugly — that's for sure," Bill replied.

"Yes, and along the way, I can expect to face an impeachment inquiry into my behavior as well. However, that doesn't bother me too much. My conscience is clear; I did what had to be done to ensure the safety of the American people. If that turns out to be wrong, then so be it. I will face the music when the time comes."

"Mr. President," James said, "for what it's worth, I can assure you if that ever happens, you'll find all of us by your side in support."

"Thanks, Jim, I appreciate that. But as I said, that's not my biggest worry now. I'm concerned about the security situation and the feeling we've unearthed only a small part of this malevolent conspiracy. What else is there we don't know about? How big is the residual threat, and how imminent is it?"

"That's true, Mr. President," Irene responded. "We have survived one battle in the war — there will be many more battles."

The President nodded. "The way I see it, the threat of the ancient nuclear weapons has not diminished one bit. It's still as real and as frightening as ever."

James looked at Bill and got a slight nod from him. "Mr. President, on that topic, I have some more disturbing information." James paused for the President to give him the go ahead.

"What is it, Jim?"

"Sir, amongst the information recovered from Xavier Algosaibi's laptop was an elaborate report about ancient nukes. Most disturbing was the discovery of an ancient nuclear explosion site in Syria."

"Give me the details."

"Sir, apparently, soldiers belonging to a group known as the True Sons of the Prophet blew up some ancient buildings close to Palmyra in Syria and discovered a tunnel system below the ruins.

"When they entered the tunnels, they found the crystallized remains of people and reported to their leader, Hassan Al-Suleiman, who is calling himself the Sultan of Syria.

"He, in turn, contacted Algosaibi, the financier of the True Sons of the Prophet. Algosaibi then contracted three Pakistani nuclear scientists to visit the site at Palmyra and investigate."

"And the plot sickens." The President sighed. "Please continue."

"The scientists provided a report to Algosaibi; we have a copy of it. In summary, they found the radioactivity levels in those tunnels to be lethal. In fact, five people who entered the tunnels without protective clothing died from radiation poisoning. The author of that report was Dr. Ishrat Sadiq of Islamabad, one of the most senior nuclear scientists who worked on the Pakistani nuclear program."

"He's not working for them anymore?" the President asked.

"No, sir, he was killed in a hit and run accident outside a hotel in Dubai, and the two other scientists who accompanied him to Palmyra have also disappeared. Our sources in Pakistan say they were picked up by members of the Pakistan Intelligence Bureau and have not been heard of since — presumably dead. The Pakistan Intelligence Bureau denies any involvement whatsoever."

"So, what were this Dr. Sadiq's conclusions?"

"Sir, he concluded that one, the high radiation levels were the result of a nuclear explosion, and two, the nuclear explosion occurred a long time ago. More than ten thousand years."

The President was staring into mid-space when James finished. After a long silence, he spoke. "That's why I can't ignore this and drop it in the lap of my successor, and neither can I waste time worrying about impeachment. We must keep working on this. And I don't mean only the ancient nukes but the entire conspiracy."

"We're in agreement, Sam. With your permission, the three of us could work out a strategy over the next few days and present it to you."

"Thanks, Bill, that's what I was about to suggest. I'll handle the media and the politicians. As for the security of our country, you three work out the strategy, and let me know what you need to make it happen. I don't have to tell you since the Mabahith did such a thorough job of the investigation in Saudi Arabia, there are now a lot more people who know about the nukes. And that makes the hair at the back of my neck stand on end."

"Sam, I take it you would like to see some of the information that was retrieved from Algosaibi's laptop?"

"Absolutely. I want to see it all. I'm also interested in this Hassan Al-Suleiman and the True Sons of the Prophet. The Sultan of Syria…" The President was shaking his head.

"Good. I'll have it ready for you at our next meeting," Bill replied.

## Chapter Six

### SEVEN DAYS IS A LONG TIME

Mayon and Aisha had their father's very precise instructions of what they had to do and what not, whom to contact, when, where, and how, and they had followed them to the letter. After clearing customs at the Istanbul Atatürk Airport with their false passports without raising any suspicions — at least as far as they were aware — they booked into an out-of-the-way, backstreet hotel. When they were in their room, they looked at the miserable surroundings, and with repulsion clearly visible on her face, Aisha sighed. "I guess there's always a first time for everything."

Mayon shrugged. "And this is not going to be the last time, I am sure."

Ten days after their arrival in Istanbul, they had stayed at ten different backstreet hotels — a different one every night — none of them better than the first. It was time to make arrangements to get to their next destination, Rome. For that, they required new legends, which meant new identities linked to a personal history that would stand up to scrutiny, new passports, and new looks.

Their father's instructions led them to Emir Yilmiz, a restaurateur on the south side of the city. If they had learned anything at all over the past ten days, it was not to set expectations — that way they were less disappointed when they arrived at the various places on their list. Emir Yilmiz's "restaurant" was no exception, although afterward they had to admit to each other they did expect a place resembling a bit more of a restaurant than the kitchen of the house in which Yilmiz lived. Calling that place a restaurant and bestowing the title restaurateur on Yilmiz did require some imagination — maybe not for the Turks, but definitely for Mayon and Aisha, brought up in the bosom of copious extravagance.

Despite the paltry surroundings, the food was good, and they were honored by Yilmiz's personal attention from the moment they arrived — especially so after Mayon slipped a fifty-dollar bill into his hand when Yilmiz placed their coffee on the table.

Mayon's generous tip ensured that Yilmiz joined them at the end of their meal to serve them with free baklava and coffee and a private chat. That's when Mayon got the opportunity to let their host know why they were there.

After the usual pleasantries about the weather, family, politics, and other unimportant matters, a short respite in the conversation gave Mayon the opportunity he had been waiting for. He looked at Yilmiz intently, and after he was sure no one else could hear him, said, "We're the children of Nebajoth."

Yilmiz goggled, swallowed, and after almost a minute of silence managed to reply with, "Mend, Send, and Mayon."

Aisha grinned and said, "They who draw water from the desert."

To which Yilmiz responded without hesitation, "And

they who trade from the east to the west." A smile broke across his face; his guests had passed the required security check.

Yilmiz invited them to follow him to a small room in the basement at the back of the building where they could have a private conversation.

An old worn-out carpet covered the floor; the walls were in desperate need of a coat of paint, and with no windows, the air was stale. Two weathered couches that had seen better days and a chest of drawers, equally dilapidated, against the wall made up the furniture in the room.

Aisha and Mayon sat down on one of the couches, and Yilmiz took a seat on the other, facing them.

He apologized for the humble surroundings but assured them at least it was safe to talk there.

Mayon explained what they required — new legends, passports, and travel documents. They would also need a laptop computer, two prepaid, unregistered cellphones, and clothes to match their adopted persona as citizens of France.

Yilmiz smiled — the dollar signs were flashing before his eyes. "That won't be a problem at all, my friends. You have come to the right man."

He didn't ask for their real names, where they were coming from, why they were on the run, or any other details. In his line of work, the golden rule was the less you knew about your clients, the better your chances of staying alive.

"How much will it cost, and how long will it take?" Mayon asked.

Yilmiz kept a straight face. He knew he could get it all done in a few days for less than a $1,000, but he was not going to tell them that. They were in dire straits, and that was good for him. He had to make it look difficult. And that he did.

He held the index finger of his right hand up. "Please bear with me just one minute. Let me just calculate it." He closed his eyes in mock concentration, mumbled, and counted on his fingers. "It will be $9,950 US dollars. Let's say $10,000 to be on the safe side. That's without the clothes, laptop, and cellphones. You must give me the specifications for the laptop and your measurements for the clothes."

Mayon and Aisha didn't even look at each other to confirm or to start bargaining about the price. For them $10,000 was peanuts. They had dropped much more than that when dining with friends at some of the world's top restaurants. Given their circumstances, they both thought $10,000 was an absolute bargain.

Mayon nodded his agreement with the price. "When will it all be ready?"

Yilmiz had a hard time suppressing the smile that threatened to occupy his face. He had readied himself to negotiate and would have come down to $2,000, maybe even $1,300. He went through the closed-eyes-finger-counting routine again. "Seven days is the quickest it can be done."

Aisha sighed; she was heartily fed-up with living in Istanbul's bughouses, the so-called budget accommodation. Nevertheless, she knew equally well there was nothing she could do but endure it for another seven days. *Maybe the bughouses in Rome would be better than the ones here.*

"Seven days is a long time, but I guess we also have to be careful," Mayon replied. Yilmiz concurred. "When can we get the laptop and cellphones?"

"Just give me the specifications, and I will have them

delivered to this address for you tomorrow at three p.m." He wrote the name and address of a restaurant on a piece of paper and handed it to Mayon. He got up and retrieved a brown, faux leather briefcase from the chest of drawers and gave it to Mayon. "Carry this with you when you go to the restaurant. A man with a briefcase that looks exactly like this one will join you at some stage. You will swap briefcases, and you will pay him for the cost of the items."

"Understood," Mayon replied.

For the next hour, they went through all the details of where and when and by whom packages would be delivered to them, and Yilmiz took several photos for their new passports.

At the end of the conversation, Aisha took an envelope out of her handbag and counted out $10,000 in one-hundred-dollar bills and handed it to Yilmiz, who didn't count the money — it would have been an insult to his guests if he had.

## Chapter Seven

### UNWAVERING AND STOUTHEARTED

Understandably, King al Saud was shocked and heartbroken when he was told of the two Royal family members who were involved in the planned subversion of the House of Saud. However, the King had to put the safety and well-being of more than two hundred powerful princes and twenty thousand plus family members above the interests of two dissenting family members. Therefore, like a true statesman, the King was firm in his decision not to interfere with due process in any way, shape, or form. Justice had to be seen to be done.

Although the investigative and trial processes were conducted in secret, there was nothing secret about the outcome of those processes. Therefore, justice was seen to be done by the many thousands who attended the mass public execution of the condemned, twenty days after the Minister of Interior gave his first instructions to Hamza Kouri, the Director of Mabahith.

The photographing of public executions was forbidden. However, the Saudi police did not strictly enforce this prohibition. They felt it should be treated as a rough guideline of expected behavior at events such as public beheadings.

If there was one wisdom the spectators took away from the executions, it was that although there were many things one could not do in the kingdom of Saudi Arabia, the consequences of ignoring the prohibition on criticizing the House of Saud topped them all. If you had any criticism of the Royal family, it was highly recommended to keep your ideas in your head if you had any desire to keep your head connected to the rest of your body.

The lackadaisical enforcement of the law against the filming of public executions assured the world media of a news scoop in almost real-time.

It was twelve days after Carter, Mackenzie, and the children arrived on Freydís that the news about the public mass execution in Saudi Arabia broke.

Carter was alone in the living room when he saw the news. Mackenzie was busy bathing and feeding Beth, and Liam was out somewhere with Jeha and Ahote.

This time, the news had a different effect on him.

He and Mackenzie had thus far not discussed their plans for the future. It was as if there was a tacit understanding between them that the time for that had not arrived yet. For now, it was more than enough to be reunited and to enjoy every moment of it.

However, the initial excitement of being together again, to be free and without danger, had started to wane. What was beginning to surface now was the inexorable psychological damage that followed in the wake of the ordeal that had begun ten months ago.

The beheadings in Saudi Arabia added another thirty to the mounting death toll. Many of the dead were entirely innocent, being in the wrong place at the wrong time, or just being friends and family of the wrong people. How could anyone look upon all those mindless killings, injury, and destruction and not be affected? And Carter knew he was directly responsible for at least one of those deaths.

Beth was too young to be directly impacted. Carter and Mackenzie were keeping a close watch on Liam for signs of any adverse effects. For now, he still seemed to be unscathed. Maybe part of it was because Jeha, Ahote, and Bly kept him so busy there was no time to dwell on the dark and depressing thoughts Carter and Mackenzie had to deal with. And maybe another part of it was because Mackenzie made sure that during the time of their captivity, she never spoke to him in negative terms, always supportive and full of appreciation for how brave and strong he was.

Mackenzie was emotionally exhausted, however. Many a night, she would still break down in tears, even though Carter held her in his arms and reassured her that she and the children were safe, back together, and he would make sure they would never get in harm's way again.

Carter's emotions were fluctuating between fury, gratefulness, guilt, and fear that his family would never be the same again. He was finding it hard to come to grips with killing a human being. As much as he knew he had no choice but to shoot that guard when he went for his gun, the bullets out of *his* gun, held in *his* hand, still ended the life of another human being.

Was there a right and wrong here? If so, what was right and what was wrong?

An eye-for-an-eye, a tooth-for-a-tooth, or turn the other cheek?

Certainly, the news about the executions was disturbing. Although no graphical images were shown of the explosion that began the nightmare of the past ten months, Carter knew what it entailed. In his mind's eye, he imagined the pandemonium of the bomb explosion, the twenty-three dead, and the many wounded including himself. Mackenzie and Liam, a six-year-old boy, captured and held like animals in cages below ground for more than ten months without a single ray of sunlight, under constant threat of harm. Beth born in captivity . . .

As was the case with George Robertson's death, the death of thirty more didn't amend anything. It didn't restore life, nor did it heal physical and emotional injuries. And the chain of events set in motion with that bomb explosion in Jerusalem ten months ago, was still raging. How much more before it would end?

It was a nightmare, which he, Mackenzie, and Liam to a lesser degree, would have to live with — wounds would heal but scars would remain.

Carter was so deep in brown study he didn't see Mackenzie come in nor hear her talking to him.

After getting no response, she tried a different tactic and changed her voice to sound like that of Steven Spielberg's ET character. "ET calling Carter. Carter come home." That had the desired effect.

"Huh, what...? Sorry, Mackie, my mind was in a different place. What did you say?"

When she saw his face, she didn't answer his question; instead, she asked, "Carter, what's wrong? You look . . . upset . . . out of sorts . . . What's bothering you?"

Carter was quiet for a few moments before he spoke. "Mackie, our lives have changed in so many ways the past ten months. You and I should make time to talk about everything that happened."

She didn't say a word. She just came to him, sat down

on his lap, embraced and kissed him. Then she said, "Yes, I know, there is a lot to talk and think about."

"Mackie, I'm aware you might not feel up to it yet. There's no rush. We can do it when you're ready."

She shook her head. "I'm ready. Tonight, when the kids are in bed, we'll get a bottle of fine red wine out of the cellar and tackle this thing head-on."

Carter smiled. *That's my Mackie—unwavering and stouthearted.* That night, he was going to find out just how unwavering and stouthearted his Mackie could be.

## Chapter Eight

WE WILL BE FREE

Mayon and Aisha, masquerading as a husband and wife couple from Dubai, had taken delivery of the laptop, mobile phones, new passports, clothes, and other items piecemeal as Emir Yilmiz supplied them over the course of seven days. The two of them remained ever heedful and tense. Television and radio news channels, as expected, showed their names and faces. In adherence to their father's instructions, they stayed off the Internet. The Saudi government wanted them for subversion, conspiracy to overthrow the government, and corrupting the children of Allah.

They understood the first two charges; however, they had no idea what the charge *"corrupting the children of Allah"* meant. Indeed, very few people did. It was an offense that lacked specifics and included anything from loitering in public to high treason. Such a nonsensical charge was a joke, except for the fact that it carried the death penalty — that much they comprehended. However, it would make no difference whether they understood or not.

They were innocent. If arrested, they would eventually

be found guilty of all charges by their own confessions. But their only true transgression was that they were the children of Xavier Algosaibi — an adversary of the House of Saud.

To quickly bring the two of them to justice, a one and a half million US dollar bounty was placed on each of their heads by the Mabahith. And although it was not mentioned in the news, Mayon and Aisha knew that meant dead or alive.

Thus far, their changed appearances, relocating to a different hotel every day, and staying out of the public eye ensured that they were not discovered.

Nevertheless, being on the run from the terrifying Mabahith and no doubt some of the world's best contract assassins meant seven days was an agonizingly long time. Mayon and Aisha felt the tension, uncertainty, and idle waiting was becoming too much for them. Aisha was constantly complaining about their miserable accommodations, food and surroundings, and being treated like delinquents and plebs. Mayon's patience was wearing thin. Aisha didn't seem to understand there was nothing they could do unless they wanted to take the grave risk of going back to Emir Yilmiz to try and speed things up. Their father's directions were unambiguous — *use a contact like Yilmiz once and once only. The first time you meet the person is also the last. No exceptions.*

The straw that almost broke the camel's back was the breaking news about the mass public execution in Saudi Arabia. Their father was the first one to be executed. It was not shown on TV, but Mayon and Aisha knew how gruesome and inhumane those public executions were.

A bit of respite came the day after the bad news. It was the morning of the seventh day after meeting with Yilmiz that Mayon entered the hotel room with their new passports in hand. Aisha broke down sobbing with relief. She already had their luggage packed, and thirty minutes later they were in a taxi on the way to the airport. Another personal safety tip from their father — *if you can prevent it, don't use the same airport or border crossing twice* — meant they didn't direct the taxi driver to the Istanbul Atatürk International Airport where they had arrived seventeen days before. Instead, they headed for Istanbul's Sabiha Gokcen International Airport.

Mayon took his sister's hand when the plane lifted off the tarmac. She was still shaking. "Don't worry, Aisha, we are going to make it."

They were seated in economy class. Being in first or business class, where they were used to traveling, would have exposed them too much. "Within a few weeks, no one will ever be able to track us down. We will be free," Mayon whispered to her.

She nodded, closed her eyes, and let out a long sigh. "I hope you're right about that, my brother. I don't know how much longer I can endure this kind of stress."

Emir Yilmiz's cell phone rang, and he answered. There were no pleasantries, just a voice saying, *"Alitalia 4755 to Naples."* The phone went dead, and Yilmiz immediately made a call to his contact in Paris.

## Chapter Nine

### WE DIDN'T WIN; WE ONLY SURVIVED

Liam and Beth were fast asleep. Carter and Mackenzie had settled on the couch in front of the fireplace. Mackenzie was reclining on her back with her legs over Carter's lap, and he was massaging her feet.

"Okay, Carter, let's talk about it," she started. "I can see it's been bugging you, and to be honest, it's the same with me. But I think you should go first. I don't have all my ducks in a row yet."

"Mackie, that's what I admire so much about you — untiring and courageous."

"Flattery will get you nowhere. Out with it." She smiled.

"The thing is, Mackie, you and the children went through a horrible ordeal, and I blame myself for everything that happened. I—"

"Stop it right there!" Mackenzie said firmly. Her eyes were blazing. "If I ever hear you say that again, I won't answer to the consequences. It isn't true. I know it, and you know it—"

Carter interjected, "No, wait, let me finish. If I'd never

taken the position with A-Echelon, you wouldn't have become part of A-Echelon, either. And even if you didn't take the role with A-Echelon, you would've been with me. And as we know, I was the prime target of Algosaibi and his cronies."

"Now, just tell me how on earth were you supposed to know all of that was going to happen? Hmm? Are you going to tell me you have some sort of hidden prophetical ability you neglected to use when you were supposed to? Only then would it make sense to blame yourself."

"That's not the point, Mackie—"

"What is the point then, Carter?"

"The point is that if it weren't for my work on the ancient nukes, none of this would have happened."

"Now listen to yourself, Professor Carter Devereux. If one of your students would have given you an argument like that in an exam, I'm sure he or she would have failed. Right?"

Carter shrugged.

"Of course, you would fail the student. Let me ask you a question based on your logic." She didn't wait for him to agree; she just continued. "Why only blame the moment you started working for A-Echelon? Why not go back to the moment you stepped on my toe? Why not the day when you asked me to marry you? Those are the incidents that triggered the chain of events. Not only your work at A-Echelon. We — Liam, Beth, and I—became part of your life the day you stepped on my toe there at the University. Yes, even before they were born they were part of your life."

Carter shrugged again. He knew Mackenzie was right, and her pure logic was somehow helping to straighten out his mind. He could feel the weight of self-blame slowly lifting off his shoulders.

"I don't want to disrespect the memory of your parents and siblings, but what about that situation? You were only a little eight-year-old boy then. The gas truck lost control on a dry road and swerved into the oncoming lane, colliding with your parents' car, killing them all. Do you blame yourself for the fact that you weren't there at the time? That you were at your grandparents' house?"

"No, of course not," Carter whispered as his memory flashed back to that fateful day.

"But this time it's okay to beat yourself up over something you had no control over either?"

There was a long pause.

"Oh, and one more thing," she said. "You remember these words? *'I, Mackenzie Anderson, take you, Carter Devereux, to be my lawfully wedded husband. To have and to hold, from this day forward, for better, for worse, for richer, for poorer, in sickness and in health, until death do us part'?* Hmm? You remember them?"

"Yes, very much so, Mackie. It was one of the happiest moments of my life."

"Well, just to let you know, I was serious when I said those words. I understood every single word of that vow. I meant it, and nothing has changed — including the *'for better, for worse'* part of it."

It was as if a ton of bricks suddenly fell off Carter's shoulders. He pulled her over to him and kissed her like it was the first time. "You are the most amazing woman in the universe, Mackie," he whispered through the kissing.

When they both got their breath back, she laughed and said, "Okay, now that we've sorted that one out, what's next?"

Carter looked down at Mackenzie, who was now resting her head on his lap. "We need to think about the future. Where do we want to live, and what do we want to do? I'm sure we haven't seen the last of evil people, and it's my duty to protect my family."

"I understand that, Carter, and I agree it's important that we do everything humanly possible to keep our family safe. The question is how? How do we keep our family safe?"

"Well, for starters, I'm going to resign from A-Echelon, and then—"

But Mackenzie didn't let him finish his sentence. "And that will make the ancient nuclear weapons evaporate into nonexistence?"

"No, it won't, but it won't be a threat to my family anymore."

"Really? Not even if some lunatic finds and activates it? You told me they might have used fusion bombs back then — a thousand times more powerful than our nuclear weapons. How is ignoring their existence going to protect us?"

"What are you saying, Mackie? You want me to continue with that research? How can I, after what happened to you and Liam and Beth?"

"So, you want to walk away from it—make it someone else's problem — just dump it and forget about it? That will make you feel better . . . safer? More at ease about your family's safety?"

Given the ordeal she and the children went through, Carter was more than a little surprised by Mackenzie's reaction. "I'm not sure I understand your reasoning, Mackie. Can't you see that it's my, our, involvement in this research that's placed us in this precarious position?"

"Carter, I had a lot of time to think in that hellhole in Saudi Arabia. Desperate and depressing as it was, what kept me alive was that I didn't want to give them the satisfaction of giving up. Giving up would have meant they won, and I was not prepared to let them have that satisfaction. After months in that place, I gave up on being rescued, but one thing stuck in my mind; *if* we ever got out of there, we *must* continue our work. I don't want them to win—ever. We have to beat them."

The strength of mind revealed through her words and the determination radiating from her eyes surprised him. He knew she could be very determined, and he loved that trait, but this was going way beyond anything he had experienced on any prior juncture. She had an unyielding vigor.

"What about the discoveries you've made?" she continued. "The Golden Garden in Peru, the city of the giants in Egypt. Does that mean nothing to you? What about the library of the giants — are you just going to dump it somewhere? Don't you want to know what we can learn from it? What if there is something about the ancient nuclear weapons in there or in that city?

"What about the respirocyte research? It holds so much potential for the good of humanity. Yes, of course, it can be used for evil purposes as well, but we have the only copy of the Sirralnnudam on the planet. We are light-years ahead of anyone else. Or are you saying you just want to dump it all and walk away?"

"Mackie, there are two things at stake here — one, the safety of our family, and two, the research. Believe me, I would very much like to continue everything we have been working on but . . ." Carter paused for a moment, "at what price?"

"Those things can't be separated, Carter. You can't choose one above the other. It's only through continued research and discoveries that we can ensure the safety and future of our family. Even if we don't play leading roles in the research work in the future, we *must* be involved. I don't want to become a spectator — a passenger in a vehicle driven by someone who hasn't seen the map of where we're supposed to be going."

Carter's brain was working overtime. What Mackenzie was saying was true. In fact, he wanted to get back into it, but he couldn't get his mind away from the horrors he and his family had been through in the past ten months. Nodding slowly to acknowledge his understanding of what she was saying, he was silent, not yet ready to answer. He needed more time.

"Carter, your knowledge about the ancient nukes is unique. No one else has any idea. Think about it carefully. We didn't win; we only survived. What we went through — all of us — was only the first shots in a long war."

"For someone who didn't have her ducks in a row at the beginning of this conversation, I would say your ducks are now all toeing the line." Carter chuckled.

"Well, they organized themselves while I was talking." She laughed.

Carter became solemn again. "Mackie, there are a few things I love above anything else — God, you and the children, Freydís, and archeology. The only things I won't give up are God, you, and the children. Everything else comes second, especially if giving up everything else will keep my family out of harm's way."

"Carter, believe me, I understand how you feel about our safety; I respect that. I can only beg you to not give up . . ."

"I need time to think about it," Carter said.

Mackenzie, with a naughty little smile on her lips, knew it was time to back off and give him space to think and decide. She grabbed him and pulled him down to her, wrapped her arms around him, and rolled them onto the carpet, where she landed on top of him. She sat up and started giggling, "Okay, now that I have your attention, here's how it's going to work . . ."

But she didn't get any further. Carter had wiggled himself out from under her, lifted her into his arms, and carried her to their bedroom.

Much later, with Mackenzie nestled in Carter's arms, they decided that for the time being they would stay on Freydís. Liam would be homeschooled, and they knew the boy was going to jump over the moon when he heard that. And to be honest, they had to admit they were thrilled with the idea as well.

## Chapter Ten

### APPROPRIATE STEPS

With the benefits of modern technology available to them, the Council of the Covenant of Nabatea didn't have to meet in person like they had to do in the old days. With their almost incalculable wealth, they could afford the services of the world's best information technology and telecommunication engineers. These days, they would have face-to-face meetings maybe once a year, and for the rest of the time, they met via video conference. Not the typical widely used video conference over the Internet — they were using their own top-secret, custom-built, impenetrable, holographic, telepresence technology through their own satellite links. Holographic video conferencing was still in its infancy in the rest of the world. Many IT professionals and businesspeople would give their left eyes to get their hands on the Nabatean's knowhow — if they knew about it.

At 11:05 p.m., Graziella Marie Nabati stepped into the Council of the Covenant of Nabatea's meeting chamber ten stories below her house in Paris. As always, she wore no jewelry. She was as always, dressed in white trimmed in gold, a regal figure of sophistication and elegance.

The holographic images of the ten people waiting around the oak table arose, bowed, and in unison said, "Behold the daughter of Hagar of whom God said, '*I will multiply thy seed exceedingly, that it shall not be numbered for multitude.*' The mother of Ishmael of whom God said, '*I will make him into a great nation.*'"

Graziella bowed in acknowledgment and took her seat. She looked at the empty seat of Xavier Algosaibi, and an expression of sadness washed over her face for a fleeting moment before she spoke.

"I have called this urgent meeting as there are three important matters to discuss. First, Councilor Algosaibi's heartrending death yesterday, second his replacement, third his children." She paused, and while she waited for everyone to let her know if there were any other urgent matters to be addressed, she looked around the room at the images of the attendees. They were so life-like it was difficult to accept they were only cleverly manipulated beams of light.

There was nothing else to add to the agenda.

"Councilor Algosaibi's death fills me with sorrow," she started the eulogy. "Not only will he be deeply missed as our brother, his absence has left us leaderless in the land of our origin. Xavier was a good man, a good leader, clever and loyal to the cause of our forefather, Nebajoth. He has left a legacy that is going to be hard to repeat. He had a powerful sphere of influence that his successor must rebuild. It's going to take willpower, motivation, time, resources, and money. We honor Councilor Algosaibi's memory." With that, Graziella stood and bowed her head.

The rest of the council members did the same, and all

said, "And he will be gathered to his people." With bowed heads, they remained standing in silence for another minute in adherence to their age-old tradition to honor the memory of one of their members. But the truth was none of them were grieving Algosaibi's demise — they were relieved at his empty seat. He had become a thorn in their flesh over the past few years. His incessant political ambition and religious fanaticism was a big headache for them, because it was undermining the secrecy and vision of the Nabateans.

More than half of the council members had already begun contemplating Algosaibi's end — the Mabahith had done them a big favor. Otherwise, they would have been forced to place it on the agenda of one of their meetings very soon.

"Thank you," Graziella said after one minute and took her seat. "Let's proceed to the second item on our agenda." She looked at the holographic image of her son, Mathieu Nabati, and nodded for him to speak.

"Honorable councilors," Mathieu started. "As you know, we, the children of Nebajoth, have a proud and illustrious lineage that spans more than 6,100 years and 245 generations. Everyone in this meeting tonight can trace their bloodline back to our patriarch, Nebajoth. Without that lineage, you would not be serving on this council — that is how it has been for more than six millennia.

"Our success, and I dare say our supremacy, is embedded in our bloodline. To be Nabatean is in our DNA — we can draw water from the desert."

The councilors gave a round of applause and nodded at Graziella, who had the smile of a proud mother.

"Therefore, when we do our research and create a recommendation for the council, we start with heritage.

And then, only after that, do we consider education, personality, achievements, influence, contacts, and wealth."

Mathieu continued and revealed the name of Hassan Al-Suleiman, leader of the True Sons of the Prophet, referred to by many as the Sultan of Syria.

The councilors were not entirely surprised by the name. They had all heard of Hassan and his True Sons of the Prophet and the inroads they were making in Syria and Iraq. And they all agreed with his vision for the Muslim world.

Mathieu pushed a button on his laptop to activate a presentation on the computer screens of each of the participants. First, he stepped them through Hassan Al-Suleiman's bloodline to assure everyone that the man met the ancestry criteria. There were a few pleasant surprises in Hassan's family history. The relationship to the Saudi Royal family was probably not much to be excited about, but on the other hand, to be able to count King Darius I of Persia and Cyrus the Great amongst your family was a great honor.

Twenty minutes later, everyone was convinced that the heritage box was well and truly ticked.

It took another hour to step through the rest of Hassan's profile and to get a unanimous decision about his appointment. That was part of their tradition — new councilors had to be elected undisputed.

Councilor Alireza Karimi-Shah, a very wealthy engineer, businessman, and humanitarian from Iran, was tasked to get in touch with Hassan Al-Suleiman and invite him to take his rightful place on the Council of the Covenant of Nabatea.

Graziella introduced the final item on the agenda — Algosaibi's children, Mayon and Aisha. "Our sources in

Saudi Arabia confirmed that the two of them have managed to escape and are on the run.

"I've received information that they were in Istanbul and have been in contact with one of our providers there. They are in Rome now and are being closely monitored. I am of the opinion they are planning to come to Paris, as this is where they lived and studied for many years."

"Do you have reason to suspect that they might cause us trouble?" one of the councilors asked. He was the American Secretary of the Treasury — concerned with all financial and monetary matters in the USA, member of the President's Cabinet, and a non-statutory member of the National Security Council. His was considered one of the four most important cabinet positions with that of the Secretary of Defense, the Secretary of State, and the Attorney General.

Graziella replied, "They are part of the bloodline, and if required, we should protect them. But not at all costs."

The councilor frowned.

Graziella continued, "We have been living and trading in the world around us unnoticed for about two thousand years. As you know, we have been very successful at what we do, and one of the reasons for that — probably the only reason — is that we have done it all in secret. What we do and who we are has been kept secret from everyone, including our families. We would have achieved nothing if we didn't do it in secret.

"You can study the chronicles of the Nabateans, and you will see that every time one or more of us failed to abide by the oath of secrecy it led us to the brink of disaster."

"Do you have reason to believe that Algosaibi broke his oath of secrecy?" the Secretary of the Treasury asked.

"No, I don't. But to be safe, I have ordered surveillance be placed on them to find out. If it turns out that the late Councilor Algosaibi broke his oath and passed our secrets on to his children . . ."

"Then we *must* take appropriate steps to protect our secret." He nodded in agreement.

Graziella looked at each of the councilors in turn and got their approval.

## Chapter Eleven

### CONSIDER HER WAYS AND BE WISE

Carter rose early the morning after he and Mackenzie's discussion about the future. He saddled his horse and rode out, turning towards the river flats. He needed some thinking time, and riding out on Freydís land was his way of meditating. He hadn't seen the wolves for a while, not since he, Mackenzie, and the children had first returned to Freydís. He was aware the wolves often changed hunting grounds during the summer months, so thought they may have gone farther afield, giving the four young ones more experience.

His head was spinning with the conversation he and Mackie had the night before. He was glad they had decided to stay at Freydís for the moment.

Was he willing to return to the work that had been the cause of the last ten months' turmoil? He was loath to continue for fear of the harm it could bring to them again. Carter loved his work, but not at the risk of his family — he would never be able to live with himself if something happened to them again.

On the other hand, he understood Mackenzie's desire to continue. While she had been imprisoned, her research had kept her sane, and she and Liu had achieved a great deal.

Suddenly he stopped, his musing broken as he stared down towards the river flats and spotted the Freydís wolves. That small pack of two adults and four pups moving through the grasslands intent on hunting was unmistakable.

One of the pups spotted a lonely bison standing at the water's edge — likely an old one and not able to keep up with the rest of the herd anymore. Carter could see a distant herd farther up the valley.

Carter took his binoculars out and watched. One of the young wolves approached the bison. Carter drew in a breath. "No, leave it alone," he whispered. "It's too big for you." He thought to turn away and leave them to it, not wanting to see injury or death come out of the curiosity the young wolf was displaying, but he couldn't — he had to watch.

The pup crept on its belly slowly, closer to the beast, which had spotted him and put its head down, making it seem even more massive than it was, intent on deterring the pup. But the youngster would not be put off. His curiosity had gotten the better of him. He advanced closer, and the bison charged a short distance at him. The wolf leaped sideways from it, only to return.

Loki spotted what was going on, approached the animal, and put himself between it and his pup. He judged this was not the time to take on something of this size and clearly wanted to get the youngster out of the way.

But then the bison charged.

Carter grew pale. It had been known for a single adult wolf to bring down a bison, but it was rare.

Keeva, by this time, had joined Loki. It was clear their

only option was to bring the creature down despite its size. Maybe there was little choice now it had been woken from its apathy, and the pups were now creeping in on the prey, refusing to leave.

"It's too big, Loki," Carter muttered. "Leave it. Someone's going to get hurt."

The bison was now swinging its huge head back and forth watching the circling wolves, its immense shoulders tensed with muscle, tail twitching, its feet planted firmly, ready to charge once more.

The wolves fanned out around it, and Carter judged there was no turning back. Now stirred, the animal was dangerous. Neither was it in the wolves' nature to turn and run.

He realized watching the wolves' movements that Loki and Keeva had taught the pups the pattern of a hunt and bringing down an animal, but he guessed nothing as large as this.

It was going to take time. The wolves circled, the bison moved back and forth, testing every avenue of escape, but each time it made a run for it, one of the young out-maneuvered it.

*I can't watch this. One of them will be injured — killed. I need to do something.* But Carter knew better than to interfere. Whatever the outcome, he could not move in on them. He had to watch helplessly as the bison charged at one of the young, who only just escaped the hooves smashing its head in.

Slowly Loki moved closer, and then, choosing his moment, charged at the nose. He gripped the soft, tender flesh in his teeth as the angry animal shook his head, blood spraying, in an attempt to dislodge him.

One of the over-excited young raced in behind Loki and received a nasty nip on the rump from Keeva before she circled and leaped on the bison's back, sinking her teeth into its rump.

The erring child shook its head. The nip had hurt, but it rejoined its siblings to harass the feet of the beast, running in, biting, nipping, dodging, leaping sideways and in again, distracting him.

Carter watched them avoiding the slashing hooves close to their heads and bodies while he held his breath. *This won't end well — I just know it won't.*

His pulse was pounding as he watched Loki slowly drag the head down, cutting off the air supply on the beast's nose. It was breathing through its mouth and bellowing.

Keeva was pulling hard on the rump with her teeth, her hind legs digging into the side of the beast to get purchase and to bring the creature down.

It ended quite suddenly as the bison toppled, then hit the ground in a cloud of dust and a thump he could hear even as far away as he was. Keeva leapt to one side, while Loki continued to grip its nose. Keeva joined him to sink her teeth into its neck, reaching quickly to the carotid artery and aiding the animal's rapid death.

Carter was shaking as he counted heads. They were all there, and no one was hurt. He watched as Loki broke into the bison's soft underbelly and began to feast. He was followed by Keeva, and shortly afterward the young were allowed to join them.

Once fed, the wolves would carry a lot of the flesh and bones off to be buried for later, still leaving enough for more ravaging creatures to dine upon.

Carter turned his horse and slowly continued his ride, thinking of what he'd just witnessed. It was as if there was a lesson in it, but what was it? Obviously, the young wolves had been taught a great deal about hunting since they were weaned, but he knew that at their age a bison would not have been a chosen beast of prey for the young wolves. However, Loki and Keeva had no option once the pup roused the animal.

He frowned. *Am I being a coward wanting to keep us out of harm's way? Would we be happy living a secluded life here on Freydís? Isolate ourselves from the rest of the world and the perils within?*

Suddenly the words of Solomon flashed before his eyes. Proverbs 6:6 *"Go to the ant, thou sluggard; consider her ways, and be wise."*

Then it struck him — the analogy between what he'd just witnessed and his own situation. He and Mackenzie's work had stirred up a bison. The bison came after them and their family. Now they had no choice — they had to attack and defeat it. Just like Keeva and Loki had to lead dangerous lives if they wanted to survive, and their young had to be trained how to fend for themselves.

Yes, the beast was enormous. They'd seen it, but it shouldn't deter them. There was work to do that only they, with their experience, could continue — it was time to reactivate the project work.

He turned and headed home to talk to Mackenzie.

## Chapter Twelve

THE STRATEGY

James had deliberately postponed the phone call he had to make to Carter. Bill, Irene, and he had developed a new operations strategy for A-Echelon, and the President had accepted it. James's problem was that the strategy called for Carter and Mackenzie's involvement, but they had no knowledge of it yet. James was saddled with the task to get them onboard, failing which the President would step in and use *his* powers of persuasion.

What kept James from contacting Carter was that he knew him better than anyone else in the group. That meant he knew that if Carter had decided to quit A-Echelon, nobody would make him change his mind — not the Pope, not the Dalai Lama, not even President Samuel Houston Grant. Given what had happened to Carter and his family, nobody could blame him if he decided to keep them as far away from A-Echelon and its activities as possible. Moreover, with a net worth north of two billion dollars, Carter was a very wealthy man. Neither he, nor Mackenzie, or for that matter their children, would ever have to work for anyone or at all.

Irene's knock on his door startled James out of his silent deliberations. "Morning, Jim. Just checking in to find out if you've had time to speak to the Devereuxs?"

"Haven't had time yet," he growled without looking up.

Irene smiled. She knew James loathed the task assigned to him and recognized what he was doing — kicking the can down the road in the hope it would just disappear. "James Rhodes, look at me," she said, sounding like a mother who'd caught her four-year-old boy with his hand in the cookie jar. "Stop procrastinating, pick up that phone, and call Carter now."

James looked up — and indeed, he looked like that four-year-old boy. "I don't see the point. I already know what he's going to say, and I don't blame him. I feel like a criminal having to talk to him about it."

"Jim, you participated in the planning, and you agreed that Carter and Mackenzie have vital roles to play—"

James put his hand up and stopped her mid-sentence. "Yes, and as you know, I also told you, Bill, and the President I'm sure they won't do it, and we might as well start looking for someone else—"

Irene interrupted him. "Yes, Jim, and the President told you he would support that notion, but only after you got a definite answer from Carter and Mackenzie."

"Dammit, why didn't he make the call? Now I must harass the poor people. I already have few friends as it is — I don't want to . . ."

James's secure phone started ringing before he could finish — it was Carter. "Speak of the devil," he mumbled as he picked up the phone and pushed the answer button.

"Jim, how are things inside the Beltway?" Carter asked, obviously in a cheery mood.

James indicated to Irene to take a seat.

"I'm surviving, Carter, but only just — I would much rather be walking around Freydís. But hang on, I have Irene with me. Would you mind if I put you on speaker? She was just asking about you and Mackenzie and the children." He winked at Irene, who just shook her head about James spinning the facts.

"No, of course not. Let me call Mackenzie so we can all have a chat — the more, the merrier." Carter chuckled.

When Mackenzie arrived, she and Irene took over the conversation for the first ten minutes, talking about the health and well-being of their families. Finally, there was a lull in the conversation, and James and Carter got a chance.

"Carter, I'm sure you didn't call me just to facilitate a conversation between Irene and Mackenzie." Irene rolled her eyes, pressed her lips together, and made a fist at James.

"Well, there is that, of course." Carter laughed. "But the original reason for the call was to find out when we're getting the show on the road?"

Irene started smiling, and James had slack-jaw. "Umm . . . ah . . . are you talking about what I think you're talking about?"

"Now, Jim, how on earth would I know what's going on in that corroded, antiquated mind of yours? The psychiatrist who would be able to do that does not exist."

"Watch it, boy! I know where you live." James chortled and then continued in a serious tone. "Of course, I know what you're talking about, Carter; it's just that I'm surprised — really, pleasantly surprised. But then, I must confess, I've been under Presidential decree to contact you about that. I just couldn't scrape the courage together yet to do it. I was so convinced you and Mackenzie would want out, and of course, you are entitled to it . . . God knows you and your family more than deserve it."

"The decision didn't come easy, Jim," Carter said. "But in the end, there was only ever going to be one right decision. Mackenzie nailed it on the head when she told me the other night, '*We didn't win; we only survived.*' She and I agree we have to get back to it, and the sooner, the better."

"And we are both raring to get started," Mackenzie rejoined. "Irene, what are the prospects of you and Jim paying us a visit here on Freydís? That way I won't have to disrupt Beth's routine at all."

Irene and Jim smiled and nodded quietly at each other. They never required persuasion to take a trip to Freydís. "Done deal, Mackenzie. Give us a day or two to make the necessary arrangements. I'll let you know when we're ready."

## Chapter Thirteen

### THE HUMAN TAIL

The one thing most professional assassins were lacking was not money, adventure, or excitement. It was the prospect of longevity. By its very nature, theirs was a treacherous job. Clients willing to pay obscene amounts of money to get their problems taken care of by a third party soon had a conflict of interest. Almost without exception, clients wanted no evidence left that could lead back to them — that's why they outsourced their problem in the first place. But the problem existed for as long as the assassin was alive. Footprints back to the client, however faint they may be, always remained if the assassin continued to live after the job was done.

Picking clients very carefully, making use of agents and go-betweens, dead letter boxes, and other measures helped to a degree, but it was never watertight. With enough time and resources, anyone with the motivation to do so would be able to find the dotted line back to the client. It was nearly impossible to wipe it out.

In many cases the contract ended in one of two scenarios; either the client got rid of the assassin, or the assassin got rid of the client. The only alternative was for one of the parties to run and hide and hope never to be found.

These thoughts were front and center in Perrin Durand's mind as he was on France24.com, a news website he visited three times a week from different Internet cafes. As always, he had typed in just one keyword in the search box, "enduring."

This day, there was a message for him in the rooms for rent section. It read:

Enduring views of Rome from two-bed apartment. €150 per day. Applications close on the 10th.

His surname, Durand, was of Norman origin and meant "enduring" — the message was for him. No phone number or email address, and the link in the ad led to a website that sold outdoor furniture. That was his confirmation.

The message meant there were two people (two bed) in Rome to be placed under surveillance (views), the contract price was one and a half million Euros, the price mentioned in the ad times ten thousand. He had one day (the date divided by ten) to lodge his expression of interest or not.

*A shitload of money for a surveillance job! What is so important about them?*

He was more than intelligent enough to know that when something looked too good to be true, it probably was.

Durand was an ex-officer in the GCP (*Groupe de Commandos Parachutistes*), an elite parachute unit within the French Foreign Legion. They were trained for commando type missions, which included recon, target marking, raids, hostage rescue, and extraction or destruction of high-value targets.

He'd left the Foreign Legion five years before, shortly after he was promoted to the rank of captain. He'd had enough of it after ten years, and for someone with his expertise, there was real money to be made on the hit man circuit. If played shrewdly, a few carefully selected and perfectly executed contracts would assure a life free of money worries in an exotic location of his choosing.

If he accepted this contract, it would be his third. He had to relocate from the USA to Italy after his first hit and from Italy to Paris after his second. Those two contracts earned him one and a quarter million US dollars, and he had stashed away a little over a million of that in a few anonymous numbered accounts in tax havens across the world.

He had his qualms about this project. But that was the nature of the job. Since his last hit, he had been waiting and preparing for a new one. His next vanishing was already prearranged in detail — Thailand. The money was good. Just two more contracts of this size and he was out of the game, set up for life. Durand never made rash decisions, but twenty-four hours was enough time for him to evaluate before responding to the agent.

---

When the plane leveled out at cruising altitude, Mayon and Aisha leaned back in their seats, and their minds turned to the events since they'd fled from their home country twenty-one days ago.

Since they got the laptop from Yilmiz and could connect the miniature portable hard drive given to them by their father, they had been reading a lot. At times, while they were devouring the information on the hard drive, it was as if their father's parting words were still hanging in the air.

*"This contains your promise — this is my blessing to the two of you. With this in your hands, you can start a new life and become very successful. Keep it with you always and use it wisely."*

Mayon and Aisha cleared customs at Naples without any problems, and then got a cab to the train station from where they would make their way to Rome.

When they left the airport building, despite being on high alert, they didn't notice the human tail following them.

## Chapter Fourteen

### BACK TO BUSINESS

With Carter and Mackenzie's agreement about the future also came Carter's decision to keep up his Special Forces training routine. The next morning at six a.m., when he was outside stretching before his run, he was surprised to see Mackenzie appear next to him dressed in a tracksuit and running shoes.

"What's this?" he asked. "You're going for a run with me? What about Beth?"

"Beth will be okay. I've asked Liam to take care of her if she wakes up. I fed her an hour ago, so she should sleep for another two hours. I've put the baby monitor next to Liam, and he knows what to do."

"And?" Carter frowned.

"What do you mean and? I'm going for a run with you, and you're going to teach me everything you have learned during your Special Forces training. Self-defense and weapons . . . all of it."

"Huh. You want to become GI Jane now?"

She just smiled and aimed a friendly kick at him. "Yep, something like that."

Mackenzie had given him no indication that's what she planned, but if she did, he had no problem with it. In fact, it was something he'd been thinking ever since their conversation about the future. It would be good if she could take care of herself when the need arose.

"Okay, the track is ten miles. I suggest you do as much as you can and build it up over time. The first few days are going to be the worst, but don't get despondent. It gets better after the fourth day."

Mackenzie managed to keep up with Carter for the first mile, then dropped back. At the two-mile mark, she stopped, took a few deep breaths, turned, and walked back home. It was a good start.

When Carter arrived home, Mackenzie had already completed the Five Rites routine, which she and Liam had been doing religiously every day since they were captured.

They both had a drink of water, and then Carter started teaching her the Krav Maga close combat techniques. The self-defense system employed by the Israeli Defense Forces to neutralize threats utilized concurrent defensive and offensive tactics sourced from aikido, judo, boxing, Brazilian jujitsu, and wrestling.

Forty minutes later, Mackenzie plonked down on the lawn, exhausted but happy. "That was a lot of fun." She laughed. "But now I'm pooped."

Carter laughed and pulled her up. "You did great, Mackie. I'm impressed. You should have seen me on my first day. I'm sure I looked much worse than you do now. The secret is to keep on going every day and get past those magical but excruciating third and fourth days. If you get past that, you'll be okay. Those guys who trained me had a good motto. *'Yesterday was the worst day.'*"

Mackenzie's weapons training would start in a few weeks, when she'd be in better shape. They went inside and showered together. "You know, Mackie, I can get used to this new routine very quickly." Carter chuckled as Mackenzie was washing his back.

"Me too, absolutely!" She laughed.

Carter made breakfast for them. Liam must have smelled the bacon and eggs as he appeared at the kitchen table just when they sat down.

Carter produced the plate of bacon and eggs he'd put aside for Liam while the boy told them he and Ahote had plans to go fishing for the day.

Mackenzie packed lunch for them, and soon after, they watched as Liam and Jeha disappeared in the direction of Bly and Ahote's house.

"So, I guess while we're waiting for Irene to let us know when they are coming up to visit, I can get started on the Sirralnnudam and you on that library of the giants," Mackenzie said.

He nodded. "I'll help you with the translation of the Sirralnnudam as much as I can, and as soon as you are settled, I'll take another look at that library from the City of Lights. Last time, I couldn't make head or tail of it, but then it was under different circumstances. Maybe I'll make better progress this time."

They both got busy with setting up their workspaces and computers in the study, where there was more than enough space for both to work.

A few hours later, Carter looked up from his computer at Mackenzie. She didn't see him looking; he smiled. *What a fortunate and blessed man I am.* He got up, walked over to her, gently turned her face to him, and laid a kiss on her that took her breath away.

"Ah, now that was very nice! What was it for?" she asked when he moved his lips away from hers.

He smiled. "Because I am the happiest man in the universe, because I am so grateful to have you as a wife, and because you are right here with me. What else can a man desire?"

Before Mackenzie could respond, the secure satellite phone rang. It was Irene. Mackenzie answered. Carter went to the kitchen to start the coffee machine. When he returned with the two mugs of coffee, he was just in time to hear Mackenzie ending the call with, "Don't worry. There's enough space for everyone. Yes, I'm sure. Looking forward to see you tomorrow, Irene, and I'll let Bly know you're coming. We'll expect you around ten o'clock then. Have a safe flight."

Carter handed Mackenzie her coffee. "Who's coming? Sounded like it's more than just Irene and James."

"Yes, Sean and Dylan will be coming as well."

"Sean and Dylan . . . Hmm, I wonder what they have in mind. I actually planned to talk to them but first wanted to run the idea by you."

"What were you thinking?"

"Well, I am of the opinion, now that we are back in the snake pit, it will be wise to get a security detail in place again. Like I had before."

"Great minds think alike!" Mackenzie laughed. "I was actually going to talk to you about that."

"In that case, we'll have to think about extending the cabin or building separate quarters for them. What do you think?" Carter asked.

"Let's discuss that with Sean and Dylan when they're

here, but I would prefer them having their own quarters — if that's practical."

"Agreed. It would be easy to build a few single bedroom cabins out there. Ahote could oversee it — he constructed their cabin," Carter replied. "If it's the same guys who were on my protection detail, they can also take on the task of training the two of us. They're tough, but they know what they're doing."

"Just as long as I get a nice back scrub from you, like this morning, every day during our after-training showers." Mackenzie chuckled.

"That's a deal." He laughed. "Okay, where were we before the phone rang? . . . the kiss and the reasons for it?"

"You already gave the reasons, and I love it. Can we now have a look at the Sirralnnudam before you get distracted again?" she said sternly.

"Ah, well if you insist." Carter grinned. "After all, it is this book that led us to find you."

"Well, it seems to me the old saying 'crime doesn't pay' has been proven wrong then. At least in this instance," she said.

"Mackie, if ever there was a grateful man for a crime his wife committed, you are looking at him. I just don't know how we would ever have reached you, Liam, and Beth if it wasn't for your crime when you copied this book."

"I know I should feel guilty, but somehow I can't. It's what saved us and brought us back to each other."

Carter nodded quietly. "Let's just hope my criminal deed of stealing the library of the giants produces the same lifesaving results as yours."

"I won't exactly call that theft, Carter. I like to think of it as crime prevention — or rather terrorism prevention."

"Thanks, Mackie. You have a way of making me feel a

bit better about it. But I'm sure that's not how my archeologist colleagues will see it, and neither would the courts, especially the Egyptian courts."

He sat down next to Mackenzie and looked at her computer screen, where she had the book open. She handed the mouse to him. He scrolled back to the first page and started reading, mumbling inaudibly as he looked at the words.

"Hey, I am here." She waved her hand in front of his eyes. "Tell me what you're reading."

"Huh? Oh, sorry. It's written in proto-Arabic. In other words, an ancient version of Arabic. The name Sirralnnudam literally means '*the scroll of secrets of blood.*' It says that this book was compiled from several older sources and information passed on through the ages . . . wait, no, not ages . . . that word there means millennia — thousands of years."

"Carter! That's amazing! Wow! I mean you can just read it like that. Does it give the names of the other sources?"

"No names yet. I think we'll see the names later in the text. A pity these old scripts didn't have an index. That would have made it a lot easier to know what's inside."

"Well, let's scroll through and see if you can get the gist of what it says."

"It's not going to be *that* easy — my ancient Arabic is a bit rusty. It's going to take some effort to get back into the swing of it. I think it's best if you get on with something else. I'll copy it to my tablet. Then I can carry it around and read it anywhere. I'll make notes for you as I go."

With the book copied onto his tablet, Carter walked out and sat down on the deck, reading, highlighting text, and annotating. Hours later, he thought his tablet had run out of power, but when he looked up, he saw that the sun was setting. He'd been so fascinated he didn't hear Mackenzie getting busy with dinner preparations in the kitchen.

Carter went back to the study, plugged the tablet in to recharge, and joined Mackie in the kitchen. Beth was in her carrycot on the couch. She was almost three months old, and to the delight of everyone, a week or so ago she'd started smiling and laughing whenever she saw one of them. It quickly became a contest for all of them to make her smile and laugh. Carter tickled her tummy, and she started giggling. She was elated to see his face and made happy sounds when he picked her up.

"Any interesting stuff in the Sirralnnudam?" Mackenzie asked as she handed Carter a glass of red wine.

"Oh yes, I found—"

He didn't get any further as Liam and Jeha came bursting through the door. "Mom, Dad, have a look here!" he shouted. "I landed four big ones! Uncle Ahote filleted them for us." Proudly, he held up the plate with fish fillets for them to see.

"Oh my, Liam! That's a big catch," Mackenzie said. She gave him a hug while she took the plate from him.

Carter smiled. "It certainly looks like you two had a good day, son. That's an excellent catch. But you'll have to go back tomorrow and get us some more; we're having four guests arriving."

Liam's face exploded with pride. "I will go and tell Uncle Ahote."

"Wait, I'll go with you. Let me just put the beanie over Beth's head, and she can come with us."

Mackenzie smiled and nodded. "Dinner will be ready in about an hour."

Later that night when the children were asleep, Mackenzie nestled in Carter's arm, they returned to discussing the Sirralnnudam.

Carter explained he found references to other sources, which they would have to try and track down. Some would probably be somewhere in the Middle East, if they still existed. Others would be in India or Pakistan, and some could even be in China.

Mackenzie was getting excited. "That means we've got some traveling coming up?"

"It appears to be the case," Carter replied. "But we won't be going out there alone. We'll need a protection detail to go with us. I'm not putting us in danger again."

"Agreed. One more thing to put on the agenda to discuss with Sean and Dylan," she replied. "So, apart from the references to the other scripts, did you manage to get an idea of what is covered in the contents?"

Carter nodded. "Yep, some of it. So far, I gathered that the document is categorized into topics covering the functions and composition of blood, the human circulatory system, blood-borne diseases and ailments, treatments and cures, but there is a lot more to read. So far, nothing about respirocytes, although I doubt, even if they were familiar with the concept, that they would have referred to it by that name."

"Hmm, I can understand that. I've been thinking how I could get Liu involved again. She was such a good friend during our ordeal in Saudi Arabia, and not only that, she is a genius when it comes to the translation of ancient texts."

"Strangely enough, that thought has crossed my mind a few times. My only concern is about her security and safety if she is working on the translation off-site and on her own. Maybe it's another topic to discuss with Sean and Dylan."

"Yes, let's do that. I would love to continue working with her. We understand each other so well, and she knows exactly what I'm after."

"By the way, I got the impression there was a thing going between her and Dylan," Carter said. "Or was that just because she felt lonely and scared during the rescue mission?"

Mackenzie chuckled. "No, you're right about the thing going. I speak to her often, and all I hear is Dylan this, and Dylan that, and Dylan and I . . . Reading between the lines, it seems to me Dylan has been spending more time in Boston than D.C. lately. I'm not surprised — after all, he carried her in his arms out of her room and up those stairs. Very romantic."

"Huh, what was so romantic about that? It was a do or die situation, no time for romance," Carter mumbled.

"Carter, let me educate you a little about women. Any woman gets rescued like that by a man — it's romantic."

"As opposed to stepping on her toes in a dark alley at the University?" Carter laughed.

Mackenzie replied with an elbow to his ribs.

"Ouch! You will never let me forget about that, will you?" He laughed.

## Chapter Fifteen

### THEY'RE INCONVINCIBLE

The next morning, Carter and Mackenzie continued their training regimen, followed by a tantalizing shower, which included the contractually-agreed mutual back scrub, and finally breakfast before they settled down in the study to work.

Right on time, ten a.m., they heard the plane approaching, dropped what they were doing, scrambled out to the electric carts, and drove out to the landing strip. They arrived just in time to see Sean Walker landing the Executive Advantage twin-engine, four-seater Beech Baron 58.

Soon after, Bly turned up in another electric cart to welcome the visitors and help transport them and their luggage.

Sean taxied the plane into the hangar next to Carter's plane, where they all emerged, greeted each other with hugs and handshakes while packing their baggage into the electric carts, and drove off.

A little while later, they were all gathered around the

kitchen table at the Devereux cabin, where Mackenzie and Bly treated them to coffee and carrot cake.

Later, they all strolled up to one of the vantage points close to the cabin, from where they enjoyed the stunning scenery over part of the eastern side of Freydís. On the way, Sean's and Dylan's whispering and exchanging of a few meaningful looks and nodding didn't escape Carter. He didn't ask what it was about — they would tell him in due time why they were there.

Right after lunch, Bly left as they all retired to the comfortable living room to talk about the projects.

James started by giving Carter and Mackenzie an overview of the meetings they had with President Grant and the Director of the CIA, Bill Griffin. He nodded for Irene to continue.

"You can't imagine how relieved we were when Carter called us a few days ago to say the two of you are ready to jump back on the wagon." She smiled. "We, especially Jim," she mocked, "thought the two of you would never want anything to do with us again."

"It took a bit of convincing, Irene." Mackenzie grinned, but didn't explain that Carter was the one who had to be swayed.

*"Go to the ant, thou sluggard; consider her ways, and be wise,"* Carter mumbled.

"What was that, Carter?" Irene asked.

"Proverbs 6, verse 6 — Solomon." Carter grinned and then told them about the conversations he and Mackenzie had about the projects and how watching the wolves helped him change his mind.

"Those wolves are the most remarkable animals," Irene replied pensively, as she remembered how the wolves had been instrumental in discovering Mackenzie and Liam were still alive and their eventual rescue. "Well, the most important part is that you're back. We admire you for that and are grateful that you're ready, willing, and able to continue."

For the rest of the afternoon, they delved into the details of Carter's and Mackenzie's projects and what A-Echelon and others could do to help so that the work could be progressed at the best possible pace.

Mackenzie told them they had decided to make Freydís their home base for the foreseeable future and that Liam would be homeschooled until he was old enough to go to a private boarding school — maybe in Quebec City or Montreal.

Sean and Dylan traded a quick *this-is-going-to-work-out-just-fine* look between them while Mackenzie was talking.

Carter explained that he planned to contact the University and hopefully renegotiate his contractual arrangements with them. He was keen to continue his association with them and hoped they would agree to him becoming a guest lecturer and researcher. If necessary, he could give lectures via the video link — if the Dean was agreeable.

"While we're on the topic of the University," Mackenzie said with a small conniving smile, "Dylan, we, Carter and I, were thinking of asking Liu to take a break and come and help me with the translation of the Sirralnnudam and other documents. Do you think she might be interested?"

"Mackenzie," he grinned, "let me answer both your questions."

"What do you mean both? I—"

"Yes, both. I know you and Liu talk at least three times a week." Dylan chuckled. "And I'm sure she is keeping you informed about what is going on between us. The answer to your hidden question is yes, I'm in love with her. The answer to your other question is I think she'd like it very much, but you'll have to ask her yourself."

Irene and Mackenzie stood and started clapping their hands in applause. Irene laughed and said, "Now all you have to do, Dylan Mulligan, is to tell her what you told us — both of your replies."

The men were just shaking their heads at Irene's and Mackenzie's antics — women! Incomprehensible, yet impossible for men to live without them.

Mackenzie had just gotten up to start the espresso machine when Beth let everyone know she'd woken from her afternoon sleep and required attention. Carter went to her room, changed her diaper, and brought her out to the living room, where she immediately became the main attraction. She was not shy of strangers.

James got the first honor of holding her on his lap and coaxing a smile from her, followed by Irene. Even Sean and Dylan, the two hardened Special Forces operators, succumbed to her charms.

With coffee in hand, the conversation turned to the ancient nuclear weapons — Carter's project, which came to a halt when Mackenzie and Liam were abducted and the search for them was begun.

Carter told them although he may not have been actively working on it, he'd been thinking a lot about it and had some ideas.

"We'll have to cast our nets much wider — expand our search efforts. That information retrieved from Algosaibi's laptop about the nuclear site the True Sons of the Prophet discovered at Palmyra, Syria, is worrying. And what is more worrying is it was found right in the heart of ISIS country.

"We'll have to assume by now there's more than one

fanatic out there who knows about the ancient nukes, and I'm willing to bet is also out looking for them.

"From that report, I gathered the radioactivity levels in those tunnels are lethal, and the people who entered the tunnels without protective clothing died from radiation poisoning."

"Music to ears of the radicals," Sean muttered.

Carter slowly nodded. "I have no doubt anymore. Actually, I stopped questioning the reality of those weapons a long time ago. They are as real as the sun out there.

"The challenge we have is to find out who built them, where, and how they did it. And my guess is that's exactly what the extremists are thinking — who, where, and how."

"Any ideas how we can stay ahead of them?" James asked.

"Digging, Jim, digging — with picks and shovels."

"Where?" Jim was serious.

"Start in the east and dig our way to the west . . . ." Carter started laughing.

James snorted as he realized Carter was having him on. "I should've known you'd pull a fast one on me at the first chance you got."

"Don't worry, Jim, there won't be *that* much digging," Carter said. "I think we have to do more underground surveying of those sites we identified before and dig them up to see if we can find information. I'm hoping at least one, maybe more, will produce written records that could give us some clues."

"What about the library of the giants?" Irene asked.

"I'm about to start working on that again. I might need help with it though — the last time I looked at it, I couldn't make heads or tails of it. But then that was in the midst of the planning and preparations for the rescue operation.

Maybe I'll do better now that I can apply my mind to it . . . without distractions."

Mackenzie smiled as she remembered how distracted Carter got the previous day when they were working in the library and couldn't help herself. "I'll make sure he stays focused."

Irene started giggling, and then the men caught on when they saw Carter's embarrassed look.

Before anyone could prolong Carter's suffering, Liam and Jeha came to his rescue as they arrived with a big noise and a bucket full of fish fillets.

Liam stopped in the door when he saw all the people and went quiet. Then he recognized them all, handed the bucket with fillets to Mackenzie, and went around quietly greeting everyone — the smell of fish following him like a wave.

He also gave Beth a little hug and kiss, which made her laugh out loud.

Jeha followed Liam, sniffing out everyone. She showed she was happy when she recognized them from their previous visits and allowed each of the guests to give her, to her delight, a little pat or ear-scratch.

Liam's arrival brought an end to their discussions — they would continue after dinner. Bly turned up shortly after with some salads and dessert and to help Mackenzie and Irene prepare the rest of the dinner. Ahote would join them shortly.

Carter produced some wine, beer, and other refreshments and made sure everyone had something to drink and nibble on before he took Beth for her bath, after which Mackenzie would feed her. She would stay up for another few hours before she went back to sleep around eight p.m.

# The Alboran Codex

Until then, the young red-haired lady would be thrilled with all the attention she got from the adults.

---

With Beth and Liam asleep, Ahote and Bly returned home, and the conversation returned to the projects.

"Carter," Sean started, "I always wanted to ask you about those giants and the 'City of Lights' as you call it. I know you have evidence of the size of the people who lived there, thousands of years ago. So, I'll have to accept they existed, but where did they come from, when did they cease to exist, and why?"

"That's quite a mouthful, Sean." Carter grinned. "We don't have enough information to say where they came from yet. A few anthropologists are busy with DNA studies, and hopefully we'll be able to get answers to that question soon . . . ish, maybe . . . I hope."

"Why the hesitation?" Sean frowned. "I would've thought scientists would be swarming all over that place by now."

"No, not really." Carter shook his head. "I guess you already know it was a very controversial discovery — as in, it doesn't fit nicely into the squared evolution box. So, there are quite a lot of scientists for whom the whole thing has become a bit prickly, and they are trying to distance themselves from it — doing everything they can to ridicule the discovery as a hoax and doing their level best to dissuade funding of further excavations."

"Are you saying they have seen the evidence, they have read the reports, and they still deny it because they can't explain it?"

"You whiz kid! Ten out of ten for that answer!" Carter laughed.

"What a bunch of jackasses," Sean mumbled.

"Okay, so leaving the featherheads aside for a moment," Irene interjected, "what're your theories about their disappearance?"

"Well, as far as I can see, they didn't disappear until 'recently'—and by recently, I mean they were still around 3,400 years ago."

"You call that recently?" Dylan asked, half surprised, but then corrected himself. "Yeah, well, if you think the City of Lights was abandoned fifty thousand plus years ago, I reckon 3,400 is recent."

"Wait a minute, 3,400 years ago, you say?" Sean replied. "That means they were around in the time of Moses and those guys?"

"Yes, even after Moses. You guys all attended Sunday school, didn't you?" Carter smiled. "Remember David and Goliath? The big guy who got his butt kicked by the shepherd boy with a slingshot?"

"Of course, I remember that," James growled. "Ah, so you reckon the big fellow could have been family of your giants?"

"It's possible, but compared to my giants, he was a bit on the short side."

"What do you mean?" Sean said. "I always thought Goliath was . . . gigantic."

"The Bible says he was 'six cubits and one span'," Carter replied. "A cubit is approximately eighteen inches and a span six inches, so he was around nine feet, six inches tall. My guys are more than fourteen feet — on average."

"Ah, I see what you mean," Sean replied. "But that then

doesn't explain your theory that some family members of your giants were around thirty-four hundred years ago, does it?"

"No, but my theory is not entirely based on the story of David and Goliath. Are any of you familiar with a guy by the name of Og? Also a biblical character."

Everyone except Mackenzie looked at him, dazed.

"Og? Like in O—g?" James asked.

Carter nodded.

"Never heard of him. Weird name, if you ask me."

"Okay, time for you people to sit down for a short Bible study session. Just give me a second." Carter laughed as he got up and retrieved his Bible from the bedroom.

Mackenzie offered everyone something to drink. All of them opted for tea, and she got up to get the kettle going.

Carter returned with his Bible in hand. It was the Bible his grandfather, Will, gave to him when he went to University. It had a personal message from Will in the front, which read, *"Carter, my son, in this book you will find wisdom and peace. Read it often — let it be the lamp for your feet and the North Star of your life."*

"Okay children, are we ready?"

They all nodded and smiled.

"Deuteronomy 3:11 - *For only Og king of Bashan remained of the remnant of the giants. Indeed, his bedstead was an iron bedstead. (Is it not in Rabbah of the people of Ammon?) Nine cubits is its length and four cubits its width, according to the standard cubit.*"

"Wow! That's like what . . .?" Dylan was making quick calculations. "Fourteen feet? Huh?"

"Yep." Carter nodded. "In Jewish literature, Og is said to be a descendant of the giants who survived the flood."

"This is fascinating stuff, Carter!" Irene exclaimed.

"Oh, learned and wise one, please tell us more," Sean quipped.

"Let me give you a few examples. The earliest mention of giants is found in Genesis." Carter continued, "Throughout the Old Testament there are references to giants when talking about Amorites, Emim, Zuzim, Rephaim, and Nephilim. Here are a few examples.

"Genesis 6:4 — *There were giants [Nephilim] on the earth in those days, and also afterward, when the sons of God came in to the daughters of men and they bore children to them. Those were the mighty men who were of old, men of renown.*

"Genesis 14:5–7 — *In the fourteenth year Chedorlaomer and the kings that were with him came and attacked the Rephaim in Ashteroth Karnaim, the Zuzim in Ham, the Emim in Shaveh Kiriathaim, and the Horites in their mountain of Seir . . . Then they turned back and came to En Mishpat (that is, Kadesh), and attacked all the country of the Amalekites, and also the Amorites who dwelt in Hazezon Tamar.*"

Carter stopped and said, "Genesis 14 does not specifically say that the Rephaim, Zuzim, Emim, or Amorites were giants, but just hang on, and I'll show you how they are linked.

"The Amorites are mentioned more than eighty times in the Bible. Early on, they were allies of Abraham, and apparently, they were the descendants of Noah's grandson, Canaan.

"Amos 2:9–10—*Yet it was I who destroyed the Amorite before them, whose height was like the height of the cedars, and he was as strong as the oaks; yet I destroyed his fruit above and his roots beneath. Also, it was I who brought you up from the land of Egypt, and led you forty years through the wilderness, to possess the land of the Amorite.*

"The reports provided by Moses's spies, which he sent through the land of Canaan, supports the notion that the

Amorites were giants. Numbers 13:28 — *the people who dwell in the land are strong; the cities are fortified and very large; moreover, we saw the descendants of Anak there.* Numbers 14:6–9 — *all the people whom we saw in it are men of great stature.*

"Let's look at the Emim. Deuteronomy 2:10–11 — *The Emim had dwelt there in times past, a people as great and numerous and tall as the Anakim. They were also regarded as giants [Hebrew rephaim], like the Anakim, but the Moabites call them Emim.*

"The Zuzim or Zamzummim, Deuteronomy 2:20–21 — *The land of Ammon was also regarded as a land of giants [Hebrew rephaim]; giants [rephaim] formerly dwelt there. But the Ammonites call them Zamzummim, a people as great and numerous and tall as the Anakim. But the Lord destroyed them before them, and they dispossessed them and dwelt in their place.*

"And for an encore, just a few more from Samuel." Carter smiled.

"2 Samuel 21: 15 to 22 —*Then Ishbi-Benob, who was one of the sons of the giant, the weight of whose bronze spear was three hundred shekels, who was bearing a new sword, thought he could kill David. But Abishai the son of Zeruiah came to his aid, and struck the Philistine and killed him.*

*"Now it happened afterward that there was again a battle with the Philistines at Gob [or "Gezer"]. Then Sibbechai the Hushathite killed Saph [or "Sippai"], who was one of the sons of the giant.*

*"Again there was war at Gob with the Philistines, where Elhanan the son of Jaare-Oregim [or "Jair"] the Bethlehemite killed ["Lahmi"] the brother of Goliath the Gittite, the shaft of whose spear was like a weaver's beam.*

*"Yet again there was war at Gath, where there was a man of great stature, who had six fingers on each hand and six toes on each foot, twenty-four in number; and he also was born to the giant. So when he defied Israel, Jonathan the son of Shimea, David's brother, killed him."*

"What extra-Biblical evidence of giants do you have?" James asked when Carter ended.

Carter held three fingers in the air. "Three sources that spring to mind. First, for more than a century now, archeologists have been discovering enormous bones, tools, weaponry, and other artifacts that only a giant could have used. Some of those giant-sized artifacts exist in museums, much of the evidence are eyewitness accounts and pictures.

"Second, the illustrations of huge people found on Egyptian jars and inside tombs. Some historians say they are simply representations of deities and kings drawn in a way to show their importance or high rank, but there are other explanations which postulate that those images are of real giants.

"Third, written accounts outside of the Bible can be found in the Book of Enoch, the Book of Jasher, and in the writings of the Jewish historian, Josephus, all of which support the Bible narratives.

"All three of these books talk about the existence of giants. For instance, in one of Josephus's writings, there is a passage about the Israelites moving to Hebron, where they encountered '*the race of giants, who had bodies so large, and countenances so entirely different from other men, that they were surprising to the sight, and terrible to the hearing. The bones of these men are still shown to this very day.*'"

Carter's audience looked at him with mouths agog.

Glancing at his watch, he said, "Okay, it's getting late, children. I can show you some images and texts tomorrow, if you're interested."

"I'm now convinced there were giants, and that they were still around not too long ago — well, at least within the timeframes we are talking about," Sean said.

"After a lecture as stimulating as this, who wouldn't be convinced?" James added.

"The jackasses and featherheads Sean and Irene referred to earlier." Carter laughed. "They're inconvincible."

"Yeah, well, tough luck for them. They are missing out big time," Sean concluded.

## Chapter Sixteen

### I TOOK THEIR ADVICE

The next morning, Mackenzie and Carter were up early and went for their run. They skipped the self-defense training but didn't skip their pleasant shower routine. They prepared a big breakfast for everyone, after which they all went out for a short hike to see more of the picturesque beauty of Freydís.

In their bedroom, the night before, Mackenzie said, "Maybe it's just my imagination, but I get the distinct feeling Sean and Dylan didn't come along just for the fun of it — it's as if they've something important to talk about."

"So, you've also noticed it," Carter said.

"Any idea what it could be?"

"No, but I'm sure we'll hear about it tomorrow. If it were anything serious, they would have mentioned it by now."

"Well, curiosity killed the cat, so I guess we'll just have to be patient and wait then."

The previous night, after dinner, they had covered all the details about the two projects before they got into the discussion about the giants. What remained to talk about was the setup of the communications infrastructure, security arrangements for the inhabitants of Freydís, and the hitherto undisclosed matter on the minds of Sean and Dylan.

Carter had Beth in a baby carrier on his back. She fell asleep while they were walking but opened her eyes when they settled on the grass under a nice, big, old tree on top of a lookout point.

Mackenzie took Beth out of the carrier, and the little one looked around — dazed for a few moments. When she spotted Irene, she began smiling, prompting Irene to immediately take the baby in her arms.

Carter and Mackenzie didn't have to wait long to get the answer to their speculations of the night before.

"Carter, Mackenzie," Sean started. "I'm sure you have already surmised that Dylan and I came along on this trip because we have something important to discuss with you — a proposal we want to make."

"Sean, Dylan — Mackenzie and I are offended. Are you saying the purpose of your visit was anything other than to be in our wonderful company?" Carter tried to look hurt.

Sean laughed. "Yeah, well, there is that, but maybe not entirely as much of it as you would like to imagine."

Irene and James knew what Sean and Dylan were going to put forward, so they just sat back and enjoyed the jesting.

Carter grabbed the left side of his chest in a mock gesture of a stab to the heart. "I'm floored, my friend. Totally devastated. Here poor Mackie and I are living in the illusion that you two are our best friends and would like nothing better than to spend a bit of time with us."

"Carter, cut it out! Let Sean talk now." Mackenzie laughed as she aimed a playful punch at him.

"Well, if you accept our proposal, we might be able to work on those friendship issues," Sean replied.

"We're all ears, Sean. Please continue, and don't mind Carter. He's still hyperactive from all the coffee he had this morning," Mackenzie said.

"Okay, so let me get to the point before Carter gets his nose out of joint about our friendship going south." Sean laughed. "We want to know how you would feel about us, Executive Advantage, setting up a Special Forces training facility here on Freydís?"

Carter and Mackenzie looked at each other — they opened their mouths, closed them, and just stared at Sean and Dylan in turn.

After a long pause, Carter said, "What exactly do you have in mind?"

Mackenzie's mind was working at light-speed.

Sean continued. "Jim and Irene told me you know a little about the history of Executive Advantage — that we are a type of international mercenary force — much like a mini French Foreign Legion."

Carter nodded.

"Almost like the NATO of black ops — in other words, we are the free world's top-secret country-less antiterrorism organization with very little red tape or bureaucracy. Just a bunch of good guys hunting and eliminating the bad guys — agile and extremely effective thus far. We are independent, apolitical, areligious, anti-dogmatic, et cetera, and therefore we have the support of intelligence agencies across the globe.

"EA was established when leaders of a few security agencies from around the world got together and agreed to form an independent, global Special Forces unit with a deep pool of expertise. We are officially part of the American black ops community, but we are funded by all the member countries. It's a unit of specialists who can assure swift and successful clandestine missions anywhere in the world. The result of this international interagency agreement is that Executive Advantage has access to the skills of former Special Forces members from around the globe. That means we recruit people from the Navy SEALS, Delta Force, Green Berets, AFSOC, British and Australian SAS, Canadian Joint Task Force 2 - JTF2, French Foreign Legion, Israel's Kidon — part of Mossad, Oman's Desert Phantoms, India's Gurkhas, and others.

"We're an organization of last resort, which means we're called upon whenever security and intelligence agencies find themselves with an intractable problem that must be dealt with when commercial, diplomatic, and political solutions have failed or are not an option.

"However, and I'm sure you can imagine, politicians of the member countries don't want to have any 'knowledge' about us or our activities — they want results and no links to them — plausible deniability."

Carter and Mackenzie both nodded and waited for Sean or Dylan to continue.

Dylan took over. "So, what we have in mind is to set up a secret training facility in a place where no one would expect it, isolated, away from populated areas, prying eyes, spy satellites, and such. And Freydís ticks all those boxes."

"Hmm, that's an interesting idea," Carter murmured. "What type of training, and how many people?"

"There'd be no worry about environmental issues," Dylan replied. "What we have in mind is to blend in with nature in every way possible. We don't want to build open air rifle ranges or train demolitions experts and turn the place into a simulated war zone. What we have in mind are training in things such as survival skills, field craft, tracking, stalking, fitness, hand-to-hand combat, electronic communications, surveillance, spy craft, and the like. In other words, no noise pollution."

"Mackenzie?" Carter looked at her. He was not going to decide without her — Freydís was Mackenzie and Mackenzie was Freydís. If he detected even the slightest hint of hesitation from her, he was not going to agree, neither was he going to put any pressure on her. Although Sean's proposal came as a big surprise, for some unknown reason, the idea appealed to him. He had to think about it first, but one thing was immediately clear in his mind — if Mackenzie didn't agree with the proposition, he was not going to agree to it either.

Her mind was still racing. The absence of humans on Freydís was the reason for its unadulterated natural beauty and special charm for her. Freydís was the one and only place in the universe where she felt she belonged; it was as if she had been part of this land for thousands of years. It was as if her DNA was somehow interwoven with this land.

*Was that about to change? Should I allow it to change? Do I want it to change? Is this the price we must pay for our decision to continue? Am I selfish to want Freydís just for myself and my family?*

Conflict was battling in her brain.

Carter noticed Mackenzie's impasse and came to the rescue. "Mackie, I don't think" —Carter turned his eyes to Sean and Dylan— "they want us to make a decision right now. Right, guys?"

"No, there's still a lot to talk over," Sean replied. "Take your time."

Dylan added, "And please don't feel under any pressure to agree. We'll not be disappointed if you decide against it."

"Thanks. It's good to know there's no pressure. I guess

the important thing for us" —Carter pointed to Mackenzie and himself— "is to find out how something like this would impact on our lifestyle here. I know that might sound self-centered, but Freydís is a very special place for us, and we want to keep it that way."

Mackenzie slowly nodded. "Yeah, what Carter said — Freydís is special to us, but I have to say I'm not experiencing any immediate allergic reactions to the idea." She smiled. "I would like to hear more and think about it."

"Well, in that case, I am sure we could work it out," Sean said, sounding relieved. "Let's talk about the details then. If that's okay with the two of you?"

Carter and Mackenzie both nodded.

For the next hour and a half, Sean and Dylan provided the specifics, with Carter and Mackenzie stopping them every so often with questions.

Their idea was to assign two or three semi-permanent staff members, who would be instructors to take care of the training of new recruits. Semi-permanent because they would rotate them every few months. The trainees would number no more than six to seven at any given time, depending on what type of training they had to undergo.

They had already studied the aerial maps and satellite images of Freydís and identified a valley about two miles to the east of the homestead that looked like the ideal place to set up the training base.

Sean explained that President Grant had approved the idea, and the Director of the CIA, Bill Griffin, had discussed the plan with his counterpart in the Canadian Security Intelligence Service, who was also positive about it.

Dylan explained how Rick Winslow would set up impenetrable communications links, which would give them secure high-speed access to D.C. and any other location in the world via satellite.

"Are we not setting ourselves up as a target by doing all of this?" Mackenzie asked.

"Yes, Mackenzie." Sean nodded. "That is a possibility. I'd be dishonest if I told you otherwise. But I can assure you that we'll take all the necessary security steps to protect you as well as us. Rick will be setting up twenty-four seven drone and satellite surveillance and other electronic protection measures.

"As far as possible, we'll make sure that our buildings and presence here are invisible to drone and satellite detection by unfriendlies or snoopers."

Just then Mackenzie saw movement amongst the trees and bushes about a hundred yards away. She squinted. Keeva and Loki were standing under a tree quietly observing them.

"Excuse me for a few minutes," she said as she got up and walked over to them.

Everyone went quiet. Sean and Dylan were worried they may have said something to upset Mackenzie. Carter's eyes followed the direction she was going and saw the wolves.

"The wolves came to say hi to her." He pointed towards the trees.

"Those wolves will never cease to amaze me," James said. "It's just the most unusual thing I've ever experienced — at least as far as animals are concerned."

They all watched in awe as Mackenzie approached the wolves and sat down with them. Putting her arms around them in turn, scratching their ears and backs while she was talking to them. They were clearly listening to her, and with a bit of imagination, one could be forgiven for thinking the wolves were talking back to her.

Maybe they were.

About ten minutes later, she got up and walked back to the group — the wolves followed her.

Everyone watched her and the wolves approaching.

She saw the inquisitive looks and smiled. "Oh, Keeva and Loki said they haven't met Beth yet, so they want to meet her and just wanted to say hi to all of you. Apparently, they have met all of you before."

"Wha . . . how . . . Mackenzie, what the . . ." James stuttered. "You can't be serious!"

Everyone started laughing except Carter. He'd told her about James's meeting with the wolves but not that the wolves had met Irene, Sean, and Dylan before — she had no way of knowing that.

She led the wolves to Irene, who was still holding Beth. She took Beth in her arms and knelt in front of the animals — they sniffed and made little joyful sounds, wagging their tails while they looked at the little human bundle. After a while, they had seen enough and went around to everyone, sniffing and licking the hands held out to them.

Mackenzie handed Beth back to Irene, looked at Keeva and Loki, and said, "Come," as she started back to the trees where she'd met them.

Loki and Keeva followed her back. She spent another few minutes talking and rubbing them, and then they left.

Mackenzie watched them disappear amongst the trees and then returned to the group with a beaming smile. They guessed there was something for her to pass on and were waiting for her to tell them.

She did. "Sean, Dylan, I've made up my mind. If Carter agrees, then I agree."

"Advice from the wolves, Mackenzie?" Sean quipped.

She just laughed. "In a manner of speaking, yes."

"Well, in that case," Carter said, "let's get back home and start planning. We need to bring Bly and Ahote in on this as well. Any problem, Dylan, Sean?"

"No problem, of course, they must know," Sean replied. He and Dylan were smiling broadly. It had gone a lot better than they anticipated.

Beth was placed in the baby carrier on Carter's back, and they wandered back to the homestead.

Carter fell in step next to Mackenzie. "Mackie, I hadn't told you Irene, Sean, and Dylan met the wolves before. How did you know?"

She shrugged and laughed. "Just an intelligent guess, Carter. I know they've been here before, so I imagined they had met them then."

"Of course," Carter replied with a grin. "And what about making up your mind so quickly after meeting with Keeva and Loki?"

"I took their advice." Mackenzie giggled. "Just like Sean said."

"Come on, Mackie, I'm serious."

"I don't know, Carter. I told them about my dilemma, and they started licking my hands, and . . . well . . . the next thing I knew, I felt convinced it's the right thing to do. It's impossible to say how it happened. But that's what happened, and I feel relieved about it."

"Mackie, you and your wolves . . ." Carter was shaking his head. "One day I'm going to write a book about it!"

## Chapter Seventeen

### IT AIN'T OVER TILL THE FAT LADY SINGS

Perrin Durand had been watching Mayon and Aisha for a few days, and it was a dreary job. The subjects were observably nervous. They didn't appear in public much, and whenever they did, they were constantly looking around and over their shoulders. It was clear as daylight that they had no idea about counter surveillance — how to blend in and look inconspicuous. Their behavior made them stand out like sore thumbs. For him, there was no challenge in this, no excitement. If not for the money he would earn for the job, and keeping his mind occupied about his tropical island retirement plans, this mission would have been utterly mind numbing.

For the first few days, Durand kept a distance to get an idea of his subjects' routine and to see if anyone else was tailing them. The only thing they did that remotely resembled evasion tactics was moving to a different hotel, motel, or backpacker's every day. That guaranteed that Durand could practice boredom in a different location daily.

By the fifth day, he was confident that no else was

following them and decided he knew enough about their habits to get closer. He needed to plant surveillance bugs on their luggage and perhaps install a little GPS tracking program on their mobile phones — if they had mobile phones, because he had never seen them use one thus far.

It was 1:20 in the morning when Durand approached the door of the motel room on the ground floor. He had been watching the area since early evening. Mayon and Aisha's room lights had gone out two hours ago. There were not many guests — the place was practically deserted — all factors that favored his plans. He had studied the door locks and the poor excuse for a security system — antiquated electronic door locks, no security cameras, only fire alarms — no challenge. He stopped at the door and swiped the electronic lock jammer. Exactly five seconds later he heard the click of the lock.

Slowly he cracked the door open and dropped a small canister containing a non-lethal dose of the powerful knockout agent Fentanyl. He closed the door and slowly counted to twenty while pulling out and donning a small gas mask from his backpack before entering.

He had thirty to forty minutes to finish the job. He did it in ten — planting small inconspicuous bugs on each piece of their luggage, and the laptop bag took him less than two minutes. Finding their mobile phones and laptop and loading the GPS tracking and remote activation software took him another eight minutes. The two never moved once during the time he was in their room.

*Apologies in advance. Unfortunately, the two of you are going to wake up with a bit of a headache.*

When he was done, he checked the hall outside carefully for a minute, making sure he would not be spotted by anyone, before leaving.

With the bugs in place, Durand's observation mission became much easier, and he also hoped a bit more eventful than the past five days. At least now he would be able to listen to their conversations.

It was shortly after seven a.m. when Durand heard the voices of his subjects for the first time.

"Aisha, it's seven. We have to get moving," the male voice said in Arabic. "I have a terrible headache. Come on, Aisha, wake up!"

"Huh . . . what . . . Oh! My head!" It was a female voice, which Durand assumed belonged to Aisha. "Mayon, what's going on?"

"We've overslept. We have to get going; otherwise we'll miss the appointment at the clinic," replied Mayon.

"Good. From now on we will be on a first-name basis." Durand smiled. "You may call me Perrin." He'd once been stationed in North Africa for many years and spoke fluent Arabic, both the North African dialect and the original.

For more than half an hour he listened to their irritable voices, bickering and complaining about their headaches, the miserable room, bed, food, and people, nearly every time they opened their mouths.

*Spoiled brats.*

Finally, they made their appearance, their baggage in tow. Mayon went to reception, dropped the room keys off, and returned to help Aisha move their stuff to the parking lot where a taxi was waiting for them.

On his GPS tracker, Durand saw one of their mobile phones was on — probably the one they used to call the cab. Once their vehicle pulled into the traffic, he allowed three more cars to pass before he pulled out onto the road and followed them.

He had no trouble tailing the cab, but other than

knowing they were going to a clinic and that for the past hour had been heading south, he had no idea about the location or purpose. Nothing came over his earphones except the sound of the taxi's engine and other street noises —no conversation, not even *"look there"* or *"what's that"* or *"that's beautiful"* or anything else tourists in Rome would usually be saying.

*Maybe they know Rome well enough that there is nothing to impress them anymore, or maybe the language barrier is preventing them from talking to the driver, or maybe . . . stuck-up, rich, spoiled Arabs never satisfied with anything.*

Almost ninety minutes after leaving the motel, they were in the peaceful, exclusive *Appia Antica* neighborhood about twenty minutes south of the city center. Secluded villas with gardens and swimming pools within the boundaries of the *Appia Antica* Park, a regional nature and catacombs park, created a rural atmosphere.

The cab pulled up to a gated entrance to a villa, which was not visible from the road. The driver spoke into the intercom, *"Mr. e Mrs. Zaid per la loro nomina."*—Mr. and Mrs. Zaid for their appointment — the gates rolled away.

Durand drove past the entrance and tried to take in as much as he could without looking too interested. He parked a block away, still within range of the signal from his listening devices, took out his tablet, and called up Google Maps.

*Family, friends, or business contacts?* he wondered.

He didn't have to wait long to get his answer when a woman's voice welcomed them and asked them to take a seat, saying, "Doctor Bordereau will see you in five minutes."

*Okay, so it's a private clinic. Hmm . . . wonder what could be ailing them?*

Again, Durand didn't have to wait long for an answer as he heard doctor Bordereau explaining the plastic surgery procedures and expectations to them in French — his mother tongue. Bordereaux was good — he took time to put his patients at ease. He gave them a bit of an overview of the history and methods used during cosmetic surgery.

"Don't worry, I won't be implanting plastic into your bodies. The word plastic, in this case, refers to shaping or, as in your case, reshaping some of your facial and body features."

There were some muffled sounds from Mayon, which Durand could not hear.

"Contrary to what many people believe," Bordereau continued, "plastic surgery is not really a modern branch of medicine. In fact, it has been around for thousands of years.

"Did you know that the 'plastic' repair of a broken nose was common practice in Ancient Egypt? There are texts about this procedure that go back to 3000 BC.

"I have seen documents coming from India that describe reconstructive surgery techniques performed in 800 BC. In the late 1700s, British surgeons went to India frequently to learn how to perform rhinoplasties, nose-jobs as we call them these days.

"The first major nose-job in the West was done by the British surgeon Joseph Constantine Carpue at the Duke of York Hospital in Chelsea in 1815.

"But let me give my host country some praise as well." Bordereaux chuckled. "More than two thousand years ago, the Romans also performed cosmetic surgery. More simplistic than the Egyptians and Indians, but still they repaired damaged ears and other parts of the body.

"The first American was John Peter Mettauer, who performed the first cleft palate operation in 1827."

Another muffled noise, which Durand couldn't hear properly and thus made him swear. "They must be sitting on one of the damn microphones."

"Yes, don't worry. It is not invasive surgery. I'm not going to cut you open — all of it will be happening at the skin level. It is not like the old days when these procedures were performed without anesthesia. You will be fast asleep while I do it, and with the proper painkiller administration, the most you will feel will be the anesthetist's needle when we put you to sleep."

"How . . . long . . . can . . . leave . . ." was all the frustrated Durand could make out of Aisha's words.

"Ten to fourteen days," the doctor replied. "I prefer to keep my patients here to make sure there are no infections or any other complications. The day when you walk out of here, not even your own mother would be able to recognize you."

More muffled speech followed.

"Good. Now let's look at exactly what it is you want. "

For the next hour, Durand listened while the three of them looked at and discussed various images the doctor was bringing up on-screen, after he had taken pictures of them. The software the doctor used showed what they would look like afterward with different nose lines, eyebrows, contact lenses, bleached skins, changed hair color, and other features.

To Durand's surprise, he even heard a few bouts of laughter coming from Aisha and Mayon. He'd thought they had no sense of humor.

The operations were scheduled for the next morning at seven a.m. for Aisha first and then Mayon. Each would last between two and three hours.

They were already booked into the clinic and had paid the $200,000 USD cash in advance as agreed.

*Not a bad rate for six hours' work.*

Durand started the car and drove back to his hotel. There was not a lot more he could do but wait until the "new" subjects made their appearance outside the clinic in ten to fourteen days.

Back in his hotel room, he typed up his progress report and copied it onto a small flash drive, which he would leave at a dead drop location — a coffee shop close to the Vatican —the next morning. For the next ten to fourteen days, he would visit the clinic once a day to "check" on his subjects' recuperation. The rest of the time he would be sightseeing Rome and the surrounding areas.

*If this mission continues on this trend, it might just be the easiest $1.5 million any hitman has ever earned.* Durand grinned at that thought — he knew, as the American's say, *"it ain't over till the fat lady sings."*

He had to follow them until they reached Paris, if that's where they were heading.

## Chapter Eighteen

### TALA CAMP

James, Irene, Sean, and Dylan extended their visit to Freydís by two days to finalize the plans for the training center. Ahote and Bly were now involved as well. The group visited the canyon about two miles from the Freydís main house, which Sean and Dylan spotted on satellite maps before. The area was about twenty acres, surrounded by high cliffs on three sides and covered with lush, dense vegetation and tall spruce trees right up to the cliff walls. It was the perfect cover from prying satellite or drone cameras. A perennial stream would supply fresh water, and a small turbine could generate electricity. An abundance of timber ensured they had enough building material to construct as many log cabins as they wanted. Carter showed them a cavernous rock overhang, about nine hundred square feet, on the eastern cliff wall. With a little bit of imagination and carpentry, this area would serve as their communications center and office.

It was the ideal place — secluded, quiet, and easy to secure. The high, vertical cliffs, fitted with strategically placed solar powered laser "trip wires", would make it all but impossible to approach the area unnoticed, other than from the narrow cleft in the rocks on the south side.

While inspecting the perimeters, and arriving at the opening, Sean remarked, "This reminds me of the Battle of Thermopylae. In 480 BC, Leonidas, the king of Sparta, and three hundred of his warriors, in a place that looks a little like this, stopped a Persian army of one million men in their tracks for two days. Had they not been betrayed, they could very well have stopped them completely and made them go back home."

"Those were the days." Dylan sighed and smiled wryly. "Swords, spears, bows and arrows, blood, guts, and glory. What more can a soldier desire?"

Carter laughed. "Dylan, it almost sounds as if you were there!"

It was settled. This was the best place to set up the training camp.

Back home over coffee and more of Bly's cake, it was apparent they were all excited about the plans. Ahote, who had experience with building log cabins, was appointed as the construction manager.

Sean arranged with six of his men to prepare themselves to relocate to Freydís for a few weeks to start the work. Initially, the construction team would be put up by Mackenzie and Bly until they had their first cabins ready at the base.

A target move-in date was set for ten to fourteen days from now. Within two months, the first trainees would arrive.

Carter and Mackenzie were delighted to find out that some of the EA training staff were married and had young children, some of them Liam and Beth's age.

On the last night before James and company had to go back, Irene brought up the inevitable question. "What do we call this new place? Let's be creative — not something like EA Camp Alpha, or the like." She smiled.

Carter looked at his old friend. "Ahote, I remember Grandpa Will told me you were the one who named Freydís all those years ago. What do you think?"

"Hmm, well I'll have to think about that . . ." Ahote murmured.

A long debate followed, but James's fascination with the wolves of Freydís since the first day he met them must have influenced his chain of thought. "We called our rescue team 'the Wolves of Freydís'. I suggest we stick to those magnificent creatures and call the place 'Tala', the Sioux word for wolf. How does that sound?"

Everyone went quiet. Mackenzie started grinning — anything to do with her wolf-friends had that effect on her. She smiled as she said, "Tala Camp or the Wolf Camp. I really like that." She already had her hand up when she asked, "Shall we vote?"

James's proposal won by a landslide, getting one hundred percent of the votes. There were no abstentions or dissent.

The mention of the wolves and seeing how Mackenzie interacted with them the day before must have reminded Irene about the many thoughts she'd had about this strange phenomenon. She was looking at Mackenzie and Carter when she started, "Is there a clear scientific explanation for the origins of human language? How did language develop in humans? Rather, I should ask, did it develop, or was it always there?"

Everyone stopped and looked at Carter.

"Professor?" Mackenzie asked with raised eyebrows.

"You are a receptive bunch of students!" Carter started laughing. "But this time, I might disappoint you. My knowledge is superficial. Liu should be here — I know she did some in-depth research on this subject a while ago."

Dylan smiled. "Well, I will ask her when I see her again. But in the meantime, I'm pretty sure what you refer to as 'superficial knowledge of the subject' is still going to be much more than I know."

The group went quiet again, waiting for Carter to start.

"Well, it is said to be one of the most controversial subjects you can imagine. The answer of how language came about as a human trait depends on whether you are listening to evolutionists or creationists."

Mackenzie chuckled. "Well, we haven't had one of those evolutionary discussions in a long time. I'm all ears."

"The debate has been raging for centuries," Carter continued. "The problem that scientists have is the lack of direct evidence, which makes for a lot of confusion and conjecture. There was even a time when this shortage of fact led many scholars to abandon the entire topic because it was regarded as *'unsuitable for serious study'*.

"I've read somewhere that in the late eighteen hundreds, the Linguistic Society of Paris banned all debates on the subject. It was as if everyone agreed to that prohibition, and the subject sort of stayed off the agenda until late in the twentieth century. And despite a lot of scientific breakthroughs and new methods since the eighteen hundreds, it is still referred to by many as *'the hardest problem in science.'*"

"Keep on going," Irene prodded when it looked like he was going to stop talking. She was enjoying every moment of it.

"Well, the two main schools of thought come from the continuity and discontinuity theorists.

"The continuity believers say *'human language exhibits so much complexity that one cannot imagine it simply appearing from nothing in its final form; therefore, it must have evolved from earlier pre-linguistic systems among our primate ancestors.'*

"The discontinuity theorists use that same argument to say *'human language is a unique trait, which cannot be compared to anything found among non-humans, and must have appeared fairly suddenly during the course of human evolution.'*

"Some say language is genetically encoded while others say it's learned through social interaction. Noam Chomsky, a well-known American linguist, said something to the effect that some sort of mutation occurred in one individual about a hundred thousand years ago by chance, which suddenly created the language ability in *perfect* or *near-perfect* form."

"Yeah, right!" Mackenzie started laughing but stopped abruptly. "Oops, not too many years ago I was one of those *mutation by chance* believers myself."

Carter chuckled. "I told you way back then Will and I were going to make a creationist out of you."

"Yes, I remember, and at the time, I thought *'we'll see about that'.*" She laughed.

"But seriously now, what do *you* believe? How did we learn to speak?" Irene asked.

"I don't think humans ever evolved into speaking creatures from non-speaking creatures. I believe we were created with the capability to speak. That's obviously a very simplistic view of it because human language is an extraordinary thing. It's complex and for the most part controlled by a set of in-built automated rules. Steven Pinker calls it *'the language instinct'*. I think it's present from birth, and as we grow, we are influenced by the language of our parents, teachers, friends, et cetera."

"That sounds fairly logical to me," Mackenzie replied, while Irene and James nodded.

"But why are you interested in this, Irene? I get the idea you have something else on your mind," Carter observed.

"It's actually the wolves that got my mind into overdrive since the first time I met them. They made me wonder about humans and animals and communication. I always thought language is a human trait only, but since meeting the wolves, I'm not so sure anymore. It's as if they somehow have a way to communicate with us — a language we don't understand, but it's definitely there."

Mackenzie nodded. "Just look at Jeha and Liam. Sometimes that little dog looks like she understands everything Liam is saying, and at times I get the impression she knows exactly how to talk to Liam. I've read somewhere that even the average dog can learn 160 human words, and Border Collies, the sheepdog breed, can learn up to a thousand human words."

"On the topic of dogs," Sean added, "Dylan and I have experience working with war dogs on some of our missions. It's mindboggling to see what those dogs are capable of. I've personally experienced that military war dogs can not only understand diverse commands but can follow a string of orders such as *'search ahead, stay, watch.'* In some situations, the handlers fit the dogs with tiny earphones so that they can communicate with them when they are out of sight, which means they must understand specific words and sentences, not just the intonation of our voices."

"What bothers me is we don't even know one word in dog language," Mackenzie noted. "What do we miss by not being able to have conversations with the animals? I know animal vocal cords are not capable of producing human sounds and vice versa, but with computers these days, it must be possible to bridge that gap. Wouldn't you think?"

"You've got a point there, Mackie," Carter replied. "I've been thinking about that for years, in particular since I saw you and the wolves interact the first time and ever since. And . . ." he paused for a moment, "how can we ever forget how they practically *told* us you and Liam were alive, and not only that, they also *told* us about Beth? We just didn't understand at the time when Keeva got pregnant it was the same time as Mackenzie discovered she was pregnant. And also why they gave Liam's toys back to us."

"Yes," said Mackenzie, "and how they kept me company in my darkest moments in that hellhole. It was as if they really were there. I know psychologists will have a lot of mumbo jumbo about it, but for me their presence was real."

The group was staring at each other for a while before Mackenzie continued. "What about primates? Like Kanzi, that bonobo ape capable of demonstrating his understanding of more than 3,000 English words. And not just single words but sentences with instructions or questions."

"What about dolphins?" James said.

"Don't even get me started on dolphins," Mackenzie said, laughing.

"No, no hang on there. Don't stop now. I want to hear about the dolphins," James said as he leaned back in his chair.

"Okay, you asked for it," she said with a big smile when everyone was looking at her to continue.

"So, do dolphins have a language? That's a question I've been asking since I was a little girl. And here is my take on it.

"First, I don't want to get bogged down in the academic

definition of the word language. For me, the word 'language' just means a communication system. It could be verbal and non-verbal, sounds and gestures. So, I'm of the opinion that we humans don't have a monopoly on language.

"Dolphins have a communications system; there is no doubt about it. The fact that we don't understand it is not proof they don't have a language. In fact, all animals and most living things have some sort of communications system. Just think about it. Even plants, like flowers, have a way of communicating with the bees when they are ready to be pollinated. The cells in our body communicate with each other. Just cut yourself with a knife, and a message goes from the wound to the brain, to the vocal cords and out comes the word 'ouch!' Without *'the language of cells'*, we wouldn't have a body.

"For ages, people have tried to teach human language to animals—anything from dolphins, dogs, chimpanzees, gorillas, elephants, to parrots, and results have been remarkable. But scientists agree that only a human can fully learn a human language. To make their conclusion complete, I think they should have admitted that by the same token, humans are incapable of learning animal language.

"I mean, if 'dolphin scientists' were doing the same experiment on humans, they would probably conclude that no matter how smart humans seem to be, they just can't learn how to swim like dolphins."

James replied, "Well, when you put it like that . . ."

Everyone exploded in laughter.

Mackenzie continued. "So, I'm saying in the same way humans have a verbal and non-verbal communication system, animals have verbal or, to us, audible and inaudible communication systems. Audible sounds or what we call language is part of our communications system, but the sounds we make are not the entire communications system. Our smiles, hugs, laughs, frowns, handshakes, hand gestures, and movements, et cetera are all an integral part of our communications system.

"Animals also use vocalizations — barks, growls, whistles, creaks, chuffs, screams, squawks, pops, chirps, and others— for communication. They also incorporate gestures in their communications, like dogs baring their teeth or wagging their tails.

"Dolphins have been shown to use communicative methods such as vocalizations, physical contact, and postures to express their emotional state.

"Now hold onto your chairs," Mackenzie said. "Scientists showed dolphins communicate emotions such as anger, frustration, contentment, affection, and others. And not only that, they also express information about their reproductive state, age, gender, and more.

"Furthermore, like many other animals, they can interpret each other's behaviors and communicative signals and coordinate activities like feeding or just swimming together. In the town of Laguna, Brazil, dolphins have been communicating with fishermen to help them catch fish, they have saved people from drowning, and that famous story about the dolphin approaching a human diver and *'asking'* him to help it remove the fishhook from its fin.

"Dolphins, just like humans, use physical contact for communication with each other — a gentle nuzzle, a playful bite, an aggressive bite, a soft petting with the pectoral fin, and much more. Signals to convey their frustration, threat, or anger include forceful bobbing of the head, gaping mouth, flared-out pectoral fins, and such.

"There are scientists, not all of them ready to admit it in

public though, who believe that those chirps and whistles are in reality used to refer to things more than just general emotional states. They are adamant that dolphins can refer to objects in their environment, communicate about abstract concepts, refer to things in the past and the future, and best of all, learn and commit to memory the meanings of hundreds of thousands of ideas and link them to specific combinations of vocal patterns.

"They, those scientists, say the only stumbling block in the way of a major breakthrough is our inability to decipher their language. It's as if the dolphins are holding out on us — waiting for us to ascend to their level."

Mackenzie's audience was gawking at her when she stopped talking.

"So, are you saying, Mackenzie, that dolphins have a human-like language, and the only issue is that we haven't decoded it yet?"

Mackenzie nodded. "Yep, that's what I believe."

"Do you reckon we can bridge the gap and speak *'dolphinese'* sometime soon?" Sean asked.

"I like that, *'dolphinese'*." Mackenzie laughed. "I think it's not too far away. Like I said before, with the use of computers, vast amounts of data can be collected, mapped, and interpreted. I think it's just a matter of time."

"Man, that would be great!" James exclaimed. "I've got a lot of questions for those dolphins."

## Chapter Nineteen
### SOUNDS-LIKE

After their guests' departure, early the next morning, Carter and Mackenzie settled down in the study to continue their research. Mackenzie got Liu on the phone and tried to convince her to take a break from the University and come up to Freydís for a visit.

Liu started hemming and hawing about taking off and missing lectures, et cetera, when Mackenzie's face broke into a devious little smile. "Oh, did I forget to say Dylan is coming up again next week?"

The line went quiet for all of about two seconds before Liu replied, "Let me see what I can arrange. I'll let you know before the end of the day."

Mackenzie beamed. She didn't even have to explain why Dylan was visiting again so soon — knowing that Dylan would be there was more than enough motivation for Liu. All Mackenzie had left to do was let Dylan know to pick Liu up on his way to Freydís.

"You are a crafty little devil, Mackie," Carter smirked when she ended the call.

She just shrugged and grinned, replying, "I had to think of something to get her here without telling her too much over the phone."

Carter shook his head and returned his mind to the library of the giants. He stared at the image created by the electron microscope from the original flimsy, metallic-looking sheets he and his team had smuggled out of Egypt on their last trip to the City of Lights.

He still had no idea what material the sheets were made of, and neither did he have any idea what language he was looking at.

*Before Adam and Eve? It looks familiar . . . Semitic almost.*

After a while, he was so deep in thought he didn't even realize he was talking to himself in an audible voice. "Definitely Semitic, no doubt about that anymore."

He was oblivious to the fact that Mackenzie was staring at him. She didn't say anything. She had seen that look many times — he was about to figure something out.

"Aramaic. Some say it's the language Adam and Eve spoke . . . . Aramaic is also Semitic." His voice turned into muffled mumbling and then stopped completely.

Mackenzie got up and went to the kitchen to fetch them both a mug of espresso and a cookie. When she returned, she could swear he had not moved, blinked an eye, or even realized she was gone. She placed the coffee and cookie in front of him and returned to her desk, still watching him.

Another minute or so passed before Carter's eyes moved as his olfactory senses made him aware of the aroma of the coffee drifting out of the mug in front of him, and he looked at her as if to ask *where did this come from?*

She smiled and waved her hand. His starry eyes focused on her, and suddenly he was back in the present. "Where were you for the past twenty minutes, my dear?" Mackenzie laughed.

"Amongst the giants." He grinned. "Trying to get them to tell me what language they spoke and how I can understand it."

"And?"

"Nah, no such luck. Maybe they are annoyed because I stole their library . . . but I told them I'll return it soon."

"I thought I heard you talking to them about Semitic, Aramaic, Adam, and Eve."

"What?" He laughed. "Could you hear me talk to them?"

Mackenzie nodded. "Every word of it."

"Mm . . . just as long as you didn't hear them talking back, we should pass all sanity-related psychiatric tests."

"I would certainly hope so." She laughed. "Carter, maybe if you explain to me in simple terms what you're thinking and wondering about, you might just perchance get your answer. If you can't make any progress with my method, then Liu might be able to help when she gets here."

"Not a bad idea — definitely beats having a soliloquy or talking to giants who refuse to reply," he said. "Okay, let's begin at the beginning. All we know up until now is that the giants left that city about fifty thousand years ago — in other words, long before Adam and Eve and long before the flood. We also know, as I explained the other night, giants lived until long after the flood, until about 3,400 years ago — fairly recently."

Mackenzie nodded. "No brain damage yet."

"It's difficult to say, at least until I can do more research, whether the giants of the City of Lights and the giants of the Bible spoke the same or related languages."

"But that's a possibility, is it not?" Mackenzie asked.

Carter nodded. "Yes. Absolutely. In fact, for now, I am assuming that's the case, because the language of our 'modern giants' was almost certainly Semitic. And the language of the 'old giants' bears a strong resemblance to the Semitic languages."

"And the Semitic languages are?"

"There are scholars who believe that the name Semitic refers to Shem, one of the three sons of Noah, and that might be so, but I'm convinced he was not the father of the Semitic languages. Aramaic is classified as Semitic but was spoken long before Shem's time. In fact, many people believe that was the language spoken by Adam and Eve. There are some who believe they spoke Hebrew."

"Aha, now I know what you were saying before when you were talking to the giants." Mackenzie chuckled.

"There are more than 330 million people today who speak one form or another of a Semitic language, such as Arabic, Amharic, Tigrinya, Hebrew, Aramaic, and Maltese. In the era 3000 to 2000 BC, Semitic languages were widely spoken in the Mesopotamian, Akkadian, Babylonian, and Assyrian civilizations."

"But what about the verse in the Bible that says all people had one language?" She opened her Bible on her desk to find the correct verse. "Here it is, Genesis 11 verse 1 *'Now the whole earth had one language and one speech.'*"

She stopped for a few moments and then continued reading out loud to the end of verse nine. *"And it came to pass, as they journeyed from the east, that they found a plain in the land of Shinar, and they dwelt there. Then they said to one another, "Come, let us make bricks and bake them thoroughly." They had brick for stone, and they had asphalt for mortar. And they said, "Come, let us build ourselves a city, and a tower whose top is in the heavens; let us make a name for ourselves, lest we be scattered abroad over the face of the whole earth."*

*"But the Lord came down to see the city and the tower which the sons of men had built. And the Lord said, "Indeed the people are one and they all have one language, and this is what they begin to do; now nothing that they propose to do will be withheld from them. Come, let Us go down and there confuse their language, that they may not understand one another's speech." So the Lord scattered them abroad from there over the face of all the earth, and they ceased building the city. Therefore, its name is called Babel, because there the Lord confused the language of all the earth; and from there the Lord scattered them abroad over the face of all the earth.'*

"So, if I understand what I've just read correctly, Adam and Eve must have spoken the same language as Noah and everyone else before and after the Great Flood, until the Tower of Babel event?"

"It's one of those 'maybe' answers," Carter said. "It certainly looks like there was just one language up until the time of the Tower of Babel. And the Tower of Babel has been the subject of a legion of religious and scholarly debates over the ages, even though the whole account given in the Bible consists of just nine verses.

"And just as the chronicle of a Great Flood is present in the history of every civilization on earth, there is a similar narrative about the confusion of languages — in other words, their versions of the Tower of Babel.

"I'm not supporting any version, as you know, although I believe the Bible is true, I also believe that the Bible does not cover everything that has happened in human history or the history of the earth for that matter.

"The Bible's description of the beginning of creation creates a lot of questions for which I have no clear explanations, only theories. It's clear in the early parts of

Genesis that there were other people around at the time of Adam and Eve. For instance, in Genesis 4, after Cain has killed Abel and God confronts him about it, verses 13 to 15, *And Cain said to the Lord, "My punishment is greater than I can bear! Surely You have driven me out this day from the face of the ground; I shall be hidden from Your face; I shall be a fugitive and a vagabond on the earth, and it will happen that anyone who finds me will kill me." And the Lord said to him, "Therefore, whoever kills Cain, vengeance shall be taken on him sevenfold." And the Lord set a mark on Cain, lest anyone finding him should kill him.'* The question is, who were they who could kill him? The Bible mentions only three people on the earth at the time — Adam, Eve, and Cain. So, there must have been other people around at the time, but the Bible does not tell us who they were.

"It's only around the time of Abraham that the questions start to become fewer for me."

Mackenzie nodded. She and Carter and his late grandfather, Will, had many of these discussions.

Carter continued, "So I guess what I'm trying to say is there is no other evidence in the Bible about the dispersion of Noah's family across the face of the earth to cover all the continents, yet we know that people have lived on all continents for at least two hundred thousand years. Long before and after the Great Flood."

"Okay, so let's assume for now that Adam and Eve and everyone up to the Tower of Babel *in that region* spoke one language," Mackenzie said. "Which was it? You did mention early on that some scholars believe they spoke Hebrew or Aramaic. Didn't you?"

"Yes, I did. But what I see here is not Aramaic or Hebrew. I suspect it's proto-Semitic, or in other words, an earlier version of one of the Semitic languages."

"So, what is the reason why some academics are saying the first language was Hebrew?"

"Some Jewish researchers base their viewpoint on the fact that the Bible is the only historical source providing trustworthy data of the origin of the Hebrew language."

Carter picked up his Bible and read some verses out loud as he explained. "Genesis 14:13 starts like this: '*Then one who had escaped came and told Abram the Hebrew* . . .' Abram descended from Noah's son Shem, Genesis 11:10-26. God blessed Shem, Genesis 9:26, and they believe that it is reasonable to assume that Shem's language was not affected when God confused the language of the disapproved people at Babel. In other words, Shem's language would have remained the same as it had been before Babel.

"There is no secular source that explains the origin of Hebrew or for that matter any of the ancient languages, such as Sumerian, Akkadian, Aramaean, and Egyptian, so that's how they concluded that Hebrew was the first language."

"Really? I would have thought there would be some explanations about Sumerian and Egyptian at least. Why would that be?" Mackenzie asked

"That's a question with a very interesting answer." Carter smiled. "Those languages appear already fully developed in the earliest written records found by historians. That means, any arguments that Hebrew stemmed from Aramaic or some Canaanite dialect are hypothetical."

"Hmm, interesting, very interesting," she murmured. "Okay, so, let me see if I've got this whole thing correct. Your giants wrote on those metallic sheets with nanotechnology or something akin to it. The language they used bears semblance to the Semitic languages. On track so far?" She smiled.

"Yes, one hundred percent."

"Okay, so far so good then. I take it that all or most of the Semitic languages, the same as most other languages, have been captured electronically in dictionaries and writings?"

"Mm . . . yes, all of them, even Sumerian and the Egyptian hieroglyphs . . ." Carter paused suddenly, his eyes almost popped out of their sockets. "Mackie! You beauty, you . . . oh my goodness . . . you did it!" By now he had reached her and lifted her clean out of her chair, swinging her around in his arms, screaming and shouting.

Liam and Jeha heard the commotion from outside where they were playing and stormed into the study, and Beth started crying. Carter looked around as Mackenzie wiggled out of his embrace and went to Beth's room.

"What's happening, Dad?" Liam asked, out of breath. "Why were you screaming and shouting like that?"

Carter became aware of Liam and Jeha's presence. He took a deep breath to calm down before he spoke. "Sorry, Liam. I didn't mean to scare you. Mom just discovered something very, very big. It's so exciting I couldn't help myself."

"Ah, okay," Liam said in a deflated tone, "then Jeha and I will go and play again."

Carter nodded and smiled at his son.

---

Mackenzie came back to the study after she'd lifted Beth from her crib and pacified her. With her she brought the little one, who, when she saw her dad, started smiling and put out her arms to him.

With Beth, happy and content on his lap, Mackenzie

continued the discussion. She wasn't exactly sure if she and Carter were thinking about the same thing.

"So now that you have scared the living daylights out of your entire family and the poor dog" —she giggled— "let's see if you and I are thinking along the same lines?"

"You first," Carter said, smiling broadly.

"Well, I was thinking maybe you could get some computer genius to set up a data warehouse consisting of all the Semitic languages and the language of the giants. Then you can get him or her to write sophisticated queries to compare the giants' language with all the Semitic languages.

"I've seen some pretty intelligent questions developed by those database sages while working in the biology labs on campus. I know there is a query called 'SOUNDS-LIKE', and if I'm not mistaken, that command will search a database for words that not only match the word or phrase you're searching for, it will also find anything that sounds like it. That's apart from partial matches and exact matches and a lot more than I can even remember."

"Mackie, you're the best," Carter said with a big smile. "Absolutely, undeniably, without doubt, I am the luckiest man on this planet."

Mackenzie was beaming. "You're not too bad yourself," she jested as she winked at him.

"Okay, let me get hold of Rick Winslow," Carter said as he handed Beth off to Mackenzie.

"Sounds like a good plan," Mackenzie punned.

"I've got a few databases to query."

After the call with Rick ended, Carter called up the calculator on his laptop and spoke as he typed in the numbers. "There are close to ten thousand of these metallic sheets, each with 3,750 nanodots, and each dot contains about eight hundred thousand words. The print collection of the Library of Congress is said to be ten terabytes. If the giants' library consists of text only, it will be almost three hundred times bigger than the print collection of the Library of Congress. Mind-bending, to say the least."

Mackenzie did a quick search on the Internet and quoted from the official website, "The Library of Congress is the largest library in the world, with more than 162 million items on approximately 838 miles of bookshelves. The collections include more than thirty-eight million books and other print materials, three-point-six million recordings, fourteen million photographs, five-and-a-half million maps, seven-point-one million pieces of sheet music, and seventy million manuscripts."

"We've got a giant task in front of us — pun intended." Carter smiled.

"I'd be willing to bet there's much more than just text. Surely there will be pictures, drawings, and music in there," Mackenzie said. "Considering their technological advancement — in many ways far, far ahead of us — I'm sure they would have stored information not only about their history but also about their technology and culture and the world around them. Who knows? We might just find a few fifty thousand-year-old videos in there! Won't that be great? The giants' version of Netflix." She chuckled.

"That's what I'm hoping for," Carter replied. "I'm expecting to find an answer for our ancient nuclear dilemma in that library. And who knows? Maybe even something about respirocytes."

## Chapter Twenty

### THE NEW MEMBERS

Councilor Alireza Karimi-Shah, had a rewarding meeting with Hassan Al-Suleiman three days after the council meeting. The fact that the two of them came from bitterly opposed religious sects in the Muslim faith — Karimi-Shah a Shiite and Al-Suleiman a Sunni — never featured in their conversation. It might be possible that they thought about their religious differences, but neither of them voiced it. The councilor was impressed with Hassan and extremely pleased with Graziella and her son Mathieu's choice. Hassan was an intelligent man with rapidly expanding influence in the Middle East, and his political views did not clash with those of the Council of the Covenant of Nabataea. Hassan was definitely not going to be another Algosaibi.

Karimi-Shah kept the first part of their conversation at a high and inquisitive level as a final measure to ensure that they were not making any mistakes with Hassan's appointment. When he was convinced that they were doing the right thing, he started to lead the discussions to the real purpose of the visit and lifted small parts of the veil of secrecy.

Even with the little bit of information he got, Hassan was speechless. He could not begin to explain how it came about that these people knew so much about him. In some cases, they literally knew more about him than he knew about himself. Karimi-Shah was careful not to reveal the name of the organization and skimmed over their purpose and objectives. Nevertheless, when it was time for Hassan to say yes or no to taking the next step, it didn't take him long to accept the offer — The Sons of the True Prophet just got another lease on life — and the backing of unlimited funding.

With his acceptance to proceed came the conditions. Once he accepted and arrived in Paris and went through the induction ritual, there was no turning back. He was in it for life. And "for life" meant exactly that—it was made very clear to him that he could not resign nor walk away, ever. If he ever tried to do that, it would also be the end of him.

Hassan understood all of it and agreed. The next step was for him to travel to Paris, where he would undergo a three-day induction process culminating in a formal ceremony. At that time, he would meet all the councilors, take the oath, and take up his position as new councilor.

Karimi-Shah accompanied Hassan to Paris three days later. From the airport, Hassan was taken to a house on the bank of the Seine in the third district of Paris. When they arrived at the house, Karimi-Shah led Hassan to his quarters, five levels below ground, where he would remain for the duration of the induction.

Hassan was surprised at what he learned during his meetings with Karimi-Shah prior to his arrival in Paris, but he had no way of preparing himself for what he was going to learn over the course of the next few days.

---

Late afternoon, a few days after James Rhodes and company departed, the Devereux family was out for a walk. Beth was in her usual place in the baby carrier on Carter's back making happy sounds and laughing at Mackenzie and Liam. Jeha, full of energy, was running around chasing butterflies and making a lot of noise.

About two miles from the Freydís homestead, Jeha stopped in her tracks, lifted and wiggled her nose as she smelled the air. Next, she pulled her tail between her legs and scurried back to Liam, as if she wanted his protection. Her eyes were fixed on some trees about two hundred yards away.

Carter noticed the little dog's behavior and turned in the direction she was staring. "Aha, that's what got your knickers in a knot — it's Mackie's wolves."

"Where? Where?" Mackenzie wanted to know.

Carter showed her and Liam where the wolves were waiting for them under the trees, and they changed their course to meet with their four-legged friends. When they got closer, they could see that the whole family was there — Loki, Keeva, and the four pups.

Carter and the rest of the family stopped about ten yards from the wolves and waited for them to approach, which they did immediately. Jeha made sure she was behind Liam, clearly respecting these big animals. The wolves undoubtedly noticed her right away, but as always ignored her as if she didn't exist. From a human perspective, it seemed as if this tacit arrangement suited Jeha well — as long as she had Liam between her and the wolves at all times.

After the usual interspecies greetings and socialization of sniffing, licking, tail wagging, talking, patting, back scratching, and rubbing, Loki turned and disappeared behind some trees.

Carter and Mackenzie found it strange that Keeva and the pups stayed behind with them. But the mystery was short-lived when Loki returned a few minutes later followed by a wolf mother and two pups they'd never seen before. The newcomers were very human shy, staying about twenty yards behind Loki. Despite him turning around, looking at them, and making soft noises as if to say *don't worry, we know these people — they are our friends. You can trust them; come now, don't be shy*, they remained where they were — suspicious of the humans.

Mackenzie and Carter knew it was not a good idea to approach the strangers. They had to wait for the new wolves to build up enough trust to draw nearer to them when they were ready to do so.

"Carter, this is weird. I've been reading a lot about wolves and their behavior since I met Keeva and Loki years ago, and they almost never allow other wolves into their packs. As far as I know, they will only allow outsiders to join their pack if the outsiders were in some sort of danger or hardship. But more often than not, they are just left on their own to die or survive."

"Well, looks like your wolves have been good Samaritans by taking in this family. Their emaciated condition gives me the impression that they went through some tough times. They look really starved and scruffy," Carter replied. "I'm wondering how she and her pups got separated from their pack."

"It's possible that her pack was killed by poachers or by some kind of culling program," Mackenzie said. "You think they'll be okay now that they're on Freydís? Even if they are kicked out of Loki's pack."

"Absolutely." Carter nodded. "No one is going to bother them here, and there is enough space and food for them."

They stayed a while longer, and the new wolves did take a few steps closer to them but did not go all the way. The best Mackenzie and the others could get out of the new arrivals were wagging tails and a few soft but friendly sounds, and that was good enough for the first encounter.

Mackenzie looked at the new she-wolf and whispered, "Nadia. It means 'hope'. Let's call her Nadia. What do you think?" She exchanged looks with Carter and Liam.

"That's a nice name, Mom. I like it," Liam responded.

"I agree with my son," Carter replied with a smile.

## Chapter Twenty-One

### INDUCTION

Hassan's induction into the ancient mysteries of the Nabateans commenced early the morning of the day after his arrival in Paris. Karimi-Shah knocked on his door at seven a.m. and led him to a meeting room on the same level, where they would have a working breakfast and spend most of the next three days.

The room, carved out of the limestone below the house, was about eight yards square, with an oval oak boardroom table and six luxury chairs. The lavish lighting and air-conditioning inside the room made the absence of windows all but unnoticeable. The floor was covered with elite Persian carpets, and the wall decorations included paintings and rugs displaying ancient scenes and water features, birds, animals, and a center piece depicting all the known marine mammals.

A typical French breakfast consisting of coffee, croissants, pastries, *tartine* (toast with jam), *grillé* (toast with butter), and every flavor of jam one could imagine was waiting for them on a small table to the side.

They loaded their plates with the delicacies, poured some coffee, and then took their seats at the boardroom table.

"There are many people who know about the Nabateans," Karimi-Shah started. "All of them, except for a very small group of selected people, only associate the Nabateans with Petra, that ancient city in the southwestern desert of Jordan. Lately it has drawn a lot of attention, not only amongst archaeologists, but also the public at large — especially since that movie 'Indiana Jones and the Last Crusade'. It has become Jordan's most popular tourist attraction. The Arabic name for the city is Al-Batrā, but the Nabateans called their capital Raqmu. It has been a UNESCO World Heritage Site since 1985."

Hassan nodded. "Yes, I have read some articles about the city and have seen a few pictures, but I'm afraid I haven't studied it in much detail."

"Not to worry," Karimi-Shah said. "I've got all the information here." He started his laptop and connected it to an overhead projector to display the slideshow on the screen hanging on the wall. He provided commentary as he clicked through the slides.

The first slide was a map of Jordan and surrounding countries. "Here is the city on the slope of Jebel al-Madhbah, also known as Mount Hor, mentioned in the Bible. As you can see, it is situated in a basin on the eastern side of Wadi Araba which is part of the large valley stretching from the Dead Sea to the Gulf of Aqaba.

"The city dates back to about 300 BC. And here is the access to the site via that narrow canyon called Al Siq. The place is sometimes also called the 'Rose City', which I suspect comes from the pink sandstone cliffs into which the tombs and temples were sculpted." He brought up a picture of the majestic temple with an elaborate Greek-style façade. "This is probably the most famous feature in Petra — it's called Al Khazneh."

"I'm honored to learn that I'm a descendant of the people who built that place." Hassan grinned.

Karimi-Shah nodded. "I can assure you, over the next few days you'll hear and see a lot more to be proud of.

"According to modern day historians, the Nabateans were originally nomadic people, but later in their history they constructed, or I should rather say, carved out the city of Petra. The location of the city was strategically selected on the regional myrrh and frankincense trade routes of the time, and it quickly became a major center.

"And it was not just the location of the city but the fact that the Nabateans were masters at collecting water from the barren and hostile desert environment. That meant the travelers and traders on those routes had no choice — they had to go through Petra to get water. The name Nabatean has come to mean '*they who draw water from the desert.*'

"Petra stayed out of the eyes of the western world for almost two thousand years, until it was discovered in 1812 by the Swiss explorer, Johann Ludwig Burckhardt. Since then it has become famous. *'A rose-red city half as old as time'* as John William Burgon wrote about it in a poem. UNESCO described it as *'one of the most precious cultural properties of man's cultural heritage'*. It was named one of the new seven wonders of the world, and the Smithsonian Magazine selected it as one of the *'28 Places to See Before You Die.'*"

"This is fascinating!" exclaimed Hassan. "And to think, until a few days ago I didn't even know these people were my forefathers." He shook his head and paused for a breath. "But what is the importance of the city of Petra for us today? I mean for the group that I'm about to become part of." Other than knowing now that he was a Nabatean, he still did not know the name of the organization he was going to belong to.

Karimi-Shah smiled. "I will get to it as I lay it all out for you over the next few days. But for now, just keep in mind what I have shown you so far is only recent history. Our history goes back much further."

"How much?" Hassan asked.

"Way before Adam and Eve — could be over one hundred thousand years . . ."

"Wait!" Hassan's eyes were wide in shock. "Before Adam and Eve, you say? But the Holy Koran and the Torah and the Bible—"

"Are religious books," Karimi-Shah interjected. "Not history or science books."

"But the Holy Koran—" Hassan tried again to make his point.

"Hassan!" Karimi-Shah interrupted him resolutely. "Listen carefully. I told you right from the beginning we are not a pious organization. Religion is no reason for why we can't serve together for the greater good. If you are not comfortable with our areligious views, then you'd better tell me now."

The full implication of the man's words slowly dawned on Hassan— *it was for life* — he had committed to that by agreeing to come to Paris. Slowly he nodded. "My apologies, Alireza. It's just that religion has been so ingrained in me since my birth . . . I guess it will take a little while to unlearn the habit of seeing everything through religious colored glasses."

Karimi-Shah nodded as he watched Hassan's face carefully for any signs of hesitation before he continued. "That doesn't mean we are disbelievers, agnostics, or atheists.

Everyone is permitted to believe what he or she wants. But we will never allow any religious dogma to influence our group — *never*."

Hassan got the message, loud and clear, particularly the emphasis on the word *"never."*

"Amongst this group there are Muslims," he pointed to Hassan and himself, "like us, Buddhists, Hindus, agnostics, atheists, Christians — and hold onto your chair for this one — even Jews."

*Jews!* Hassan almost exploded but managed to keep his mouth shut and nodded as calmly as he could. *Serving with Jews! How can Allah ever forgive me?* But he remained quiet.

His tutor was silent, watching him with raised eyebrows to see if he was ready to continue. He knew all too well that the news about having to pull in the same yoke with Jews would have been a bitter pill to swallow.

"Please continue," Hassan said softly.

"No doubt or hesitation?"

"None whatsoever." Hassan managed to muster a slight grin.

"Good. Let's continue then.

"Our history goes back more than seventy-five thousand years, and some data indicates it could be as far back as two hundred fifty thousand years. Obviously, there are big gaps in our knowledge of prehistoric times prior to Adam and Eve. After Adam and Eve, although still a bit haphazard until Abraham and Ishmael, when data became more accurate, and kept on improving in exactness up till now.

"As I've said before, many people know about the Nabateans of Petra in a historical sense, but very few know of those who are progeny of our forefather Nebajoth, and are aware of their lineage.

"The providence of modern-day Nabateans settles in

the hands of a secret council of twelve, the Council of the Covenant of Nabatea — in existence since 106 AD. Hassan, note the emphasis here is on the word 'secret'. We work in secret; we are a shadow, a phantom, our work known only by the selected few on the council. You are about to become one of those selected few when you take the place of your benefactor, the late Xavier Algosaibi."

Hassan's squinted. *Another fact I thought only I knew about.* "Is there anything you don't know about me?"

"I'll be very disappointed if there is," Karimi-Shah said matter-of-factly. "We have the best information collection system on the planet, bar none. Yet we fly so far below the radar that whatever footprints we leave are all but invisible or effortlessly wiped away. Only Council members know how large the Nabatean community is, how wide our influence reaches, and the technology we have at our disposal.

"Our members and influence have spread to every corner of the globe — all in positions of power in governments, businesses, media, science, technology, even criminal activities from time to time. Any industry and study discipline you care to name, we're in.

"We're almost certainly the only group in existence where not only the two major Muslim sects, Sunni and Shi'a, peacefully coexist, but also the other religions I've mentioned before."

"What's our aim?" Hassan asked.

"What's our aim?" Karimi-Shah repeated and grinned. "What everyone wants. Power, money, control of world events."

Hassan nodded as if he understood, but his face betrayed his confounded mind. "Yet you have no army, no country, no nation, no visible followers. How is it possible?"

"With power of the magnitude we have, human politics

and religion become irrelevant. In 106 AD, the elders of Nabatea decided to hand over their empire to the Romans without a fight, and everyone believed their distinctiveness had disappeared. But that is what historians believe— *'their distinctiveness disappeared'*. The Nabateans only vanished from the public eye, not from the earth. We are still very much alive and here. But nobody knows, and that's how we are going to keep it." Karimi-Shah ended that last sentence on a higher note — a questioning tone accompanied by raised eyebrows.

Hassan got the cue and nodded. "Absolutely."

"In the beginning, and I am referring to the time after *'capitulating'* to Rome, the Nabateans formed the Council of the Covenant of Nabatea and started infiltrating every aspect of the Roman society like termites. They were motivated by the desire to restore the glory of their kingdom, and that remains our goal to this day. That's why we want power, money, and control of world events. In the early centuries, if only in small ways, their infiltration and invisible influence were successful and gained momentum and continued to this day. I will tell you more about that shortly.

"However, as you can imagine, world power has shifted several times, new religions, wars, conflict and strife, new cultures, countries, languages, and technology had made the original goal, to return to Petra, obsolete. I doubt it very much that any one of us would want to go back to Petra to live in the Jordanian desert anytime soon."

Hassan had a hint of a smile. "Yes, I can see that, but what, then, is it we are after in the present-day?"

"What are the two most important, most valuable commodities today?" Karimi-Shah answered.

"Mm . . . gold and oil?" Hassan responded hesitantly.

Karimi-Shah shook his head. "You want to try again?

Think about it carefully. In today's society, what would be as vital as the water of the Nabateans was to the traders traveling through the desert in ancient times?"

Hassan stared at him for a while, his brain working overtime. "I am tempted to say, computers and electricity, but I am not sure."

"Close, very close indeed." Karimi-Shah chortled. "It's information and energy. In today's world, if you don't have information, you might as well live in the dark ages. Information is knowledge, education, science, technology, computers, progress — it's everything — information is power. The one who has the right information at the right time wields the power. Remember this — no information, no power."

"I can see that," Hassan replied slowly, deep in thought. "What about energy?"

Karimi-Shah stood and walked to the array of switches on the wall and flipped them all off. The darkness in the room was absolute. "Need I say anything more?" he asked after a minute of silence as he turned the switches on again.

Hassan started laughing. "You've illustrated that point so well, Alireza, how can I ever forget it?"

There was a protracted silence as Karimi-Shah took his seat and studied Hassan's beaming face. In the silence, Hassan slowly poured his tutor and himself another cup of coffee and said, "Please tell me more. I want to know everything... if I'm allowed."

Karimi-Shah chuckled. "You're a Nabatean, Hassan, from a noble bloodline, about to become a member of the Council of the Covenant of Nabatea, the highest order in our society. Of course, you're allowed to know. It's your duty to know."

"How much of the world's information and energy do

the Nabateans control or can they control? Surely, we can't physically take control of all the oil, coal, and gas fields of the world. Can we?"

"No, of course we can't. You're right. But we can destroy all or most of it and replace it with our own."

"What . . . how . . . ah . . . say again? How will you do that?"

Karimi-Shah held his hand up for Hassan to relax. "Are you familiar with the concepts of quantum physics?"

Hassan slowly nodded. "I've only a layman's knowledge about it. I've read a few articles, but I don't understand much of it. I know Einstein gave up on the quantum theory and once said *'God does not play dice with the universe.'*

"Nevertheless, it remains a fascinating concept — the idea that a particle can be in different places and states at the same time reminds me so much of the omnipresence of Allah."

Karimi-Shah replied. "Yes, to some it has the fingerprints of a higher power. However, despite Einstein's reservations about the theory, he was man enough to acknowledge the extraordinary empirical successes of the quantum theory.

"However, don't let me mislead you into thinking I know much about the subject either." Karimi-Shah smiled. "For that part of your induction I'll bring in one of the world's top scientists in this field. For now, just accept that it is as NASA has said *'the most precisely tested theory in the history of science.'* Its predictions and projections have been substantiated over and over again with eerie accuracy.

"It is said that close to thirty percent of our modern economy hinges on our current comprehension of quantum physics. Think about computers, cell phones, lasers, and such."

Hassan looked surprised. "Am I to understand from what you are saying the Nabateans have developed or have control over quantum technology so advanced it can manipulate the world's information and energy?"

"Yes and no — *'no'* because we have not yet achieved one hundred percent of what we want. And *'yes'* because we have already achieved so much, and we are so close we can almost smell it. What you will learn over the next few days will blow your mind away."

"What is holding you back?"

Karimi-Shah went quiet for an uneasy long spell while contemplating how to break the next bit of information to Hassan without causing another religious temper tantrum in the man.

Finally, he spoke. "Hassan, my friend, what I'm about to tell you is going to rock your boat. So please hear me out before you respond. Okay?"

Hassan nodded agreement.

"Human history has been distorted beyond recognition by religion, historians, scientists, evolutionists, zoologists, anthropologists, archaeologists, and the like. All in an effort to fit in with their ideologies. Many people believe the human species has only existed for about six thousand years since creation — Adam and Eve. Despite unquestionable evidence that humans have been on earth for much longer than that.

"Others believe in evolution and that we are related to the apes. Their view is hominid creatures originated from a bunch of apes who one day about two hundred fifty thousand years ago, got it into their heads to leave the jungles and go and live in the grasslands. What a sad goodbye that must have been. And when those deserters arrived on the savannah, they decided it was time to change a few things.

They decided it was time to walk on two legs instead of four. Shed all their body hair, which would have protected them from the glaring sun in their new habitat. Maybe because they thought they would look sexier with no body hair and a nice tan. Then they decided to make themselves tools and weapons to hunt and fight, and just for kicks, they changed their diet from herbivorous to omnivorous.

"And while they were at it, they said 'you know what? We need to teach ourselves how to speak a proper language. This ape language is no good. And just to set ourselves apart from those idiots who didn't join us, let's increase our brain size and become more intelligent than they are.'"

Hassan couldn't stop himself from exploding in laughter at Karimi-Shah's laconic version of evolution. He didn't believe in evolution either. He was one of those six thousand-year-old human species believers, but this crack at evolution was the most entertaining version he had ever heard.

"The thing is," Karimi-Shah continued once Hassan stopped laughing, "our data shows something very different. And I don't want to get into the evolution or intelligent design deliberation. Some of it might be true and some not — it doesn't concern us. The Nabateans, I mean."

Hassan looked at him inquisitively but kept his promise to wait for his teacher to finish the narrative before commenting or asking questions.

"Here is the kicker. Not only did humans exist for hundreds of thousands of years in antediluvian times, but there were also civilizations far more advanced than ours. They had technologies so progressive we can't even begin to understand them. We are physically holding some of those ancient technologies in our hands, but we have no clue about its purpose or how to operate them."

Hassan looked as if he could be knocked over with a feather.

"As you already know from your men's discovery of that site in Syria, they had nuclear weapons. And not only that, they understood and harnessed the power of nuclear fusion, quantum vacuum zero-point energy, faster than light communications, quantum entanglement, nanotechnology, quantum computing, neuroscience, advanced medical technology . . . I can carry on and on.

"Those hairless, bipedal apes from the jungles of Africa were apparently very clever."

Hassan could not control his urge to speak any longer. "That's absolutely mindboggling!"

Karimi-Shah nodded. "Yes, without a shadow of a doubt — it is a game changer. As I've said, we have already acquired some of those ancient technologies—"

"Such as?"

"We are already using some of their quantum computing and nanotechnology, as well as some neuroscience and medical techniques. We have the most comprehensive library of ancient technology knowhow in the universe.

"There is no computer on the planet that can do what our quantum computers can — not even if you combine the computing power of the world will it standup against ours. There is no computer or communications network on earth we cannot access, or hack, if you will.

"We are on the verge of a medical breakthrough that will double the human lifespan. There are more . . ." He paused as he saw Hassan's bewilderment.

Hassan had gone slack-jawed as his brain was bombarded with thousands of thoughts per millisecond. He tried to say something but was unable to produce any sound. *Medical . . . longevity . . . neuroscience . . . free energy . . . nuclear weapons . . . quantum computing . . . faster than light . . . faster than light . . . faster than light!* Random words were triggering electrical impulses through the synapses in his brain and must have short-circuited something.

"Huh. Wow! Stop," were the only comprehensible sounds that came out of his mouth.

Karimi-Shah smiled. "Another coffee while you gather your thoughts?"

Hassan just nodded. By the time the cup of coffee was in front of him, he had managed to regain his composure. "I don't know where to begin. But let me ask you this. Where do you get all this information?"

"Remember what I told you about our quantum computers?"

Hassan nodded.

"Well, if there is an electronic record of any piece of information available on a computer anywhere, we can access it. The only computers we can't access are those that are not connected to the Internet or are switched off. I'm not a technology expert, so how they do it I won't be able to tell you. But don't worry, tomorrow is your technology induction day, and our experts will answer all your questions.

"When it comes to archaeological discoveries, we keep a close watch on archaeologists across the globe. We know exactly what is going on — what has been discovered, and what is suppressed by authorities. You will be stunned to know how much information is concealed and never sees the light of day."

"So, if I understand you correctly, there is still some information out there you are hunting for?"

"Yes, and there's a lot of it, and we want it. We have

been looking for it for millennia. We know it's there because the ancient texts and manuscripts talk about it.

"You see, there was a race of giants on earth in pre-Adamic times. In fact, many thousands of years before Adam, maybe even hundreds of thousands. And the most amazing thing is, they survived through all of it until about 3,400 years ago. And what's important for us is the evidence that points to the fact that those giants were the most advanced human beings ever to walk the earth."

Hassan's mouth was agape again. But Karimi-Shah pushed on. "I take it the name Professor Carter Devereux rings a bell?"

Hassan nodded cautiously as he recollected how his special forces botched the mission on behalf of Xavier Algosaibi to capture Professor Carter Devereux and his wife, Dr. Mackenzie Devereux, and their son, Liam, in Jerusalem.

They succeeded in capturing his wife and son, but Carter miraculously avoided capture as he was in the bathroom at the time when they arrived at the restaurant. The operatives detonated a massive car bomb in the restaurant where the Devereuxs were dining to make it appear like a suicide bombing and wipe out the evidence of the abduction.

Their failure to capture Carter Devereux came back to haunt them when Devereux and a group of United States Special Forces operators discovered where his wife and son were being held near Mecca in Saudi Arabia and launched a successful rescue mission.

That mission was what blew Algosaibi's cover and led to his and his co-conspirators' public beheading in Saudi Arabia.

Suddenly, Hassan was unnerved. He certainly didn't

expect anyone else would know about his involvement in that mission. On the other hand, he was not entirely surprised, because since his first meeting with Karimi-Shah, back in Syria, there was not one single piece of information this man didn't know about him. It was a real worry. But there was also nothing he could do about it — other than to take note of the fact that nothing about his life was ever going to be private nor secret anymore.

Karimi-Shah must have noticed his discomfort, for he said, "Don't worry, my friend, that's water under the bridge. Nothing will happen to you. We've taken care of that. But I trust you have learned from that experience — the Council of the Covenant of Nabatea operates above country political strife and ambitions. There is nothing but trouble to gain from it. We repeatedly warned Xavier to heed our advice but to no avail.

"His meddling in politics and his devouring ambition only succeeded in putting Carter Devereux and the United States' security establishment on alert. The Saudis have no doubt by now leaked some of the ancient nuclear weapons information to some radicals, amongst them your erstwhile comrades in ISIS."

Hassan visibly relaxed and sighed with relief as he slowly nodded. "I most certainly have learned a lot from that experience."

"Good. Let's return to the topic of Carter Devereux. That man has made history-changing discoveries of pre-Adamite civilizations in the past few years. His work is nothing short of astonishing. We have been following his and his wife's research with great interest for some years now." Karimi-Shah shook his head and paused as if in deep thought. "It's such a misfortune that he's not of the Nabatean lineage.

"To us, the most important of his discoveries is that city of the giants in Egypt. That city dates back more than fifty thousand years. Correction — that is, according to geologists, the last time it was occupied — the city itself could be much older. And the city hasn't even begun to give up its secrets. Were it not for Xavier's dimwitted interference, we might have had a lot more information from that site by now."

Hassan nodded his assent.

"We are convinced that those giants must have left written records behind, and we were waiting for Devereux to discover them. Algosaibi's little ego trip endangered Devereux and his family and almost caused him to retire from archaeology. That would have left us with no choice but to get involved in the exploration of that site ourselves — not something we would have liked to do.

"Fortunately, a few days ago, we got some good news. It seems that Professor Devereux has decided to continue with his projects, and most promising of all, we have learned that he has indeed discovered written records in the city of the giants—"

"Really? Do you know how much information it contains?" Hassan leaned forward, his eyes wide and glittering.

Karimi-Shah shook his head. "Too early to say. So far, we have seen only one image of a metallic looking plate, containing what we believe could be nanodots with information. Then we saw a set of documents, which we believe was produced by an electron microscope that converted part of that metallic plate into an unfamiliar language. But his computer was online for only a short while. We didn't have enough time to get everything he has on it."

"Any ideas what language?"

"Definitely proto-Semitic in origin but nothing that our linguistic expert could read. We didn't want to send the document to other linguists yet. We want to keep it very quiet until we can get more information from Devereux's computer."

Hassan grinned.

"We have a recording of a telephone conversation between Devereux and Rick Winslow, a computer expert at the CIA. It was about setting up a database of Semitic languages to use for translation purposes. That's what led us to the conclusion that Devereux's got more of those plates. We'll wait and monitor."

"For how long?"

"A month or so. If progress is not to our satisfaction . . ." he shrugged, "we'll have to step in and take over."

## Chapter Twenty-Two

### CLOSE ENCOUNTERS

Shortly after dark, ten days after Sean and Dylan had reached the agreement with Carter and Mackenzie about the establishment of the new training facility, Dylan, accompanied by Liu and six EA employees, arrived on Freydís. They arrived in an Alenia C-27J Spartan, a medium-sized cargo aircraft of the United States Special Operations Command. The plane, which had a payload of more than twelve tons, was packed to the brim with equipment and material.

Years ago, when Carter's grandfather, Will Devereux, constructed the mile-long landing strip, he built it so that larger aircraft could land and take off. When Will settled on Freydís, a lot of material and equipment to build the farmstead and outbuildings had to be flown in. This extra-long runway came in very handy again for transporting cargo and people to and from Freydís.

In the days before their arrival, Dylan had arranged with their connections in the Canadian Joint Task Force 2

— JTF2 — to deploy a security detail, equipped with surveillance drones, close to Freydís to prevent and warn them about any uninvited prying eyes. This was going to be a standing arrangement while the construction of Camp Tala was in progress until EA could shoulder the responsibility for their own security measures.

Carter and Ahote had ascertained that the runway was in good order and had constructed numerous torches from long sticks, the ends wrapped with cloth and soaked in paraffin. When they got the message from Dylan that the plane was about twenty minutes out, the two of them went out to place and light the torches on both sides of the runway.

The pilot taxied the plane as close as possible to the hangar, and the men got busy unloading the cargo while Mackenzie and Liu went home to finalize the sleeping and meal arrangements.

Liu and Mackenzie were ecstatic to see each other. Liu got teary-eyed when she saw Liam and hugged him. When Bly appeared with Beth in her arms, Liu couldn't fight the tears anymore and let go.

"This . . . is just so . . ." She shook her head, searching for the words while tears of joy were streaming down her face. "I don't know what to say, Mackenzie. I've missed you all so much. And the children — just look at them. They have grown so much."

Mackenzie stepped closer and hugged her. "The same for us, Liu, the same for us. We are so happy you finally came to visit us."

It didn't take long for Beth to smile at Liu and hold her little arms out, which caused another round of tears in Liu's eyes as she took Beth in her arms.

About two hours later, they heard the plane's engines coming alive. The men turned up at the house shortly after it took off, all begging for food and coffee.

Dylan and his men, with Ahote as the site foreman, would set out early the next morning to do a final inspection of the location where the camp would be established. Then they'd start moving the equipment and material onsite, using the electric carts as much as they could.

The plan was to enclose and configure the large area under the rock overhang on the eastern cliff wall as their temporary sleeping quarters and kitchen as soon as possible. Before they could move in and become self-contained, they had to get their electricity and water supply set up, build shower and toilet facilities, et cetera.

The next morning during the site tour, one of the young guys, Conrad Westley, was heard saying, "I'm glad my dad made me read the story of Robinson Crusoe when I was a kid."

Dylan smiled. "Well, at least we have airplanes, food, electricity, and friendly people on our island."

"And wolves!" shouted Ryan McGraw, pointing to a pack of nine wolves standing about fifty yards away. Everyone stopped dead in their tracks, turned, and saw the animals staring at them.

Carter, Dylan, and Ahote exchanged quick looks without saying a word. *"Shall we have a bit of fun?"*

Dylan nodded ever so slightly.

"Okay, guys, we might have ourselves a bit of a problem here," Carter started, struggling to keep up the pose of earnestness. "Those wolves look really mean and hungry to me, and they have now blocked our way out of here, which is through that cleft behind them . . ."

"No shit, Sherlock! And we don't have our weapons

with us. We can't even shoot our way out of this one," Ryan whispered.

"Okay, I suggest we don't do anything stupid, like running away from them," Dylan added. "Let's just stand here and look back at them. Maybe they will lose interest."

One of the men, John Ruschin, was an experienced war-dog handler who had been embedded on many missions with Special Forces operators with his dog. He had just recently been recruited by EA with the view of starting a war-dog training program for them.

"I know about dogs and how to handle and train them, and I've been told that wolves can be trained the same as our dogs . . . but . . ." John said hesitantly, "reading and hearing about it is a bit different than looking them in the eyes all of a sudden."

"So, you reckon you want to give it a shot, John?" Ahote asked. He was about to explode in laughter. "You know . . . see if you can give them a command?"

John shook his head. "Nah, not really in the mood for a training session right now. I'd rather take my chances and try to climb the cliff walls."

John's answer only served to increase the tension amongst his comrades. If he, the expert dog handler, was worried, and so were Carter and Ahote who lived there, things were not looking good for them.

Carter turned to Ahote. "My friend, I think you might be our only hope now. I've heard that the Hopi people have some sort of special bond with wolves. I am sorry to put you through this ordeal, but I don't see that we have any other options."

Ahote nodded slowly while he kept his head down so that the others could not see his smile. "I'll do it. Just wait here, and don't move or make any noise. Okay?"

Everyone eagerly nodded assent.

Ahote started walking to the wolves slowly. Loki and Keeva sat down when they saw Ahote approaching, they had their heads tilted inquisitively as if to ask, *"What's wrong with you today, Ahote? Why are you creeping up on us like that?"*

When Ahote reached them, he bent over slowly and held his hands out to Loki first.

"What the hell is he doing?" John exclaimed in horror. "Those animals will rip him to pieces . . . "

Then Ahote started scratching Loki's ears and back and turned to Keeva who was patiently waiting her turn. Shortly after, the four pups surrounded him, all vying for his attention. The remaining she-wolf and her two pups kept their distance — watching everything — but made no attempt to approach Ahote.

"I'll be damned!" said Dylan. But then he could not control his urge to laugh anymore. He and Carter were doubling over as they roared with laughter.

"What's going on here, Captain?" The wide-eyed Peter Shorten demanded from his commanding officer, with all due respect.

Dylan was still trying to get over the mirth and looked at Carter to answer.

"Don't worry guys," Carter said. "Those wolves know all of us here on Freydís. Except for that female with her two pups at the back there, who are new to the pack. They befriended us years ago. They know Dylan and everyone else. I think they were just curious to see who the newcomers were. They are not domesticated, but they won't harm any of us.

"Mackenzie is the first person whom they made friends with. She's got names for all of them, and when she goes for a walk, you can bet they will turn up and accompany her sooner or later. That female next to Ahote is Keeva, and the male is Loki. The other female with the two pups is Nadia."

The six men were staring at Carter and Dylan in turn, wondering if they should believe him or not — some of their buddies had told them about the pranks Carter sometimes played on them. Yet, there Ahote was, unharmed, coming back towards them with the wolves in tow. Some of them eyed the cliffs, others eyed the rapidly shrinking distance between them and the wolves. Run and hide, or wait and see? Carter and Dylan didn't look stressed, so maybe the latter was the best choice. In any event, none of them could outrun a wolf.

A few minutes later, they were all smiles. The wolves had sniffed them all, licked their outstretched hands, and allowed them to scratch their backs. One of Keeva and Loki's pups, which Mackenzie had named JR, after James Rhodes, instantly took a special liking to John. He was all over John, playing with him.

After playing with the young wolf for a while, John said, "Okay, let's see if there is any truth in the notion that wolves can be trained as easily as dogs."

Everyone, including the rest of the wolves, watched as John got onto his knees so he could look JR in the eyes.

When he got JR's attention, he moved his hand up and over its head, pointing down while repeating the word *sit* measuredly. JR's eyes and head followed John's hand, and as he did that his butt started to lower. Once he was sitting, John made a big fuss. "Clever boy. You are so clever." He patted him and scratched him behind the ears while he brought his face close to the animal, touching its wet nose with his. JR was in wolf heaven.

John repeated the exercise a few more times and then got up. He walked a few paces away, JR following him in anticipation. John stopped, turned to JR, looked down into its eyes and said, "Sit." JR sat down immediately and waited for his reward.

The audience was gawping. "Wait till I tell Mackenzie about this." Carter smiled. "She is going to love the idea of teaching her wolves a few tricks."

"Well, as I said before" —John was obviously a lot more relaxed now than half an hour ago— "I've been told that wolves can be trained to be war-dogs as well as or better than any domesticated dog. From what I've just experienced, I think that could be true."

"I can believe that," Carter said. "Remind me to tell you what these wolves have done for us over the last year. It is an amazing story."

"Okay guys, let's get moving," Dylan said. "We've got Wolf Camp to build, and I'm pretty sure the nine of them are not going to help us, although I suspect they might want to supervise our progress. After all, they inspired the name Camp Tala."

Dylan would have been surprised if, at that moment, he knew how precisely his prophecy about the wolves' involvement in their camp construction would be fulfilled in the days and months to come.

Over the next fourteen days, Camp Tala started to take shape. The hydroelectric plant was set up in the river and worked like a charm, supplying them with more than enough electricity to operate their power tools and domestic appliances. The virtually noiseless electric pump kept the water reservoir, which they located on a cliff ledge about twenty feet above ground level to get good pressure in the pipes and camouflaged properly, filled with fresh water from the stream.

By the end of the first week, Camp Tala was ready to

take in the first occupants under the cliff overhang, which they had converted into a sleeping area and kitchen. They had to use a bit of concrete to level the floor and wood panels to cover the front opening, but other than that, the natural features of the area suited them perfectly.

## Chapter Twenty-Three

DID YOU KNOW...

While the men were occupied with the construction of the camp, Liu and Mackenzie got busy with translating the Sirralnnudam.

"Well, Mackenzie, my first observation is this is a much better work environment than the last one you and I were in when we were doing translations," Liu remarked with a bit of gallows humor.

"Can't agree with you more, Liu." Mackenzie smiled. "Which reluctantly takes my mind back to our rescue, resulting not only in our freedom, but also got you and Dylan acquainted."

Liu had a slight blush growing on her neck and cheeks. She knew which way Mackenzie was heading.

"It must have been something, having him sweep you off your feet into his arms and carry you out of that building."

Liu nodded and hemmed and hawed for a moment before she said, "You are my best friend, and I'm going to tell you something about that night that no one except Dylan and I know."

Although it was just she and Mackenzie and Beth in the house, Liu leaned in closer and whispered, "Did you know, Dylan saw me naked even before he knew my name?"

"*What?* Liu. How is that possible?" Mackenzie chuckled. "Don't tell me you had enough time . . ."

"No, Mackenzie" —Liu giggled— "get your mind out of the gutter. There was definitely not enough time for that!

"I was fast asleep when he pulled me out of bed and told me he and others were there to rescue us. I was so bamboozled I acted like a zombie and just followed orders. So, when he told me to put clothes on, I didn't even think. I just pulled my nighties off and looked for my clothes.

"But he was so modest, he turned his head away. Although he fervently denies he saw any part of my nudity, I'm sure he must have seen something. Otherwise, why did he turn his head away?"

By now Mackenzie was screaming with laughter. "Of course, he saw something. And he must have liked what he saw. This is a story for a Hollywood romance movie, Liu. I can't think I've ever heard a more romantic version of a first date than yours."

Liu now sported a full blush.

Mackenzie managed to stop laughing. "You know the man is besotted by you. Don't you?"

Liu smiled and nodded. "So am I, Mackenzie. I'm just waiting for him to say it. But how do you know?"

"Well, he told us in so many words when he was here last time with Sean, James, and Irene."

"What did he say?"

"His exact words were 'yes, I'm in love with her.'"

"Damn, what is it with men that they can't say how they feel?"

"Don't you worry. Irene and I read him the riot act and told him to say those exact words to you. He agreed. So just hang in there he'll do it. Maybe he's just waiting for the right moment."

"Okay, I'll take your word for it," Liu said.

"Now let's get going with the Sirralnnudam. After all, this book was part of the reason why we got abducted to that desert hellhole. The least we can do now is to find out what it was all about."

Over the course of the next few days, they studied Carter's notes, and Liu got a feel for the language, which was related to Arabic. After a few days, she started to read it with more ease.

"Liu, you and Carter, with your ability to pick up and learn new languages, are incredible. I'm able to speak English and French, the latter with a lot of difficulty and effort. You make it look so easy. How do you do it? Or is it all to do with genetics?"

"That's a question that's kept scientists scratching their heads for ages. It's a lot like a tool, say a pencil. All or most of us can learn to use a pencil to draw, but not all of us can draw equally well because we don't all have the same artistic talent. All humans are born with the ability to learn a language. However, the aptitude to use a language well is not necessarily innate."

"So, are you saying it's one of those either you have it or you don't situations?"

"No, aptitude is only to do with your use of a language. Just like drawing a picture. Some have the ability to draw better than others, although we can all learn to draw. When it comes to learning a new language, we all have the innate capability to learn it."

"Why then is it so easy for you and Carter and others, and so difficult for me and many others?"

"Well, scientists have used tools, such as magnetic resonance imaging (MRI) among others, to study what's happening in the brain while people are learning a new language.

"A Swedish study compared the brain activity of students studying languages with those studying medical and cognitive science subjects, and found specific parts of the brain in the hippocampus and areas of the cerebral cortex are related to language learning. Those areas in the brains of the language students increased in size, whereas the brain structures of the control group remained unchanged.

"They found that the areas of the brain that grew were linked to how easy the learners found languages, which means if you study a new language, those areas will develop, and the more you study, the easier it would become for you to learn a new language."

"Hmm, motivation to learn a new language I guess is the keyword there," Mackenzie murmured.

"Kara Morgan-Short, a professor at the University of Illinois at Chicago, and her colleagues conducted an experiment where they taught one group through explanations of the rules of the language, while they taught the second group by immersing them in the language, similar to how we all learn our native languages.

"They found that all participants learned some of the language, but the immersed learners, whose brain processes were most like those of native speakers, did much better than the others, even six months after they stopped learning.

"There is a lot more to it. For instance, students who were adept at picking up sequences and patterns learned grammar particularly well through the immersion technique. Of course, the study could help teachers to determine the best method for students to learn a new language."

Liu paused for a breath before she concluded, "I probably don't have to tell you there is overwhelming evidence showing that people who speak more than one language have better memories, are more cognitively creative, and are more mentally flexible than monolinguals. Some Canadian studies even suggest that the onset of diseases such as Alzheimer's and dementia are delayed amongst bilinguals when compared with monolinguals."

"Phew, that's good to know. I'm bilingual," Mackenzie laughed. "As for better memory, I don't have to look any further than Carter with his eidetic memory to know what you are saying about languages and memory is true."

"Well, there you have all the motivation necessary to take up language learning as a hobby." Liu sniggered.

After the morning tea break, they returned to the study where Liu started reading the translation of the Sirralnnudam into her voice recognition software, which was typing the words as she was reading.

Every now and then she would pause to look up a few words and meanings before she continued. But it was clear she was gaining speed. By the end of the day she was doing more than thirty words a minute — about six pages an hour.

## Chapter Twenty-Four
### THE MILLION-DOLLAR QUESTION

Perrin Durand was watching the taxi carrying Mayon and Aisha as it came through the security gates of the private clinic situated in the affluent *Appia Antica* neighborhood of Rome. The taxi's windows were slightly tinted, so it was nearly impossible for him to get a good view of their new looks. He gave the taxi a few minutes to get away before he started his car and made his way to the hotel where they were heading. He didn't try to follow them, as he'd gotten the address while listening to Mayon's phone call when he'd booked their room in the Rome Cavalieri, Waldorf Astoria on Via Alberto Cadlolo. A five-star hotel catering to the rich, the place offered picturesque views of Rome, extravagant rooms, opulent furniture, artwork, VIP elevators, rooftop balconies, and marble bathrooms with whirlpool tubs and chic toiletries. It was close to well-known historical sites such as the St. Peter's Basilica, the Piazza Navona, and the Roman Forum.

Durand was waiting inside the hotel lobby when Mayon and Aisha arrived at the check-in counter, and he was stunned to observe their metamorphosis. If he hadn't known who they were, he would have lost them. He quickly took a few pictures of them with his mobile phone, pretending he was snapping the frescoes and luxurious foyer. The blond hair, nose jobs, altered jawlines, skin bleaching, and blue contact lenses had turned the two of them into a young couple who would have convinced any uninformed observer of their Scandinavian roots, or, as Durand was soon to learn, French-speaking Canadian citizens from Quebec. He smiled as the thought crossed his mind that his own disguise would also have fooled anyone who knew him.

Durand waited until they had checked in before he got a bit closer so that he could hear the room number when they told the porter where to take their luggage. Once he had that information, he left and went back to his motel room to change his disguise to match one of his fake passports and legends and check out. Three hours later, Durand, now known as Julio Romeres, a Spanish businessman, checked into the Rome Cavalieri and insisted on a room with a view on the fifth floor.

By two a.m. the next morning, he was inside the room of his subjects, who were again unconscious thanks to the effects of the potent knockout gas. He worked quickly but methodically to place the surveillance bugs around the suite and replace the old ones on their laptop and mobile phones. Fifteen minutes later, he was back in his own room three doors away from his subjects.

Before he went to bed, he typed a report to his handler, included the pictures of the new Aisha and Mayon, now known as Jean and Olivia Girard, as well as pictures of their new passports. He copied it all onto a flash drive, which he would leave at a dead drop location later in the day.

## The Alboran Codex

On the second day of the mind-numbing surveillance, Durand overheard something that immediately pitched his ears.

"You know, Mayon, I've always been very proud to be an Algosaibi, and this information our father gave us on this flash drive is just proving that I've not been living in a fool's paradise. You and I have all the reason in the world to be proud of our bloodline."

Durand's mind kicked into overdrive. *Algosaibi . . . Algosaibi . . . that name sounds very familiar. Why is that?*

Within seconds he had Googled the name. Top of the results were a news article about Xavier Algosaibi, one of the ten richest people in Saudi Arabia, and his fall from grace when his plot to end the reign of the House of Saud was uncovered.

*Xavier Algosaibi is or rather was the father of these spoiled brats . . . now it makes sense . . . that's why someone is so interested in them. Who?*

Durand searched for the names Mayon and Aisha Algosaibi and smiled when Google instantly returned the information, which included their pictures, and most alluring of all, the one and a half million price tag on each of their heads.

*Three million dollars . . . I'll retire with that. This could be my last job.*

His mind was working overtime, the vision of him in Thailand on a beach in Pattaya being served exotic cocktails by scantily clothed, sexy young girls had become vivid in his mind's eye. But he hadn't survived so many battles and missions to get to this stage because he made rash decisions — this had to be planned with great care. He decided not to raise any suspicions with his faceless handler. The best was to give him or her all the information and make sure he did not set off any alarm bells until it was time to make his move.

Durand diligently reported to his handler, including audio files of the conversations, as well as video recordings and still pictures. Apart from the three-million-dollar windfall waving at him, he was beyond surprised to learn about some of the information on that flash drive. He caught pieces of a lecture in human origins and history that, even if only a fraction of it was true, would turn the scientific world into chaos. Durand often found himself with an open mouth as he followed the ensuing conversations of the Girards. At times, he got so carried away he was almost tempted to jump up and join them to partake in the discussions.

On the third day after his discovery of the real identities of his subjects, he picked up another interesting tidbit.

"Aisha, I think it's time for us to move on. As best I could tell, we are not being followed by anyone, so I feel it's safe for us to make the trip to Zürich to talk to our banker and then move on to Paris."

"Agreed," she replied tersely. "I've had enough of the damned Italians, and since I became a blonde, their disrespectful staring at me and sexually suggestive remarks have increased to the point it's freaking me out completely. So, the sooner we get out of here the better."

Mayon chuckled. "Aisha, I'm sure you have forgotten how amorous the French can be when they are around a beautiful woman such as yourself."

"Yeah, well, as you know, I'm not into men. So, the sooner I get myself a girlfriend when we get to Paris the better. Maybe that will help shoo the insolent men away."

"With your new looks, I'm sure you won't have any trouble finding someone to be interested in you," Mayon replied while trying his level best to hide his utter disgust at his sister's self-confessed sexual preferences. Although he always suspected it, it was the first time she'd openly talked about it.

In different circumstances, back home in Saudi Arabia, if this were discovered, he would have had an unavoidable duty to defend the Algosaibi family honor and have her stoned to death.

Durand's interest on the other hand, had nothing to do with Aisha's sexual inclinations. His interest piqued when he heard the words "Zürich" and "banker". It didn't take a genius to conclude that the two of them must have a secret bank account in Zürich. He was staring out the window while he listened very intently for more information.

*Which bank? Give me the name of your banker . . . come on tell me . . . I'm waiting.*

It was as if Mayon could hear him and wanted to oblige when he phoned the bank in Zürich and, after providing some information, was transferred to the personal assistant of Mr. Mathieu Nabati, the manager of a small boutique private bank. A few minutes later a meeting was set for them at ten a.m. Zürich time the next Monday — four days from now.

Durand's otherwise serious expression turned into a big smile when he heard the woman on the other end say to Mayon, "Make sure you bring with you the special security card to access your accounts. Without it, Mr. Nabati won't see you."

*The million-dollar question is, how much is in that account?*

Shortly after the telephone conversation, the Girards went out for a walk, and Durand used the opportunity to create his report. A plan was taking shape in his head. After he dropped the thumb drive off at the dead drop, he returned to his hotel room, got himself a cold beer from the fridge, pulled an old-fashioned writing pad and pencil from his luggage, and sat down in one of the comfortable reclining chairs in the lounge to start planning.

The next day when he dropped his report off, to his surprise, there was a message from his handler thanking him for a job well done and confirming that his final payment had been processed as per his instructions. It was the end of his mission — the easiest money Durand had made since he entered the professional assassin industry.

The sudden and amiable ending of his contract suited Durand to the T. It meant he got his payment and the client was happy and more importantly, unsuspecting of *his* plans.

## Chapter Twenty-Five

### THE JOB OFFER

Mackenzie had set herself up at the kitchen table where she could be out of Liu's way and out of earshot while she was dictating the Sirralnnudam translations into the voice recognition software.

She was reading through a paper titled "*A Mechanical Artificial Red Cell: Exploratory Design in Medical Nanotechnology,*" published in 1996 by Robert A. Freitas Jr., a Research Fellow of the Institute for Molecular Manufacturing (IMM) at Palo Alto, California. She had read this specific information many times before, but she often returned to it and read it again as it always stimulated her thought processes.

Although generic descriptions of potential nanomedical devices had been published by others over the years, Freitas was the first scientist of modern times who had published such an elaborately detailed exploratory design that had the potential to achieve a useful result — an artificial mechanical erythrocyte (red blood cell) or respirocyte generator.

The Nobel physicist Richard P. Feynman was the first to

propose the concept of nanotechnology in December 1959. During a presentation, he laid down an apparently "unachievable" challenge to build a working electric motor no larger than 1/64th-inch cube. He backed his challenge with a $1,000 prize. Within eleven months, an engineer, William McLellan, presented his 250-microgram, 2000-rpm motor, consisting of thirteen separate parts, and collected his reward. Since then nanotechnology had emerged in leaps and bounds in not only medical science but almost every industry on the planet, as scientists started building rigid nano parts for the medical, computer, telecommunications, apparel, military, energy, and many other industries.

Chemists had been successful at constructing self-assembling, multi-part nanomachines that could travel through the human body on missions to discover, monitor, report, and repair. It seemed as if it was just a matter of time before the first complex, micron-scale chemical factory that would overcome the shortcomings of current artificial blood technologies would make its appearance.

At least, that's what Robert A. Freitas Jr. had predicted more than twenty years ago. But after all this time, and despite enormous progress in the nanotechnology field, no respirocyte generator had been built yet.

Mackenzie was so deep in thought she didn't hear Liu calling out to her — only becoming aware when Liu waved her hand in front of Mackenzie's eyes.

"You had me worried. I've been calling you for the past five minutes. You must have been on another planet." Liu was enlivened. "Sorry to disturb your thoughts, but I have something very interesting to show you."

Mackenzie nodded, apologized for not hearing Liu's calls, and followed her to the study, where she took a seat next to Liu so they could both look at the two computer screens.

"I've got two parts I want to show you." Liu pointed at the screen to the left displaying the original text of the Sirralnnudam. "You see that part I've highlighted? Now look at my translation on this screen." She started reading.

"'*Unknown word*' air or gases are absorbed or taken up and released or set free by '*unknown word*'. There is a balance or relationship between '*unknown word's*' processing of oxygen and carbon dioxide in the human body . . ."

"Replace that first unknown word with respiratory and the other two with hemoglobin," Mackenzie said calmly.

Liu made the replacements and Mackenzie read the translation again. "Mhh now it makes sense. This is really exciting."

Liu continued. "When there is a high level of oxygen in the lungs it helps to release the carbon dioxide." She paused and looked at Mackenzie. "Makes sense to you so far?"

Mackenzie nodded.

"Okay." Liu continued. "It says carbon dioxide is generated in the body because of the burning or processing of the food we eat. Both the oxygen and the carbon dioxide in the body are transported between the lungs and the cells of the body by the red blood cells."

Mackenzie nodded again. "So far it's spot on."

"Good. Now it says hemoglobin is an important . . . I think that word means protein . . . let's call it a substance for now, in the red blood cells, which mixes or combines with the oxygen, and that about ninety-five percent of the oxygen is carried in this form. The remaining oxygen gets dissolved in the blood. I'm not sure that my figures are correct, but from what I could make out of their numbering system, it seems as if hemoglobin holds about eighty-seven times more oxygen than the blood fluid or plasma." She paused and looked at Mackenzie and noticed the stunned expression.

"Liu, it's mind-bending to think that some scientists, thousands of years ago, documented this information with such stunning accuracy. This is stuff we only discovered a hundred or so years ago. In the light of this, maybe I should use the word rediscovered.

"This information is one hundred percent in line with what we know today. If I didn't know how old this book was, I would have taken you to task about the origin of this information."

Liu smiled. She'd had the pleasure of seeing looks like the one on Mackenzie's face on quite a few occasions in the past when she'd done translations for Carter and for his grandfather, Will. "Shall I continue?"

"Please, I'm all ears."

"It says that the hemoglobin inside the red blood cells also combines with carbon dioxide and about twenty-five percent of what the body produces during food processing is carried by hemoglobin. Ten percent dissolves in the plasma and the remaining sixty-five percent gets transported by the hemoglobin inside the red blood cells.

"Now with this next part I'm struggling a bit with the medical terminology, but the gist of it seems to be that this arrangement of how the carbon dioxide is transported around in the body ensures that the acidity levels of the blood in the veins are in sync with those in the main arteries." She paused and glanced at Mackenzie.

"Magnificent translation, Liu!" she exclaimed. "I could not have explained that better than you just did. And again, as with everything else you have told me in the past few minutes, it's exactly as we understand it today."

"Well, then I am very pleased. Now I suggest you buckle up for part two." Liu laughed as she found the relevant page and brought it up on the two screens.

"Ready when you are," Mackenzie whispered eagerly.

"From what I can make out, the author is talking about an easy or simple but extremely small machine or device or mechanism that was used to simulate red blood cells. It goes on to explain that this little miracle machine can deliver about 240 times more oxygen to the tissues than natural human red blood cells are capable of. The mechanisms of the device are described in more detail in the latter parts of the text. I had a quick look at it earlier, but I will need a lot of technical help to translate that correctly."

They decided it was time for a tea break and went to the kitchen to prepare their drinks before returning to the study. Mackenzie was burning to get hold of Carter and tell him, but she controlled her excitement. She wanted to have a look at the design before she would call him.

It didn't take them long to figure out that the device was constructed out of a diamondiferous material, using a variation of chemical, thermal, and pressure sensors, all controlled by what they could best describe as an onboard nanocomputer. The apparatus apparently was powered from the abundance of naturally-occurring glucose in the body, enabling them to operate independently and virtually indefinitely.

"Liu, I can't help but wonder if some of the present-day designers of hypothetical respirocyte generators had a peek at the Sirralnnudam before creating their designs." She laughed. "Discounting my limited understanding of nanotechnology, to me this ancient device sounds so similar to some of the modern designs it's almost scary."

"Well, what we need to find now is the exact design

specifications—the blueprint if you will. I've scrolled through the text but couldn't find anything like that . . ."

"Ah . . . that's not nice of them. Why didn't they just play along and give it to us?" Mackenzie snickered.

"Maybe they were not as bad as you think. I found this paragraph here." Liu pointed at the screen with the original text. "I haven't translated it properly yet, so I'll just give you the general picture. It says here that this machine or device was developed and used by people who lived on the earth a very long time . . . wait, I think that should be translated as 'many thousands of years ago'. According to this, those were strange people who called themselves the Zamzummim, although the text also uses this word here רפאים, which is a Semitic word for Rephaim. Now the most intriguing part for me is this part here, which could have two possible meanings; the one is that this Zamzummim people were of extraordinary height and stature—"

"Giants!" Mackenzie shouted. "They were giants! Liu, this is . . . this is . . . I don't know what to say . . . staggering."

"Okay, just hang on one sec. Those words could also refer to dead ancestors or residents of the Underworld or Netherworld."

"No, I don't think so. We can check with Carter, but if my memory serves me correctly, recalling some of the facts from when Carter explained the history of giants to Sean and the others when they were here a few weeks ago — the word Rephaim means giants. That name Zamzummim appears in the Bible and is later changed to Zuzim. They were a race of giants whom some scholars believe lived from before Adam."

"I'll take your word for that. So, then that text means the giants who called themselves the Zamzummim developed and used what we would today call a respirocyte generator."

Then the reality of it all sunk in, and Mackenzie exploded. "Liu! We found it! We've got it! It's incredible . . . it's astonishing . . ."

Mackenzie was on her feet dancing and shaking her arms in the air. And the next moment, just as quickly as that outburst happened, she went unnervingly quiet. She stopped and stared out the window. Her mind had become cluttered with thoughts and emotions — remembering the first conversation she had with Will, years ago, about this. The research she had put into it, the pain and suffering of she and her children in captivity, the hopelessness she experienced at times. Liu's abduction and her unnecessary suffering — all because of this research. Guilt and remorse . . . was this really worth it? Thousands of thoughts and emotions bombarded her brain.

She should have felt jubilation, gratification, or even liberation. This was the moment she had worked for so long. But then, it had almost cost her, her life and those of her children and her husband and her friend, Liu. For so long she had expected, hypothesized, and anticipated, and now it was there. But instead of joy, she felt cold and deflated. She felt *guilty*.

Finally, after many minutes, she turned to Liu, and with tears in her eyes, she started talking. "Liu . . . I . . . I don't know what to say. Suddenly, I'm feeling so empty . . . so guilty . . ."

Liu opened her mouth, but Mackenzie held her hand up to stop her. "No, please let me finish. I've drawn you into this . . . were it not for my egotistical mania to make this discovery, you wouldn't have endured all that suffering in

Saudi Arabia . . . hell, you wouldn't even have been there . . ."

"Enough!" Liu shouted. "Have you lost your mind, Mackenzie? I won't have another word of that senseless babbling of yours. You are my best friend. I'm a linguist, I translate ancient scrolls and texts and whatever — that's my job, and I love what I do.

"The people who locked me up in that place were criminals, evil-minded people with evil intent, not you. You had nothing to do with it. I don't want to hear another stupid thought like that out of your mouth."

She stood and put her arms around Mackenzie's shoulders. "This is a momentous occasion, Mackenzie. We have all the reason to celebrate. It's almost as if this is partial reparation for what they took away from us in that evil place."

Mackenzie stood back and looked at Liu, mustering a smile through her tears. "How can anyone ever hope to be blessed with a better friend than you?"

It was time to get hold of Carter. Mackenzie phoned him on the satellite phone and asked him to come home as quickly as possible. She refused to tell him why.

---

Ten minutes later, Carter and Dylan arrived in the electric cart and entered the house to find the shell-shocked women in the living room.

"What's wrong, Mackie?" Carter asked with concern in his voice. "It looks as if you've seen a ghost." He took a few steps and took her in his arms.

Dylan followed suit and took Liu in his own arms. "What is it, Liu?"

As if on cue, the women started laughing, to the consternation of their men.

Mackenzie spoke first. "Carter, we've got it! We found it! Its beyond exciting—"

"What are you talking about, Mackie? Slow down now, take a deep breath, and tell us."

"We found the first reference to an ancient respirocyte generator, Carter!" Liu burst out in laughter again. "Can you believe it? It's been hiding in the Sirralnnudam all this time, just waiting for us to find it."

*"What?"* Dylan shouted as he lifted Liu off the floor, her feet dangling in the air almost fourteen inches off the ground. "How did you . . . hang on . . . let's sit down, I can't keep you up in the air like this forever."

"You didn't have any problems a few months ago, when you carried me up those stairs . . ." Liu giggled.

"Different time and circumstances," Dylan muttered with a big grin.

Carter let go of Mackenzie and dragged her over to the couch next to him. "Now one at a time, beginning with you, Mackie, tell us what you found."

An hour later, after Liu and Mackenzie had fetched the laptop from the study and showed them what they'd found, and Carter having checked and double-checked Liu's translations, he and Dylan were just staring at the ladies.

"Earth-shattering," was all that Dylan could get out when the significance of the discovery dawned on him.

"Mackie, it's maybe too early to say, but I've got this strange awareness that we have what you are looking for right here in this house."

"What do you . . . Of course! The library of the giants!"

Carter slowly nodded. "All the more reason to get that translated as quickly as humanly possible."

"Library of the giants? What's that? Have I missed something?" Liu asked.

Carter looked at Dylan. "I think it's time to read her in on that."

Dylan nodded, turned to Liu, and explained to her how Carter found the metallic sheets at the City of Lights in Egypt and brought them back with him. He also explained how Carter was able to access the script with the help of an electron microscope.

As Dylan's account progressed, Liu became more and more excited, and in short order she was staring at the rendition of one of the dots on one of the sheets on Carter's computer.

She started speaking under her breath, "Mhh, definitely proto-Semitic, some familiar root words that look like a mix of ancient Arabic, Aramaic, ancient Hebrew . . . and others. Wait a minute here is a word . . . large . . . enormous . . . in size. Hang on let me go back . . . humans, large or enormous . . . Giants!"

Carter and the rest started grinning. "Liu, you should have paid us a visit a long time ago. Just imagine how much we would have discovered by now."

Liu was deep in thought. She didn't even hear Carter speaking. "Mackenzie, you are not going to believe this . . . here it is, the exact same word for giants we saw in the Sirralnnudam, Zamzummim."

A deafening silence broke out as they all stared at Liu.

Carter was the first one to get his brain and vocal cords connected again. "That means Mackie's respirocyte generator might be waiting for us in those metallic sheets. Liu, how long will it take you to familiarize yourself with that language?"

"Maybe a month or two. But that is not the issue. If I

understood Dylan's explanation of the size of this library correctly, you'll need an army of a thousand linguists and ten to fifteen years to work through it."

"You've got a point there but I already spoke to Rick Winslow about developing a computer program to help us speed things up, but we'll still need a human to check and oversee everything."

Liu nodded. "Yeah, computers can help a lot, and it might be useful to at least get the rough translation of everything done quickly. That will enable you to start searching, categorizing, and indexing the content."

Carter glanced at Mackenzie. It was as if telepathic communication passed between them, and she nodded slightly.

"Liu, are you open to a job offer at this stage?" Carter asked in earnestness.

Dylan's heart missed a beat as he realized what it would mean if she said yes — she would move to D.C. — they could . . .

Liu started. "I . . . I . . ."

"You'll head up a team of translators, working on this library and the Sirralnnudam . . . and, of course, any other documents we come across. Double your current salary and of course all your current benefits."

"You'll have to give me a bit of time to think about that, Carter," she replied. Glancing at Dylan, she saw the anticipation and excitement on his face.

*Mackenzie didn't lie — he really is in love with me.*

Mackenzie saw the exchange of looks between the two and then the sudden change on Liu's face. "Oh Liu, I think Carter forgot to mention the biggest hazard with this job, and that is you'll have to move to D.C."

Liu started blushing and glared at Mackenzie in mock

annoyance. "Well, I guess I just have to endure that hardship then." She grinned. "I don't need to think more about it. The answer is yes; I'll take the job. I'd love to do this."

The next moment Liu found her feet dangling fourteen inches off the floor again. Dylan was kissing her, and in between the kisses he started whispering in her ear, "I love you. I love you, Liu Cheun."

Carter and Mackenzie were laughing as they scuttled out of the room when Dylan lifted Liu into his arms, giving them some privacy.

About a quarter of an hour later, when Mackenzie could hear their voices again, she called out to them from the kitchen. "Hey, you love birds, come and join us for cake and coffee in the kitchen."

"Okay," Liu said later while they were still sitting at the kitchen table, "I suggest instead of resigning from the University immediately, I'd rather go back and ask them if I could take a six-month sabbatical. That will give us all enough time to see how this will work out. Will that be okay with you, Carter, Mackenzie?"

"No problem for me, Liu," Carter said. He looked at Mackenzie, who nodded her agreement. "In fact, I think it's a very wise decision. Let's try before we buy."

They discussed the details of their plan for a while longer, and then Carter said, "I'll give James a call to arrange a visit to D.C. for some time next week, as soon as Sean and his crew arrive to relieve Dylan and his men.

"I need to discuss this new plan with him, and get to Rick Winslow so that I can give him the requirements for the translation software he and his team have to build for us."

Mackenzie nodded.

A few minutes later Carter was on the phone with James.

They would have been horrified to know that the moment their "secured and impenetrable" satellite phones connected, a very powerful quantum computer in a sophisticated server room, located five stories below ground on the bank of the River Seine in the 3rd *Arrondissement* of Paris, started recording their conversation.

## Chapter Twenty-Six

### THE RISK-REWARD RATIO

Mathieu Nabati had become increasingly troubled over the past few days as he read the reports and listened to the audio recordings of the activities and conversations of the Algosaibis, or the Girards, as their new passports now stated. This morning, he had a lingering uneasy feeling at the pit of his stomach. They had so far given no indication that they knew about the existence of the Council of the Covenant of Nabatea or any of its activities. They hadn't connected their laptop to the Internet at any time either, they knew or their dad must have told them what the consequences of that would be. And that was part of the reason for Nabati's unease. Parts of their recorded conversations were disturbing enough to lead him to the conclusion that what else was on that flash drive would be very damaging information.

Nabati knew he had no other option, and he couldn't wait any longer. It was a risk the Council could not accept any longer. Jean and Olivia Girard had to be silenced, and that flash drive had to be acquired and destroyed.

Before Nabati could finalize his plans, a notice popped up on his computer screen informing him about an appointment at ten a.m. the next Monday. He clicked on the message to look at the details, and a grin spread across his face as he read the names of the clients — Mr. and Mrs. Girard.

"Now what do I call this? Luck, destiny, or fate?" he murmured.

He took his custom-made quantum encrypted PDA out of his pocket and typed a message to one of the Council's trusted assassination brokers, known only by the codename "Charlie." Although Charlie and Mathieu Nabati had done a lot of business in the past and trusted each other explicitly, they had never met, never spoken a single word with each other, and would never do so. They knew nothing of each other, and that's how it would remain.

All their communications were controlled through the Council's quantum computers. There were no traces, no evidence of their dealings anywhere except on the Council's servers, which could not be hacked by anyone on the planet. The Council's quantum computing systems were light years ahead of anything else in the world — their purpose-built operating systems, coding languages, and software didn't exist anywhere else, which rendered it failsafe against hacking from other computers.

Nabati's message was short and to the point:

END ROME SURVEILLANCE. RELEASE FINAL PAYMENT TO CONTRACTOR. ASSIGN NEW CONTRACTOR TO TERMINATE SUBJECTS WHEN THEY ARE IN ZÜRICH. CONTRACT PRICE €2 MILLION. PICTURES AND OTHER DETAILS TO FOLLOW AFTER ACKNOWLEDGEMENT AND ACCEPTANCE.

Charlie's reply arrived within the hour.

ACKNOWLEDGE RECEIPT. ROME CONTRACT ENDED. FINAL PAYMENT PROCESSED. ACCEPT ZÜRICH CONTRACT - AWAITING DETAILS.

Durand did not end his surveillance of the Girards as his handler trusted he would have done. He still had a vested interest in the Girards to the tune of at least three million US dollars — the bounty on offer by the Saudis. And if lady luck smiled upon him, the money in the secret Swiss accounts. He expected that the amount in those accounts would not have been inconsequential — people didn't keep petty cash in numbered, secret Swiss accounts.

His thoughts ended abruptly when his sixth sense kicked into action and turned his brain into a state of alert. Something was wrong with the scene in front of him in Kafi Dihei, one of the nicest coffee shops in Zürich on Zurlindenstrasse 231.

There was a short, dark-haired man three tables away who started squirming in his seat the moment the Girards stood to leave. Not coincidence. The needle on Durand's alert-meter hit the amber zone when he comprehended why the man had his cellphone up as if he was taking pictures of the rustic interior with its antique furniture and old-fashioned tapestry. He could have fooled a lot of people but not Durand, who immediately knew the man was taking pictures of the Girards. And if he had any doubts, they vanished the next moment as the needle hit the red zone when he recognized the familiar miniature parabolic directional microphone embedded in the innocent-looking packet of cigarettes conveniently and strategically placed on the table in front of this man.

## The Alboran Codex

"Dammit. I'm getting sloppy," Durand chastised himself, and he felt his blood run cold when he also realized Shorty was working for the same handler as he had until yesterday. He knew because he had a parabolic directional microphone disguised as a packet of cigarettes exactly like the one Shorty was now placing in his shirt pocket. Durand's had been provided to him by his handler on his first contract.

It was Friday, and Durand had followed the Girards from Rome to Zürich the day before. The bugs in their room back in Rome helped him get their address in Zürich as well as their flight details. He landed in Zürich a few hours after the Girards because he first had to undergo another makeover to match his false Swedish passport and credentials, which turned him into a blond businessman named Karl Nilsson from Stockholm.

Shorty's appearance on the scene meant Durand had to change his plans — things had become a bit more complicated than he would have liked. Instead of dealing with two untrained, unsuspecting civilians, he now had the challenge of keeping an eye on a trained professional as well. Thus far, the operator didn't look very efficient, otherwise he would not have let anyone spot him. But Durand knew better than to underestimate any opponent.

*What was this man's brief? Can't be more surveillance . . . or could it?*

He considered his options for a few moments. The safest and probably most logical choice was to drop everything he had in mind, go back to Paris and his girlfriend, and wait for the next contract. That way he had a good chance to stay alive. But it also meant his new, earlier retirement plan had just been flushed down the toilet. *Screw you, Shorty!*

Another option was to forget about the money in the

secret account and just try to get his hands on the three-million-dollar reward — still more than enough to fund his dream retirement lifestyle. This was also a safe option — all he had to do was follow the Girards until they reached Paris, get all their contact details, contact the Saudi authorities, provide them with the intel, and claim his remuneration. Not a bad option at all, except that scenario presupposed that the Girards would be alive. However, it was quite possible that Shorty's brief was to eliminate them. *I could, of course, eliminate them myself and claim the bounty . . . mhh . . . too messy and too risky for my liking.*

Perrin Durand's entire life since the day he joined the Foreign Legion comprised of unremitting risk assessments and the management thereof. The reason he'd survived up till now was his ability to identify risks early, assess them carefully, consider the risk to reward ratio, decide whether to avoid or accept, and only then act or not.

"To avoid or accept this one?" he mumbled to himself.

*You must go one step back. You don't have enough information to determine the risk-reward ratio.* And that was his answer — he had to gather more information before he could make his choice. Which would come to him much sooner than he would have expected.

He had an advantage over Shorty because the bugs he'd planted in Rome were still fully operational on the Girards' laptop, mobile phones, and luggage, including Jean's wallet and Olivia's fancy handbag. Shorty still had to complete his surveillance, unless of course he was a really stupid operator who would take action without completing proper surveillance and risk assessment.

Back in his hotel room, on the floor below the Girards, Durand nearly choked in his beer when he heard Olivia Girard's words.

"What are your plans once we get to Paris? You know twenty million dollars is a terrible lot of money. I know we don't have to lift a finger for the rest of our lives, but I will go stark raving mad if I have to sit around and do nothing. I'm thinking with my Ph.D. in quantum physics . . ."

Durand didn't even listen to the rest of the conversation.

*"Twenty million! My dear Mrs. Girard, don't you worry. I know exactly what to do with twenty million."*

The reward to risk ratio had just gone through the roof — for that money it was a risk worth taking.

## Chapter Twenty-Seven

### THE WOLVES OF WAR

In fulfillment of Dylan's prophecy, Mackenzie's wolves had been turning up like clockwork every afternoon around five to "inspect" progress at Camp Tala. The wolves' appearance became the team's cue to stop the day's activities and spend an hour or so with their visitors. The young wolves quickly made their choices, each of them befriending one of the six men. John took it upon himself to teach the other members of the team how to train the young wolves, and it was remarkable to see how quickly all of them learned — animals and humans alike.

The parents — Loki, Keeva, and Nadia — stayed out of it, more than happy to watch while their "kids" were put through the paces. It was almost as if they appreciated the fact that someone was helping them teach the youngsters good manners and discipline.

Nadia and her offspring had quickly gotten over their reservations about the humans and joined Loki and Keeva's family in getting the humans' attention. Her pups had not been named yet, but the team took care of that and named them Walker and Mulligan — the surnames of EA's commander and second-in-command, Sean and Dylan.

After a few days of watching these training sessions, Dylan had made up his mind and raised the topic with Carter and Ahote — the possibility of expanding the wolves' training with the aim to use them on missions. The two of them were very supportive of the idea. The only remaining, and of course most important, permission required was Mackenzie's, and seeking that permission had to wait for the right moment.

They all decided to keep the training a secret from Mackenzie, Bly, and Liu. On the next-to-last day before they had to return to D.C., the team would invite them over for a surprise wolf show.

When Liam saw the secret training sessions one afternoon when he turned up at the construction site, the boy could hardly contain his excitement.

"Can Jeha and I join them? Please, Dad? John can show me how to train her. She's a very clever dog. I'm sure she'll learn quickly."

Carter smiled. "Okay, but we first have to hear what John says, and if he agrees, there will be one more condition, though."

Liam looked at his dad to hear what the condition was.

"You have to promise you won't tell Mom, Auntie Bly, or Liu about this. Not one word until I tell you so."

"I promise, Dad. This is our secret. I won't say a word."

"Good, then we have a deal. Let's go and find out what John has to say about it."

Carter couldn't help but laugh quietly when he heard Liam mumbling. "I just hope Jeha can keep her mouth shut about this."

On the afternoon of the wolf show, the six young wolves

and their handlers, plus Liam and Jeha, put on a show that had Mackenzie, Bly, and Liu ecstatic as they sat, lay down, rolled over, fetched, stayed, and navigated a makeshift obstacle course, jumping over, crawling under, and going around various obstructions with apparent ease — as if they had been doing it all their lives.

What was mind-blowing to Mackenzie was the fact that they mastered all of it in such a short time and without the use of leashes or food bribes as was required in most dog training. The young wolves and even Jeha, strangely enough, were happy to perform in return for attention. A pat on the back, an ear scratch, and a "clever boy" or "clever girl" from their handlers was all they wanted.

Mackenzie didn't require any kind of persuasion to agree to Dylan's proposal to train the wolves for combat missions.

"They were part of our emotional and physical battles of the past year," she said. "They kept me sane while I was thousands of miles away, they kept on nudging Carter and everyone else until they got their message through that we were alive, they guarded Freydís, and chased some intruders away. They played such a pivotal role in our rescue, I'm absolutely convinced they want to be part of our activities in the future. I get the impression their turning up here was their way of reporting for duty."

And with that, the deal was sealed. Camp Tala was going to live up to its name — literally.

*The wolves of war*, John thought, as he listened to the conversation between Dylan and Mackenzie. A grin broke across his face. He knew what war-dogs were capable of, and from what he had seen so far, these wolves were every bit as capable, and probably much more than dogs. He had no doubts that if the bad guys had any idea what was heading their way shortly, they would be shitting in their combat boots.

That night over dinner, John was explaining dog and wolf behavior to Mackenzie. "The fact that this pack has chosen you is important. We tend to think we chose the animals to live with us, but that's the human perspective. From their perspective, it's not — they choose us.

"They *allow* us into *their* tribe because *they* trust us. It is difficult to prove that point with domesticated animals, but with your wolves you can see the idea seems to be correct. They are free to come and go as they please. If they didn't trust or like us, they wouldn't come back. Generally, wild animals don't allow humans into their tribes. But if they do, like your wolves did, it means they have chosen you and permitted you to become part of their family."

"What is the explanation for that? I mean they don't really need us. Do they?" Mackenzie asked.

"There is no clear answer. It could be that they sense your friendly intensions and love for them. It could be that they see some sort of benefit in it for their own protection and survival. Maybe they know that teaming up with caring humans means there is some synergy. In other words, they can protect you with their skills, and you will protect them with your skills."

"There is just so much that we don't understand about these majestic creatures," Mackenzie said in marvel.

"But we must always keep in mind," John continued, "the wolves are not domesticated. They can be tamed, as we have shown, but their inherent temperament remains that of a wild animal.

"They have learned to interact with us in a friendly manner, but their wild nature remains, and they might eventually challenge us for dominance. Therefore, we should never try to handle, house, feed, or trust them to behave like a domestic dog. There is a good chance that as they become older they'll reach a stage where they won't be participating with us as they do now. That's probably why Loki, Keeva, and Nadia stayed out of it — they are too old for it."

Mackenzie smiled. "Well, as long as they are keen to help, let's take them up on the offer."

And so, with the wolves' reporting for duty, it was decided that John would become one of the first permanent inhabitants of Camp Tala. He was thirty-two and married with two children, a boy of five and a baby girl of six months. He and his wife, Jennie, had met six years before while they were both attending a military dog handler training course at Joint Base Andrews. They'd both reached the rank of staff sergeant, and both had done tours of duty in Afghanistan and Iraq. In addition, John had over the last two years been specializing in the support of special ops missions with the Navy Seals and Delta Force. Jennie had left the military about eight months earlier to have the baby and be a stay-at-home mom for a while. Her plan was to start an obedience training school for dog owners in their neighborhood.

John and Jennie were both raised on farms and loved the outdoors and animals. Hence, it didn't take Sean and Dylan much to convince the two of them to relocate to Freydís. In fact, when Jennie heard about Liam and Beth, she started packing.

John would return to D.C. with Dylan and the rest of the team the next day. He and Jennie would finalize everything over the next two weeks and be on the next plane to Freydís.

Mackenzie and Carter were more than happy to accommodate John and his family until their cabin at Camp Tala was ready. And Liam was over the moon when he heard that he might soon have a human friend who could join him on all the adventures Freydís had to offer.

Carter and Liu had coordinated their visit to D.C. so that they could both be present to talk to Rick Winslow and provide him with the requirements of the translation software he had to develop for them. Mackenzie and the children would use the opportunity to visit her parents in Boston while Carter was in D.C.

## Chapter Twenty-Eight

### WISE COUNSEL

It was exactly 1:15 a.m. Monday when Durand heard the soft click of the electronic door lock on the Girards' hotel room. These swipe card locks were child's play; it took him all of four seconds to disable it with his mobile phone. As always, he was on high alert, silenced and loaded Glock 43 pistol in his right hand, adrenaline pumping.

Other than following the Girards and eavesdropping on their conversations, Shorty hadn't done anything else — yet. And that only provided Durand with reason to be super heedful.

He stood quietly inside the room after closing the door behind him and listened for a while, hearing only the sound of someone snoring. He slipped the little rubber wedge-shaped doorstop, which he'd brought with him, under the door. No one would be able to enter the same way he did unless they broke the door down. He moved noiselessly to the bedroom. The Girards were both in dreamland. He lowered the gasmask over his face, placed the knockout gas canister on the floor, pulled the pin, and stepped back out of the bedroom, closing the door. He waited for two minutes and then entered the bedroom again to work.

About fifteen minutes later, he was done. The Girards began to stir — the effects of the gas had run its course. He replaced the gasmask with a ski mask and waited a few more minutes before he switched on the lamp on Olivia's side of the bed, farthest away from him, and started shaking them by the shoulders. Both were soon sitting up against the headboard, their arms and legs zip-tied, their mouths gagged with duct tape and their eyes shot wide with horror.

Durand was not the compassionate type, but he almost felt sorry for them. However, he was not going to put them at ease. He wanted them to be terrified—the more, the better. If he could convince them he was the only person who stood between them and an untimely entry to the afterlife, he would have their cooperation. Part of his risk mitigation strategy was not to kill them but rather just to hold the sword of the Saudi government's keenness to learn of their whereabouts over their heads.

The tears started rolling over Olivia's face as she twisted and turned and tried to scream, but only muffled sounds came out. Durand stood, pointed the gun at her, and placed his finger on his lips gesturing that she should be quiet. She went still and stared at him. Jean had not moved or made any sounds. His eyes were fixed on the intruder, radiating only shock and anxiety.

"Now, listen very carefully, Mr. and Mrs. Girard," Durand started. "Or do you prefer I call you by your real names? Mayon and Aisha Algosaibi."

Sweat was pearling on their foreheads. Their eyes could not stretch any wider. Despondent sounds could be heard through the duct tape. They didn't answer the question — it probably didn't matter by what name you were called when you were staring down the barrel of a Glock 43 about to die.

"Okay, I'll call you by your new names to go with your makeover. I must say, Doctor Bordereau certainly knows his job. I'm impressed with what he did for you.

"But I am sure you are not really interested in my opinion of your nose jobs and are *dying* to know the purpose of my visit. Please note my emphasis on the word 'dying'.

"Well, here's the story; I have a very close friend in the Mabahith. You know those guys with the white tunics and red-and-white checkered headscarves? I've been told those guys are real nasty. I don't want to upset you with the horror stories I've heard. I can't say if it's true or not . . . but what am I talking about — you are from Saudi Arabia, so of course you would know about them. No?"

The expression in their eyes and on what was visible of their faces had Durand worried that his captives were about to wet the bed at any moment.

"Now, that friend of mine told me that if I could lead them to you, King al Saud would be so grateful, he'll pay me three million dollars. Shit, let me tell you, for a poor man like me, that's an obscene amount of money. I know that's not a lot of money for the two of you, but for me . . . it's different.

"The thing is, this man and I have been very good friends for almost twenty years now. We really like and trust each other. I don't want to disappoint him, but now that very friendship has presented me with a huge moral dilemma, and that's why I came over. I would like to get your advice."

They stared at him. Confusion, or maybe it was a glimmer of hope, was now mixed with the fearful expressions.

"So, let me not keep you in suspense much longer. Here is my quandary I hope you can help me resolve. In the one hand"—he held his left hand in the air as if he was holding something— "I've got three million dollars and a twenty-year friendship." He paused for a moment. "In this hand" —he raised his right, palm up— "I've got twenty million dollars and no friend. Which hand to choose? It's a really difficult one for me. What's your advice?"

They glanced at each other, and Jean made some inaudible noises, which given the circumstances must have been something to the effect of *"take the duct tape off my mouth and I'll tell you."*

Durand shook his head. "No, can't do that. Just nod your heads when I hold up the hand you've picked." He held his right hand in the air. "This is the hand with the $20 million sans my friend." Jean and Olivia's heads immediately started bobbing up and down in sync, as if they were listening to the same tune.

"Thank you very much. I'm so glad I came to see you. I just knew from the first moment I saw the two of you that you were well educated and clever. I'll be sad to lose my friend . . . but you know . . . such is life. Everyone has a price and shit happens."

His prisoners nodded their concurrence.

"Okay, I will also need your help to work out all the details, and then I'll be on my way."

They nodded again, looking almost enthusiastic.

"Good. I'm glad you are so excited to help me out. First, let's agree about the $20 million. I had a long hard think about it and thought the best way to do this is I'll take $17 million from you and $3 million from his Royal Highness, King al Saud."

The Girards sighed through the duct tape.

"No, no, don't worry please. If everything happens the way we are about to agree, you'll have nothing to worry about. You see, I thought it best if I just leave the $3 million with the King . . . you know, sort of like in an escrow account. I take the $17 million, and I'm sure that'll be more than enough for me." He leaned towards them and spoke in measured terms. "The only time I will withdraw those trust funds will be if I find out you've decided to try and find me." He paused again. "You think that can work?"

Their heads began moving up and down in sync once more.

"Okay. Now there is one little complication we'll have to work through." He took his cellphone out, tapped a few keys, and turned the screen to them so they could see the picture.

"Have you seen this man before?"

They were staring at the picture of Shorty and slowly started nodding again.

"In the coffee shop, yesterday morning. Right?"

They nodded.

"I take it you don't know who he is?"

They shook their heads this time.

"This man has been following you since you arrived in Zürich. Did you know that?"

They continued shaking their heads.

"Well, I know that, because I've taken quite a few pictures of him since Friday. And guess what? I took it all while he was watching you. Just look here . . . there's Olivia, and there you can see this man at the table a few paces away. Ah, here's another one. Just look at that — Jean in the background and our mystery man in the front here."

Their eyes were wide again.

"That means there is at least one other person who

knows your real identities, and there could be more. So, I think we have ourselves a little problem here."

They had started sweating again.

"I've wondered how this problem could be resolved, and I'm still not sure what to do. Let me give you the options that I came up with. Option one, I pack my stuff and go home, contact my Mabahith friend, send him your pictures and contact details . . . et cetera.

"Option two, I set up a meeting with this guy and make him an offer he can't refuse, say two million dollars, on condition he drops the case and forgets he ever saw you.

"Option three, I get rid of him . . . you know . . . like permanently."

He paused a breath. "So, which option do you reckon is best?"

They stared at him, very eager to let him know what their choice was.

He held up one finger. "Option one?"

He smiled. "Okay, that was a definite no.

"Option two?

"Hmm, another strong no . . .

"Well, then it must be option three." He grinned. "Excellent choice."

Durand spent a few more minutes to explain the plan to them to make sure they understood it in the minutest detail, including the bank accounts he wanted the money transferred to. Throughout they nodded their agreement and understanding.

Durand stood, paused, and then frowned. "Mhh, I know there was something else . . . it was important . . . what was it . . . aha, now I remember.

"Just to make sure we don't lose contact, I've taken the liberty, while you were asleep, to implant a very small tracking device just below the skin in the nape of your necks. With that, I'll always know where you are and can make sure you are well protected." He grinned.

"It's very important that you understand this. Don't try to remove those implants. They have also been rigged with a small C4 charge, not big at all, but just enough to blow your brainstems away. Please make sure you don't tamper with that — it *will* explode. Oh, one more thing. I can also set it off remotely. You see this little app here on my cell-phone screen, that red button there? If I push that, you will experience the mother of all headaches right before your brains fly out of your ears."

They nodded again in unison.

Durand got up and walked over to the table in the corner of the room, unplugged the laptop and flash drive, packed it all into the laptop bag, and swung the strap over his left shoulder.

He stood back, looked at them, and said, "That's all for now. Thank you for the wise counsel; I really appreciate it." He pulled his knife out, cut the zip-ties on Mayon's wrists, and left without saying another word.

## Chapter Twenty-Nine

### DOUBLE CROSSING

It was three a.m. on Monday when Durand walked out of the Girards' hotel room and took the fire escape stairs down to the floor below where his room was. He would try to get some sleep before setting himself up at his observation post opposite the entrance to the bank where the Girards were due to have their meeting with Mr. Nabati at ten a.m.

He hadn't seen Shorty since midday on Sunday, and he still had no idea what the man's instructions were. The fact that Shorty had not done anything other than surveilling the Girards was still mystifying. If his brief was to assassinate them, there had been plenty of opportunities, unless the brief was to wait until a certain time or event — perhaps after their visit to the bank. But that meant Shorty somehow must have learned about the Girards meeting at the bank. Maybe he'd picked it up while eavesdropping on the Girards conversations with his surreptitious microphone. Whatever the reason for Shorty's actions or lack thereof, Durand was not going to take any chances. He was so close now he could almost smell the seventeen million and Thailand.

He wanted at least one hour before the Girards arrived at the bank to allow him enough time to again scout the area around his selected observation point. He had done a few inconspicuous visits to the area over the weekend and had everything planned in detail.

It was eight forty-five a.m. when Durand noiselessly picked the lock of number 704 in the apartment building across the road from the entry to the bank. As expected, there was no one in the apartment. Durand could not believe his luck when he learned through a few discreet enquiries, that 704 belonged to an elderly couple who were out of town. Once inside, Durand moved quickly to disarm the alarm system. Then he moved back to the front door and put the doorstop in place.

The apartment was ideally situated — three floors up, overlooking the street, and with an unobstructed view of the street below for more than 100 yards in both directions. No one would be able to come and go along that 200-yard stretch without his knowledge. He entered the small living area, pulled an easy chair and a little table closer to the sliding door opening on the balcony overlooking the street, and unpacked his gear — a small but powerful monocular, his Glock 43 with silencer, and his Remington Defense CSR (Concealable Sniper Rifle) also known as the Rucksack Rifle. It was a lightweight, five-piece, 7.62mm caliber sniper rifle with bolt-action, a 14-inch carbon fiber-wrapped barrel, a Leupold 3-18x44mm Mark 6 telescope, and an AAC 762-SDN-6 sound suppressor — a small but lethal weapon. If everything went per plan, and Shorty kept his unwelcome ass out of it, no one was going to get shot, but he was not going to leave anything to chance. If it was necessary to shoot people, he would not blink an eye.

After assembling the rifle, he looked through the telescope and squeezed off a few dry shots. When he was happy that the weapon was ready, he loaded the magazine and slipped it into place. Next, he checked the Glock 43, fitted the silencer, squeezed off a few dry shots, checked that the magazine was loaded, slipped it into the gun, and cocked it. He set up his electronic gear so he could listen to the Girards over his mobile phone speaker. It wouldn't do to have his hearing impeded by earphones in a situation like this where he had to keep a vigilant watch on a multitude of people.

With all his preparations done, he picked up the monocular and started scanning to make sure he had the best possible view onto the street. He had to move the table and chair a few times to get the ideal spot. Once satisfied, he opened the balcony door and returned to his seat. He glanced at his watch — only 9:20 a.m. He took a few sips of the coffee he'd bought at the corner café before he entered the apartment. Lukewarm, it was not as nice as hot coffee but still better than no coffee. He shut his eyes and took a few deep diaphragmatic breaths to stem the flow of adrenaline and calm him. It was so close now. Just another hour or so and it would be over — provided no one else meddled in his business.

"Thailand, here I come," he whispered.

It was 9:40 a.m. when he raised the Bushnell Legend Ultra HD monocular to his right eye for the umpteenth time to look at the people on the street. For some reason, his attention was drawn to an old man with shoulder-length silver hair, a walking stick, and a slight limp moving along the sidewalk on the bank's side of the street.

"I know you," Durand whispered. "I've seen you somewhere . . . where was it? Come on look up. Where was it?"

The old man arrived at the café diagonally across the street, about thirty yards away from the entry to the bank, paused for a short moment, and looked around before he entered. And that's when Durand caught a glimpse of his face. "You son of a bitch! Shorty. What the hell are you doing here? And that big briefcase? Don't tell me you are here for a business meeting . . . I'm not buying."

Durand's mind was racing. Briefcase-carrying people were nothing uncommon on the streets of Zürich, or for that matter, anywhere in the world. But briefcase carrying assassins were an entirely different story.

*Shorty's got a sniper rifle in that briefcase, and he is going to make the hit here. The only thing I don't know is whether he is going to do it before or after the meeting. After the meeting, no problem. Before the meeting, big problem.*

He kept on watching the entrance to the café, expecting Shorty to walk out again, but a few minutes later he saw the curtains of an apartment on the second floor above the café being drawn. He focused the monocular on the apartment, and there was Shorty, busy unpacking the tools of his trade — a Heckler and Koch pistol, small binoculars, and then the different parts of his Surgeon Concealable Sniper Rifle with a Schmidt and Bender 5-25x56 PM II scope — a favorite of top tier law enforcement and military groups around the world.

"Screw you again, Shorty," Durand muttered. "You are interfering in a very important business transaction. Couldn't you just stay out of it? If you want to kill them after the meeting, be my guest, but if you so much as lay a finger on the trigger of that sniper rifle of yours before the meeting, you're a dead man."

Durand settled behind the scope of his rifle and made sure he had a good, clean shot at Shorty. He had no intentions of shooting the man unless it became absolutely necessary — shooting would cause too much exposure and risk. The ideal would be if he could walk away with the $17 million without anyone other than he and the Girards knowing he had even been there.

## Chapter Thirty

### FIX THIS IMMEDIATELY!

Shorty, whose real name was known to few, and irrelevant in any case, was twenty-five minutes early. If he'd known his mission was compromised, he'd have arrived more than an hour early and scouted the surrounding area. But there was no reason to believe anyone else besides his client knew of his task today.

Secure in his eyrie, he watched the street for the Girards' arrival. He checked his watch every few minutes, but Durand was certain there'd be no way Shorty could miss the couple amongst the crowd. The twin blond heads would give them away, if nothing else. Of course, they'd be nervous, glancing around and in general acting in a suspicious manner. It would be easy to pick that out as well.

In the same moment, Durand noticed a taxi cruising in, Shorty must have seen it too. He adjusted the angle of his weapon and settled behind the scope, but his finger remained within the trigger guard but off the trigger. Durand now focused entirely on Shorty through his own scope.

With only forty or fifty yards between them, Durand could see Shorty's every small movement, every ripple of a muscle in his jaw. He fancied he could even read the man's intentions in his body language. It didn't look good. Durand put a fraction of a pound of pressure on the trigger. He'd have to react with no hesitation if Shorty's finger so much as twitched. The hundredth of a second head start with his finger already on his trigger would mean the difference between life and death for the Girards and, of course, retirement for him or not.

Durand risked a glance downward at the taxi, which had now stopped. Olivia had emerged and stood waiting for her brother. Presumably, Jean was paying the driver and would be out in a few more seconds. Durand could afford no more attention on the Girards. His eyes snapped toward Shorty, whose finger had now moved to rest lightly on the trigger. Durand cursed under his breath.

Shorty's intentions were now crystal clear. There was no more time to waste. As soon as Jean stepped out of the taxi, Shorty would take the shot, no question. As much as Durand didn't want the additional risk, he squeezed the trigger — without regret. If Shorty took his shot, the bastard would ruin Durand's retirement plans. And by now, he had too much invested in those plans to allow that to happen.

Located as he was, about two yards from the window, and with a highly effective silencer, the shot was virtually inaudible from the street. Even in the building where Durand sat, no one would have heard the whisper of the bullet as it left the chamber, no louder than a zipper being pulled.

Durand regarded his handiwork impassively. The bullet had found its mark in Shorty's left eye, continuing through his brain and exiting the back of his head to embed itself somewhere in the farther recesses of the building. Shorty was slumped over his rifle, motionless.

Durand gave little thought to the potential damage the bullet could have done as it spent its final energy. But he was plenty nervous about having to take the shot nonetheless. The longer it took for Shorty's body to be found, the better Durand's chances of pulling off his plans. Therefore, he was eager to leave the vicinity before some alert gendarme turned up.

Before he could leave, though, he had to wait to listen in on the conversation the Girards were about to have with Mathieu Nabati. It wouldn't do to have them fail to transfer the money, or worse, to enlist the banker's help. If there was the slightest hint of that, he'd finish them himself and claim the three million from the Sauidis. The only way to know what his next step would be was to hear what they said.

So, he waited nervously, one ear cocked for sirens, and the other tuned to the receiver where he'd hear the conversation that could make him rich beyond his wildest dreams.

---

Girards . . .

Unaware that they'd come within a millisecond of death only moments before, the Girards went into the building and presented themselves in Nabati's office to keep their appointment.

Nabati, almost fell off his chair when his assistant told him they had arrived. This wasn't supposed to happen! He never had any intention of seeing them — they were supposed to be dead. If he'd known that death would have occurred right outside the doors of his building but for

Durand's interference, he'd have been even angrier. As it was, he kept his "clients" waiting while he fired off an enraged message to Charlie on his secured, quantum encrypted PDA.

> WHAT THE F@!$^ IS GOING ON? TARGETS ALIVE AND IN MY RECEPTION AREA. YOU BETTER FIX THIS IMMEDIATELY!

Clearly, Charlie was at fault. He'd assured Nabati the Girards would never reach his office. He *promised* they'd be dead long before they could keep their appointment. And yet, they were here, and he'd have to act as if he'd expected them. He'd even have to pretend they were his most valuable clients.

Fortunately, there was no need to fawn over them as an American would. No — he would treat them with typical Swiss efficiency and courtesy. If you could call it courtesy when the atmosphere in his office was as frigid as the North Pole. With outward calm, he greeted the Girards as correctly as he would any valued client, while inside his gut was roiling with rage.

"Please, have a seat. What can I do for you?" he asked.

"We would like to transfer $17 million from these accounts" –Jean held up the black card with the numbered accounts from his father— "to these accounts, in the amounts listed here," Jean explained, leaning forward with the card and a slip of paper bearing the number of Durand's accounts and the amount to be transferred to each.

As Nabati accepted the items, concealing his surprise at the strange request, his mind worked furiously to understand the Girards' purpose in scattering their money into several different accounts.

"As you wish. I see you are leaving a small sum with us," he said. "May I ask, have we done anything to make you distrust our security?"

"Not at all," Jean answered, quelling his sister's comment before she could make it. "We just thought it prudent not to have all our eggs in one basket, so to speak."

Jean squeezed Olivia's hand, signaling to her to let her sharply indrawn breath out slowly and go along with him.

"I see," answered Nabati. It was all he could do to relax his clenched teeth. "I'll have this done to your specifications immediately. Please wait here." He made a measured exit from his office, still tightly controlling his temper. It made no difference to him if these children of the traitorous Algosaibi transferred their money to other Swiss banking institutions. They would soon be dead in any case, and $17 million was a paltry sum.

"Immediately" in this case meant in an expedited manner he would oversee himself. It would give Charlie time to make arrangements to correct his operative's error. That didn't mean the transactions would happen quickly, as the arrangements were fairly complex and required communications between banks outside of normal business.

Durand heard every word of the conversation. He approved Jean's sidestepping Nabati's question, but after Nabati left the room, the silence was alarming. The Girards weren't talking at all. It made the hour and a half wait almost unbearable for Durand's nerves. After all, the Girards were safe in Nabati's office, unaware he'd killed their would-be assassin to save their lives. He, however, was exposed.

If the police were to turn up, it would take a few moments only to deduce where the shot had come from if Shorty's body was discovered. And that could happen at any moment. If they found him still there, they would have all the evidence they needed to send him to prison for the rest of his life. That Switzerland didn't have the death penalty was cold comfort. Prison was not his retirement plan, after all. There were no willing Thai prostitutes in Swiss prisons.

Durand paced and checked his watch every few seconds as he waited the eternity for Nabati's eventual return to his office. He also obsessively scanned the street, on the lookout for the arrival of the police. Even though he was focused on what he was hearing — or in this case, not hearing — from Nabati's office, he was also attuned to the sound of sirens in the distance. Fortunately, none seemed to be getting closer to his location.

He noticed an attractive woman arrive at the coffee shop below, mostly because she took a seat and took a magazine out of the backpack she was wearing and started reading. As always, he took note of her appearance, not because she was an attractive woman, though she was. He was too nervous to let his libido distract him. No, it was because he always took note of people who passed through his immediate area of interest and those who stayed in the vicinity.

The woman wore a headscarf, dark glasses, and nondescript clothing — a casual shirt and jeans. Her backpack was small, doubling as a purse no doubt. She wore running shoes. His perusal of her attire made him aware she was well-shaped, but he paid no attention to that this time. His gaze moved on to watch others in the street, most of whom, if they stopped at the coffee shop at all, ordered an espresso and drank it like a shot of liquor, hardly stopping on their way to wherever they were going. Only the woman remained seated at one of the sidewalk tables as the crowds streamed past her.

At last, Durand heard Nabati telling the Girards their transactions were complete, the transfers all in order. He uttered the usual pleasantries in parting. Durand could almost visualize the handshakes all around. He sighed in relief that it was done.

He'd packed everything already, wiped all the surfaces in the apartment, and left everything as he found it. He even locked the door as he left. Exiting by way of the fire escape, he made his way out the back of the building into a quiet side street where no one would observe him. There was one stop to make before he went to the train station. In an excess of caution, he wanted to change his appearance.

Durand's interest in the Girards was over. Of course, he had no intention of giving them any more protection, and in fact would not have cared if Shorty had killed them so long as it happened *after* he had their money. It wasn't as if they could complain about bad customer service after all. He had the three million reward from the Saudis to hold over their heads, but he doubted he'd ever hear from them again. They weren't cut out for cloak and dagger. Just innocent bystanders, really. Very, very wealthy innocent bystanders, now just a little less wealthy. Redistribution of wealth is what some politicians would have called it.

Durand thought about his next moves as he changed his appearance, though he didn't bother with too radical a transformation. His assassin days were over. In fact, he'd never have to work again, his financial needs met for the rest of his life. He was on his way to Paris, $17 million richer, to pick up only the most precious of his few possessions and then move on.

He gave only a brief thought to his girlfriend of four years. Take her along? No . . . she had no idea what he did for a living. It was too risky to tell her, and besides, just hiding himself was going to take all the skill he had. Her presence would also put a damper on that fantasy of willing Thai women. It was best he just quietly disappear. She may be sad for a while, but they'd never been serious. She would move on, a little wiser maybe. And he . . . he would put that $17 million to good use having his pick of the best food and accommodation, the most beautiful, and the most willing, women he could find.

Thus, he didn't see what happened to the Girards after he left, and would only find out much later what hellish consequences there would be for him because of his murder of Shorty.

## Chapter Thirty-One
### IN TOUCH SOON

In his office, Nabati shot his cuffs and took a deep, calming breath. Charlie wouldn't dare to fail twice, he had no doubt. The Girards would shortly be eliminated, and any information they had in their possession retrieved. In fact, his expectations were met within minutes.

On the street, the Girards emerged from the bank building and turned toward the coffee shop on their way to a line of taxis a block away. They felt secure that Durand had their backs now that they'd fulfilled their end of the bargain.

"It was fun being multimillionaires while it lasted," murmured Olivia.

Behind them, a woman with long blonde hair, sunglasses, and a headscarf had stood from her table at the coffee shop. But neither noticed her as Jean pointed out they were still technically multimillionaires with three million left.

"That's not . . ." Olivia's comment was cut short as the

.22 round from the woman's silenced pistol entered her brain from the base of her skull.

Jean had no time to react as he too was cut down. They dropped to the ground, dead before they hit, with so little commotion that even the crowds around them didn't realize what happened until someone tripped over Jean's body. By that time, the killer was long gone. Her timing and precision were so seamless no one had seen the assassination.

By the time the screaming started, the assassin had walked around the corner and down the block to a large restaurant. Upon entering, she went straight to the ladies' room, where she shed the wig, sunglasses, and headscarf. The jeans and running shoes went into the garbage bin next, and she shook loose the short pencil skirt that had been rucked around her waist under the casual shirt. She tucked in the shirt and pulled a pair of high-heeled pumps from her backpack. Now she was several inches taller and a few pounds slimmer to a casual observer. She sauntered out of the restaurant in the opposite direction from the commotion she'd left behind.

Meanwhile, the street in front of the bank building had erupted in chaos. As soon as the first pedestrian tripped over a body and started screaming, other passersby started screaming as well, and not a few fled the scene. Naturally, not everyone could see what the screaming was all about, and as they began running in all directions, one or two ran headlong into the ring of horrified witnesses that had begun to form around the bodies. A few people narrowly escaped being trampled. In moments, sirens announced the arrival of the police. By that time, the knot of gawkers had become several deep from front to back, impeding the police from getting to the bodies. Tempers began to flare as the officers were none too gentle in dispersing them, while telling them to stay in the area for questioning.

Nabati acknowledged his assistant's report that something had happened downstairs but kept his smile to himself until she had left his office.

It took some time for the police to bring the crowd under control and detain as many as they could to question as potential witnesses. The streets were cordoned off, but of course that didn't stop the media. Hard on the heels of the police, both print and broadcast media were there in droves, getting in the way and annoying the witnesses whose day had been interrupted by the grisly scene. As the ambulances pulled away with the bodies, Nabati received a text on his secure device.

TARGETS ELIMINATED. RETRIEVING LAPTOP AND FLASH DRIVE. WILL BE IN TOUCH SOON.

Later, when observers were searching frantically for the moment of the murder, they would find the facial recognition software was useless. So many pedestrians had surrounded the victims when they dropped from sight that it was impossible to determine which of them had done the deed. The only thing certain was that whoever had done it had known exactly where the security cameras were and how they operated. The images were grainy, jerky, and failed to even catch the moment the shots were fired. Only the sudden ripple in the human stream gave them the moment the Girards fell.

## Chapter Thirty-Two

### ON THE TRAIN TO PARIS

Durand worked his way through the streets, finding back streets where he could deposit the pieces of his weapons unobtrusively as he walked by a rubbish bin here and there. His movements were purposeful but unhurried. Like the woman who'd shot the Girards, he knew a running person drew too much attention. Like her, he found a public place to make his transformation back to the face he saw in his mirror on any morning he wasn't working.

In his case, he went from bareheaded to wearing a clean but worn baseball cap, and from no glasses to dark sunshades. He picked up the roomy messenger bag he'd carried to his sniper position hours before, and pulled out the laptop and flash drive. The rest went into the rubbish in the department store bathroom, while the items it had concealed were deposited into a new laptop bag he just purchased.

Dissatisfied with the new-looking bag, he scuffed it on the floor a bit, picking it up just before the door opened to admit another man. He nodded to the man, but kept his eyes averted as convention required between strangers in a public restroom.

After leaving the department store, Durand made his way via the same circuitous route to the train station, where he purchased a ticket from Zürich to Basel, some eighty-seven kilometers away.

Basel, a commercial hub whose suburbs spanned three countries, was a bustling metropolis. It was situated in the extreme northwest corner of Switzerland, but extended into both Germany and France as well, where the three countries met. It was well-known among Durand's peers as the easiest place to cross any border with little notice.

Passport control in the city was understandably lax, each country relying on the other two to do a better job.

Adding to the relaxed attitude, the Euro Citizenship passport lulled border guards into complacency. Durand's was stamped with no questions asked, and even though he didn't expect a hue and cry to have followed him, he breathed a sigh of relief once seated on the train to Paris.

But, while the guards may have been lax, the security cameras and facial recognition systems worked perfectly.

## Chapter Thirty-Three
### ONE CONCLUSION

The sensational crime in the heart of Zürich created consternation among the top brass in the police department, as well as outrage among the citizenry. How, the media trumpeted, could two people be gunned down at noon on a sunny day, with hundreds of people within arms' length, and no one see it happen? In response, dozens of police were tasked with talking to everyone they could round up who'd been there when the bodies were discovered, as well as going door to door and interviewing everyone who lived or did business in the area for several blocks around.

Though the autopsy would later reveal the shots had been fired at point-blank range with a small-caliber weapon, no stone was left unturned, and no theory left untried. An enterprising police sergeant sent his men to the upper stories of the nearby apartment buildings, looking for even more witnesses. Even so, he admitted to his men that it could have been a random act of violence. After all, plenty of that went on in the world these days.

One way or another, they had to be thorough, talking to everyone in all the multi-story buildings and searching every room with a window on the street. In due time, they discovered Shorty's body. There was no question this time as to where the shooter had been. From the trajectory of the entry wound to the hole in the back wall of the room, not to mention how it had passed through the wall into the next room and embedded itself in the wall there, it could only have come from an apartment directly across the street. The floor where Shorty was found was too high to admit of any other theory. The trajectory was almost flat, no lift to suggest it had come from below, or vice versa.

The sergeant, who'd been called to the scene as soon as Shorty's body was discovered, counted the stories of the opposite building, to the one parallel with the one in which Shorty's body still rested. He sent a patrol officer scurrying down the stairs and across to the other building, where he soon appeared in a window, waving frantically. The sergeant suspected his officer had the wrong window, but a quick radio conversation explained. The occupants of the apartment where the officer had waved out the window had told him the next apartment over was currently vacant, the owners away on holiday. The officer wanted guidance, whether to wait for a search warrant or break down the door.

A third alternative was quickly found. The concierge had a key and was glad to let the police in. While there was no evidence to be found, crime scene technicians pointed out that finding NO fingerprints was as suspicious as finding those of known criminals. They had the right apartment all right. They just had nothing to lead them to a suspect.

The next piece to fall into place was the third victim's ID. Shorty had a name at last. He was Gerard Weber, a

Swiss German. From the location and the presence of a sophisticated sniper rifle, the police deduced he'd been the one who'd shot the still unknown couple on the sidewalk below. It didn't take long for the information on their ID to leak to the media. Olivia and Jean Girard, a Canadian couple from Quebec, according to their passports. The media went wild, sensationalizing the story of a couple of tourists being assassinated in Zürich.

What didn't leak was the conundrum the police had on their hands. Preliminary examination of the bodies revealed the tiny bugs hidden in their clothing. Could that mean these weren't ordinary tourists? It seemed so. Especially when they also found the access card to a prestigious bank in the very block where the Girards were killed, along with an obscene amount of cash, and their hotel keycard.

Some of the best detectives in the city were quickly pulled together to brainstorm the meaning of all this. Clearly Herr Weber was a professional sniper. The precision of the shot that had killed him suggested another pro. Were they after each other, or both after the Girards? Were they spies? And how did two wealthy Canadians fit in? The trappings of secrecy for the banking suggested that the couple weren't just innocent bystanders, somehow taken out by accident when Herr Weber lost his life and presumably control of his weapon. No, it seemed the killings were linked, but how?

The Girard's hotel, of course, being one of the elite, valued their guests' privacy. Even if the guests happened to be dead. They flatly refused to allow entry to the suite without a warrant. Which gave Charlie a head start.

Charlie, in fact, had already heard from one of his contacts within the police that no laptop or flash drive had been found with the bodies. He wasn't surprised. From the distress his client had shown, whatever information was contained in those items was explosive. Maybe literally; he had no idea. In any case, he wouldn't have been carrying something like that around with him either. It was probably in the hotel room.

He took the time to contact his female operative and received a verbal vivisection. No, of course she hadn't had time to search the bodies. She'd murdered the couple in broad daylight, on the street, as instructed. He wasn't to call her again for at least six months — it was too dangerous, even with their top-of-the-line security. No, she absolutely would not go and search their damned hotel room. Get someone else. Charlie was a bit surprised by the salty language she employed with those answers, but not by the answers themselves. But, being a careful man, he made sure to dot all his I's before crossing the T's. He called another of his "angels" as it amused him to refer to them.

This time he chose one whose looks would stun anyone into compliance. The hotel had excellent privacy and security policies in place. Though it would be best for his operative to slip in unnoticed, that wasn't likely to happen. He gave her his instructions and went back to his worried pacing, knowing that if he failed in this mission, it meant the end of his lucrative association with the man he only knew by a code name, Spider. This man had made Charlie a wealthy man over the years, but Charlie had exotic and expensive tastes and habits. Failure was not an option.

While Charlie worried, his "angel" dressed carefully. The assignment was tricky. Get in unnoticed if she could, but if not, get in somehow. The boss had made it clear that whatever she needed to do to gain entry to that room was authorized. She wasn't unaware of the commotion in the streets of Zürich. A pair of tourists had been murdered in front of hundreds of witnesses, but no one had seen it happen. A rush assignment on the same day was probably related, so when Charlie said "whatever you have to do", he probably didn't mean murder. Too messy.

Accordingly, she dressed in a pair of black leather pants that hugged her curves and a black silk button-down blouse with the top several buttons left undone. A quick check in the mirror assured her that her best assets were on display. To be absolutely sure, she added a delicate necklace with an arrow-shaped pendant to lead the eyes where she wanted them. No straight male hotel clerk alive would be able to resist her allure. She only hoped she found a straight male on first encounter.

Upon arrival at the hotel, she took a moment to get her bearings. Few guests were in the lobby this time of day, but a lone clerk stood at the desk. The woman put her shoulders back and walked toward the desk, her high heels clicking on the floor briskly. The clerk looked up. The woman knew she had him when she saw his eyes widen along with his smile.

"Good afternoon, mademoiselle! How may I help you today?"

She summoned a smile, while keeping a distressed expression in her eyes. "Oh, you are too kind. I'm afraid I've lost my key, and my . . . husband . . . is not answering his phone. If you'd be so kind as to help me get upstairs?"

"Of course, madam. Your name?"

She cast her eyes down, and then peeked at him through fluttering lashes. "Oh, I'm afraid you've mistaken . . ."

His eyes widened again in sudden understanding. Flustered, he stammered. "Of course, I, ah . . ."

She laid her hand on his arm. "Perhaps I can do something . . . nice . . . for you. After . . ."

Breaking into a sweat, he took his card and keyed the

secure elevator for her, and as the car arrived, whispered urgently, "I am off duty at five."

As the doors closed, she winked at him. "That should give me time."

On her way to the floor and room number she'd been given, she laughed silently. That poor clerk would be waiting long after five for his turn with her.

Once she reached the room, she ransacked it without finding a laptop or flash drive. She used her cell phone to inform Charlie, and then slipped down the stairs to wait for an opportunity to leave the hotel without encountering the amorous clerk again.

Charlie's heart gave a lurch when he received the report that the missing laptop and flash drive weren't to be found in the hotel room. His last hope, that they would be in the hotel safe, was dashed by his informant within the police department. The warrant had arrived in due course, and it included the fact that the Girards had left nothing in the safe. They didn't find anything of interest, either. His informant asked what Charlie was looking for. In a huff, Charlie disconnected the call. It was none of the man's business.

All the pacing he'd done, his mind churning with alternatives should the missing items not be found, had led him to one conclusion. No matter how unpleasant it would be to inform Nabati he'd failed, it would be even more so if he tried to lie and was discovered. Reluctantly, as if he was moving through a vat of molasses, he picked up his phone.

## Chapter Thirty-Four

### HE DIDN'T ANSWER CHARLIE

When Nabati's assistant had informed him of the cause for the commotion downstairs, and he'd received Charlie's notification that it was indeed the Girards who'd been killed, he breathed a sigh of relief. He wouldn't have to report failure to his mother, a truly frightening prospect.

The relief was short-lived. As soon as he learned Charlie's assassin was also dead, he knew he had a problem. Somehow, someone else knew of the contract on the Girards, and that meant the entire mission was compromised. Who could it be?

He briefly considered it was Saudi secret police, who also wanted Algosaibi's children dead. But several considerations made that idea unlikely. First, they would have wanted a public beheading, and the Girards would have been detained and deported. But then why would the Saudis have killed his man? Besides, if they'd known who the Girards were, they never would have gotten out of Rome, where extracting them would have been easier than in Zürich.

No, it was Charlie's operation that had been compromised, and not by the Saudis. Only two possibilities remained. Either Charlie had double-crossed him himself, or his first operative, the observer in Rome, had double-crossed Charlie. Either way, Charlie had made a royal mess of the assignment, the biggest mistake of his life.

Now Charlie was messaging again with more bad news. The laptop and flash drive were missing. Nabati was too angry to respond, and his silence gave Charlie all the answer he needed.

Charlie's worst scenario had come true. There was no way to save the business relationship, and only one way he could think of to save his life, and that was to find the missing items before someone else did. Even that might not prevent his death. He had reason to suspect that Spider's resources were apparently infinite, and he had no illusions that he was the only "project manager" Spider knew and used.

The alternative was to run and hide as some of his contractors would do — as he suspected Durand had done, for he was convinced Durand had somehow betrayed him. For a certainty, Durand was the most likely suspect in Weber's murder. And the most likely person to have possession of the cursed laptop and flash drive that would be the death of him. Charlie grinned ferally. They'd most certainly be the death of Durand, if Charlie had anything to say about it.

For his part, Nabati had given up on keeping the mess a secret from his mother. The news media would do his job for him if he didn't contact her immediately. May have already done so, in fact. If he waited, he might very well find himself on the business end of an assassin's weapon. He was under no illusions that motherly love would prevent her from doing what she felt she had to do to protect the Council and the ancient family.

"*Maman,*" he began. "I have bad news, and I'm afraid the Council must convene for a crisis meeting."

"I'm aware," she answered, frost riming her words as surely as if she'd spoken them from the North Pole. "Give me the details and your best assessment of what we can do now."

Nabati knew her calm words belied a cold rage that made him glad they were hundreds of kilometers apart. A crisis meeting of the Council was no small matter. They didn't have to do it often, since their reach and resources meant their affairs usually went exactly as they'd planned. They didn't like screw-ups, and this was a big one. Gigantic. Earth-shattering. As long as the information on the laptop and flash drive was in someone else's hands, it risked exposure of their ancient secret, and that could not be allowed to happen.

Indeed, Mathieu Nabati, his mother, and the rest of the Council only speculated what was on the electronics. They had to assume Algosaibi anticipated what would happen if his plot was uncovered, and to protect his children, he had informed them of the secrets, either to provide them with a bargaining chip to negotiate their safety with the Council, or out of spite because the Council wouldn't support him in his quest to overthrow and destroy the Saudi royal family. Indirectly, they were the cause of his downfall because of that lack of support. And in the past year or more, he had constantly been in conflict with the Council, refusing to bow to their instructions to abandon his political agenda.

Whatever Algosaibi's motivation, the recording of the conversation between the Algosaibi siblings, which Charlie's contractor made in Rome, left very little doubt Xavier Algosaibi recorded it all for his children's knowledge.

As Nabati laid out the analysis for his mother, who agreed wholeheartedly that they were facing the biggest crisis since the year 106 AD, he received a text message from Charlie.

> KNOW I SCREWED UP. GIVE ME A CHANCE TO FIX IT. I'LL CLEAN UP MESS; I'LL PAY.

Nabati read the message to his mother, with his editorial comment. "He'll pay all right."

He didn't answer Charlie.

---

Elsewhere in the city, a medical examiner unzipped the body bag containing Olivia Girard's remains. The naked corpse lay face-down on the autopsy table, an anxious police detective hovering nearby to get any details that would help him explain the strangeness of this case.

"Well, you are wrong about a shooter at a distance," was the first thing the ME said to him. "This woman was shot at close range, probably with a small-caliber weapon.

"See here, the gunpowder residue?

"And what is this?"

The doctor's career was brought to an abrupt halt as he reached to pry out the foreign object embedded but partially exposed in the wound. The object destroyed the evidence that would have been critical to understanding how the woman was killed, as well as taking the doctor's fingers on his right hand. Blood spattered against the horrified officer's face as he staggered back from the small, but destructive, explosion. How had that device not been triggered by the bullet that passed by it within millimeters? It would be one of the questions the replacement ME would be hard-pressed to answer. The next pathologist would have to take much more care when examining the male.

In the aftermath, the members of the investigative task force were even more confounded by the latest development. Who the hell were these people? And what the hell was happening in their city?

## Chapter Thirty-Five

### THE LIBRARY OF THE GIANTS

Carter helped Ahote squeeze the last of the luggage into the hold before taking the pilot's seat and waving goodbye to his friend. He turned to scan the faces of his passengers, Mackenzie and their children, and said, "Ready to go see Grandma and Grandpa?" Receiving a big smile and an enthusiastic nod from Liam, he took it as agreement from baby Beth as well, and started taxiing.

"It will be good to see Mom and Dad," Mackenzie remarked, once they were safely in the air. Even though Carter was an expert pilot and flying his plane back and forth from Freydís was no more stressful than driving a car to him, she never wanted to distract him during take-off or landing. Especially not with such precious cargo on board.

"I'm looking forward to it myself. And we'll be busy getting the software developed long enough for you to have a good visit with them. It's high time they had a chance to bond with Beth, too."

"I love you, Carter Devereux," Mackenzie said impulsively.

"Why, just because I happen to like my outlaws?" He grinned and winked at her, eliciting a small smack against his shoulder.

"You goof," she answered.

---

A few days later, having left Mackenzie and the children with his "outlaws", Carter met with Jim Rhodes, Rick Winslow — the computer whiz — and his colleague Samantha, as well as Irene O'Connell, Deputy Director of A-Echelon. Liu had arrived the day before, she was looking forward to the translation software development as much as Carter was.

Irene had arranged the use of three of DARPA's electron microscopes for the initial task, which was to scan all the plates in their possession, some ten thousand of them. The task, which would have been monumental otherwise, was accomplished in only fifty hours. Experts Irene had also borrowed from DARPA were feeding two hundred sheets per hour through the microscopes with no loss of fidelity in the data. After watching for a few minutes, Carter declared he was dizzy from the speed, and although Liu agreed, she said it was like watching grass grow when they could be much more productive elsewhere.

They left Irene to supervise the scanning, while Carter, Liu, Rick, and Samantha worked together to design and load a database of all known Semitic languages. Then Carter stood back and watched in awe as Rick's and Samantha's fingers started whizzing over the keyboards as they began to code algorithms for the software using a combination of machine translation and computer-assisted translation to get as close to an idiomatic translation of the language on the plates as they thought possible.

Before beginning, Rick had given Carter a thumbnail sketch as to why they were using this approach, as well as a brief description of MT, as he referred to the machine translation, and CAT, or computer-aided translation. Carter, to some extent, but especially Liu would be an integral part of the latter.

Carter was quick to get the idea. The machine translation algorithms would substitute modern English for the proto-Semitic words on a literal basis and then process the result with CAT in an iterative feedback loop until the MT began to learn entire phrases or idiomatic use of words as well as anomalies for which translations were impossible at first.

Gradually, as the AI (artificial intelligence) algorithms coded into the software became more "trained", the MT part of the multi-part program would be able to effectively take over the bulk of the translation, freeing Carter and Liu to analyze rather than simply translate Giantese (as the research group was calling the language on the sheets).

"In other words," Carter summarized his understanding of what Samantha had just explained, "as the program becomes more proficient at Giantese, the more automated the translation process?"

Samantha nodded. "Yes, we are using the latest and most sophisticated translation technology, able to use the comprehensive dictionaries of the database and the linguistic rules of the giants to completely automate the rest of the task."

"Wow, that sounds like a *gigantic task*," Carter quipped.

Rick smiled. "But you must keep in mind, all of this is going to rely on your ability to break down complex sentence structures, identify parts of speech, and even resolve ambiguities in the direct translation so that Samantha and I can code the rules of the language into the program. That will complete the development of the software. We'll know we're doing it right when the machine starts to spit out intelligible content without the need for a human translator.

"Even so, it will never reach the level of accuracy of human translation. It is only ever going to be a gisting version, meaning it searches for the main idea or most important point in the text. It will simply be a thousand times faster than human translation for finding the specifics you're looking for. Once it has found them, for the real detail and subtle, deeper meaning, you'll still have to do a final translation yourselves. Give it the human touch, so to speak."

"A thousand times faster is what we're looking for," Carter answered. "The reason is classified, but we are in a big damned hurry to have this thing translated. On a human level, it would take years. We don't have years."

Rick suppressed his curiosity. As an employee of the CIA, he knew the rules of the "need to know" game. He and Samantha didn't need to know what Carter and the others were looking for, and he knew he wouldn't get a straight answer if he asked. The answer would probably be something along the lines of "if I told you, I'd have to kill you." He laughed nervously.

Carter and Liu settled in for hours of work, the two of them barely able to keep up with the original, word-to-word translation. At first, it was arduous work, and the text made little or no sense. But gradually, as they found matches and fed the information back into the program and the algorithms processed it, they began to see patterns emerge that corresponded to the ancient Semitic languages they'd fed into the databases.

With those patterns, Rick and Samantha could develop more rules, that turned out grammatically functional sentences. As they filled in the blanks with more and more sensible information, Carter and Liu began to see more accurate translations, enough to enable them to start putting two and two together.

A few days into the process, the new software had picked up speed. Liu gave a shout. The translation of the plate she was examining appeared to be an index. With all effort brought to bear on translating the next few sheets, they discovered that the plates were uniquely numbered. With that discovery, they could map the sheets to the index and locate those most likely to contain the information they specifically sought — nuclear weapons and respirocytes.

Naturally, those weren't the words the ancients used, and considerable time was put to the task of brainstorming words or phrases that might have corresponded to them. The library, vast as it was, remained a black hole as it pertained to the topics of interest. They soon realized that it was going to take a massive amount of computing power and time. In other words, they needed access to the super-computers that were used within the no-name agencies.

James had an idea.

"Mr. President, you and Bill might want to see what we're doing over here," he said as soon as he'd worked his way through the red tape involved in calling the President directly.

"By Bill, I assume you mean the Director?" the President responded. "I know a few bills."

"Yes, Sir. William Griffin, Director of the CIA." James kept a lid on his amusement. He knew, and he knew the

President knew he knew, that the President knew exactly who he was talking about. The man did like his little jokes.

"I'll see what I can do," the President said with a wry twist. James could just imagine him poking his tongue against his cheek to keep from laughing at his own humor.

James was more than a little surprised when, an hour later, the President, with Bill Griffin in tow, arrived to inspect the progress of the top-secret project. James suppressed a little smile when the thought crossed his mind, *James Rhodes can summon the President of the United States to a meeting in one hour.*

What their visitors found, only days after the beginning of the translation effort, made their eyes pop out. The President was particularly interested in how they'd even begun to understand the language, preserved as it was in ideogram form, like Chinese, he thought.

"More like ancient Arabic," Carter corrected him. "Here, let me explain. Written language, to the best of our knowledge so far, consists of only a few types of writing systems, and those can be expressed in a table. The first thing to look at is the form of the written word, or typology. Archaeologists have agreed on what to call these systems. The next thing to know, which we can discover by statistical analysis, is how many characters exist in the written document we're studying. That will tell us whether the characters are an alphabet, a syllabary, or a logography."

Seeing the President's puzzled expression, Carter explained further. "An alphabet, such as we use, is a way of building the pronunciation of words in written form. Your brain translates the characters into sounds, which we recognize as words. You'd know what a remarkable feat that is if you had reached adulthood without learning to read.

"A syllabary on the other hand, is a larger set of characters that each stand for entire syllables. Putting the syllables together serves the same purpose as the root words of our language."

"You mean like Latin and Greek," the President observed.

"Yes, along with Anglo-Saxon. Take any word that ends in -ology. That means the study of whatever the first syllable is. Theology, therefore, is the study of God or religion. Theos — Greek for God, plus -ology, the study of."

"Gotcha," replied the President.

"In that case, you can probably work out for yourself the meaning of logography."

"Word-writing or word-picture," the President guessed.

"Precisely. An image, or a stylized image, that carries the meaning of an entire word, which are then combined to form ideas."

"And you used this knowledge to design this clever software," the President concluded, his head shaking in astonishment.

"Yes and no. We used it to begin to understand the structure of the language. We also used our prior knowledge of ancient Semitic languages to guess that this was related to them, based on where we found the plates as much as anything else. And of course, without the coding geniuses, Rick and Samantha, we wouldn't be this far along. The computer is now doing most of the work. Unfortunately, there's such a huge amount of work to do the computers we have are not fast enough. We haven't found what we're looking for yet."

"Congress is going to turn me on a spit for this," answered the President, who immediately knew why he was invited to the meeting "but on my authority, you may commandeer as much computing power as you need. I assume Bill is here because he can tell you where to find it."

Carter turned to Griffin. "The thing is, there could be any number of topics here that represent danger to our national security, not to mention world peace. I've said it before. The giants were much more advanced in certain aspects of technology than we are today, that much we know. However, thus far, we have only discovered their competency with electricity and electromagnetism, and we have no clue how they did it. The question is, what else did they know that we haven't uncovered yet? What we don't know is what's dangerous."

Griffin pretended to make a sour face, but he was as impressed with the project as the President was, and even more eager, if that were possible, to get his hands on the information in question. The possibility of ancient nukes lying around to be found by terrorists had been giving him ulcers ever since he'd heard about it. The prospect that there could be something even more dangerous was about to make him throw up.

"I'll find you your computing power," he said. "Let me know how much and if you need more after we set you up. Cost is no object. I'll let the President handle the fallout." He flexed his jaw to relieve the pressure he'd put on it from clenching his teeth.

The President, wincing at the double-entendre, had the last word. "Gee, Bill, thanks for that. I always could trust you to pass the ball at just the right moment."

## Chapter Thirty-Six
### ACCEPTED

Mathieu Nabati didn't waste much time in anguish over losing a valuable asset. Charlie had bungled the most important assignment Nabati had ever given him. Furthermore, he had to be speculating there was a valid reason why Nabati was so upset about it. It was only a matter of time before he learned more and decided to turn the tables. Charlie had become a liability as quickly as a cat twists in midair — but he couldn't be allowed to land on his feet. He had to die, and so did his subcontractor.

Six hours after his text to Nabati, Charlie was on his way from his base in Lyon to Paris, where he expected to confront and kill Durand, when he met his end in a spectacular head-on collision with a petrol tanker. The resulting explosion and fire reduced Charlie, his car, and most importantly, his special cell phone with its evidence of texts to Nabati's number, to a small pile of ash.

Miraculously, the tanker driver had bailed out of the cab at the last moment, but he had no explanation for being on the wrong side of the road. He was arrested for vehicular manslaughter, losing control of his vehicle, reckless driving, and — unfairly — drunk driving. But to the annoyance of the local police, word came down from above to release him, and he promptly disappeared.

In Zürich, Nabati received a report from his new contractor that the Charlie part of the mess had been taken care of. He thanked the man and promised more work when the occasion arose.

However, the biggest part of the mess was still at large, and Nabati was the most qualified to track down the messmaker. It was a little-known secret from the world at large that, although the Swiss banking industry was the most secure in Europe, perhaps the world, the bankers readily exchanged information amongst themselves. At least, those who were under the control, however disguised, of the Council of the Covenant of Nabatea. And that was virtually all of them.

Through his contacts, Nabati discovered everything he needed to know about the owner of the accounts to which he'd transferred the Girards' $17 million. Within twenty minutes, Nabati had a name, passport number, address, and even photos taken by concealed security cameras two years previously when the account owner had opened it. No doubt, thousands of account owners would have been disturbed to know these records existed, but the banks all followed the practice to protect themselves. Durand would have reason to be more than disturbed within a matter of hours.

The account particulars led Nabati, through yet another of his assets, to Durand's special forces record. The DRM, *Direction du Renseignement Militaire* (Directorate of Military Intelligence) supplied a current address when pressure from the government official responsible for their budget applied pressure to do so. Not only an address, but also every detail about his military history, girlfriend, friends, family — everything, in other words, from his weight and height to the brand of toothpaste he used.

Armed with the information and photos from the DRM, Nabati got in touch with Swiss border control and within a few minutes learned that Durand had crossed the border into France from the Swiss side a few hours before, at Basel. He was able to confirm visually when the images from the security cameras at the border post were emailed to him. Unfortunately, Durand had an almost eight-hour head start. But he had to be found at all costs.

Nabati had a contact he and the Council used only when in the direst of circumstances. The cost to use the services of the Sweeper, as he was known, was enough to give even the Council pause. Therefore, and also because the Sweeper took only rare assignments to avoid catching the eye of international security agencies, it had been several years since the Nabati's last had contact with him. As soon as he had all the information he could readily gather, Nabati used his secure, quantum encrypted PDA to reach out.

The Sweeper replied promptly in response to the code word indicating this was a highly sensitive assignment, and one that had to be completed at all cost, preferably yesterday. He sent back a one-word answer:

ACCEPTED.

Nabati relaxed some. There was still reason to believe the Council's very existence was in danger of being revealed, but if anyone could contain the bombshell, the Sweeper was the man to do it.

## Chapter Thirty-Seven

### A STRANGE BEDFELLOW

Durand was making his way to his apartment in Paris when the news broke of an international incident. As he already knew, but the Swiss police were just now discovering, the victims in Zürich were traveling with fake passports and IDs.

He had little doubt that the Saudi secret service was behind the murders, but he was surprised that they'd worked through Charlie to hire the assassin he shot. The Swiss police seemed convinced the Saudis were directly responsible. It was the official version of events, and the one the media was reporting. Only Durand knew he was involved at all, except for Charlie, but Charlie had no reason to suspect him. Or so he thought.

With everyone blaming the Saudis, it meant he was home free, the mystery solved and no one the wiser regarding his involvement. It only remained for him to disappear with his money, and at his leisure find out everything that was on the laptop and the flash drive to perhaps help him make some more.

Nabati, of course, knew better. His mother had orchestrated the whole diversion in the media, hoping to stop speculation, and it had. He himself had sent the anonymous tip to the police that the victims were not who they appeared to be. That tip, plus a little bug in the ear of a police contact, sent the authorities tracing the Girards' movements and surprisingly quickly turned up the information they were now reporting.

But of course, it didn't solve the Council's core problem, which was that the laptop and flash drive almost certainly contained information to expose them. Everyone who'd had those items in their hands must be killed. Only that would assure their safety.

Durand was in good spirits, whistling as he skipped up the steps to his apartment. He'd composed a speech to his girlfriend — an "I need a break" speech designed to get her out of the way while he disappeared. He was rehearsing it in his head when he opened the door and walked into a trap.

A man he'd never seen before was waiting for him inside. "I'll take that laptop. And the flash drive."

Durand hadn't made it this far in life by being indecisive. He clutched the laptop bag to his chest, prepared to fight his way out of the situation or flee, whichever seemed more likely to succeed. A bitter thought passed through his brain in a flash. If only he hadn't had to dump his handgun to cross the border.

The man opened his jacket to display a knife that, to Durand's eyes, appeared to be the size of a short sword, but didn't draw it from its scabbard. Durand's next move was too quick. He intended to retreat, but he didn't get the chance. As he whirled to go back the way he came, the man jumped to the open door and kicked it shut to cut off his escape. While the man was distracted, Durand raced toward the back of the apartment, where he could access the fire escape and maybe outrun his assailant. His plan was cut short by the sight of his girlfriend, lying in a pool of blood in the kitchen, dead.

Before he could process the image, his assailant was on his back, an arm snaking around his throat to get him in a choke-hold. With the adrenaline coursing through his veins, Durand fought like a wild animal, twisting violently out of the choke-hold and punched his assailant in the kidney with a massive blow. The man went down.

Durand ran into his bedroom, where he kept a pistol in his nightstand drawer, loaded and ready. He'd barely managed to snag it when the man was again at his back. Durand turned, shoved the gun into the man's chest and pulled the trigger. The muffled shot left a very small hole in the man's chest and heart and a large exit wound on his back.

Durand sat heavily on the bed, his heart beating wildly. *Who the hell is this? Who had I pissed off? Is it really the Saudi secret police this time? Or is this Charlie? Whoever it is must have a serious interest in the laptop and flash drive. What's on those things that is so important?*

He pulled himself together. With his girlfriend dead, there was no need for a break-up conversation and no ties to anyone in Paris now, and though the gunshot had been as quiet as a small-caliber weapon could be, he knew there was a good chance that someone, including the police, would show up at his door shortly. He had few possessions that meant anything to him, and virtually unlimited funds to replace his basic needs. Gathering what small items he needed to keep with him, he walked calmly out the door of his apartment and out of his life as a killer for hire.

Durand needed someplace quiet to study the contents of that laptop and flash drive, the sooner the better. He found it in a fleabag hotel well off the main tourist areas on the outskirts of Paris. Paying in cash for two nights in advance, he holed up and read everything. Even with what he had overheard before, he could not be prepared for what he was reading now that he had full access to all the information. Did that really say the organization Algosaibi belonged to was formed nearly two millennia ago? And that the history predating it was . . . mindboggling, to say the least.

But the real dynamite or more likely, kryptonite, was the information about the Council of the Covenant of Nabatea. Reading that sent waves of cold shivers down his spine. How could he possibly hide from this powerful organization? He had no doubt, it was they who'd sent the man to kill him in his apartment. The information on the laptop and flash drive was what they wanted and as they had so clearly demonstrated, they would kill to get it. Even for a man with no loyalties to any political party and no interest in world events except when they provided work for him, it was a terrifying prospect. To be on the termination list of an organization with worldwide influence, their hands in every government and police force, and truly unlimited funds, was much more than he could handle.

The irony, of course, was that he had no real interest in any of the information. He was interested in money and a life of luxury and peace. He would be more than happy to just hand it over to them and walk away. Maybe he could pack these hot bombshells and mail it to or have it couriered to Mathieu Nabati. But he had a gut wrenching feeling it was not going to appease them — he knew too much. Attempting to use this information for blackmail against the

Council to guarantee his own safety would be the same as committing suicide. He could just leave the laptop and flash drive here in this squalid hotel and disappear . . . and that was what he was going to do until it dawned on him that his $17 million was now in the same bank accounts where he kept all his other savings, banks that these Nabateans probably either owned or controlled.

*Dammit what an idiot I've been.*

Despair sank in. *I'd be lucky to get away with my life.*

Run and hide.

He changed his appearance to fit one of his many fake profiles, destroyed his mobile phone, packed his backpack, including the cursed laptop and flash drive and left Paris, hitchhiking his way to Eastern Europe, avoiding all forms of public transport, public places, cities, and security cameras. In some of the Eastern European countries he would be able to live in remote areas, off the grid.

Weeks of wandering around aimlessly, feeling and looking like a hobo, worrying, and contemplating his future, finally produced another idea. With the information in his possession, he could buy his life — maybe. It was a long shot. But it was worth a try — trade the information for protection — and perhaps money. Not to the Council of the Covenant of Nabatea but to the only organization he thought powerful enough to protect him from them. The CIA. It was going to be a strange bedfellow.

His time with the French Foreign Legion's, special forces had been relatively short, but filled with survival training and covert operations that gave him the skills that served to keep him alive now.

During his time as a *Legionnaire*, he'd done a life-saving favor for a CIA operative, Scott Brown, on a mission to Mali, formerly the French Sudan. Brown had been in a pickle. In fact, he'd been captured by Tuareg rebels, and if it hadn't been for Durand and his men, Brown would have lost his life then. But Durand's team had managed to set him free. He owed Durand his life, and now it was time to call in the favor.

## Chapter Thirty-Eight

THE OFFER

Durand had withdrawn thirty thousand in cash of the money he got for the Rome job when he received his payment. He had about twenty-five thousand left. It was no trouble at all to travel to Canada under one of the many pre-arranged false passports and legends he had. To be sure, he took all of them and hid them in a false bottom of his valise, covered with other papers to throw off the x-ray examination of his bag. To his relief, he went through both airport security and Canadian customs with no problem.

Once in Canada, he secured a hotel room with an in-room safe, locked the laptop, flash drive, his extra passports, and half the cash into it, and prepared for a trip across the border to the US and down the coast to Washington, D.C. It wasn't easy to reconnect with Scott Brown. The man had been promoted and brought in from the field, and it took several hours to track him down amid the security paranoia in the US capitol. However, in the late afternoon, his burner cellphone rang.

"Hello, old friend. I hear you need to talk to me."

It had been years since Durand had heard the voice, but he was reasonably sure it was Scott. Nevertheless, he took the precaution of making the man prove he was who he said, running him through several tests of information designed to trip up anyone who wasn't Scott Brown. Brown patiently answered all the questions until Durand had satisfied himself he was talking to the genuine Scott Brown. With anyone else, he might have become impatient, but he had a good idea that Durand must have something of value to convey to him, or else he wouldn't be in this part of the world, taking such precautions.

At last, Durand was prepared to give Brown the gist of what he had, hinting that he knew of a worldwide conspiracy that was heading for world financial domination, at the very least. When he mentioned Algosaibi, he heard Scott's breathing change. He'd hit a hot button! Durand knew to press his advantage, and soon he had Scott convinced there was something to his story.

That was a bite, and from a very large fish. Now he had to set the hook.

"I have a laptop and a flash drive outlining the entire organization, giving their history, secret places, leadership, and everything you would need to bring these people down. But I won't turn it over without a written guarantee of my safety, immunity from prosecution, and commitment to be placed in your witness protection program. That will need to be signed by your President himself."

Scott's tone betrayed his irritation. "You know very well I can't commit the President to anything until he sees the evidence. You've tied my hands."

"I'm sorry, my friend, but I've screwed the pooch, as you Yanks so colorfully say. I *must* have these assurances before I give up the only protection I have. You have two days to text me at this number." Durand gave the number of a new burner phone he'd purchased that day at an appallingly crass store with the oddest customers he'd ever seen. When had it become *de riguer* to shop in one's nightclothes?

After hanging up, he slipped into the restroom of the coffee shop where he'd held his conversation and changed his clothes, dumping the used cell phone in the wastebasket along with the distinctly European clothing. When he exited, he could have been any tourist from a Western state, and he carried only the cell phone on which Scott would hopefully text him with the answer. He turned in his rental car at Reagan National Airport with a ruinous one-way drop-off charge and walked to a bus stop, took the first bus that came along, and changed busses several times before hailing a taxi to take him to Dulles International, where he went through the process of renting a car again, this time under a different name, and then drove to Philadelphia to await Scott's text.

Scott, in the meantime, persuaded his boss to pass the request up the line. He arranged for a meeting between Scott and the Director. Bill Griffin knew of Scott, as he knew of every one of his top agents. Nevertheless, he had Scott's personnel file open on his desk when the man was ushered into his presence on an urgent mission with vital information.

"Do you trust this man?" Griffin asked when he'd listened without comment to the evidence Scott had.

"I do, sir. He saved my life in Mali, and he has no reason to gaslight me. He has gotten himself into trouble, I think he's telling the truth, and I think it scares him to death. I think we should take the risk and get hold of this laptop and flash drive he has."

"What do you make of this claim about giants and

ancient humans and this ancient super powerful, secret organization?" Griffin asked. "Is the guy nuts?"

"I can't say, sir. The man saved my life, I trust him. I know he believes what he's telling me is true. Whether it's indeed true, I can't say. But if it is, we have a big damn problem on our hands. Bigger than any Middle Eastern terrorist group, I'd say. If what he says is true, these people have us by the short and curlies, even if half of what he says is true."

At the mention of giants and ancients, Director Griffin couldn't help but wonder if this would somehow be connected to Carter Devereux's work. If he hadn't heard this type of talk and saw some of the evidence produced by Devereux before, he would probably have been inclined to blow this whole thing off as a lunatic's rants. However, what tipped the scales were the mention of Xavier Algosaibi's name.

"Well, I tend to agree with you. We can't take the chance of dismissing it without examining the evidence. However, before I involve the President, let's see what we can do to verify his claims," said Bill, dismissing Scott with a warm handshake. "Glad you brought it to my attention."

Bill's next urgent call was to A-Echelon headquarters. "James, we need Carter in the Oval Office ASAP. How soon can you get him there?"

James took the question in stride. He was getting used to being summoned to the Oval Office at the drop of a hat lately. Carter maybe less so, but he'd get used to it. "How soon do you want him?"

"Day before yesterday," Bill answered. The grim tone in his friend's voice told James there was no time to waste.

## Chapter Thirty-Nine

### WHERE DID YOU GET THIS INFORMATION?

While Durand was scrambling for his life and Scott was persuading Bill Griffin that a conspiracy of worldwide proportions had been afoot for two millennia, Carter and Liu were by turns elated and in the depths of frustration.

The software was performing brilliantly, and they'd found the index, but so far, no reference to the subjects they most wanted to know about. In fact, what they found was mostly history.

The race that had created the record named themselves the Zuzim or Zamzummim, and they had, according to their history, moved from somewhere else to the vicinity of the City of Lights site in Egypt some sixty-five thousand years ago. After living there for about fifteen thousand years, the Zuzim found it necessary to move away but the reason for moving away was not given in those parts of the narrative.

The records revealed that this hadn't been the only city where a substantial population of Zuzim had resided. It mentioned others, including a main location, but Carter's team couldn't make out where it was based on the names, which of course didn't correspond to modern names or those on any ancient maps. The time lapse had simply been too great, and somehow the giants had become extinct except for rare instances when, as Carter suspected, genetic traces showed up as gigantism in modern humans.

There was some evidence that the Zuzim giants were related to other ethnic groups or races of giants that lived in other parts of the world, and that those races had been in existence for some incredible two-hundred-thousand years, at the time the record was made. Even Carter, who had long suspected ancient civilizations rivaling our own admitted that was mind-blowing. The day they discovered that passage, he poured Liu and himself a bracing shot of Irish whiskey. Liu, of course, choked on it, prompting Carter to say he'd drink a shot on her behalf, if for no other reason than to calm his racing mind.

The record continued to reveal historical secrets, such as the fact they were using quantum technology to power the lights in the city. Carter was proud of deciphering that bit of information, even though he'd had to call on one or two DARPA scientists to test the ideas out. They, of course, were anxious to know more, but unfortunately the technological details were not available anywhere in the record.

The same was true of the record of wars they'd fought, using flying machines that were apparently looking very similar to the "flying saucers" of conspiracy theory. Carter's mind went racing with the speculation that perhaps some of those had been found and reactivated by persons with malevolent motives. Yet, the references to something that could only be hydrogen fusion and others venturing into quantum physics were maddeningly vague.

Liu found a section of genealogical records of the

inhabitants and worked out that the lifespans of these giants were longer than even that of Methuselah, the 969-year-old man of Biblical fame. About fifteen hundred years as near as she could make out. By then, they had uncovered so much amazing information it barely fazed her. A 1,500-year-old giant? An entire race of them? Hell, several races of them? Why not?

Liu's uncharacteristic, "Nothing turns me on a like a 1,500-year-old giant," provided a welcome humorous interlude to the serious atmosphere in the room.

It was Carter who finally found the reference to what he believed were nuclear weapons, and the appearance of the first modern humans — people whose size was more in line with those of modern humans. They wanted to destroy the giants. Initially, Carter found himself strangely torn as to whose side he was on.

The answer to what happened to the advanced civilizations, or at least the human side of the equation, was in the historical record. The giants were peace-loving, but the smaller races had developed nuclear weapons, or something like them, and the giants were forced to take preventative action. They used technology that nullified the nuclear reaction, in a way Carter couldn't understand even after he'd translated the literal words. Back to DARPA, and with their blessing, to certain colleagues in the University physics department he went, only to become thoroughly confused by their speculations about the concept of zero-point energy and other quantum physics concepts.

Within the limited circle of physics professors to whom he put the questions, some were alarmed.

"Where did you get this information?" a former mentor asked bluntly.

"I'm sorry, but that's classified," was his unsatisfactory

answer. He repeated that phrase too often for their comfort. In doing so, he was almost lynched by his former colleagues, who insisted on knowing where he'd gotten the translated texts he'd shown them.

"If I told you, I'd have to kill you," he told them, as seriously as he could manage, before beating a hasty retreat.

Back in the confines of his translation cave, as Carter called it, he learned finally that the giants had conquered the aggressors, taken away their technology, and banished them into the jungles of Africa and other remote regions.

However, Carter and Liu agreed, after exhaustive searches of anything in the index about scientific details, that the technological information simply wasn't there. The giants had apparently deliberately not left it behind. When they left the City of Lights, the Zuzim effectively disappeared into the mists of pre-history.

It was at this point, a low one for the research team, that Carter received James's urgent message to come to the White House immediately.

## Chapter Forty

### THE CONSPIRATORS

Carter arrived, breathless and bothered, in the Oval Office, where the President, Bill Griffin, James Rhodes, and Irene O'Connor waited for him.

"Apologies, Mr. President. I got here as quickly as I could."

"I'm sure you did, Carter. And thank you for interrupting your research to meet with us," the President answered. "But you look like you could use a glass of water before you begin. Help yourself." He indicated a carafe of ice water on a side table, which Carter took grateful advantage of.

While Carter was pouring the water, Bill started. "We have an unaffiliated operative who has what he describes as explosive intelligence about a group of conspirators we've never heard of. We need to determine within the next twenty-four hours whether his claims are credible. That's what you're here for."

Carter turned a puzzled face toward Bill. "I don't

understand. I don't know anything about conspiracies, except those involving ancient history" —he paused and broke into a smile— "and of course those of some of my archaeology colleagues. What help can I be?"

"That's just it, Carter. Our informant claims this group has been in existence since 106 AD. Under the radar all that time, and now they appear to be poised to take over world financial markets, energy, and pharmaceuticals, to name only a few. And we don't know a damn thing about them. We need to get up to speed right away. We figured you were the best candidate to inform us."

Carter gaped at Bill, his mind stuck on "106 AD." The date sounded vaguely familiar. He couldn't place it immediately, but then remembered. "That year, 106 AD, was the year when the Nabateans surrendered their empire to the Romans without so much as 'firing one shot.'" Carter grinned. "Is that what you are talking about?"

The four people in the room were gawping as they exchanged looks. The expressions on their faces clearly saying *now how the hell did he know or remember that?*

Bill got over the surprise, cleared his throat, and said, "Yes, that seems to be the conspirators we're concerned about. These days they call themselves the Council of the Covenant of Nabatea. We'd like you to tell us what you know about the history of the Nabateans."

Carter began slowly, his mind racing to understand the link between the conspiracy group and the ancient tribe he was about to explain. "The Nabateans? Well, no one knows much about them. They left no written record that we know of. Oddly enough, what I do know is that they ceded their empire to Rome and were absorbed into the Roman culture. But I can summarize what else we archaeologists believe we know about them, if you'll give me a moment to collect my thoughts."

"Take your time," urged the President, still spellbound by Carter's eidetic memory. "The clearer you can make it to us, the more likely we can understand how this remained a secret so long and what the risks are now."

Carter slowly nodded and wondered what the President meant with the words "*a secret so long and what the risks are now.*" He took a few moments to think, took a sip of water, and started.

"They were nomadic traders. You might call them arbitrage dealers now. They purchased goods from one place and sold them for a profit at another, but they never established diplomatic ties to the great historical empires. Instead, they lived on the fringes, kind of like ancient Gypsies. How much detail do you want?"

"Everything you can tell us," Bill interjected. "We don't know what will be relevant and what won't, so give us the full rundown."

"Okay, you asked for it." Carter took a deep breath and started. "We think the word Nabatea is related to the name Nebajoth. The book of Genesis relates somewhere around chapter 25, if my memory serves me correctly, though I can't recall the exact verses, how Esau was looking for a wife that would please his father, Isaac. He went to his half-uncle, Ishmael, the son of Abraham's slave woman, Hagar, and took Ishmael's daughter, Mahalath, as his wife. Mahalath was Nebajoth's sister. We believe that the Nabateans were an Aramaic tribe descended from this Nebajoth."

Carter looked around and wondered about the reason for the glazed looks on the faces of his audience. "Look, no one knows the whole story. But references to Nabateans pop up in the historical records from time to time, without reference to any one place we can pin them down to. There are some references to rebellions being fought by some tribes with Assyria, and they are named as a tribe that fled into the Arabian Desert and could not be conquered. Some fifty years later, they are seen supporting one of the sons of the king of Assyria in a conflict with his brother. Again, they were pushed back, but apparently not conquered.

"However, over time, the Nabateans built an imposing civilization based on commerce and constructed their first capital at the city known to us as Petra. You have all seen that Indiana Jones movie, 'The Last Crusade'?"

His audience nodded.

"Well, that temple you saw in the last scenes of the movie was shot on location at Petra. It's located in the sandstone mountains of southern Jordan. The Nabateans also built other cities in what we today call Jordan, some in the Negev and some in Northern Saudi Arabia."

Irene smiled upon noticing the looks of astonishment on the faces of the President and Bill Griffin while Carter rambled off the facts from memory as if he was reading from a book. She had seen this mindboggling performance on quite a few occasions, and it never ceased to amaze her.

"One of the anomalies of these people is that despite the advancement of their civilization, they for some reason refused to write about themselves. There is no writing on their temple walls, none of their cities has a library. To date, only a few scraps of writing have been discovered. Even ancient Greek and Roman historians chronicled how the Nabateans have succeeded in hiding their history, their trade routes, and the sources of their goods.

"The obvious question is, why? What is it that they want to hide?"

Bill glanced at the President as an icy chill trickled down his spine when he heard those last words from Carter. *These guys have been practicing the art of secrecy for thousands of years. No wonder we didn't know about them.*

Carter continued. "The reality is we still know very little about the Nabateans. I have read somewhere that archaeologists estimate they have only uncovered about fifteen percent of the city of Petra so far — eighty-five percent is still underground and untouched."

In an unguarded moment of concern, the President ran his fingers through his hair and sighed deeply. *What you don't know is what most often hurts you the worst.*

"The thing is this, for a very long time, the Nabateans were nomads, living in tents in the desert. For many centuries, the Nabateans never constructed a single house or a temple. Then suddenly, within a few short years, their civilization underwent a renaissance unequaled by any other — they started building magnificent monuments, of which Petra is one. But again, they hide that architectural marvel of theirs in a rock crevice, with access only through a narrow crack in the mountain. Why hide a city? Why build something so spectacular where no one can find it?

"During the period in history after Alexander the Great and the rise of the Roman Empire, the Nabateans became the most successful mercantile society in the area we today call the Middle East. Their knowledge of caravan routes and sea routes enabled them to become a kingpin in the trade of goods between the east as far as China, to the west as far as modern day Europe.

"They managed to create their own caravan routes through the hostile desert where no one else could go. They developed a method of transporting goods in the desert without the need to use the local water wells, which earned them the name *'people who draw water from the desert.'*"

"Very few things can make my day like when a bunch of surreptitious, ancient, merchant-architects from the Sandpit arrive at my doorstep," Bill mumbled, loud enough for everyone to hear and send them into a fit of laughter.

Bill held his hand up in apology for interrupting and nodded for Carter to continue.

"The Nabateans also transferred ideas and inventions between eastern and western civilizations. Over time they gained a monopoly on most of these trade goods, started manipulating the prices, and of course, managed to annoy the hell out of the Greeks, Egyptians, and Romans. The rumblings started as the merchants of these countries complained that their empires were being bankrupted by the hold the Nabateans had. They persuaded their politicians to mobilize their armies and crush the Nabateans."

"Nothing ever changes," the President muttered.

"However, every time, the Nabateans managed to escape without ever entering battle," Carter continued. "But their time eventually ran out in 106 AD when the Roman legions marched on them. They again avoided battle, this time by handing their empire over to the Romans. After this, they seemed to have faded from history . . ." Carter hesitated for a moment.

The President completed Carter's sentence, "But apparently not. It looks like they have just been doing what they do so well — hiding, and that for the past nineteen hundred plus years."

The President thanked a very curious Carter, dismissed him without further explanation, and then called in his security advisors, who quickly concluded that these were a people who were resilient as well as adept at hiding in plain sight. The fact that they indeed existed at the time Durand claimed the Council of the Covenant of Nabatea came into being led them to believe the truth of the matter. What was worse, these Nabateans could very well be much worse than Durand indicated.

They were about to find out just how much worse.

## Chapter Forty-One

### THE COUNTEROFFER

The question remaining was, what was on that laptop and flash drive? Durand claimed it was evidence of a widespread conspiracy, but the only hints he'd given about the nature of the conspiracy were that they involved world finance and energy control. He'd hinted that the mystery assassinations in Zürich were linked, as well, leaving the President and Bill Griffin to assume the worst about the victims' ties to extremist groups.

Nevertheless, Durand had asked for the moon with little upside for national security if he was inflating the importance of the information on the laptop. Therefore, they made a counteroffer. Scott was tasked with getting back in touch with him, since he'd made himself scarce after the first contact, but all he could do was wait for the forty-eight hours to run out before he could make contact again, as he agreed with Durand.

Precisely forty-eight hours after Durand's call, Scott dialed him. "Well?" Durand asked.

"We're interested," Scott said carefully. "But just as you

need guarantees, so do we. We have conditions, and a counteroffer."

Durand sighed. The ploy was a classic negotiation strategy. The first to name a price or concede interest was at a disadvantage; therefore, he didn't want to ask. But Scott was a master of the game. He remained silent, waiting for a response.

Durand considered his options. He could shop the information to another government, but he didn't know of another one that could keep him as secure as the US could, nor had he saved the life of one of the secret service operators of another country. Not even Israel had the resources of the US security agencies. Deciding he could at least hear the counteroffer, he responded at last.

"What is your counteroffer?"

"We're willing to give you what you ask — *if* the information is thorough and as volatile as you say. You can trust us to keep our word on that. We'll place you in protective custody to keep you safe until we can examine the goods. If they're bona fide, we'll sign off on the deal, and you'll have everything you asked for."

"And if your agency arbitrarily decides they aren't? What are *my* guarantees?"

"Then we'll escort you out of the US with a protective detail to any country of your choice. We'll give you a written guarantee of immunity from our prosecution. In other words, we'll leave you alone. We won't come after you."

*But Switzerland might.* Durand couldn't help being bitter about the consequences of going rogue. Someone knew of his involvement, and if someone knew, anyone could know. Which likely meant he was wanted for murder in Switzerland even now. And the $17 million might as well have been nothing for all his ability to reach it. One step of getting some of it would be like an insect stepping foot on a spider web. He'd be trapped as surely as if he walked into the headquarters of this accursed Council and gave himself up. He had less than $20,000 left.

Furthermore, because of his betrayal of Charlie, he could expect no more jobs. Contractors in their industry made it their business to know of each other, and know of each other's circumstances, if not the details of the jobs they completed. He could expect that apart from a big black X on his forehead as far as work was concerned, he probably had a hefty bounty on his head as well.

"Will you give me back the laptop and flash drive?"

"I can't guarantee that. You can ask for it, but whether you'll get it is above my pay grade."

"I suppose I don't have much choice," Durand answered in defeat. His tone was bitter, but at the same time, he knew the information was going to be extremely valuable. If Scott and his employers were to be trusted, his future would be secure. "Where shall I bring the items?"

"Tell me where you are. We'll pick you up."

Reluctantly, since it went against all his tradecraft, Durand gave his location. "I have a rental car to return also," he mentioned. "And by the way, I'll have to retrieve the goods from a secure location. I'll need a couple of days."

"We'll bring someone along who can drive the rental back. As soon as we get to you, you're under our protection. I'll escort you to pick the items up."

Somehow that statement didn't seem as comforting to Durand as it was no doubt meant to be. To him, it sounded like *"we've got you now."*

Scott didn't waste time in socializing with Durand when

he saw him. As far as he was concerned, the favor he owed was paid back in spades. A curt nod was all he afforded the man when they met. He wasn't very happy that to retrieve the laptop and flash drive would require a trip into Canada, either. But he made the arrangements that got them there and back in record time.

Then, with laptop and flash drive in hand, he drove at top speed to the A-Echelon offices, while others handled getting Durand to a safe house and his rental car back where it belonged.

Within twenty-four hours of delivering the laptop to A-Echelon, Scott, along with James and Irene, were once again in Bill Griffin's presence, with corroboration that turned his blood to ice.

"It's all true," James said. "Unbelievable, but this came straight from the horse's mouth, and it's undeniable. Algosaibi clearly created this record to assure his children's safety, but somehow, they were discovered, and it did them no good. However, knowing what we know now, I'm damned glad he did. Even if I haven't mourned his passing one iota."

---

"What's your assessment?" the President asked. "What kind of threat does this organization actually pose?"

Bill's voice was grim when he spoke. "Every kind. What's mind-numbing is that they — these Nabateans — have been right under our noses, right under *everyone's* noses, since fucking 106 AD, and no one has ever heard of them. Sorry, Sam, but this has me shaken up, I'll admit.

"Their goals are total world domination, in every sense of the word. Political, financial, control of all energy, and every other technology you might care to mention. And damned if they aren't capable of it. They're right on the brink of accomplishing everything they've been working for all this time.

"And it should come as no surprise that with Algosaibi's involvement, they also know everything about Carter Devereux's work at that city of giants in Egypt and his search for the ancient nukes, as well as his wife's research into ancient medicine."

"In other words, the shit is about to hit the fan," the President said, though his smile didn't reach his eyes.

"Wait for it, sir. That ain't a fraction of the bad news. Their systems, their communication technology, and in fact their surveillance technology, is superior to ours. It's more advanced than ours or any we know of, and in fact, they've been spying on us and everyone else all along, including the CIA, NSA, FBI, A-Echelon, DARPA, Homeland Security — you name it, they have it. And you can bet your life they already knew we had this information in our hands. And that poor fool Durand? He doesn't stand a chance. He's already compromised, and I doubt we can do a damn thing about it."

A moment of silence fell as they spared a bit of regret for the man who'd given them critical information barely in the nick of time. But they couldn't focus on him now. He'd be given their best efforts, but those would have to be delegated to others while the implications of what they'd learned were studied by the best minds they could gather.

They'd be handicapped at first by the fact that Algosaibi hadn't revealed the names of all the council members, only those of Graziella and Mathieu Nabati, and that the Council have their headquarters in the catacombs below a house located on the bank of the River Seine in the third district of Paris. Clearly, more intelligence about these two was required, but how to get it when they couldn't even guarantee the secrecy of their most sophisticated techniques? If they were to storm in there and setup a spy operation, they would immediately be compromised and have the tables turned on them.

Every time Griffin thought about the fact that the Nabateans had probably been spying on not only his operation, but his predecessors', for decades, he suffered a heartburn attack. This job was going to kill him if he didn't get a handle on this threat soon. His only chance was to pull together the best minds in his organization for a summit meeting.

## Chapter Forty-Two

### SUCCUMBED TO HUMAN NATURE

As Carter was the reigning expert on the Nabateans, at least within the circles of people with top secret clearances, he was invited to sit in. He eagerly accepted. *Maybe now I'll learn what got the sand into everyone's asses the other day.* At the meeting, though, held in as unlikely a place as he could think of, a restaurant in Tyson's Corner, he got rather more than he'd bargained for.

Carter couldn't have known, but the restaurant where he sat around a massive makeshift conference table, was owned by the IRS, the result of a raid on its tax-evading owner. Through a series of face-to-face meetings designed to foil the superior espionage of the Nabateans, it had been borrowed, thoroughly swept for bugs, and then protected by the most powerful jamming electronics known to the CIA. None of that was in evidence at the meeting. The only thing Carter knew about it all was that he'd been given specific instructions about how to approach and arrive at the location, handwritten and passed to him during a handshake. His limited spycraft training when he joined A-

Echelon was enough to alert him to follow the directions to the letter.

With him at the table were several people he didn't know, introduced as CIA analysts and technology experts. When he shook hands with his friend Sean Walker, he managed to hide his surprise and immediately concluded that something serious must be afoot. Executive Advantage was only called in as a last resort whenever security agencies find themselves with an obdurate problem that couldn't be dealt with through commercial, diplomatic, and political channels.

The meeting began with a PowerPoint presentation that summarized the information on the laptop to the extent the group needed to know in order to formulate a plan.

The most puzzling and therefore frightening piece of information had to do with the 1900-year-old secret. How was it possible they'd gone unnoticed for so long?

While the presentation was running, Carter was fully focused on it, storing every bit of information on the hard drive of his brain. But the minute the floor was opened up for brainstorming, his quick mind put what he knew of the ancient Nabateans together with what he'd just seen, and he had a theory.

"It may be that the current group's interests have only been focused on international control since World War One," he remarked, almost as if he were talking to himself.

"What was that?" James had heard him mutter and wanted the others to hear it, too.

"Maybe at first, they just wanted to protect their trade secrets, maybe to rebuild Petra and maintain their cultural identity. They weren't a great political influence in the world, or even in their region. Historians have even thought they had completely blended into Roman culture after 106

AD," he explained. "They wouldn't have been noticed until they began to form their current agenda. That had to have been after World War One, or maybe even after 1948, when Israel was carved out of the area. But I would say we've been focused in the wrong direction, and that's how they've avoided detection."

"How do you figure?" asked an analyst. "We've always backed Israel. Or did, until . . ."

"Let's keep it focused," snapped Griffin. He, of course, had his own political opinions, but he'd served under several presidents, and he didn't intend to have any of them thrown under the bus during this discussion. No matter how much he agreed or not.

"What I mean," explained Carter, "is that we have been focused on the unrest in the Middle East, for as long as I can remember and probably even before that. Yet the ringleaders of this group are apparently based in Europe. Specifically, in the bastions of finance, which underpins every other aspect of global affairs. Hell, they may have even finagled intelligence, or disinformation, to keep us focused elsewhere."

Heads began to nod around the table, and James exchanged a knowing wink with Irene. Carter's ability to reason and analyze was almost as spectacular as his memory, but the analysts he'd only just met didn't know it yet. James thought privately that they might all get a wake-up call during this meeting.

The analyst who'd questioned Carter's thought process took up the flag. "That sounds about right, especially in light of the passages where Algosaibi states his dissatisfaction with the Council's hands-off policy with regard to Middle Eastern politics and any form of religion. That would keep them under the radar unless and until they made a move."

"Here's something else," said a woman halfway around the vast table from Carter. He cocked his head to better hear her. Noticing it, she raised her voice. "From what I can see, it's pretty much this tight group, this council of 12 members, who have run the organization from the beginning, under threat of death if they reveal the secrets. They could have thousands of operatives around the world, but all it would take is a buffer of several contacts between the principals of the organization and the people who are doing the work, but have no idea who they're working for. Or even, for that matter, what their little tasks might accomplish when part of a whole. Probably the business end of the organization is so disseminated that the big picture is impossible to see."

Carter nodded. "That makes sense."

Bill tapped his water glass with his spoon to call everyone's attention back to him, as low-volume conversations had broken out all around the table. "So, to summarize, what we have determined so far, although it's unverified as yet, is that it's highly probable these Nabateans have infiltrated not only finance and technology interests, but likely governments across the globe. Perhaps to the extent that they're in a position to give orders to those governments. Moreover, it's potentially true that our own government is among those they have the means to control."

Carter, who had continued to pull together threads of information, some of which was unknown to most of the participants, was suddenly convinced beyond all doubt. "Yep, that's about the size of it," he said, staring over the heads of the people across from him as he drew his own conclusions, unconscious he was stating them aloud. "This Council of the Covenant of Nabatea is not unlike any dictatorship or totalitarian government or organization under the guise of religion, be it Nazi, fascist, communist, or even Muslim. It exists for one purpose and one purpose only — to amass power so they can control world events for their own advantage. What may have begun as a noble enterprise eventually succumbed to human nature. They must be stopped."

One by one, the analysts began to applaud. Soon, the applause broke through Carter's daze of rumination.

"My boy, you've hit the proverbial nail right on the head," Bill said. "Now let's go repeat that to the President."

Bill would have been appalled had he known his elaborate precautions for secrecy had done no good at all. All the technology in the world couldn't make up for one mole on the team.

## Chapter Forty-Three

### THE BIGGEST CRISIS

It was midnight in Paris, not all that late in some quarters, as locals ventured back to their favorite haunts for the night life after the terrorist attacks of the previous year. Despite the time differences and the distances that separated them, Graziella Nabati waited for each member of the council to check in. This was a mandatory meeting, and it wouldn't begin until they were all present.

There was no chatter and no friendly banter between council members as, one by one, they all made their presence known. Beijing, Geneva, Washington D.C, London, Moscow, New Delhi, Paris, Riyadh, Shanghai, Syria, Tehran, and Tokyo. For some, the meeting was taking place in the dead of night, appropriately for its content. For others, it was midday, the juxtaposition of the somber mood not at all in keeping with the sunlight streaming in their respective windows.

Though most of them didn't yet know what was wrong, it was the second emergency meeting within a week. *Something* was clearly wrong. Graziella wasted no time in getting to the point. After the opening ritual, she skipped the usual welcome and greetings, her agitation plain for all to see over their secure links.

"We have a serious problem. One of our operators in America has sent a message about a top-secret meeting held just five hours ago, this afternoon in Washington, D.C. Such elaborate precautions of secrecy were taken that our operative was lucky to have been included in the planning; otherwise we would not have the recording of the meeting. However, he was able to place several sophisticated bugs in the meeting place, so we have a complete recording of the proceedings.

"Please bear with me while I play that recording. It will explain everything."

Not a reply or cough was heard as she clicked the icon with her mouse. No question was raised as each member of the council listened with growing apprehension to the clip in its entirety. The first part they already knew; Durand had obtained the laptop and flash drive with which their former colleague Algosaibi had betrayed them and their ancient secrets.

The shock was that Durand had gone to the American CIA and traded the information on them for his life and protection. The CIA now knew everything — all their secrets, of their assassination of Algosaibi's children, and of their mission and goals. The Council's biggest threat to existence — the CIA — now knew something about the advanced technology the Nabateans had, along with the extent of their influence. Most alarming, they knew the names of the leader of the group and her son, Graziella and Mathieu Nabati, and disturbingly much about the location of their headquarters.

The meeting at hand was to determine what to do

about it. But Graziella wanted to talk about the future of the council first.

"This has come about because we didn't take effective and immediate action against Xavier Algosaibi when he insisted on following a political religious agenda. I warned you at the time that he should be sanctioned.

"The principles of our Council have always been to steer clear of politics and religion. The famous American author, Mark Twain, said '*I am quite sure now that often, very often, in matters concerning religion and politics a man's reasoning powers are not above the monkey's.*' This proves it. By his stubborn meddling in matters that don't concern us, Algosaibi has brought us to the brink of disaster, and although he has paid the ultimate price for it, he also set in motion this catastrophe. Before we do anything else, we must be certain it never happens again."

Graziella's solution was that the very moment any council member stepped out of line again, he or she would be terminated without warning. The Council members immediately acceded in unison. Not a few of the members silently gulped as they remembered voicing political opinions about the status of their ancient homeland in Jordan, but they all assented anyway. Assuming the Council survived this crisis, they would all be under threat of death if they developed agendas like that of Algosaibi.

Naturally, it was decided, again without dissent, also to spare no effort to locate and eliminate Durand. Even if he was no longer in possession of their secrets, he knew them. He and everyone else who came into that knowledge would be summarily dealt with, until the last fading echo of a rumor about it was silenced.

Only then came the discussion of what they should do about their immediate danger. Graziella and Mathieu of course had to disappear, and with them every trace of records of the Council located in the catacombs below Graziella's residence. The others weren't certain their identities had been compromised, but those two knew everyone, not only their public personas, but also who they really were. They could not afford to be interrogated.

Briefly, they considered making their move for world domination immediately. They had achieved a superior position regarding power and influence. They had access to advanced technology in the fields of computing, energy, and medicine. If they wanted to move, albeit prematurely, they could probably succeed.

There was no question they could collapse the Internet and satellite communications worldwide. They could probably collapse or control most if not all world stock exchanges and money markets. They'd long since mastered a way to predict, with their über-powerful quantum computers, the appearance of an unlikely correlation and had grown exceedingly wealthy on that knowledge. They could probably use it now to create chaos in the markets, for a short time anyway, before the regulatory agencies shut them down.

Or, they could flex their muscles and use the evidence of their superiority to form alliances with existing governments, although that idea didn't float long because of their aversion to politics. And because they would likely have to trade their exclusive knowledge for the protection. In the end, they decided the chance of failure meant they could not move before the fullness of their plan was in place. It was best to fade into the background, as they'd done so many centuries before, and protect all of it so they could use it when the time was right.

It was just as in the old days, when the ancient

Nabateans had withdrawn from conflict and survived on so many occasions in their past. And just like they did the last time, in 106 AD, when they quietly ceded their empire to the Romans, they would lie low, suspend activities, and bide their time. The American Secretary of the Treasury who resided in Washington, D.C., pointed out that he was in the very bosom of the enemy. He'd have to disappear, too, but in a way, that didn't excite speculation. If it became known he'd been a member of the council, everything he'd touched in a long and illustrious career in the capital city would be brought under suspicion. Discovery of only some of it would dismantle a significant portion of their network and cripple them.

Again, the decision was made without discord.

There was one agenda item remaining, and that was the most important of all.

It hadn't escaped the attention of anyone on the Council, least of all Graziella, that the most accurate assumptions being made in that meeting were those of someone whose research focus they knew well. Carter Devereux.

Ever since he'd gained credibility with the discoveries of the ancient city in Peru, outside Cusco, and then the City of Lights in the Egyptian desert, the man had been a thorn in their sides. They knew, through their spy networks, about all his top-secret research. They knew he was in possession of the library of the giants, and their most coveted goal was to get their hands on it.

Only the Council had known for all those centuries that there was a record somewhere of technology so advanced it put even theirs to shame. And then in one stroke of luck, Devereux had found it before they could put someone in place in the dig to retrieve it once the city had been located. Worse, he had defied every rule of honest archaeology by removing the precious artifacts that comprised the library from their environment! It went against his nature, so they hadn't expected it and were not prepared for it.

They knew his reasoning, because they'd listened to him talk it out with James Rhodes many times. He still felt guilty for it, though he knew taking it was the only way to keep the ancient knowledge of nuclear fusion technology out of the hands of terrorists and fanatics like Algosaibi.

Over the last few weeks they learned that Devereux had in his hands everything they themselves had been hunting for, for nearly two millennia; greater advances in quantum physics, zero-point energy, medical technology, and more.

And to crown it all, now he was aware of *their existence*, as well. And he'd predicted with deadly accuracy the threat their goals represented for his country and indeed the rest of the world. The only hope they had of fulfilling those goals was to get their hands on Devereux and that library. Or, in fact, they didn't even need *him*. They had their own brilliant scientists and translators. All they needed was the library, and they'd stop at nothing to get it. Even if it meant killing him and his family and anyone else who dared to stand in their way.

Aside from disappearing and sweeping their tracks behind them, it was their top priority. Durand had forced their hands—they had to get that library immediately and no cost or effort would be spared.

## Chapter Forty-Four

### COUNTER MEASURES

Even though they didn't know their summit meeting had been compromised, the revelations about the Nabateans and what they were capable of gave everyone the jitters. Especially Bill, James, and Sean. The three of them agreed they had to take drastic measures to safeguard their communications, as well as the translation efforts and the research the Devereuxs were doing.

After studying the facts, there was only one way to secure those things. Everything important had to be taken offline. Even with the most sophisticated anti-hacking security known to them, the Internet was still a huge threat. Since they'd reluctantly conceded the Nabateans had superior snooping technology, they couldn't afford to connect anything sensitive to that vast labyrinth of secret and not-secret connections. Who knew? Some people speculated that "the Internet" was some semi-sentient entity on the verge of becoming self-aware. Maybe they were right. Stranger revelations had been proven to them that very week.

So, no device containing sensitive information could be connected to the Internet for even a fraction of a second, the wireless network features on those devices were disabled. Furthermore, all electronic means of communications, even secured and encrypted cell phones, were off-limits. No written records, whether electronic or the old-fashioned paper kind, were allowed. Everyone's memories, except Carter's of course, would be taxed to the limit.

James remarked, "Carter is the only one who won't have a problem with these new measures. His brain is already a mass-storage device."

They all had a good laugh at Carter's expense, but when the decree was implemented, he was the one with the last laugh.

When the Executive Advantage leadership considered the safety of the primary people involved in the translation or research, Sean's assessment was they couldn't keep them safe and happy both anywhere near Washington, D.C., and that included Boston. It was either lock them in a concrete vault, or take them to a remote location whose perimeter could be secured.

Faced with this assessment, Carter brightened. "Of course! What better location than Freydís?"

"We have to assume they know about Freydís," Bill countered. James and Sean exchanged looks. They had a feeling Bill was about to have his ass handed to him, and Carter didn't disappoint.

"We have to assume they know everything about everyone and every place," he began hotly. "Freydís can be secured. Sean's outfit has their training camp there, and every precaution to keep it secret and camouflaged has been taken. I have the financial means to provide whatever other buildings we need, and don't forget Mackenzie's freaky clairvoyant wolves to warn us of trouble. I insist."

The stubborn set of his jaw convinced even Bill that any further argument would be futile. "All right, you win. But you have to let us help your security team prepare."

"Not a problem." Carter didn't bother to say so, but he'd been missing the daily training he and Mackie were doing with the commandos before they'd left for the States for the translation effort. Mackie had told him on the phone that she missed their home, too, despite enjoying her visit with her parents. He'd have to think about whether Mackie's parents were in any danger from the Council. If so, they'd better think about bringing his "outlaws" to Freydís as well.

Once the decision on the location was made, it didn't take long for James and Sean's team in the person of Dylan to determine that Liu, Rick, and Samantha were critical to the translation and should be moved there as well. Dylan was over the moon. To be full-time on Freydís, and Liu with him? *Don't throw me in the briar patch, Brer Fox!*

In fact, before the previous plan had been interrupted by the need to take the translation project to the States, work had already begun on a nice little cabin for Dylan and Liu at Camp Tala. The finishing touches were just now being added.

The move was made in stages, as the work couldn't be interrupted to get all the plans in place. With the bulk of the coding on the translation software done, Rick and Samantha were detailed to Freydís to oversee the planning of an addition to the main homestead to accommodate a server room with temperature and humidity control, along with a couple of secure rooms for the research projects. Fiber optic cable would be utilized to network everything, so the more insecure wireless technology wouldn't create a vulnerability to snooping.

Carter arranged for prefabricated offices to be flown out. All the planned facilities would be housed in them and become the translation center. Dylan's team of trainees would place both physical and electronic security devices to protect the outbuildings, all hooked up to Camp Tala's electronic guard system.

He also approached Mackenzie about the idea he couldn't shake — that leaving her parents and brother unprotected was as good as an invitation to the Council to take them hostage and force one or both to give up their secrets.

Her eyes went wide. "Do you really think that?"

"Mackie, I would never joke about such a thing. I think we need to persuade them to move to Freydís with us. At least until we have the Nabateans neutralized. The only problem I see—"

"—is that we've invited them before and they refused," she completed for him. It was true. Her parents had both recently retired, and before the extended visit occasioned by Carter's need to be focused on the translation project, she had begged her parents to join them on Freydís. They hadn't thought long enough, in her opinion, before reluctantly turning her down. It was too isolated, they'd claimed. And although they'd love to be around Liam and Beth more, they felt they'd miss their friends.

"We'll have to clue them in on why we're insisting," Carter said. "But it's imperative. And your brother needs to come, too."

"What about his job?"

Ray Anderson, a horticulturist, was Mackenzie's younger brother. He'd spent most of his twenties "finding himself", and it had been a relief to Mackenzie's parents when he settled down to a career. She was worried that uprooting him from his job would send him drifting again, professionally anyway. She wasn't at all sure even Carter's powers of persuasion would be enough to convince them or her brother.

"I'll offer him another. At least he doesn't have a wife and kids to uproot, too. It's important, Mackie."

"You won't get any argument from me. But it's your job to convince them. And I just thought of a good argument. Liam is going to need more schooling than Bly and I can provide soon with our other duties. Tell them they're needed to homeschool their grandson and his new-found friend, Shane, John and Jennie Ruschin's boy, and any other kids who come with the trainers to live at Camp Tala for any length of time.

"In fact," she said, getting more excited, "come to think about Ray, we need someone to establish a horticultural system to produce fresh vegetables and fruit for all the people year-round! Ray would love to do that. And I am sure he will find a very enthusiastic Bly at his side with an undertaking like that."

"Thanks for the tips, Mackie. Are you sure *you* don't want to make these arguments to *your* family?"

"Nope. *You* still have to convince them. I'm not touching it."

"If I must, I'll kidnap them," he deadpanned.

---

Even as the Executive Advantage team worked to get everything ready, the Nabateans observed every move. They knew when their information stream dried up the translation project had gone offline, and the flurry of activity in a remote area of Canada that they'd already connected to Carter was too big a coincidence to fool them. They began making plans to raid the place and take possession of the precious library.

What they didn't know about, because such stealthy precautions had been taken to keep it a secret, was Camp Tala. It had every security device possible guarding it from observation, from trip-wires and infrared motion and heat detectors far from visual range on the perimeter, to trainees on virtual guard duty twenty-four seven. The monitors were never unobserved, and regular patrols made sure the remote surveillance equipment was never down and never interfered with.

Even the airspace was patrolled, as surveillance satellites were tasked with a sweep every few hours to detect "unfriendly" drones.

## Chapter Forty-Five

### WHERE DID THEY GO?

Carter was anxious to get back to his research, and once Mackenzie's parents and brother had been persuaded to move to Freydís, he saw no reason not to leave the security in the hands of the experts and continue his research.

The translations had progressed to the point where Carter found a passage that hinted where the giants had gone when they abandoned the City of Lights. It also confirmed that they had indeed abandoned it, rather than surrendering it. That explained the tidiness of the city as it emerged from the sand. Indeed, the sand had preserved it in remarkably pristine condition.

> *The small ones continue to make advances, and we fear now that they have the means to travel in air, along with fearful weapons of great destructive power. The air machines have been observed more and more often in recent days. Here we have not the devices to disarm or neutralize their weapons, those our informants say harness the power of atoms as we once did, before we discovered less destructive ways to utilize this energy.*

> *At the meeting of the government today, it was decided we will leave, all of us, for the capital. There they have the defensive weapons. Even now, conveyance is being prepared for everyone, and everyone must go with virtually none of their possessions. At dawn, we will set out in a great caravan to the northwest. May the gods look with favor upon our journey.*

"Liu, come quickly!" Carter called. "Look, I think I've found the answer to the abandonment of the City of Lights."

Having worked with the language for so long now, Liu quickly checked the original and then the screen with the translation, reading it aloud in almost the same words Carter had chosen.

"They left under threat of attack and went to the northwest. Carter, I wonder if they ever meant to come back?"

"We'll probably find that answer in a record left wherever they went. Why couldn't they have just said where that was?" Carter slammed his palm on the table in frustration. "Another damn mystery. One on top of the other."

"Calm down, Carter. They did say where they were going. They expected whoever read this record to know exactly where the capital was, just as we'd say the same thing in the States and anyone would know we were talking about D.C."

Carter's frustration melted at Liu's unperturbed explanation. "Too bad they didn't know how long it would take for someone to find it. And how ironic it's 'the little ones' who are finally unearthing their secrets. But we could have used some coordinates."

"Which wouldn't necessarily have been the same as what we use today," Liu pointed out.

"Would you quit being so damn reasonable?" Carter said with a smile.

"We just have to keep looking for clues. But we do have one. They went northwest. We need a map and a big red pin to mark the City of Lights," Liu offered.

"I'll dig one up or order one online."

"No, you won't order it online. Ask James to procure it for you. Remember?"

"Of course, I remember. I remember everything. But it's d— it's inconvenient, even though you're right. Sorry I keep swearing."

Liu smiled. It seemed Carter wouldn't be unaffected by the restrictions after all.

## Chapter Forty-Six

### THE HUNT IS ON

*The problem with knowing you have a problem is you then must do something about it.* Bill Griffin had more than one problem. Sure, he now knew about the Nabateans and the threat they posed to the US and all other countries of the world. However, it wasn't ideal that the group was headquartered in Paris, where the woman with the sexy name lived. Graziella. Sounded elegant. And maybe deadly. The intel they had from the Algosaibi laptop gave her address in the 3rd *Arrondisement*, and based on where it was located, directly above a section of the Parisian catacombs that was probably the headquarters of the whole thing.

And, though there had been plenty of times when his organization had needed to do it before, it really wasn't nice to spy in a friendly country. Nor was it easy. Just as it hadn't been easy to cut off the ready flow of information from the CIA and indeed all sensitive government agencies to the Nabateans. Even less easy was getting close enough to the Nabateans to gather information while dodging the attention of all European spy agencies. It would be slow and tedious.

They would have to rely on some old but effective tradecraft to elude the sophisticated technology of the Nabateans, too. It was like walking a tightrope in a high wind with a thunderstorm raging. And no safety net.

In fact, they were certain there was no way to spy on Graziella or get close to her home. But they did have hope they could get to her son. It was a start, at least. While it was true that Swiss banks had strong security technology, there was reason to believe it wasn't necessarily superior to the CIA's infiltration techniques. So, the delicate task of trapping this spider without getting caught in the web would begin in Zürich.

The Spider in question, Mathieu Nabati, had just about reached his breaking point when it came to controlling his temper. His mother was the Ice Queen, but Mathieu had a passionate side from his late father that occasionally made him impulsive and often caused him to act based on emotion rather than the cold calculation his mother employed.

A child could have predicted the CIA, NSA, and a host of other alphabet-soup agencies would be coming after the Council of the Covenant of Nabatea. Their cover was blown, and they knew the CIA knew of both their existence and their extensive infiltration of all those agencies. Not to mention the myriad other infiltrations that had given them virtual control of the major countries and industries of the globe. That they hadn't chosen to exercise it except in limited operations was irrelevant. They couldn't be allowed to continue, and they accepted that. There was no way they wouldn't be hunted down and stopped now that they were no longer undercover. Even their power couldn't prevent it; so, they'd have to do as their ancestors had done in 106 AD — disappear.

Most of their secrets would go underground with them, to be employed when the time was right.

Mathieu accepted the decision, but he didn't have to like it. He exacted one concession from the rest of the Council. It had been his operation, and he was due some revenge. Along with that, his plan would send a message to the agencies that dared to pursue them about their reach and power.

Thus, it was that Perrin Durand, while under the protection of the US Marshall Service's Witness Protection Program, managed to throw himself off a bridge. But not before he'd also stabbed himself in the back seven times. Mathieu's enjoyment of American movies provided the detail that would leave no doubt the "suicide" was in fact murder, and who had committed it.

It was a spine-chillingly clear message to everyone about the reach of the Council of the Covenant of Nabatea.

That detail taken care of, the Council soon found evidence they hoped would allow them to take similar revenge on the man who was the biggest thorn in their flesh and the sole barrier in the way of getting their hands on the library of the giants. Carter Devereux. Within days, they had information regarding which satellites overflew Devereux's Canadian property and to whom those satellites belonged. With the schedules in hand, they pulled silk strings with their Chinese contacts and obtained their own satellite time to surveil Freydís.

Each member of the Council who were compromised then made his or her own arrangements to effectively disappear from their former lives. While the world would think them gone, they would blend with their surroundings, while secretly staying in touch to continue carefully chosen operations. But for the time being their grand scheme was on hold.

## Chapter Forty-Seven

### A NEW EXPEDITION IN THE CARDS

Six weeks after Durand's untimely and unlikely death, the group at Freydís had settled into a routine that, while acknowledging their vulnerability, didn't dwell on it. Camp Tala had been fully operational for a couple of weeks, and the combat training that Carter and Mackenzie had interrupted for their trip to the States resumed.

Liam was in heaven with not only Ahote but his grandpa to take him fishing and on other adventures, teaching him everything his little body and quick mind could handle. Carter participated in some of the activities, too, bonding with his father-in-law as never before, while silently admiring his son. What a man the little guy would become!

Beth enjoyed similar quality time with the women of the extended family and was thoroughly spoiled by all the Executive Advantage team, both the security details and the trainees. It was clear she would become a beauty like her mom, and like Mackenzie, she had every man in the vicinity wrapped around her little finger. Except Dylan, of course, who was wrapped around Liu's. He was very fond of Beth, too, though, and secretly hoped his and Liu's first child would be a little girl as engaging as Beth. The son to follow in his footsteps couldn't come soon enough, either.

The research, along with the translation of the library, continued with all due speed. Each day while Carter spent time with his children or the men, Liu and Mackenzie would search for a couple of hours in the library and in other resources Mackenzie had obtained over the years for any mention of respirocytes or anything that could be construed to mean the same thing.

The rest of the time was dedicated to locating information about the ancient nukes. They were the most urgent of the dangers to put to rest. While other tantalizing mentions had been found here and there, Carter's conviction that the bulk of the answer would be found in the giants' capital city seemed more and more likely to be correct. Accordingly, he spent most of this time poring over maps and texts for clues to its location. Everything he could find added to his sense that it was probably located in an area that was now underwater, in what was known currently as the Alboran Sea.

When he could no longer keep his speculation to himself, he called everyone together for a discussion.

"I can't believe no one has done anything about this yet," he began, turning all the eager looks around the table to bewilderment. Noticing the puzzled faces, he started again.

"I think I know where the giants went. Where their capital city was." Various expressions of surprise went around the table, but the loudest was Liu.

"And how is it you haven't said a word to me?" she all but screeched.

Carter made a quelling motion with his hands, and the

others settled down. Liu, however looked as if she might chew nails. Or perhaps Carter, if she could cut him into small enough pieces. He gulped and hastened to explain.

"We know they went northwest, because they said so. I've been combing the translations for anything more specific, but when I ran out of material, I had to concede that if it's in the library, it hasn't been translated yet.

"So, I went to other sources. And I could kick myself, because I've *known* about these sites. An undersea wall off the coast of Morocco has stones, some of which are the size of 2-story houses. How could a normal human, even with our current machines, maneuver such a thing? Had to be giants. There's a temple in Lebanon with similar stones in its foundation. But there's more under the Alboran Sea."

Carter paused at Mackenzie's tilted head. "That's between the Iberian Peninsula consisting of Spain, Portugal, and Gibraltar on the one side and Africa on the other, at the west end of the Mediterranean. In other words, when you go from the Atlantic Ocean through the strait of Gibraltar you enter the Alboran Sea.

"I don't think it's a coincidence that many of the legends about Atlantis have it located in that area. There are numerous documented ruins under the sea in that area, but not only there, it can be found along the coastlines of almost all landmasses, on the continental shelves. Mean sea level has risen and fallen many times with climate changes, from ice ages to melt-offs. Right now, it's at one of the highest levels ever determined, and you've all heard the political debate over global warming. Never mind whether humans and their activity have contributed to it; the climate changes in both directions and has always done so.

"What makes it interesting is that over the past few centuries, it happened rapidly enough that we have ancient maps showing just how much of the coastlines, especially along the Mediterranean and the Atlantic coastlines of Spain and Morocco, have been inundated by rising sea levels. People used to live in cities that are now underwater. Explorers and archaeologists have observed giant relics of cities, and the Bible has mentioned giants, as we've seen before, so why hasn't anyone put it together before? Giants lived in those giant relics.

"And I've got one site in mind where I think the capital city could have been. I want to take an expedition to make a more thorough exploration of that site, and if I'm right, we'll find the rest of the answers we've been looking for."

Pandemonium erupted among the participants. From Mackenzie, who wasn't on board with letting Carter out of her sight while they were all still in danger from the Nabateans, to Rick, who had always been a believer in Atlantis, to Liu, who was terrified of water, or at least of being underwater — everyone had an opinion.

Gradually the noise died down and Carter continued, "Obviously, I'm going to need a crew. But I'll choose who goes and which of you stays. Don't worry, Liu. I do need you, but I don't need you to dive. Mackie, I understand your concern, but I'll be fine. Dylan, I trust you can round up some of your people who have underwater experience. It's only a matter of time before someone does put all this together. I don't want them to interrupt my investigations. We have an expedition to mount."

Out of respect for Carter, everyone had heard him out during the mini-lecture, until he mentioned the expedition. His calming words after he'd dropped that bomb on them served to focus their minds on both the truth he'd stated about the urgency and what would need to be done before an expedition could be ready. Underwater meant a boat as a base of operations.

Remote control mini-subs would be best for the initial site survey, and Rick immediately volunteered to man the computers that would take the data from the subs and create a map. Carter himself was the most qualified to interpret the images the sub would record and decide where would be the most productive areas to dive. But he would need a team of divers. The quicker they got in, drew their conclusions, and got out, the less likelihood they would come to the attention of people they didn't want to invite. Like pirates, or Nabateans.

Carter accepted the need for his bodyguards and other security professionals to go along, and in fact welcomed them. No matter what uninvited guests might show up, the Executive Advantage folks would take care of it, he trusted. Naturally, they'd do all they could to keep the preparations and the expedition itself a secret. But with a project of this complexity, it would be a challenge.

They couldn't just fly into Morocco, hire a boat, and start diving. Too many eyes and ears in that part of the world. The best course of action would be to fly to Casablanca and from there make their way to the coast. With such a large group of people to transport, it would have to be done a few at a time and with care. They had to have trusted allies to gather the supplies for the boat. There were a million details.

This was going to take a while.

## Chapter Forty-Eight
### GIANTESE

While the planning and staging of the expedition went forward, Mackenzie distracted herself from the danger Carter intended to walk into by throwing herself even more intensely into her research. But with Liu fully involved in the expedition planning, Mackenzie often found herself handicapped by the temporary loss of her translator.

The solution was to redouble the efforts of the coders to improve the software, and it fell to Samantha to visit Freydís regularly to update the code and the algorithms with the latest requirements. On one such visit, she had been invited to stay the weekend and relax a bit on the beautiful property, which she eagerly accepted. Finishing her work early on a Friday afternoon, Samantha felt guilty about starting her weekend early.

As she looked around for something else she could work on, she noticed a stack of plates that had been set aside and asked Mackenzie about it.

"Oh, those . . . something's different about them. The

computer couldn't make anything of it when we ran it through. I'm afraid it's damaged."

"Mackenzie, remember when we talked about how odd it was that we've only found text on all these plates? How even our early encyclopedias had pictures? And now, with electronic records, there are sound files included?"

"Yeah. What brought that up?"

"Well, you know we put that on the back burner because Carter was so certain the information you both are looking for will be found in text files. But what if this plate isn't damaged? What if it contains images, or even sound files?"

"It would be great to find information in those formats. Go for it."

The images on the screen showed nanodots on the plate, just like the others. Yet processing it had produced no text. Interesting. She increased the magnification of the image — and jumped back in surprise when what showed up was an actual image. She could make out what it was! The dots were organized much like pixels, and when she reduced the magnification again, the image proved her earlier impression correct. It was a human face.

"Holy Toledo," she breathed. She looked over at Mackenzie, not yet ready to trust what she'd found. It was so simple! Yet the tiny dots were too small for the naked eye to make out a pattern. Only by enlarging it to a size too *large* to make out much, could she see that there was a happy medium, and she'd found it. A picture of an ancient . . . giant?

With trembling hands, Samantha shifted the image to the next nanodot, this time at the exact magnification to see the image immediately. And then the next and the next. By the time she'd gone through the first row, she was about to jump out of her skin with excitement. She couldn't wait any longer!

"Mackenzie!" she shouted.

Mackenzie jumped and hit her head on a lamp that was bent over her work. *"What?* Jeez, Sam, you scared me to death!" Then she looked up and saw the excitement on Samantha's face. "What is it? What have you found?"

"You'll never believe it. Come here and look!"

After an intense half hour of poring over image after image of the giants, Samantha noted they'd been keeping this all to themselves for too long, and they were going to be in serious trouble.

Mackenzie just laughed. "You're right. We need to call Carter and Liu in right now. Let's show them. But wait. Carter's always pulling jokes on us — let's turn the tables."

"I'm not touching that one with a ten-foot pole," Sam said, rolling her eyes. "It's on you."

"Okay, just go along with me then." Mackenzie's eyes sparkled with mischief as she left the room to go and get the others. A moment later, she spoke to Carter. "Honey, something's wrong with some of the plates."

Alarmed, Carter looked up. "What do you mean?"

"Well, Sam was running the ones that wouldn't translate under your electron microscope, and, well . . ."

Carter jumped up and ran toward the other room. "Don't tell me the microscope damaged them! Those are irreplaceable—" He stopped short when he saw Sam, who had managed to put on a contrite expression.

"I'm not sure," she said. "Here, have a look for yourself."

Carter slowly approached, the trepidation on his face

nearly making Mackenzie lose it and start laughing. She managed to save the joke by turning the laugh into a cough. Carter took one look at the viewer and started shouting.

"Oh, you have got to be kidding! Pictures! How? What? Mackie, I have a good mind—"

At that, Mackenzie did lose it. She laughed so hard that tears started rolling down her cheeks.

"You clever girls! How did you do it?"

"I have to confess, it was a total fluke," answered Sam. She explained how she discovered the photos.

Carter nodded. "I can see why you say it was a fluke," he began. "But it wasn't. You tried something and it worked. That's the scientific method. At least if you can repeat the process. Are there any more pictures on that plate?"

"Hundreds of thousands."

"Wow. We're going to need to look at every one of them and catalog them." Growing even more excited, he exclaimed, "What if there are pictures of those nukes? This is critical! Sam, you've made an important discovery."

Sam blushed.

"Can you stay and begin the cataloging process? I'm assuming it's possible to automate it . . ."

"Hmmm. I can write a routine that would identify the major components. Or at least sort the faces from landscape and large objects . . . it would make it faster to get to the images you're interested in."

"Trust me, I'm interested in *all* of them. But some are more time-sensitive than others. That sounds like a good project. Can you get in touch with Rick and arrange to spend some more time here?"

"I'll try," Sam answered. "I've got another day before my pickup is scheduled. I can at least do some more before then. Let me get back to work." She sent an encoded text message to Rick. *Remember Kelly's birthday is in five days.*

After everyone settled down from the excitement, Sam went back to her quick scan of the images, moving the plate carefully from one to the next under the microscope. Hours later, she stretched her back and took a break. She hadn't mentioned it to anyone else yet, but there were some nanodots that didn't translate or expand to an image. Something about them tugged at a memory she couldn't quite bring to the front of her mind.

Sam went to the kitchen, selected an apple from a bowl of fruit on a counter, and went outside for a walk. The beauty of this place never failed to awe her, and this day was no different. Late afternoon sun lit the trees, highlighting their subtly different shades of green. As she gazed upward, the contrast of the clear blue sky peeking between the treetops and the green of the leaves made her sigh with contentment. In a light voice, she began to hum a favorite song about the woods from her childhood. And then a thought struck her like lightning.

Music! That's what some of those dots reminded her of! They had a pattern, just not one that she'd recognized. As much as she was enjoying her walk, she turned and rushed back to her work to test her theory.

Sam thought hard about how she could go about translating the dots into recognizable music. There was little chance the notation she thought was in the patterns would be the same as modern music notation. But she had to start somewhere. Before she could form a plan, her cell phone received a text.

*5 days. Thanks, I would have forgotten.*

Just then, Bly rang the dinner bell, and Sam composed herself to look as if everything were business as usual. She was quiet during the dinner, but no one remarked on it. Maybe they just thought she was tired, but nothing was further from the truth. She planned to work all night.

The idea she had was to run a few songs through a program she wrote quickly to identify major chords of "modern" music, though she would use the oldest she could find. She began with Arabic music, since the scale was different from European. Her reasoning was that because these plates came from that area, the music probably did, too. And modern music had to have evolved from the ancient.

Her program was designed to do something similar to codebreaking. It charted the notes and chords from most common to least common. Then she copied and modified the translation program to create a new one — this one to sort the data on the nanodots in question in the same way. Once the charts were complete, a third part of her experiment assigned notes to the dots by correlating the two charts.

By morning, she had the first iteration of her experiment ready to "play", using computer-generated music. She'd lost track of time and had forgotten it was 4 a.m. and the others were asleep when the first "song" blared from the computer's speakers.

Scarcely thirty seconds had passed before Carter ran into the room closely followed by Mackenzie. "What is that awful racket?" he shouted.

Sam had been trying to make the music sound like any Arabic music she could remember hearing. There were some resemblances, but when Carter's shout broke her concentration, she realized she needed some refinement of the program.

"I think it's music," she explained sheepishly. "It may need a little work."

"Definitely needs some work, especially if this is going to be our morning wakeup call," Carter mumbled. He smiled to take the sting out. "I need some coffee before I hear that again."

Over a very early breakfast, the four of them, periodically interrupted by Liam's questions, discussed what Sam could do differently to make the sounds something their modern ears wouldn't find too bizarre. Sam pointed out that most Westerners found Asian music jarring, and Arabic or Indian music if not jarring then at least foreign.

"It's the difference in major and minor scale," she said.

"That may be," Carter allowed. "By all means, keep working on it. It would be fascinating to know about their instruments and whether they sang like we do. But don't forget, we need the pictures of the nukes day before yesterday. If there are any of those left to process, the images are most important."

Sam began working on a database that would store the images by subject and cross-reference them by position on the numbered plates. As soon as she had the database designed, she planned to work on code that would recognize certain patterns so the database could be automatically populated. But before she had the database matrix worked out, Carter arrived in the room where she and Mackenzie were working. He was breathless, and his face was redder than Sam had ever seen it.

"Carter! What is it?" Mackenzie was clearly concerned by the way he looked.

"Sam, I'm sorry, but I'm going to have to pull you off the sound files for a while. We've just found a plate . . . Well, here. Read it for yourself."

Sam took the paper he waved at her and began to read, at first to herself, and then aloud as Mackenzie continued to ask what it was. "'. . . had no choice but to disable and confiscate the weapons of mass destruction . . .' Carter, did the translation seriously say that?" she interrupted herself.

"It did! How's that for irony?"

Sam shook her head and continued. "'From the [enemy warmongers]. I am deeply concerned about storing them within our capital, but there is no better place to defend them.' Carter! You've found the nukes!"

"Well, we now know they're out there, and we know where, more or less. But we still don't know where the capital is, or was, located. I need all eyes searching for any clues. Mackie, can you break loose and help Sam scan pictures?"

"Of course, I can, but it seems as if there's something you aren't telling us?"

"I planned to. Just got word from James. There are many ships in the area where we plan to send our expedition. We know the Saudis are in the area, as well as Russians, Chinese, and others. The sooner we find the right place to look, the better. Before one of the others stumbles on it."

"In that case, we need another microscope or two and another body. There are literally thousands of images on each microdot, and we have maybe fifty plates set aside that don't have text on them. That's a lot of scanning," Sam remarked.

"I'll have everything you need here within twenty-four hours," Carter said. "Meanwhile, I think we should move to round-the-clock in three eight-hour shifts. Of course, you'll need to eat and sleep."

"Thanks, boss," Sam said with a wink. "Appreciate a job where there is time to eat and sleep every now and then."

Carter, whose good nature had been suppressed by the alarming news, changed his serious expression for a smile. "Welcome. Don't make me regret it." He winked back.

Sam asked Mackenzie whether she wanted to take the first or second shift. Despite the need for her to get some sleep, she wanted to use the opportunity to work a bit more on her sound-recognition programs. Now that they knew some of the non-text, non-image nanodots contained sound, she was eager to identify them all pull them into a database and find if any were of speech rather than music. What Carter didn't know wouldn't hurt him — at least for the next twenty-four hours. She set her alarm for six hours later and promptly went to sleep, a talent she'd cultivated during her college years.

Sam came awake instantly in response to the soft ping of her cell phone alarm. She was rested and ready to work. She checked on Mackenzie, who said she had another two hours in her if Sam wanted to get something to eat and clear her mind. Ten minutes later, a sandwich in hand, Sam was again at her computer, working on a nanodot that had produced a particularly horrible sound when converted as music.

Her theory was that dot might represent speech instead. Because of the type of language, they'd previously determined, she had a head start on assigning common sounds to the data on the dot. She had only to borrow the chart of what sounds they'd identified in the language, which in turn they'd based on the Semitic languages they'd determined to have sprung from this one. Once again running a common statistical analysis program to analyze the text they'd translated so far and correlating it with the dot patterns, she was able to synthesize the sounds represented. To her delight, an artificial voice started speaking recognizable syllables into her earphones.

By the time Mackenzie turned over the microscope to Sam, the latter had set the computer to automatically synthesize all the relevant dots. She figured there'd be something to show for her work at the end of her image-scanning shift.

When Mackenzie turned up after eight hours of sleep to take over again, Sam checked the computer files. To avoid another incident of jarring noise, she put on earphones to play the files the automation software had created. The first couple were hauntingly beautiful music in the minor keys she expected. The third, however, was a male voice speaking rapidly in a language that sounded to her like the proto-Semitic syllables she'd heard while Carter, Rick, and she were creating the translation software. Eureka! Although it was now midnight, she thought it was important enough to wake anyone who might be sleeping. "Carter!" she called.

Carter had been working still, desperately searching for more of the translation that mentioned the weapons of mass destruction. When Sam shouted, he wasn't aware that Mackenzie had taken over the scanning again, and he rushed in expecting to see an image of an ancient nuke. His disappointment quickly turned to elation when instead Sam played the speech file for him. Even though it was a boring recitation of a crop report, hearing the language he'd been reading for weeks was exciting.

"This is the second breakthrough you've made in as many days. I could kiss you!" Carter shouted.

"No, you couldn't," Mackenzie interjected. "A hug will do, and only one." She smiled.

"I agree. A hug will do," Sam echoed. She winked at Mackenzie.

"All right," Carter said, ignoring the teasing the women were giving him. "Now we need someone who understands the language to come and listen to these files and alert us if anything about the nukes is discussed on any of them."

"The more, the merrier," Mackenzie said. "But where will everyone sleep?"

"Tents if necessary," Carter answered. "Everyone get back to work, and I'll wake up James in a few hours with our latest request. Good job, Sam."

Within a week, Carter had two more electron microscopes and an expert in ancient Semitic languages James had "borrowed" from the University. The borrowing was somewhat traumatic on the elderly Jewish professor, given the rush job of clearing him for top secret information. But once he understood what he was hearing and what he was listening for, he became a wholehearted member of the team. His remark was he'd been through one Holocaust already, and a nuclear one was not on his bucket list.

Everyone settled into a routine now that there was enough equipment to go around and they didn't need to work in shifts anymore. Midnight to six a.m. was for sleeping. First thing each morning, Carter and Mackenzie had their training session with the Executive Advantage team, while the others each pursued their favorite exercise — which for some was a stroll in nature and for some it was sleeping another 30 minutes. Then they all met for breakfast where they discussed their progress and the day's goals. There were lunch and dinner breaks, but on average the work consumed more than twelve hours of each day.

Carter was convinced they were under a deadline. The only problem was they didn't *know* the date. A lot like someone on death row waiting for the day of execution. Despite the interesting work, no one was free of the pressure of knowing their efforts might well be the difference between a world at peace and a world at war. Or more precisely, a world annihilated by ancient nuclear weapons.

## Chapter Forty-Nine

DOLPHINESE

It was on the third day after he arrived that Professor Wasserman had a question for Sam.

"I understand, young lady, that you are responsible for the sound synthesis of these files I'm listening to. Is that right?"

Sam smiled. "It is. Did you have a question about them?"

"Yes," he answered. "What is the meaning of the squeaks and whistles in the files? These are not sounds I recognize as part of the language."

"Squeaks and whistles? I'm not sure what you mean."

"Please, come and listen. I will put it on speaker."

Sam smiled again. The professor must be an octogenarian, yet he said things like "on speaker" as if he were part of her generation. She waited for him to queue up the file and listened in astonishment as the voice pronouncing the familiar sounds of the language was interspersed with, exactly as he'd described, squeaks, whistles, and other sounds, like hoots, similar to electronic beeps, and others.

"I have no idea what that is," she said slowly. "I'll have to check the original dots and see if they've been corrupted."

Sam took the time to notify Carter, and while she examined the dot that corresponded to the file in question, Carter, Mackenzie, and Liu all listened to the odd sounds.

"That sounds familiar," said Liu. "I can't quite place it."

Just then, a series of high pitched squeaks that sounded like "ack, ack, ack," followed by chittering noises comparable to a chimpanzee's laugh came through the speakers.

"I know! It's dolphins!" Liu clapped her hands in delight that she'd remembered. "I used to hear them on my parents' boat. When we would go fishing, sometimes the dolphins would come and beg for scraps of our catch."

Mackenzie looked at her strangely. "That's interesting. How did you know they were begging?"

"Oh, by their body language, and they always made the same sounds. They'd come upright and halfway out of the water, and lurch backwards like they wanted us to throw something. And they made the same sounds every time."

"You sound almost like you could communicate with them, Liu."

"It seemed like we could. At least, we thought we knew what they wanted. And when we threw them some, they'd make something like a bow, and a different sound, and then they'd swim away."

"Remarkable," muttered Carter, who was still attuned to the squeaks and other sounds. "Is it possible that person talking there and the dolphin were having a conversation?"

"That's it!" Mackenzie cried. "I'll bet anything they were. It's been proven they communicate in a language we don't understand yet, and that they are self-aware, and even have names!"

"Well, having names sounds a bit rich to me, but it certainly seems this female giant and a dolphin were having a conversation," Carter marveled. "So maybe at one time humans *did* understand dolphins and vice versa. How can we verify this is indeed the case?"

"I can check the wavelength, frequency, and patterns and confirm if the sounds are within the dolphin audio spectrum," Samantha volunteered.

"It is, I'm sure," Mackenzie and Liu said, almost in unison.

Carter said he would ask Professor Wasserman to spend some time translating the parts of the file that were uttered by the giant in her language, and that would give them some idea of what the "conversation" was about. He was still having trouble wrapping his mind around the real possibility that a giant and a dolphin were conversing. "What if it's just some giant mimicking a dolphin?" he asked.

"I'd just about guarantee it isn't," said Mackenzie. "But there's an easy way to find out. Dolphin sounds are in a much broader range of the audio spectrum than we have. Sounds we can't even hear. We need to get some sound analysis of these files going, and see if there's anything recorded that we can't hear. If there is, we can be certain it's genuinely dolphins, speaking genuine Dolphinese."

"Maybe there's something about it in the index of the text files," Sam suggested. "I could write a search routine and find it pretty fast."

"People, we have our work cut out for us. Sam, nukes first, then dolphins.

"Liu, I need you to help me with the text translations as soon as Sam has identified them.

"Mackie, you have an interest in dolphin intelligence. Could you put together a white paper on how this communication could be possible, including any references you think relevant?

"Professor Wasserman, would you translate the conversation on this file and on any others like it you can find, and work with Sam to try to figure out the dolphin language, if this is indeed a conversation? After she finds the references, that is. Translation first, then analysis."

Each person agreed to their assignments and went to work immediately, paying no attention to the fact they'd only had two hours' sleep. A bombshell of this nature was a remarkable energizer.

Carter experienced a twinge of uneasiness but kept it to himself. He'd discovered some controversial stuff in his time and had always been able to back it up with fact. This . . . whatever it was . . . interspecies communication, might be the most controversial discovery of his career. There was no doubt that, although it took his entire research team to make and verify the discovery, it would be his reputation on the line when they announced it. If they *were ever allowed to* announce it. His imagination was running wild with the implications.

What if they could send dolphins to explore under the water and never had to mount a dangerous expedition until they knew exactly where to look? What if the dolphins would know where that city was, help them find those nukes? He brought himself up short. There was still a lot of work to do before any of those things would be possible. He had to stop chasing squirrels and focus on the most important thing — finding those nukes before someone else did. But still, wouldn't it be cool if they had dolphins as allies?

Meanwhile, Liu and Sam were chattering like magpies about the wonder of it all with Mackenzie listening. Interspecies communication, proven and demonstrated for the first time! And if the dolphin language of today was the same or similar to that of fifty thousand years ago, maybe they themselves could talk to another species for another first!

"Not for the first time," Mackenzie pointed out. "What about my wolves, and Jeha with Liam? We've had this conversation before. The more we experiment and learn, the more I'm convinced that many species of animals are just as intelligent as we are, and some are more so in some ways. We should approach this as if we fully believe the giants, whom we know have been far more advanced than we are now, and the dolphins could communicate and collaborate. Stranger things have been proven true."

"Your wolves?" Sam asked. Of course, she'd seen the wolves on occasion, but she hadn't been told about their behavior during the time Mackenzie and Liu had been captives of Algosaibi. While Mackenzie made a list of the subjects she wanted articles for from A-Echelon, since her computer would not be connected to the Internet, Liu filled Sam in on the case of the clairvoyant wolves.

When she'd finished, Sam whistled, a low sound of astonishment. "That is the coolest thing I've ever heard," she said.

"Stick around, and you'll hear a lot more," Liu assured her. "It's like Shakespeare said in Hamlet, 'There are more things in heaven and earth, Samantha, than are dreamt of in your philosophy.'"

"Hmm, I'm pretty sure that was Horatio Hamlet was talking to, not me," Samantha said, laughing. "But I get your point."

## Chapter Fifty

### HOLD ONTO YOUR SKIVVIES

At dinner, a few days later, Mackenzie couldn't wait to share some of her research about dolphins. So much of it confirmed what she'd always believed or suspected. Even people who didn't know much about dolphins usually knew there were legends about people riding on them or them rescuing humans in trouble. The enormous data dump about dolphins she got from A-Echelon, contained several documented stories about individual rescues, including one where three dolphins put themselves between a man who'd been swimming with them and a Great White shark, protecting him until he could be rescued by fellow sailors.

"That's remarkable," Sam said. "Don't Great Whites prey on dolphins?"

"Well, yes, presumably. But full-grown dolphins aren't easy to prey on. They are more intelligent than sharks and have been proven to strategize and cooperate in many pursuits. Attacking sharks is one of them. Dolphins will ram them in the gills to try to kill them. In this case, the shark eventually gave up and left the area. I guess it was smart enough to know that the human the dolphins were protecting wasn't worth the price of the meal." Mackenzie laughed.

"There are so many stories about dolphins interacting with humans. Do you remember in the news not long ago, a dolphin came and asked a diver for help with a hook and some fishing line?" Liu asked.

"Oh, yes, and I watched that video today. It was amazing. The dolphin stayed close to the diver and remained very calm as he removed the hook from its fin and used scissors to remove as much of the line as he could. And then it just swam away. I'll tell you, from everything I had already read, I almost expected it to say 'thank you' and tip its hat."

"What else, Mackenzie?" Liu asked, very keen to hear more.

"Well, I've confirmed that they 'talk' among themselves. Scientists have identified bursts of sound that may represent sentences. They're polite, too. They don't talk over each other. One dolphin makes sounds, and then another responds. So, my belief that they communicate complex ideas and instructions isn't farfetched. Oh, and they do have 'names.'" She looked at Carter. "Or rather, a unique whistle that identifies them to others."

"That's wild," Carter remarked with a smile.

"Not as wild as this. We know already that they exhibit a real interest in interacting with us. Did you know they can solve problems? And that they may consider solving puzzles that humans set as a fun game to play with us?"

"Seriously?"

"Yes! There are some interesting studies going on that the marine biologists who designed them think may indicate dolphins can actually count, add, and subtract."

"No way!"

"Yes, it's true. The tests are simple. They give the dolphins several objects, something to play with, like buoyant objects they can push around and toss to one another. Then they take some away and hide them underneath or behind barriers in the pool. Every time, the dolphins go looking for the missing ones. And they keep looking until they find all of them."

"Amazing!"

"Did you know the Navy has been training them to do underwater missions since 1978? We really should talk to some of those trainers about it. Although I don't know if I could deal with it if I found out the missions were dangerous. From what I'm learning, if they do suicide missions, like placing mines on enemy ships, it would be just like sending a human to do it."

Carter took Mackenzie's hand. "Mackie, you know that sometimes a human does have to do something like that. I'm sure the Navy doesn't lightly risk a valuable asset, whether human or dolphin, without a damn good reason."

"Still. They are such beautiful and gentle creatures. What if they just want to please us, like dogs do? And then we send them all unknowingly to do something that could kill them."

"Mackenzie, if what you're saying about communication is true, don't you think they tell each other what the consequences may be?" Liu's thoughtful expression and tone made the others stop and consider it.

Mackenzie finally answered. "You may be right." She continued. There's also evidence that young dolphins learn in groups that we might call a school in the human sense of the word. Maybe they're taking safety classes or even history." She spoke lightly, as if making a joke, but the others could tell she believed it. She'd been pulling dozens of articles and scholarly research together all day, they didn't doubt she had a valid idea.

Mackenzie brightened with her next revelation. "They have a sense of humor, too. I watched a video several times that showed a dolphin in an aquarium watching a girl turn cartwheels. When she went over, the dolphin would circle its head and then, I swear, it would smile or laugh. The sound didn't include any noise the dolphin was making, but you could just tell it was delighted by the unexpected behavior."

"You're convinced they have emotion, then?" Carter asked.

"Oh, of course! I mean, they aren't the only animals that do. It stands to reason that as one of the three most intelligent species, they'd have developed emotion. They seem to grieve when one dies, especially the mothers of young calves that don't make it. But elephants, apes, even dogs do that. It takes a highly-evolved animal, and in fact a self-aware one, to have humor. In fact, I read a quote from a psychologist saying something to the effect that he defines humor as seeing improbable connections in the mind. That's what makes a joke funny. You're not expecting it, and then suddenly . . . bang! It comes from the ability to put very strange, often illogical things together."

"So, you're saying that when a dolphin sees something that doesn't fit with its prior knowledge, it could find humor in that?"

"I guess. We'd have to ask them, wouldn't we?"

"Mackie, you sound as if you're pretty sure we are going to have a chat with the dolphins soon." Carter chuckled.

Mackenzie's comment made the others laugh, too.

"See, that kind of proves my point." She said. "You all thought asking the dolphins was illogical, so you laughed. But I think we could actually do it — if someone were to study it long enough. Maybe we'd better bring on a marine biology PhD candidate in search of a dissertation topic."

Carter sighed. "We've already got half of the University here. Not long before we'll open the University of Freydís. Not that Professor Wasserman and Liu are unwelcome.

"Nevertheless, I think your idea about consulting the Navy is a good one. Is there anything else you learned that we should know about tonight?"

"There's so much to tell! But I'll be pulling it all together in a PowerPoint presentation with videos and sound embedded. I can probably contain my enthusiasm until I'm done . . . It will be better organized."

"That sounds good. Let's call it 'Hold Onto Your Skivvies: Interspecies Communiqués'."

Mackenzie aimed a playful punch at Carter, and when the laugher receded, he asked, "Anyone have any questions before we move on?"

"I do," answered Professor Wasserman. "Have the scientists who discovered they talk among themselves discovered any of the meanings of the sounds?"

"A few, tentatively. I don't think there's a serious effort to document an actual language, though. That's where your assignment comes in. If we can understand the conversation from the giants' side, then maybe we can begin to interpret the dolphin language as well. Because dolphins do listen to each other and respond, the back and forth nature of those files with Giantese and Dolphinese together leads me to believe they are indeed having a conversation. We just need to figure out how, and what they were talking about."

"That's the million-dollar question," Carter concluded. "And I'd give just about that to find out they were talking about the nukes."

Everyone at the table laughed, but Carter was serious.

In fact, he'd give his entire fortune to discover that the ancient dolphins had communicated with the giants about those nukes, and that they'd passed the knowledge of where they were down through the generations. If Mackie was right about those history lessons, why not believe they also remembered that?

A few hours later, as they prepared for bed, Mackenzie whispered to Carter, "Did you know dolphins also have sex for pleasure?"

"And you're telling me this, why?" Carter asked with a mischievous smile.

"Well, I think we've been working too hard . . ."

## Chapter Fifty-One

### EVERYTHING YOU THOUGHT YOU KNEW

It didn't take long for Sam's algorithms to find references to the translation device the group knew *had* to have existed if humans and dolphins were to talk. In fact, they found the plans for it almost as quickly as they confirmed it was real. By then, the idea of interspecies communication was not a matter of belief and speculation anymore, it was a foregone conclusion. That didn't keep them each from experiencing a sense of unreality and heart-pounding excitement whenever the thought hit them.

Meanwhile, Mackenzie had uncovered even more facts about dolphins, such as the growing controversy surrounding dolphin therapy. Some people swore that the dolphins were somehow healing people, even mental or emotional disorders, by some sort of supersonic communication. Others maintained that any pet therapy could produce the same results, without the New Age mumbo-jumbo, and that keeping dolphins confined for such a purpose was cruel.

The discovery that there was indeed a translation device

that they could duplicate energized everyone. It also solidified the notion that they should talk to the Navy about it, but there were some barriers. The Navy's use of dolphins was for the most part classified, and their own project was above top secret as well. To bring the parties together to share information was going to require some high-level intervention and mutual vetting.

It was no surprise then that the Navy, when approached with the idea by James Rhodes, wasn't keen to share their secrets. They would have been singing a different tune if they knew what James knew, but he was not authorized to share it with them — at least not yet. When James reported that the Navy wasn't on board with sharing information, Mackenzie almost had a melt-down.

"I knew it! Those bastards are endangering the dolphins. That's why they don't want to tell us. We have to get through to them that it isn't okay," she pleaded. In fact, she'd already uncovered allegations that they were being deployed in waters that were too cold for them and were also trained for kamikaze missions to destroy enemy ships. Other revelations were that they were being used to guard harbors against human invasion from underwater and to guard nuclear sites.

Carter could swear that Mackenzie's red hair was about to explode into flames while she was ranting.

Mackenzie was so distraught that a visit from the wolves made her realize she had to calm down. In broad daylight, they appeared and paced nervously around the cabin until she went out and soothed them. "I'm all right," she crooned to them, but only the touch of her hand reassured them enough to leave.

"Mackie, if you're going to be involved in the discussions with the Navy, can you avoid calling them bastards?"

Despite the droll question, Carter was serious. They all, A-Echelon, the military, and the top security agencies, had to be on the same page on this issue.

"I can do my best," she replied. "But I'd better not find out they've ever harmed a single one of these creatures. The Navy has denied these allegations. If I find out they're lying, I'm going to kick some butt."

The mental picture of his Mackie kicking an admiral's butt sent Carter into raucous laughter. "I'd like to see that!" Sobering, he went on. "I've got my own doubts, Mackie. There are already a lot of people who know about this. And while I trust all our colleagues who are here, it takes only one unguarded moment to bring utter chaos. Can you imagine what would happen if the Nabateans got hold of this information? That there exists a library from the ancients with the plans for an interspecies communication device? Never mind all the rest of it. Forget about the Nabateans for a moment, do you think there is a country on earth who wouldn't want to have this for themselves? We'd have to stave off an armed invasion."

"Believe me, I understand," Mackenzie said. "I just don't want anyone to hurt these beautiful animals. But I understand that what we have here is revolutionary. It's pretty much an 'everything you thought you knew is wrong' situation. It's mindboggling, and we haven't even scratched the surface. So, what's next?"

"Well, we have to get Bill involved if we want to talk to the Navy, and I think we have to. Of course, that means the President. James and Irene, too. I'd say we're in for several days' briefing and debriefing at the very least. Do you have your presentation ready?"

"Yes, just a few last-minute details need to be added. I'll be ready as soon as you can set up the meeting."

"I'll hold you to that. Give me forty-eight hours."

Carter sent James an encoded message that they needed to have a face-to-face meeting and then went to notify Dylan that he, Mackenzie, and some of the team would soon be leaving the safety of Freydís for a few days. He wasn't looking forward to it, especially since it meant leaving Liam and Beth behind. He'd miss them. But risking their safety wasn't an option. They'd be much safer here with their grandparents and Bly and Ahote.

## Chapter Fifty-Two

### WE CAN TALK TO THEM!

To say that the Navy top brass who were present were blown away by Mackenzie's presentation would be an exaggeration. In fact, they didn't have anything complimentary to say at all. They called it a bunch of anecdotal claptrap and waved off the scholarly papers and studies she'd cited, saying they were nothing new. She barely kept her temper in check as she whispered fiercely to Carter, "Make them listen."

Carter wasn't in too forgiving a mood when it was his turn to show what they'd found in the giants' library. No one treated his Mackie that way. Consequently, he didn't give much background on what they were about to hear and see before going straight to his presentation. He watched with satisfaction as the dim light in the room revealed how all but a few diehard Navy officers in the audience dropped their jaws.

His presentation consisted of still images of the giants in their cities, some in the City of Lights to provide a sense of scale, and some of the giants on quays or docks in attitudes

## The Alboran Codex

of conversation with what were clearly bottlenose dolphins. The kicker was when he played the sound files of Giantese interspersed with the characteristic squeaks and whistles of the dolphins. Although they found the images convincing, a few were still holdouts on the conversations, some even openly accusing Carter of a hoax.

However, when Professor Wasserman, whose reputation was well-known and impeccable, gave *his* presentation, even the holdouts couldn't deny it any longer.

"Exactly what do you want us to do with this information?" asked the Chief of Naval Operations, who'd insisted on being present for the exchange of classified information.

"We'd like the cooperation of your dolphin project personnel in turning over anything they think could help us in our studies. We may also want to interact with your dolphins, both youngsters that haven't been conditioned or trained yet and veterans that have. In return, whatever we learn about dolphin language and the plans for the communications device we'll share with you."

"Fair enough." The Chief of Naval Operations replied but just because he had orders from the President to cooperate. "But anyone in your group *must* have Top Secret Clearance first."

The Chief of Naval Operations was stumped when Carter grinned and said, "which all of us already have, but any of *your* personnel will need Level Q Clearance in addition to *their* Top Secret Clearance."

Startled, the admiral sent Carter a questioning look. Carter in turn looked at James Rhodes, who answered the admiral's unspoken question. "What the dolphins may be able to tell us will require that level of clearance, unfortunately I can't tell you more until you *have* that clearance."

Q-type clearance was a Department of Energy (DOE)

security clearance required for access to Top Secret, Secret Restricted Data, and DOE "security" areas, the highest-risk sensitivity levels in the country. People with these clearances held exceptional accountability because of the potential to cause grave and immeasurable damage to the national security of the United States. It was required for anyone with access to "SIN-widee," CNWDI (Critical Nuclear Weapon Design Information).

Mackenzie tried her best not to grin with satisfaction.

A very unsettled admiral decided not to delve any deeper and left the gathering just before the Freydís group and the excited Navy dolphin scientists began an informal discussion among themselves, while enjoying a catered lunch. It didn't take long before the two groups came to consensus that a translation device should be built at once.

"Of course, you realize," Professor Wasserman began in his classroom voice, "the giants weren't speaking English, but rather a proto-Semitic language we've only just begun to translate. We have a great deal of work to do to program the device so that the dolphins can understand us."

"We've observed the older ones teaching the young ones," one of the marine biologists said. "Not everyone agreed with our superior officers dismissing your presentation, Mrs. Devereux. You did a great job of pulling together nearly everything we know and then some."

Mackenzie was still fuming about the treatment she received earlier and was on the verge of telling him to address her as doctor when Carter winked at her, reading her feelings perfectly. "Can we all dispense with the titles and just go on a first-name basis? We're on the same page now, yes?"

The Navy personnel quickly agreed it would be much simpler. Several of them realized that if they wanted to be in on one of the greatest scientific leaps of humankind, they'd better apply for Q Clearance immediately.

---

Within a few weeks, Professor Wasserman had translated enough of the conversations to be able to work with Sam and Rick to build a database of equivalent English words. A DARPA engineer was tapped to build the device and soon it only remained to work with the dolphins to begin the process of understanding their sounds and map it to English words so the databases could be populated.

After that, the sophisticated sound synthesis engineering within the device would allow actual conversations. Mackenzie was in a constant state of jubilation that the creatures she'd loved and admired all her life might soon become true friends.

As soon as the device was ready and programmed with as many of the words as they could be sure of, Carter made the arrangements for himself, Mackenzie, Sam, Liu, and the directors of A-Echelon, James, and his second-in-command, Irene, to meet with the head of the Navy's dolphin project, and of course, with the dolphins themselves. On hand, would also be Lieutenant Gerald Hooper, Gerry to his friends, who worked directly with the dolphins.

The Freydís group and their Executive Advantage security detail arrived in San Diego by chartered jet early in the afternoon. With a pang, Mackenzie thought about how much Liam would have loved to see the dolphins. Even baby Beth, loved animals. Both had been raised with the benevolent wolves in attendance, and with childlike faith in the goodness of all living creatures, approached all the wildlife on the ranch with arms wide open. Liam, Shane,

John and Jennie Ruschin's boy, and Jeha had already learned that skunks didn't particularly appreciate human friendship. Especially when they were frightened or startled.

The group followed Gerry straight to the training pool. He had done his best to prepare his dolphins, because they were going to listen in on the trained dolphins' "chatter" first. Gerry had always believed the dolphins understood his full English sentences at least as well as dogs would, so he'd told them that there would be some visitors there to listen to them talk, and they should feel free to talk about whatever was on their minds. Nevertheless, he made sure he was alone when he did it.

"Folks, I'd like you to meet John and Jason, our pair-bonded males. You know of course, about dolphin social structure?"

As Mackenzie started to say yes, Carter also spoke. "Some of us are more familiar than others. Why don't you go ahead and explain?"

"All right. Well, pods of dolphins are what you might call ad hoc groups. They get together for certain purposes and later disband and gather for other purposes. However, the males tend to pair up as sort of best friends, and a pair-bonded duo will do everything together. As far as we know, that's a lifetime bond. Groups of females also hang out together, and since it's a matriarchal society, you'll find them helping each other with the calves when they're newborns, teaching the older, immature ones in groups, and cooperating in hunting. In fact, mixed pods will do the latter or come together for protection. Dolphins also socialize by mating, and we think they and the apes are the only other animals, besides humans, who have sex for pleasure."

Gerry's fair skin was a bit pink as he said the last

sentence, and he sent an apologetic glance at Mackenzie and the other ladies present. She nudged Carter.

"Okay," Carter said, studiously looking anywhere but at his wife. "So here we have John and Jason." He noticed the two dolphins were close to the edge of the pool and could almost imagine them eavesdropping. Evidently, they were more mature than humans, since they hadn't appeared to be as amused as Mackenzie by the lieutenant's discomfort. A few feet away but also close to the edge, several other dolphins swam back and forth in a tight arc. "And who are these lovely ladies?"

Gerry named the females, Nola, Jewel, Jessie, Michele, Bess, and Dakota, and then explained their complex relationships. Nola was the only one not born within the program. She had been rescued by a Coast Guard patrol some twenty years before after a shark attack had left one fin dangling from her body, useless. Today, she had a prosthetic attachment that replaced the part of her fin that had to be amputated. She didn't seem to notice it wasn't part of her. Jonah and Jewel were her offspring by the same sire, and Bess by a different male. Jessie had been born to another captive dolphin at Sea World, as had Jason and Michele, the latter to a different dam. Dakota was Bess's half-sister, through their sire.

"Is there going to be a test later?" quipped James, whose head was spinning.

Irene muttered, "Lord, I hope not!"

Gerry smiled. "You'll get to know them and be able to tell them apart soon. I can tell you that from experience. They've all been in the program longer than me."

Carter, who'd been given detailed instructions by the engineer who constructed the translation device, programmed it to recognize each one by asking Gerry to have them "speak".

"To tell you the truth, each sound they make, whether a hoot, whistle, or squeak, sounds different to me, but I can't tell the difference between two whistles, for example, or two hoots." Gerry said.

This time Mackenzie did dissolve in laughter. The bewildered lieutenant gave her a look, and she explained, "So the dolphins do give two hoots?"

Carter shook his head. "You've been around me too long, Mackie."

After that bit of silliness, they got down to business. For now, they wouldn't try to speak to the dolphins. Gerry showed the dolphins pictures, and Sam made a notation of which picture was being shown each time one of the dolphins vocalized. They noticed that it was usually Nola who responded to the pictures, but occasionally one of the younger dolphins would also respond. Everyone found it fascinating that the sounds were similar in those cases.

What they didn't recognize was that when pictures of different items of the same objects were shown, the dolphin sounds were the same. Mostly this was because these pictures weren't shown in succession, but were all mixed up. In this way, they hoped to verify that the dolphins were indeed recognizing and "naming" objects, rather than just making random noises. It would take careful analysis of the sounds on the track to distinguish the noises and map them to the pictures.

Most puzzling was the times when the dolphins opened their mouths, but no sound was emitted. Until Mackenzie reminded them that dolphins could make sounds humans couldn't hear. Then they could only hope the device was recording them, and they'd be able to use various devices to measure the properties of the sounds and assign words to them. That was when Sam asked Gerry to show the pictures again that the dolphins had reacted to but no sound was heard. This time she notated every reaction and the picture that caused it. This was going to be more complicated than she'd thought.

After several hours and dozens of pictures, the dolphins signaled that they were tired of this game by swimming away. Bowing to the unmistakable withdrawal of cooperation, the Freydís group retired to on-base accommodations to spend the night. They were all exhausted by that time anyway, as jet lag caught up to them.

In the morning, Sam, Liu, James, and Irene stayed behind to see what they could learn about the first experiment, while Carter and Mackenzie met with the commander in charge of the project to arrange for future visits.

First Sam fed the sounds into the database along with the pictures that went with them. While uploading the sound files wasn't difficult, identifying the beginning and end of each sound required careful comparison on a sine-wave chart. Especially when more than one of the creatures got involved in the conversation. Liu, James, and Irene provided extra sets of eyes, with Sam both teaching them what to look for and verifying their work.

At the beginning of the recording, there was quite a bit of chatting among the dolphins. Sam would have given a pretty penny to know what they were saying. Maybe someday they would.

The first breakthrough came when she located identical words for images of various people, not only pictures of the individuals involved in the experiment, but those of random people, and even a couple of silhouettes with no features visible. Every time an image of a human was shown, Nola made the same sound. The first translated word in the database was "human". The next was "ball", and then as they distinguished "word" after "word", it was time to declare the experiment a success.

Sam was afforded the honor of telling Carter, Mackenzie, and Gerry. "Guys! We've done it! We know the words for human, ball, fish, bucket, and a whole bunch of others! We can talk to them!"

While everyone was excited and in fact elated, giving high-fives all around, it was nothing short of what Mackenzie had expected all along. She hugged Liu, and whispered, "I never would have thought this possible before hearing those sound files."

Liu had been overcome with emotion most of the morning. All she could do was cling to Mackenzie and nod. "When are we going to try to talk back to them?" she asked.

"We have more work to do before we attempt that. Today, we're going to try to show them images that convey action and abstracts," Mackenzie answered. "Only then will we be able to get ideas across. Let's see what comes of today's work before we schedule a talk-back with them."

In fact, no one, not even Gerry, knew whether the dolphins would cooperate today. And it seemed they weren't in the mood, as they insisted on playing hide and seek for about half an hour before they would come to the side and look at the pictures.

Now the pictures were of people in action, like running, swimming, eating, and so on. In the afternoon, there were pictures of humans hugging and dolphins swimming close together and other images meant to evoke abstract concepts like love, help, arguments, and more. The dolphins again cooperated for several hours and then signaled they were done. Interestingly, it was about the same time in the afternoon when they swam away from the humans.

"I wonder how they know it's quitting time?" Carter asked. It was a rhetorical question, but Gerry answered it in all seriousness.

"Probably the changing quality of the light," he answered. "We can never get them to do anything after five o'clock."

"I'll be damned. Do they have a union?"

Once again, the earnest young lieutenant was caught short by Carter's joke. When he failed to laugh, Carter decided some people just had no sense of humor.

As it turned out, though, they discovered the dolphins did. Of course, Mackenzie had *known* it, but there was no question in anyone's mind now. The dolphins had the same sound-wave reaction to a picture of a child being tickled as to one of a dolphin hiding from a human. Even more interesting, they had the same reaction to a picture of a human running as they did to a dolphin with a shark in the same picture.

"What word should I assign to that?" Sam wondered. "I don't get it."

Mackenzie and Carter were observing the process, and Mackenzie answered. "Fear. But I wonder what they've seen that makes them think a running human is afraid? Like they are, of the shark, I mean."

It was an interesting enough phenomenon that they called Gerry to come and brainstorm with them. He supplied the answer. "Oh. I don't think they've ever seen anyone running, except the time when Dakota was trapped underwater by an obstacle that came loose from its moorings. The others were trying to lift her so she could breathe, and one of the other trainers and I had to run from one of the other pools to get to her in time. We could hear the commotion in here, and it sounded like they were all very agitated. When we saw what was happening, we dived in and lifted the obstacle so she could get to the surface, it was a close call. They can only stay under water for about fifteen to seventeen minutes."

"That has to be it. Wow. Can we do an experiment tomorrow? Can you run from one end of the poolside to another, and let us record any vocalizations they make?" Mackenzie asked. Mentally, she noted they weren't using the word "noises" anymore. The sounds the dolphins were making were words, if not sentences. Vocalizations was a much better word than noises. And in fact, they should be calling the dolphins people, because it was beyond doubt that they were sentient. Tomorrow's experiment would also determine whether they could identify their emotions. She almost hated to do it, because she was certain some of the emotions they would evoke weren't pleasant.

Each of the planned experiments and the added one Mackenzie had requested went exactly as she thought they would. When Gerry ran from one end of the pool to the other, the dolphins made the same sounds of distress that they did when shown a picture of a dead orca on a beach.

That idea had come from one of the stories Mackenzie had collected during her research. It seemed a pod of orcas had been caught by low tide, and while people did their best to keep the beautiful creatures alive until high tide could lift them, the orcas were too distressed and confused to swim in the right direction by then. To the amazement of the onlookers, a pod of dolphins had swum in, nudging the orcas and then leading them out into the deeper water at considerable risk to themselves.

Mackenzie wondered two things. Were these captive

dolphins as compassionate as those wild ones had been, and did the younger ones know what an orca was? The answer was a resounding yes to both questions. And the latter one proved that Nola had indeed been teaching the younger ones, because they had never seen an orca in their lives, despite a pod of them living in a different pool on the same base.

How did she do it?

## Chapter Fifty-Three

SIR, I NEED A BOAT

Back at Freydís, everyone worked together to translate what they could of the random conversations the dolphins had had among themselves, as well as to upload both the sounds and the images of the sound waves to the main database. They made sure to indicate the dolphins' unique sound to identify everyone, and programmed the database with the individuals' names associated with their unique sound. When they could string a few words together, they got snippets that sounded like broken English from a foreign speaker: Human . . . play. Give food . . . fish. Sad . . . give food. Happy/funny Nola play . . . ball. Sad . . . human fear.

Strangest was they didn't seem to differentiate between humans and dolphins when they said "human". After an intense brainstorming session, the Freydís group substituted "person" for human in the database — and it meant an individual, whether dolphin or human. Mackenzie's thought had been validated.

Carter was choked with emotion when he made the pronouncement they all knew to be true. "We are no longer alone as intelligent beings on this planet. My God, what can they teach us?"

Clearly, this news had to be conveyed to the President immediately. Because they had no code that could contain the enormity of what they'd discovered, Carter and Mackenzie left the others to continue the work while Carter flew the two of them to D.C. James and Irene met them at the private airport, with some idea of what they had to say but curious as to the extent of it.

"You're not going to believe it," was all Mackenzie would say. No amount of cajoling on the way to the White House would move Carter, either. They had to wait until they heard it along with the President. To Carter's delight, the President had taken it on himself to invite Bill, to hear the news as well.

With the entire group expressing surprise in every way from "you've got to be kidding me" to "shit, no way", Carter and Mackenzie told what they'd discovered. The President managed to keep his remarks politically correct when he asked what the next experiment would be.

"Well, we can stop calling them experiments. That's insulting, when we're talking about intelligent beings with a sophisticated language we've only just begun to understand. I'd rather call it interspecies diplomatic relations." Mackenzie beamed.

"All right, call it that. In that case, I should name one of you ambassador to the dolphins. Or should it be 'Dolphins,' with a capital D?" he asked, making air quotes with his hands.

"I think that's all got to be worked out, and we don't even know enough about them to know if they have a worldwide organization, or only work in their relatively small pods. First things first, though. We must discover if we can reproduce some of their ultrasonic sounds well enough for them to understand us. So, the next encounter will be us trying to speak to them," Carter said.

"This I've got to see," said the President. "Keep me posted. I'll meet you in San Diego any time. Just give me a couple of days to clear my calendar."

"Yes, sir, of course," Carter agreed.

A week later, the same group, with the addition of the President and his Secret Service entourage, met again with a nervous and overwhelmed Lieutenant Gerry Hooper — so nervous he didn't know whether to salute or offer to shake hands. The President helped him by saluting first, against protocol, but the President was a compassionate and informal man. He didn't mind.

"Let's see these remarkable marine people you work with," he said, after a flustered Gerry returned his salute. "I can't wait to meet them."

"Marine people, sir?" Gerry repeated.

"Hasn't Carter filled you in? The Dolphins call themselves people with the same word they use for humans."

"You're kidding!" Gerry exclaimed. And then flushed. "Sir."

"That's what they tell me. Carter, why haven't you filled this young man in?"

"Classified, sir, and no way to code it. This is the first time we've been back. Same reason we told you in person."

"Oh, well, that makes sense. Anyway, I'd like to meet them."

This time, Carter carried a modified version of the device. If it worked correctly, he could speak into a microphone, and the device would translate and broadcast dolphinese to the pod. Furthermore, its programming now included the AI routines that would allow it to learn and refine the translations on the fly.

Before he spoke to them, though, Gerry went through the same introductions of the seven dolphins to the President as he'd given Carter's group before. The dolphins had gathered as before at the side of the pool. This time, Gerry had told them an important person was coming to visit them. Unbeknownst to the humans, the dolphins understood quite a few English words, including the gist of what Gerry said to them. All the dolphins identified the different person right away. They were silent, waiting for whatever the humans intended to do.

Carter was more nervous than he'd thought he would be when he prepared to speak to them. What if it was all a fluke? What if the dolphins didn't respond to his speech at all? Mackenzie gave him an encouraging pat on the hand. "Go for it, Carter. You'll do great."

Carter cleared his throat and then spoke into the mic. "Hello. We humans hope you can understand us. We want to talk to you, and we want to be friends."

At first, the Dolphins thrust their upper bodies out of the water and twisted their heads, looking for all the world like curious dogs do when they hear a sound they don't recognize. Then they all raced to the underwater speaker where the translated dolphinese broadcast Carter's words. Nola gently bumped the speaker, and then lifted above water, looked at the humans, and chittered. Carter interpreted it to mean "play it again, Sam", and directed her to do so. Sam fiddled with the file for a moment, adding "Nola" to "hello," and played it back.

They all saw Nola's mouth open as if in astonishment, and Sam yanked the earphones away. "Wow, that excited her." She turned a knob and a cacophony of high-pitched vocalizations emerged from the speakers, prompting some of the listeners to clap their hands over their ears.

"What in God's name?" cried the President. Sam turned the knob back and the speakers fell silent.

"We've assigned some high-pitched sounds we *can* hear to their supersonic sounds," she said, a bit sheepishly. "Sorry about your ears, sir. It seems they're excited."

Indeed, the Dolphins were swimming in circles, and when Sam again made the sounds audible, this time at a lower volume, the device was attempting to translate but getting the words all jumbled. The only thing they could make out was "happy, happy, happy", along with the names of the Dolphins.

Mackenzie grabbed the mic. "Please. One at a time. We can't understand."

This time, Nola spoke to her pod. "Silence. Nola talk." Everyone's mouth was wide open as they heard, for the first time in real time, a Dolphin talking to another Dolphin. They continued to stare in awe as Nola swam toward them while the rest hung back. "So, that's what she was saying in the first recording," Sam muttered. No one else heard her. They were too busy being astonished by what they heard from the speakers."

"Nola. Nola. Talk. Friends. Talk more. You . . . name. Sun head."

"Uh, oh," said Carter. "We've jumped the gun. I don't have a clue—"

"She's asking my name," said Mackenzie in awe. "My hair. She's talking about my red hair. But they don't really understand hair, I think." She said, "My name is Mackenzie."

Nola gave an unidentified whistle and then said, "Sun head. [whistle]"

## The Alboran Codex

Sam quickly looked at the sine wave for the whistle after "sun head" and compared it to the first one. "She's named you in their language. That whistle means Mackenzie."

Nola identified each person as well as she could, asking for each name. Some of her remarks were less than flattering, they noticed, as she used "You. Ball head. Name" while noticeably staring at the bald, somewhat rotund President. His reply translated as "Leader", they discovered, when she laughed.

"Leader, ball head. Sun head female. Mackenzie beautiful. Mackenzie leader sun head."

"Well, I guess I've been put in my place," said the President, laughing. "I have to agree. Mackenzie's much better looking than I am. I'm lucky that isn't how they decide the vote."

Mackenzie blushed. "I'm sorry, sir."

"No need. These are obviously highly intelligent creatures. What did she mean by 'Talk. Friends. Talk more' when you first spoke to her, Carter?"

"I haven't a clue."

Nola, who had followed the conversation, turning her head back and forth as each man spoke, whistled again. This time the translation was, "I said, 'It's good to talk to you again, our friends.'"

Now it was the humans' turn to be dumbfounded. "How the hell?" the President asked.

"The translation device has artificial intelligence. Obviously, it's been hearing both the Dolphins and us and working in the background. But where it got the syntax routine, I have no idea." In his own mind, Carter stumbled over the "again" part. They'd never spoken to the Dolphins, not directly. Maybe the device wasn't translating correctly.

Sam spoke up. "My fault, I'm afraid. After the broken

snippets, we got back at Freydís, I wrote up a routine to fill in the most likely meanings based on English syntax. It doesn't do it in the other direction. You're probably still speaking pidgin English to them. I'd have to know a lot more about their language and how it's structured before I can make it sound smooth to them."

"Have I ever mentioned to you that you're a genius, Sam?"

"Once or twice, maybe." She grinned.

While they were having this conversation, the others were taking turns with the mic, excitedly talking to the Dolphins. Still stung though amused by Nola's pronouncement that Mackenzie should be the leader, the President asked about Dolphin politics. Nola responded, "I don't understand."

The President then explained at length about the political process in America, and about people voting. Diplomacy obviously not being her strong suit, Nola responded that it was the stupidest idea she'd ever heard. "Do land-people have a death wish? How can you survive if you aren't led by the strongest and cleverest female?"

Nonplussed, the President handed the mic back to Mackenzie. "I'm glad I didn't have to debate *her* in an election."

By then, Carter understood what Sam's initiative had done for them but was still trying to figure out what Nola meant by "again". He gestured for Mackenzie to hand him the mic. "Nola, what did you mean when you said it was nice to talk to us again? When did we talk to you?"

"Before I was born. Land-people and water-people used to talk to each other all the time. Then we didn't. Many generations."

Carter thought carefully before he spoke again. "How do you know this if it was before you were born?"

"I learned from my mother and she from her mother. Many generations."

Carter thought some more. Of course, the Dolphins wouldn't have the same concept or measurements of time. None of them would be able to tell him how many years, centuries, or millennia it had been. "Many generations" was all she could tell him. How could he verify that she meant the giants? Did Dolphins even recall that humans used to be much bigger?

"Nola, do you know if your people and mine talked with each other using a machine before you were born?" He held up the mic to let her know what he meant by machine.

"Yes, many, many, many generations."

Nola's answer confirmed that land-people had used a translator, but Carter wondered if there was a difference between knowledge in Dolphins on this side of the world from those on the Atlantic Ocean side — if the Dolphins here had spoken with a different group of land-people than the giants. He decided that to learn any more, they'd have to communicate with Dolphins closer to where they believed the ancient nukes were to see if they too had any knowledge of speaking with land-people in the past before they began their expedition in the Alboran Sea.

Carter told Nola they would talk again soon and signaled the others that they were through for the day.

After leaving the area, he turned to the President, bypassing the chain of command. "Sir, I need a boat."

## Chapter Fifty-Four

### I WILL TEACH YOU

With the President's help, Carter had his "boat" within days. In fact, he had a fully-equipped marine research vessel and crew along with a Coast Guard escort. Everyone essential to the Dolphin language research was along for the first short expedition from the Hampton Roads Coast Guard base into the mouth of Chesapeake Bay, where Dolphins had been observed for centuries. The mission was to contact wild Dolphins and attempt to talk to them.

No one knew whether the language they'd learned from the San Diego captive Dolphins would be recognizable to Dolphins on the other side of the continent who only had incidental contact with humans. Carter, Liu, and Professor Wasserman, as the foremost experts on language within the team, had discussed it at length, concluding that they couldn't even guess at the outcome. The only thing to do was broadcast a greeting underwater and see if any Dolphins accepted the invitation.

For this expedition, Rick joined them. He and Sam greeted each other professionally, but Mackenzie's matchmaker eye detected that there was more to the relationship than professional congeniality. No wonder Sam hadn't responded to any overtures from the Executive Advantage trainees or staff! Mackenzie didn't mention it to Carter, but determined to the best of her ability to give the young couple every opportunity to be alone. What better way to advance a relationship than on a romantic cruise!

Of course, the research vessel lacked any amenities one might find on a cruise ship. Quarters were cramped, and single members of the expedition were assigned bunks in shared two-man cabins by gender. There was no spa, no swimming pool on the vessel, and no round-the-clock gourmet buffets with fancifully-carved fruit and too much dessert. Nevertheless, every member of the team was excited to cast off and find Dolphins as quickly as they could.

Mackenzie had continued her research into everything known about Dolphins, and did have a project she wanted Carter to talk to Rick about. While the others set up the device and began broadcasting as soon as the boat reached a point midway between the mouth of Back River and Fisherman Island on the east side of the mouth of Chesapeake Bay, Rick, Carter, and Mackenzie met briefly.

"Rick, Mackie has turned up something interesting in her research, and we're hoping to piggyback an experiment on this expedition. Since Sam has the translation algorithms working so well, we were wondering, if we captured the sonar recordings from any Dolphins we encounter, could you work on something different?"

"Sure, if that's what you need from me. I guess you didn't invite me along only for my good looks and the pleasure of my company."

"Of course, we did," Mackenzie answered, smiling in a

way that Carter recognized as meaning she had ulterior motives. *What could that be about?* he wondered. But she was already continuing, so Carter pushed it aside and listened.

"But we do need your expertise, too. You see, some scientists think that Dolphins can interpret sonar communications as images. In other words, they think Dolphins can send pictures to each other as a more efficient way of communicating than words. We'd like you to work on the sonar recordings and see if they can be translated as images."

"Wow, now that's a challenge," Rick answered. "But hey, I'm game. Can't let Sam have all the glory, now, can I?" He winked at Mackenzie, who winked back.

*What's going on here?* Carter wondered.

Leaving Rick to think about how he'd go about his assignment, Carter took Mackenzie's elbow and steered her to a sheltered area on the deck. "What are you scheming with Rick?" he asked.

"Oh, nothing, or at least not in the sense you're thinking. Have you seen how Sam acts when Rick's around?"

"Like she usually does, I guess. What are you talking about?"

"They're interested in each other." Mackenzie waited for Carter to get it. When he still looked puzzled, she said, exasperated, "Men! You are so clueless. They like each other. *Romantically*. Come on, Carter, open your eyes!"

Now that she'd spelled it out, Carter said, "Oh! You mean like this?" He kissed her so thoroughly it left her breathless. All she could do was nod, before returning the kiss in kind.

"We'd better get back to the others. I wonder if we have any RSVPs to our Dolphin reception yet?" he said. He was trying to pretend his own heart wasn't racing after that kiss.

Mackenzie smiled at him. "I will get my revenge, you know."

"I know. And I can't wait."

Arm in arm, they strolled to the foredeck, where Sam, Liu, Wasserman, and a Coast Guard electrician were fiddling with the translation device. "What's going on?" Carter called.

"We just sent out the invitation to come and talk," Sam replied. "Switching to receive, so we can hear them if they respond."

"Put it on speaker, and Mackie and I will watch for Dolphins in the water nearby."

"You got it, boss."

For several minutes, nothing happened, and the group was beginning to think they'd have to move farther into the Atlantic. Then, just as he was about to go and find the skipper to say so, Carter spotted a Dolphin in the water several yards off the port side of the boat. At the same time, the speakers blared.

"Who?" the translated whistle sounded. "Land-people, are you in metal-fish?"

"Carter! They understood us! Answer her! Hurry!" Mackenzie was so excited she was shouting.

"How do you know it's a she?" Carter asked.

"I just do. Answer her!"

Shaking his head with amusement at his wife's childlike delight, Carter keyed the mic. "My name is Carter. Yes, we're on the metal-fish. What is your name?" Sam had created the translation algorithm in such a way that the names of the people were associated with the whistles Nola had assigned to them, and a database of names was available to assign to the new unique whistles any Dolphins they met.

"My name is Joanna," the Dolphin replied. As soon as she finished speaking, she leaped from the water to show herself. "I am the leader of my pod. Where is the leader of your pod?"

A hurried consultation followed. "She means you, Mackenzie," Sam urged.

"No, Carter is the leader."

"But they expect a female."

Carter handed the mic to Mackenzie. "Go ahead and talk to her. Maybe you can make her understand that leaders of land-people can be either male or female."

Mackenzie noted his use of the "land-people" designation rather than "human". The more the group associated with Dolphins, the more they were beginning to accept them as equals, not animals. She took the mic and keyed it confidently.

"Hello, Joanna. I am Mackenzie. Carter is my mate, and he is the leader of this pod. Land-people have males and females as leaders. Sometimes we lead together."

While they waited for Joanna to respond, Mackenzie said to Carter, "Do you think that was too much at once? What if the translator couldn't keep up?"

"Let's wait and see," he said, rubbing her arm to reassure her.

A moment later, Joanna responded. "I understand. Thank you. It has been many, many generations since land-people and water-people spoke. I am happy we speak again."

As the words were broadcast over the speakers, everyone within hearing expressed their joy — some by jumping up and down, others by offering high-fives to all who would return them. A few of the Coast Guard crew were there as well. They'd been told only that the researchers were going to try to communicate with dolphins, which amused them. Who could make anything of those weird dolphin sounds? Those who heard the exchange over the speakers were overwhelmed with shock. They'd expected whistles and hoots, not full, English sentences. What kind of hocus-pocus was this?

Carter paused to collect his thoughts. Diplomacy was required, yet the need for information was urgent. What could he say, and how could he say it, to avoid making a faux-pas in Dolphin culture?

"Joanna, we are happy as well. I am happy to meet you. Land-people have forgotten the time when we were friends and could talk together. We have much to learn from you. I might make a mistake — please help me when I say the wrong thing."

"Carter," said Sam, sotto-voce, "I don't know if the device got that concept across. I don't remember a translation for wrong."

"It's done a pretty good job so far. She seems to be thinking about it. Let's see what happens."

After several tense moments, Joanna spoke again. "I teach you. Like teaching my children. You can learn. We were taught land-people are almost as intelligent as water-people."

Sam slammed the mic pickup off as the group erupted in laughter. It wouldn't do to insult their new friend by laughing at the "almost". When Carter had his mirth under control, he keyed the mic again. "Thank you, Joanna. That is very kind of you. Land-people are very excited to learn."

Over the next few hours, Carter learned that when greeting another pod, the correct thing to do was first exchange names. Because Dolphins formed and reformed pods according to their needs, they had wide circles of acquaintances, and the pods both needed to know who among their friends were present. Accordingly, Joanna introduced every individual in her pod, and Carter introduced his group. Joanna assigned whistles to each human name that didn't already have one from Nola, and the computer assigned human names to the pod members. All names were automatically entered into the database.

"There's going to be a problem when someone with the same name as one of us joins the group," Sam observed.

"I don't think so," Carter said. "The whistle will be different. We just have to make sure to use full names to differentiate."

Joanna was already explaining that the next information to convey was what the pod was doing just then. Were they feeding, fleeing from an enemy, teaching the youngsters, or was it playtime? Her pod, she explained, had been teaching the youngsters when they heard Carter's original call from a long swim away. It was then that Carter realized they needed a way to identify location. "How can you tell us where you were?" he asked Joanna. In response, she didn't whistle or make any other vocalization. Instead, a sonar pulse went out, to be captured by the special equipment Carter and Mackenzie had set up for Rick.

At the time, Rick had no program set up to translate it, but Carter assured Joanna they were working on understanding. She seemed content with that.

By the end of several hours, Joanna showed signs of tiring. "I must rest," she signaled. "Dark is falling, and tonight has no moon. Come back when the sun is high again."

A quick check of a moon calendar revealed she was right; it was the new moon. As they sailed back to base, Rick was in his room, which doubled as an office so he was on a small bunk but luckily alone, working feverishly to convert the sonar pulse Carter was most interested in — the one Joanna had sent when he asked about location. He translated it using wavelength as a measurement, but the resulting printout didn't make much sense to him. After thinking about it for a while, he got up and went to Sam's cabin, where he knocked lightly on the door.

Sam came out and went into Rick's arms. "What are you doing up? I thought you'd get some sleep?"

He kissed her quickly and answered, "Nah, too early for that, and plenty of time once we get to shore. Listen, if you were a Dolphin, how would you recognize where you were?"

Sam, who'd been working with the language long enough to have some idea of Dolphin thought processes, answered promptly. "Well, you know they navigate by echolocation. They probably have some mental picture of the coastline or bottom where they usually hang out. Kind of like the map we carry in our minds of our surroundings. Maybe more accurate. Why?"

"Carter has me working on translating the sonar signals to an image. Come see what I have. Maybe you can make something of it."

As soon as Sam saw what he had, she asked if he could make it appear in a 3-D representation. Rick applied some binary filters to the data, first slicing the sinewaves into even sections and then assigning ones and zeros, grouped in bytes, to indicate grayscale values. When a 3-D image appeared onscreen, they both gasped. "It looks like a map of the bay bottom," Rick whispered in awe.

"Yeah, and I recognize this part," Sam answered, pointing to a couple of complex indentations on the right side of the screen. "Bet you anything you want to name that those are the Poquoson and Back rivers."

"But they're on the wrong side," Rick objected.

"Not if you're a Dolphin swimming south," she answered. "They wouldn't recognize our maps, which are from an overhead perspective. What we're seeing is the shoreline from their perspective — in the water, fairly shallow, and swimming south. You'll have to apply algorithms to rotate it to what we're used to seeing, with north up, et cetera."

"You've been a big help, Sam. When did you get smarter than me?" he joked.

"Haven't you heard? According to the Dolphins, females are always superior." She squealed as he lunged for her and captured her in his arms, tickling her for good measure. "I've missed you, Rick," she whispered before he started kissing her.

The next morning, they set out for the same location, but this time they carried supplies and food for several days. Too much time was lost in sailing back and forth, though it took only a couple of hours each way. Because of the traffic in the area, the speed had to be relatively low, and they didn't want to attract more attention than was necessary. It wasn't lost on Carter that the Nabateans most likely had his team under surveillance.

In fact, the Nabateans didn't have to look far or employ highly sophisticated tactics to learn where Carter and the team were. They had only to intercept the Skype conversations between Liam and Beth and their homesick parents. Each day just before the kids' bedtime, Mackenzie and Carter would take time to call and greet them, ask about their day, and if there was time, one of them would read a bedtime story. Liam and Beth were always happy and upbeat about their day, relating stories about what they'd done with their grandparents. Liam's stories were of course more comprehensible than Beth's babbling, but Carter and Mackenzie listened to both with equal attention.

After closing the call one night, Mackenzie said to Carter, "I don't think they miss us at all!"

"Thankfully, with one set of real and one set of honorary grandparents, I don't think they have time to miss us. Be glad they're happy and not worried."

"You're right, but I miss them like crazy."

"We'll be home soon, Mackie."

Listening in from separate parts of the world, Graziella Nabati said to her son, "Trace that feed. I want to know exactly where the doting parents are and what they're doing."

The next few days were spent in a steep learning curve about Dolphins, their social structures, their history, habits, and what they knew about ancient times and land-humans of those times.

Carter finally felt it was time to broach the subject of giants and the Alboran Sea with Joanna. And he was particularly keen to know if there was any association between her pods and those from across the Atlantic.

Joanna's answers were enlightening to put it mildly. Befuddled by Joanna's explanation that Dolphins could communicate with other pods via their pod leaders anywhere in the world, Carter called Rick and Sam in to try and make sense of what he was hearing.

Carter apologized to Joanna and asked that she explain it to Rick and Sam again. The two of them listened carefully and looked at the patterns on the screen of the translation device. After a quiet consultation, they nodded at each other and Sam confirmed, "No mistake Carter, she is talking about instantaneous communications."

"Ansible communications . . ." Rick mumbled, while shaking his head in disbelief as he stared at Sam.

"Ansi . . . what?" Carter asked.

"Ansible communication, Carter," Sam replied. "It's . . . it's . . . well, as far as our human scientists are concerned, it's a sci-fi concept — fiction. Impossible, but whatever we humans think, what Joanna just described is instantaneous or superluminal (faster than light) communication. That is what we call ansible communications . . . messages are sent and received over any distance, with no delay. Our scientists, or I should rather say, our land-human scientists, believe superluminal communication of any kind is impossible."

Carter whistled in awe. "They have just been proven wrong."

Carter sent a coded message to James, who notified the President and Bill. The three of them and some of the National Security Council arrived by helicopter the next day. It took the whole team on the boat and several replays of the recording to half-convince the President and his entourage about the Dolphins' mindboggling communication capability.

Once the President accepted it, almost (and although he wouldn't admit it, he was still trying to come to grips with the idea that it was possible to have an intelligent two-way conversation with another species), he asked to speak to Joanna.

She was happy to talk to him, although she probably was having her own emotional battles to come to terms with, such as the strange protocol of these land-humans to have a male as a pod leader. The two of them spoke at

## The Alboran Codex

length, and Joanna indicated she understood there was some serious danger to land-humans and agreed to help them. She would let the leaders of the Alboran Sea Dolphins know to expect them.

"I guess we should call that a Dolphinogram," the President muttered to no one in particular.

After that, the expedition ended, and the team returned to A-Echelon headquarters to analyze their data.

## Chapter Fifty-Five

### BIT BY AGONIZING BIT

Carter and his team had been forced to stay close to shore with their expedition because of their need for speed. An ocean-worthy research vessel could have been had, but not within the time frame they wanted. The down side to that compromise was that they were carrying out their research within a high-traffic area at the mouth of the Chesapeake. Not only commercial boats plied those waters, but hobby fishermen swarmed the numerous areas both near shore and in the middle of the bay. And all of them saw the research vessel anchored in the same spot for nearly a week.

It took only a day or two for speculation to surface in the media. Pictures of the boat and a pod of dolphins surrounding it made it to social media, where it was picked up by conspiracy theorists. Identification of the boat as a Coast Guard research vessel brought out the animal activists and rumors ran rife. The dolphins were being trained to carry out kamikaze missions to plant mines on enemy ships; they were being fitted with listening devices to spy on everyone from foreign dignitaries to domestic politicians, including aliens — if someone could imagine it, the claim was made despite lack of proof.

With the pictures to bolster the claims, it was bigger news than a sighting of Elvis Presley. Even the mainstream media got involved when they bombarded the President for information about his visit to the boat. At some point, an imaginative reporter came up with the idea that the unidentified people on the boat had cracked dolphin language. It was too close to the truth for comfort.

With eyes and ears everywhere, the Nabateans soon caught wind of the strange activity, especially the unprecedented helicopter drop of the President onto a nondescript boat while it was anchored in the Chesapeake. The same boat they knew the Devereuxs were on. Something significant was going on. Well aware that his last mission had ended in chaos and his credibility was on the line, Mathieu Nabati vetted his operatives personally, no longer trusting a middle man to do so. Their mission: spare no expense or mercy in getting every scrap of information pertaining to that expedition.

Months before, Mathieu and his mother had been forced to flee. In an uncharacteristically emotional goodbye, Graziella told her son that they would be able to be together in person again sometime, but the time was not now. For now, they would have to run the Council from opposite ends of the earth.

Mathieu took up residence in a remote location in the Ural Mountains in the western part of Russia. Even the other Council members didn't know where his new hideout was, only that it boasted the latest in quantum computing and communications equipment possible.

Graziella, on the other hand, retreated to her similarly-equipped mountain stronghold high in the Andes in Peru.

Not too far from the Incan citadel Machu Picchu, she felt as at home as she'd felt in the ancient catacombs of Paris. Something in the atmosphere of the ancient and mysterious fed her connection to her forebears and was as necessary to her sense of well-being as food and water.

Machu Picchu, built as it was in the fifteenth century and later abandoned, was modern compared to her ancestors' holdings in the Middle Eastern desert. Its lush green was far from the austere sands of her birthright. Nevertheless, as she looked down from her neighboring home into the Urubamba River valley, she felt the tug of the astronomical alignment of the temple nearby. She nodded.

Her decision to come here had been the right one. She could feel the strength of the ancients filling her with purpose. Her mission would soon be complete.

It was short work for the two-person team, a couple based in the US, to locate A-Echelon headquarters and place every member of the team under surveillance. After a couple of days, they focused on one member who wasn't as heavily guarded as the others. Despite their knowledge that Carter Devereux was the head of the group, they couldn't get close to him or his wife. Equally well-guarded were the core team, those who usually resided on Freydís. But one was local, and they homed in on him — Rick Winslow.

Though Rick had been instrumental in writing the initial code that translated Giantese with Sam's help, he had been assigned to other projects when she was called temporarily to Freydís a few weeks before. Then her return had been delayed, and finally he had been called back into the project for the Dolphin expedition. Now he was only loosely associated with that project as his others required time as well. Because he wasn't considered a core member, his security wasn't as high a priority; but that turned out to be a grave error.

Only three days after the Nabatean operatives had been told to get the low-down, Rick failed to show for work one morning. When Sam called his home, his recorded phone message stated he was feeling under the weather and he'd be off for a couple of days. Sam left a message wishing him a speedy recovery and that she would miss him. She thought no more of it.

However, Rick had been forced at gunpoint to leave that recording. He was in the hands of the Nabatean operatives, and they'd threatened to harm Sam if they had to shoot him because he wouldn't cooperate. He decided to spare himself a gunshot wound and Sam an equally horrifying fate and did exactly as he was told.

Fortunately for the team, but unfortunately for Rick, he didn't know everything, nor did he have any of the information stored on his personal computer. Bit by agonizing bit, he gave up what he did know under torture. The library of the giants, the progress they'd made translating it, the surprising knowledge of the Dolphins, and even the plans to go to the Alboran Sea, and with the help of the Dolphins, locate the ancient nukes hidden in the giants' capital. Because he didn't know the timeline for the last revelation, he died pleading for them to spare Sam. On the third day after he didn't show up for work, his body was found in his burned-out car in a vacant lot in Southeast Washington.

Identification was from dental records, the autopsy revealed that he was badly beaten but everyone assumed it was a hate crime because of the neighborhood, but no one could explain what Rick was doing in that neighborhood. The police had their hands full, and Rick's parents were grief-stricken but believed the police. Sam was inconsolable and unable to work.

Carter and his team as well as the Executive Advantage were shaken by the loss of one of their most valuable team members. The suspicious circumstances of Rick's death also set off alarm bells for Carter and a few others. At the insistence of the senior management of A-Echelon, Executive Advantage rushed most of them back to the safety of Freydís. There was still so much they wanted to learn from their new found marine friends, but it wasn't going to be. They'd have to work with what they had.

However, Carter and Mackenzie sided with Samantha when she refused to go until after Rick's funeral. Despite their desperate need for her expertise and experience with the code, they understood her desire — no, her absolute need — to grieve for Rick. Only their concern for their children made them go before paying their respects to their colleague as well. James, Irene and Sam would all represent the entire A-Echelon team at the funeral. Sam would rejoin the others on Freydís within a week afterward. Meanwhile, more security was assigned to her. Sean and Dylan promised they wouldn't let so much as a mosquito get within two miles of her.

Mackenzie hugged Sam goodbye as they boarded the plane to return home. "Take care of yourself, honey," she said.

"I will, and thank you. I'll be there as soon as I can; I promise. I know your beautiful Freydís is the best place to recover. You, Liu, and Bly have become like family to me."

"We feel the same way, Sam. Hurry home."

## Chapter Fifty-Six

### WE MUST HAVE THAT INFORMATION

The report from Rick's torturers electrified Mathieu Nabati. Another emergency Council meeting was called, this time to present a coup. He had vital information and a decision was required.

After presenting what he knew and how he knew it, Nabati made his proposal. "We MUST have that information. All of it. It's time to move in on Carter Devereux's ranch, Freydís, and get it at all costs."

"We have only minimal intel from our observation satellites and drones," objected one of the members.

"Nevertheless, we have to strike before their planned expedition. We cannot allow them to find those ancient nukes, and we cannot allow them to be the only guardians of the knowledge of the giants. We should have captured that library and those weapons as well. This is no time to be cowardly," Nabati concluded, eyeing the objective member with a frown.

"I can help." It was the member from Russia, who also happened to be the Director of the Federal Security Service

(FSB) of Russia. "I have a team of ex-Spetsnaz on my payroll, standing by for just such a mission. Let them earn their keep. These puny guards on Freydís won't stand a chance."

No debate was needed. With the one naysayer duly chastised, the vote was unanimous — attack Freydís. Take Carter Devereux and anyone else they might find useful alive if possible, but priority number one was to get the library and anything pertaining to dolphins at all costs, up to and including the killing of everyone on the ranch.

The council left the details up to the Spetsnaz team, and they made their plans with their usual efficiency. Over the next week, sixteen men would arrive separately at different locations within Canada, either alone or traveling with a fake partner or family. They would make their way, one group of eight to Montreal and another group of eight to Quebec City, meeting up there within ten days. When they were assembled, they would use two private jets to fly them over Freydís to be parachuted in from high altitude, collect their information and hostages, if any, and then be extracted from the private airstrip on Freydís.

Assuming everything went per plan, they would fly back to Quebec, turn over their booty to a Council operative, and then make their way back to where they'd arrived in the first place and leave the country in a reverse of their entries. Each was trained to improvise. If the unthinkable happened and the mission failed in any way, only the leader knew they were hired by the Director of the FSB. The others would protect whatever information they garnered from the mission itself with their lives and kill anyone they couldn't extract.

## Chapter Fifty-Seven

### THE BATTLE OF FREYDÍS

At first, everything did go according to plan. One plane dropped its deadly load to the west of Freydís, and the other to the east. Each group assembled, made sure they were all there, hid their parachutes, and then split into two four-man teams to observe from four separate high points in the mountains surrounding the ranch. For two days, they observed the homestead, taking note of the comings and goings of Ahote, Bly, and the people living in the cabin and surrounding outbuildings.

During this time, Keeva and Loki had noted the presence of the newcomers. Put off by their furtive manner, they had posted their pups, Nadia, and her two to observe what these strange humans were up to. They made sure to stay out of sight until they had some signal from Mackenzie, their special human, that the newcomers were friends. For the time being, the new humans weren't making any threatening moves, but the wolves were on alert.

After observing with high-flying drones during the day and infrared imaging by satellite at night, the Spetsnaz team had enough intel. At two a.m., they began making their stealthy way toward the main cabin, where they knew Carter Devereux and his family would be sleeping when they arrived after a forced march. Tough as nails, none of them were unnerved by the faint howl of wolves in the distance. They all knew that wolves in the wild would not approach humans, and they were confident in their numbers and weapons.

Communicating with their pups and Nadia to stay put unless called, Loki and Keeva raced for the cabin. Something was very wrong about these new humans, and they had to warn Mackenzie to protect her pups. At three thirty a.m., both adult wolves arrived at the cabin and set up a howling like never before. Carter and Mackenzie, startled out of a sound sleep, were up like lightning, Carter grabbing his semi-automatic weapon as Mackenzie threw on a robe over her nightgown and checked that the children were still asleep.

"Mackie, take a look and see who's out front, while I take a look around back," Carter said.

Mackenzie looked out the front windows and saw only Loki and Keeva. Both were still howling, their heads pointed skyward. "It's just Loki and Keeva. Where are the rest of them? Do you think something's happened?" she called to Carter.

He called back, "No, I think they're trying to warn us." Just then, his peripheral vision caught movement. Two human figures were crouched at the side of the barn. As he watched, they made a dash toward the translation prefab. *Shit*. This wasn't good.

Carter ran toward Mackenzie's position, and she met him in the middle. "Get the children and take cover in the hallway," he whispered urgently. "Stay down."

"But Carter . . ."

"No buts, Mackie. We have armed intruders out there. I'll raise Dylan while you get the kids. Try to keep them quiet. If you can get to the guns and ammo, please get them to me ASAP."

Mackenzie's blood ran cold when she heard "armed intruders". Her concern for the wolves took immediate second place to her fear for her children. She hurried to Liam's room first, gave him quick instructions to go quietly into the hallway, lie down, and keep quiet. To Jeha, she said, "Guard." The little dog followed Liam at a trot and lay down on top of him. Mackenzie moved quickly into Beth's room and lifted her from her bed, blankets and all. "Shhh," she soothed, as the little one began to stir.

Once in the hallway, she asked Liam, "Can you be mama's big boy? I need to help Dad. Can you stay here no matter what happens, and keep Beth here?"

"Yes, Mama. And Jeha will help me. But I'm scared."

She took a moment to hug him. "I know you are, sweetheart. But Dad and I will protect you. Loki and Keeva are here, too. Stay down, now, and keep Beth with you. Can you do that?" Seeing him nod, even though his eyes were wide with fear, Mackenzie squeezed his shoulder. As she duck-walked to the end of the hall to get the weapons out of the gun safe, she spared a thought for her parents and brother, two miles west in a secluded cabin. When Carter had built the cabin and its attached apartment for them, the distance was a way of giving both families some privacy. Now she worried that they were unprotected, although her brother had begun training with them and could probably hold off a normal break-in until help arrived. This was no normal break-in; she knew in her heart. All she could do was pray they'd be safe until the EA team secured the ranch.

She heard Carter speaking firmly on the two-way radio. "I saw only two, but there could be more. Be careful. We'll hold the fort until you get here." Apparently satisfied with Dylan's reply, he laid the radio down and turned toward her position. She handed him his Sig Sauer P226 pistol, his bulletproof vest, belt with a spare magazine and high-powered flashlight, and a throat mic. She'd shrugged on her own vest and throat mic as soon as she'd gotten the safe open. Carter took his weapon and accessories with a quick smile of reassurance and then did a double-take as Mackenzie pulled her own weapon from the safe.

"I never thought I'd see the day . . ." he muttered as she slammed a magazine home into the pink-trimmed weapon. But now was not the time to razz her about her sissy gun. It would do just as much damage as his, and Mackie had proven herself a crack shot in their training sessions. He was silent as she buckled her own combat belt around her slim waist.

"Do we stay put until we have more information?" she asked. "Dylan and his team are on the way. Are they not?"

"Yes, they are. But I don't like the idea of staying inside. If we're in here with the children when they attack, there may not be time to protect them. They can throw a grenade through the window. Let's go outside, reconnoiter, and keep them away from the house and the children. The wolves are out front, so it must be relatively safe in that direction. We can radio Dylan with whatever we learn, too."

"Good point. Okay, stay low," she replied.

Carter led the way as they bush-crawled through the living room and out the front door, first opening it a crack to see if the wolves were still in position. Loki and Keeva paced back and forth on the cabin-wide front veranda, closer than Mackenzie had ever seen them come to the house.

"Keeva, Loki. Who's out there?" Mackenzie asked, almost believing they would answer her. For a minute, she truly thought they would, as both their ears pricked up and rotated toward Camp Tala. They gave a series of sharp yips, and then resumed their pacing.

---

Within minutes of receiving Carter's distress call, Dylan had his ten-man team up and in full gear, only waiting on the order to move out from Camp Tala. The wolf-handlers each put a dog whistle to their lips to call the wolf pups. They'd had enough training to be of assistance in a nighttime operation and were nearly the size of their fearsome parents already. No sooner than the whistles were employed, at frequencies inaudible to humans, a series of yips from the direction of the Devereux cabin let them know the wolves had heard. Within a few moments, the six juveniles and Nadia, the lone female, reported for duty — Loki and Keeva having given their permission for the pups to leave their assigned posts.

Dylan gave the signal to move out, and the ten men and seven wolves set out at a brisk trot for the cabin with orders to hold up and assess the situation before rushing in with guns blazing. As he was wondering how intruders got past the passive security measures — laser trip wires, motion sensors, and others — he and the others heard all hell break loose at the cabin.

A couple of gunshots, the sound of a wolf yelping in pain, and a high-pitched scream — it was Mackenzie —

followed by a firefight with too many gunshots too quickly to count. He halted his men in their tracks.

"OK, we've got real trouble. You three, circle the cabin clockwise. Assess and report. You three, go the opposite direction and do the same. Don't shoot unless you can absolutely identify your target as an unfriendly. You two, come with me. Hendricks, Johnson, separate and cover us." He motioned the last two men right and left, and then began trotting toward the cabin in a zigzag manner, with two men following.

---

Back at the cabin, Carter motioned Mackenzie to go to the east side of the veranda while he took the west to see if any of the intruders showed themselves. Loki and Keeva maintained their pacing, but nosed Mackenzie each time they passed her. As she gained the corner and cautiously peeked around, she saw a man wearing night-vision goggles peering through the windows of the master bedroom with a handgun at the ready. Slowly, she raised her weapon. Before she got it fully raised, a blur of gray-brown raced out of the woods and leapt on the man's back.

Under attack by one of the young wolves, the man panicked and turned toward it, reflexively firing as he turned. The wolf pup yelped and landed on the ground, still. Mackenzie lost it. With a blood-curdling war cry, she leaped over the railing and charged the man, pulling the trigger as she went and spewing obscenities she didn't even know she knew. Her cry had alerted the man, and he turned toward her, raising his gun. But it was too late. Her first round took him between the eyes, taking almost half his head away — he was dead long before he hit the ground.

# The Alboran Codex

Mackenzie, wild with grief for the wolf, kept shooting. By the time she reached the man, he was hamburger. She fell to her knees beside the wolf pup to examine its wounds. Keeva was right beside her.

At the same moment when Mackenzie saw the man on her side of the cabin, Carter looked around the corner on his side and saw two men at each of the children's windows. Noting that they were each wearing night-vision goggles and had their guns raised and pointed to the inside of the rooms, he quick-drew his flashlight and blinded them with its high-power beam before dropping them both, each with a single shot to the head. Carter was infuriated that these attackers would go after kids.

As his two villains dropped to the ground, he heard the commotion from the other side of the house. A gunshot, and a yelp! Mackenzie's scream galvanized him. He yelled her name and whirled in place. He reached the other side of the veranda in time to see her charging a man on the ground and firing at him on the run. There was little he could do. He cleared the railing with a long high-jump and fell to his knees in a shooting stance in case she gave him the chance to defend her.

When she veered from her straight run at the intruder, Carter saw the man torn to shreds by her bullets and watched as she fell to her knees beside the wolf pup, Keeva right next to her. Carter breathed a sigh of relief that Mackie seemed safe, but in the blink of an eye, the relief turned to terror as a man appeared from the back of the cabin and grabbed her from behind.

Carter raised his gun again, but once more Mackenzie was between him and his target. As he roared in frustration, Mackenzie dropped into a dead weight and the man lost his grip on her. Before Carter could react, Mackenzie whipped her head back, connecting solidly with the man's unprotected groin. As the man doubled over in pain, Mackenzie shot up, spun around, and brought one knee violently into the man's face. The assailant was done for when Keeva got into the act. As soon as his back hit the ground, Keeva was at his throat, and it was over in seconds. All Carter and Mackenzie heard was his gurgling as Keeva ripped his throat out. Keeva raised her head to the sky and howled, an eerie sound of triumph and grief, before going back to tend to her wounded pup — JR, named after James Rhodes.

Carter spoke to the corpses of the two intruders. "Can't say that I'm sorry, assholes. On this ranch, no one messes with the women. And apparently, you didn't know about our arrangements with the wolves." He looked up to find a feral look on Mackenzie's face. "Didn't you know that wolf moms will kill you for messing with their pups?"

Just then, one of the EA men rushed out of the woods, too. Mackenzie saw him and looked down at the wolf pup, with Keeva guarding him. "He needs first aid. Hurry! Keeva, let the man help your pup." Keeva relaxed and whined, then licked the hand of the startled soldier. He flashed a grin at Mackenzie.

"I'd give my left nut to have your way with these wolves. Don't worry, I'll take care of our young soldier here."

"Come on, Mackie, let's go check on the kids," urged Carter.

## Chapter Fifty-Eight

### RELIGIOUS EXPERIENCES

At Ahote's cabin, as soon as the first shots were fired, Ahote was out of bed and reaching for his .308 Winchester before he even knew he was awake. He'd instinctively analyzed what woke him before fully coherent. Gunshots, yells, and howling, to the south in the direction of Carter's cabin. Bly was also alert and waiting for Ahote to speak.

"Stay here and lock the cabin. I'm going to see what's going on."

Bly felt the shivers down her spine. "The last time Mackie's wolves were howling like that it was bad, very bad news," she whispered.

The Spetsnaz group nearby had been ordered to standby but were getting ready to go to the aid of their comrades as they heard the chatter in their earpieces from the two attacking teams that things weren't going well. What was that about wolves? As they stood to move out, the two bringing up the rear suddenly felt as if a ton of bricks hit them in their backs as two sixty-pound wolves hit them mid-leap, throwing them face first into the dirt.

The two in front turned at the sound of their teammates' cries and bodies hitting the ground along with low growls as the wolves stood on their backs, holding them as they'd been taught — by the backs of their necks. One Spetsnaz raised his rifle, but halfway through the act, the .308 round from Ahote's rifle hit him in the chest, lifted him off his feet, and slammed him into a tree trunk two paces away — dead on arrival. Ahote, who'd seen them from yards away, had worked his way toward them as they got ready to move out.

With two of his comrades quivering with fear of the wolf fangs around their necks, and the third dead from an encounter with a .308 Winchester, the fourth man lost all interest in the mission, dropped his weapon, and raised his hands.

Before tonight, he did not believe in heaven or hell, God or Satan, but he had just changed his mind and become a very religious man. He was convinced that these wolf-demon creatures, accompanied by a humanlike demon appearing from nowhere, could only be from one place — hell.

How many more of these creatures were still lurking out there? "Stay still," he managed to advise his two terrified comrades in a very shaky voice. "They haven't torn you apart yet. Don't give them a reason. And pray my comrades, pray to God. Pray for all of us. Tonight, we've stepped into the devil's lair. Only God Almighty can save our souls now."

His two dirt-eating comrades, each with one of the wolf-demons still on their backs, were so preoccupied with controlling their breathing, bladders, and stomachs, they didn't hear a single word of their newly converted team leader's profound sermon.

Ahote had moved silently from his position behind a tree as soon as he took his shot. He was surprised to see the fourth man drop his weapon, but he grinned when he heard the man's tone of voice as he spoke to the two on the ground. Although he didn't understand the Russian words, he understood the fear behind them, and he didn't know why, but the man's tone of voice sounded kind of pious to him. Then he had his own spiritual experience when two EA guys appeared silently next to him. He had to clench to hold his water before recognizing them.

The EA men gave their wolves the command to let the enemy up, but they kept their guns trained on them.

"Who are you?" one asked. When the frightened Spetsnaz troops didn't answer, they cuffed them and herded them toward Carter's cabin, unaware that the translation center was also under attack.

---

When they had taken care of the four men at the cabin, Carter and Mackenzie assumed it was over and went inside to comfort their frightened kids. Liam was pale but held his little sister in his arms, rocking her back and forth and crooning one of his mom's lullabies to calm her. Mackenzie rushed to them and gathered them in her arms, with Carter completing the group hug by enveloping all three in his.

Only when they'd assured themselves the kids were safe did they spare a thought for the others. Carter jumped up to go and see about them, but Mackenzie grabbed him around the leg. "Wait. What if there are more out there?"

"Dylan and his men are here now, and they brought the war-wolves. It should be safe."

"Be careful, Carter"

"I will."

Carter moved cautiously to the front door, checked the status of his ammunition, and then slipped out, hugging the front of the cabin. Loki and Keeva were nowhere to be seen, but from the direction of the translation cabin, Carter heard John Ruschin's voice.

John had led the counter-clockwise group, and as soon as they realized the situation at the cabin was under control, had directed them to check on the translation cabin. When they were in position, they noted an intruder at one corner. Further observation revealed two others at other corners, and a fourth at the door. It looked like he was placing a charge to breach the reinforced door.

John was keenly aware of what was going on all around him. A single shot had come from the north. Sounded like a high-caliber rifle, but since there'd been only one, he assumed it was Ahote, and he probably had the situation under control. In any event, there was an EA team with wolves out there to help if he required any. The gunshots from the cabin had stopped moments before, and he'd observed Carter and Mackenzie openly entering their front door, as well as seeing Dylan trotting toward the cabin. No one else was covering the translation center.

He called out, "Drop your guns and put your hands—" He didn't finish the sentence as the intruders began firing toward the sound of his voice. A double-tap from each of his men dropped the four bad guys. They'd never had a chance, having been in the sights of the EA team from before John's instructions to drop their guns. They didn't even have time to regret their stupid decision.

## Chapter Fifty-Nine

### WE HAVE YOUR MEN

Only one Russian team remained. The south team, also on standby, had heard everything over open radios. The commander of the operation was with them, and with the last shots, the howling and yipping of the wolves, and the silence from the north team, he knew he and the three men with him were so deep in shit that there wasn't enough water in the Black Sea to wash it off.

He gave the command to retreat to the north and south groups, knowing already that the east and west groups were done for. From the north group, a drawling voice in English replied to him. "We have your men. Give yourselves up, and we won't set the wolves on you."

The Spetsnaz leader spoke perfect English and knew he had no other choice but to retreat as quickly as possible. Without answering, he turned to signal his three squad members to head out. Only he couldn't see them — they were already gone. He turned tail and ran as if the wolves were after him, and they were. Nadia and her brood tracked him and the three squad members silently, waiting for the command to take them down.

Back at the cabin, Carter and Mackenzie had come out again, after cautioning the children to stay where they were. Carter went to the EA team and began helping them make sense of what happened, while Mackenzie ran to the side of the cabin where she'd last seen the wounded wolf pup. She found the handler sitting beside a pup who was too still, his face in his hands, his shoulders heaving. Keeva lay with her head on her pup's side, keening softly. Mackenzie drew up short.

"No! What happened? He was fine . . ."

The security guard lifted his tearstained face. "No, he wasn't. I don't know how he lived as long as he did. The shot nicked his heart. He . . . stopped breathing right after you left."

Mackenzie burst into tears and went to her wolf friend. "Keeva, I'm so sorry!" She buried her face in the rich fur and sobbed. From far away, she heard Loki howl, a heart-rending wail that came from a broken wolf heart.

Dylan had reached his men and assessed the situation, meeting up with Carter as he examined the bodies of the men at the translation center. Carter had knocked on Wasserman's door and told him it was safe to come out. The old man also stood looking at the Spetsnaz dead. He spat on the ground nearby. "Barbarians," he snarled. When Dylan reached Carter, the latter grabbed him by the shoulders.

"Liu?" Carter asked.

"At the camp. I'm sure she's fine." He raised his radio and contacted the men he'd left in charge of guarding Camp Tala, verifying that they'd seen no action there. "I guess they didn't know about us. Liu is safe, but I'll send two of these guys to get her and bring her here. Where's Mackenzie? And your kids? And what about your in-laws?"

"Safe. The kids are in the cabin. Mackie went to check on one of the wolf pups who was wounded. We need to make sure her family is safe ASAP."

Dylan signaled John to come over. "Can you take your guys and check on Mackenzie's family in their cabin?" He followed Carter to the side of the cabin where Mackenzie had gone. When they rounded the corner, they took in the tragic scene. Mackenzie stood up, covered in the wolf pup's blood. "If there are any left alive, I want them," she snarled. Her red hair flew around her head, crackling with early-morning static electricity and making a terrifying halo as he shined the flashlight toward her.

"Mackie . . ."

"No! Don't say it. I want to know who came into our sanctuary, threatened our children, our family and friends, and murdered one of *my* wolves. They'll wish they had never been born."

Carter wisely kept his mouth shut. He'd never seen Mackenzie so beside herself and wasn't about to get in her way. She'd suffered a terrible shock — killed a man, which was no small thing, and had seen another have his throat ripped out by her wolf friend. She needed time. Carter nudged Dylan, and the two of them left the mother wolf, the handler, and Carter's vengeful angel to grieve in peace.

When they'd gone around the corner of the cabin, Dylan put his hand on Carter's shoulder. "My men are bringing in three of them. Ahote shot a fourth. It looked like they were being held on standby. What happened here?"

Carter mechanically recited the facts as he knew them,

his heart and half his brain with Mackenzie. And then he registered what Dylan had said. "A third squad?"

"Yeah, and from what I've observed, they're Special Forces. Which leads me to believe there's a fourth one out there somewhere. I can only assume the wolves broke up their plans and maybe unnerved them enough to run."

"Which of the wolves are accounted for?"

"Three of Loki and Keeva's litter are guarding the attackers they helped capture. One dead, . . ." he took a deep breath and continued, "Keeva is with Mackenzie, Loki is out there somewhere — I heard him howling a moment ago. I don't know where Nadia and her two are."

"I think Mackie will want to know if the rest are safe."

## Chapter Sixty

### WE SPEAK ENGLISH ONLY

Dylan noticed the three captured men coming into the clearing followed by three wolves, Ahote, and his two men. He spoke to them. "Hey, who's handling Nadia's pups?"

"I think it's the guys in the counter-clockwise squad, but I think I know where the wolves are, if you're looking for them. I had radio contact with the southern attack force, and I'm pretty sure they're on the run. The wolves are probably following them."

After exclamations all around about another squad of attackers, Dylan dispatched the handlers to find and guide the wolves who were presumably following the fleeing attackers. Then he and Carter secured the three captives to trees. Carter spared no mercy in tightening the cuffs.

Dylan ordered his men to retrieve all the bodies of their dead comrades and drop them in front of the captives where they could see them. All of this was done in total silence except for the grunts escaping from the prisoners as each body was dropped on the ground before them.

With that done, Dylan looked at the three men and said

in a soft and measured but deadly voice, "Now, let's have a nice little chat. Yes? Let's start with something simple. How many of you came here?"

When they refused to speak, two of Dylan's men stepped up and commanded the wolves to approach them. The two who had been pinned by the wolves before began trembling and stuttering incomprehensibly — in Russian.

"On this farm, we speak English only," Carter said in perfect Russian. "As you can see" —he pointed to the bodies on the ground— "we and our wolf comrades don't really like anyone who speaks Russian."

They nodded eagerly, the message was very clear. When the two wolves started growling, all three of them tried to speak at the same time. By this time, their britches were soaked with urine. But their new leader, the recently converted believer, got the upper hand and started in perfect, almost unaccented English, "We were sixteen men. You and your demons have killed nine. So, there are seven of us left including the three of us here. Our mission leader and three more have escaped."

The fugitives had a head start, but Dylan had a secret weapon. The last two wolves, and possibly their mother, Nadia, would be on their trail. They couldn't outrun horses, and they surely couldn't outrun wolves.

He turned to Carter and whispered, "Get hold of Ahote and saddle some horses for us." Carter nodded and left, while Dylan continued the chat with his new Russian friends.

## Chapter Sixty-One

### HOT PURSUIT

By the time Dylan, Carter, and two more EA men mounted their horses, the fugitive Russian team had nearly an hour on them. But Dylan wasn't worried. The horses would make up that distance quickly, as they proved when they caught up with the two wolf handlers and handed them the reigns of their horses, which Carter and Dylan had led. Keeping the pace at an easy trot, within half an hour they spotted the fleeing Russians in the distance.

The handlers used their dog-whistles to signal the wolves to break off their pursuit and come to them, keeping them safe from friendly and unfriendly fire. Nadia and her pups arrived in short order, panting from their exertion. The handlers gave them permission to stand down, and the wolves dropped to their resting position, but with their heads still high and on alert.

Carter pointed Dylan to the ravine, about three miles ahead of the Russians, and said, "They're heading for the cover of that gorge. I know that place like the back of my hand. There is an ideal place to ambush them."

Dylan nodded and told the men they would be circling wide around the Russians and setting up an ambush.

On arrival, Dylan made a quick tactical assessment and nodded at Carter. "It is exactly as you said, *'an ideal place to ambush them.'* They'll have to form a single file to get through that narrow cleft opening and those ledges up there" —he pointed to the outcrops, between twenty and thirty feet high on both sides— "will give us very good cover and put them under the crossfire from perdition if they are stupid enough to try and make a stand. I hope they don't — I really want to have a bit more of a chat with these assholes, especially their fearless leader."

Dylan ordered the two wolf handlers to take the wolves and all the horses and hide about a mile farther down the gorge and to keep their radios on in case they were called in for support.

Carter and Dylan, each accompanied by one of the EA men, took up positions on opposite sides of the gully.

About five minutes later, the four Russians came into sight. It was immediately obvious they had thrown caution to the wind. Their clothes and faces were drenched in sweat, and they didn't even look around them, their eyes fixed on the ground in front of them as they were jogging along.

They were right in the middle of the killing ground when Dylan called out to them in Russian not quite as fluent as Carter's, but still unmistakable, "Halt!"

Instead of obeying the command, the Russians looked toward the sound of the voice frantically, but the echo off the rocks made it impossible to pinpoint a location. Two of them dropped into shooting stance and started firing wildly in all directions. The firefight was over in less than three seconds — the score was Freydís 2, Russians 0. One dead

Russian and another wounded. The leader had thrown down his weapon, raised his hands above his head, and shouted, "*My sdayemsya!* We surrender!" in Russian and English.

Two of the men gave up their horses to carry the dead Russian and his wounded comrade, the EA men marching behind the captives with the wolves pacing on either side to ensure cooperation. It was a long walk.

Along the way, the wolves lifted their heads as if they heard something in the distance, and then set up an eerie howling they kept up all the way back to the ranch headquarters. Dylan thought he knew why but kept it to himself. Everyone else shivered, especially the Russians.

The mission leader had time to think things over.

*These wolves have really spoiled our party and made complete asses out of all of us. Maybe they are just taunting us now with their howling.*

*And where the hell did these Special Forces operators come from? We never had any information about them. Someone has fucked up big time with the intel.*

*Whatever the reason for our botched operation, if any of us ever get out of this alive and are sent back to Russia, they'll probably reopen the Siberian gulags just to accommodate us for the rest of our lives.*

*Maybe the best tactic would be to give up all information and plead to be locked away in a Canadian or American prison?*

Once back at Freydís, Dylan and Carter asked that everyone except a few of the EA men and the wolves be relocated to Camp Tala until further notice. They didn't want the women and children to witness what was going to happen next. Mackenzie was still in a foul mood, and it took a lot of persuasion to get her to go with everyone else. As far as she was concerned, she had the right to lead the interrogation. But Carter and her parents finally convinced her that the children needed her attention now more than the Russian intruders.

When everyone had cleared out as requested, the new captives were treated to the same wolf-enhanced interrogation techniques that their other comrades had enjoyed earlier.

"I don't want to be accused of workplace discrimination by treating some Russians better than others," Dylan explained through Carter to the new captives as they were tied to the trees next to their other comrades, and the wolves were called in closer.

Carter was there to hear and interpret any muttered Russian that passed between the two groups. He might have been amused at the characterization of the wolves as demons had it not been for the seriousness of the morning's attack.

And as the "chat", as Dylan liked to call the interrogation, progressed, Carter got more and more worked up. Hearing the admission that the group had instructions to retrieve all the information about the library of the giants and the Dolphins was sort of digestible, but when the leader told them they were to abduct Carter and Mackenzie and kill everyone else, including the children, Carter pulled his Sig Sauer from the holster, popped the magazine out, checked that it was fully loaded, slammed it back into place, cocked the gun, and walked up to the nearest captive.

"Carter! What are you doing?" Dylan shouted.

Carter didn't even look at Dylan. He had his eyes fixed on the first target. "I'm going to shoot vermin, my friend. All of them. One by one, I am going to put a bullet in their heads, and don't you dare stop me."

"Carter! Stop it! Right now, that's not how we do it. There's no honor in that. Don't do it! We'll get a lot of information from them. They'll help us track the Nabateans down. They'll help us get Rick's killer. Come on, Carter, stop it."

Somewhere in all of that, Carter got his senses back and stopped in his tracks. Tears of fear were streaming down the face of the Russian in front of him. Slowly he turned around and put his gun away. He didn't say a word, but his face was ashen with rage.

Dylan continued with his questioning for another half hour or so before he contacted Sean to arrange for transport of the fugitives to D.C., which required a round of diplomatic jockeying with Canada. The Canadians were naturally keen to understand how and why a group of sixteen former Spetsnaz operatives had entered their country, not to mention the individuals who had entered with them to provide cover. But they were also not very keen to get into any unfriendly discussions with the Russian government. Especially when they heard that the Russian Director of the Federal Security Service (FSB) might be involved. That sort of "diplomatic" discussions were best handled by their big brother to the south.

Eventually, the President managed to "persuade" the Prime Minister that the attack had to do with an ongoing mission, and that when all was said and done, he'd provide a full briefing for his Canadian ally. And Canada was welcome to the cover people if the US could have the soldiers. "Reluctantly," the Prime Minister agreed to look the other way as the illegals were transported out of his country. *If* the President would promise to brief him fully.

## Chapter Sixty-Two

### A FUNERAL

While these negotiations were going on, JR, the wolf pup, was afforded full military honors in a hastily-arranged burial next to the grave of Will Devereux. Keeva and Loki, JR's brothers and sister, Nadia, and her pups mourned in the wolf way, keening softly at times, and at other times howling their anguish.

Each sound of grief uttered by her beloved wolves ripped through Mackenzie's heart and soul. It seemed to Carter that the howling was in response to Mackenzie's tears and heartfelt tribute to JR. He couldn't decide who felt the most pain, Keeva and Loki or Mackenzie. A chill went down his spine when he thought of how easily it could have been Liam or Beth they mourned. If it took him until his dying day, he vowed to keep them safe, and along with them, all the world's children. Monsters who sent armed Special Forces against kids could not be allowed to walk the earth. He'd find out who it was or die trying.

# The Alboran Codex

After the wolf funeral, a teary-eyed Liam and sleepy Beth were put to bed by their equally exhausted mother. Mackenzie told Carter she needed just a short nap, and then she'd be at his side to help with whatever came next. Carter agreed, but he couldn't rest himself.

Two questions vied for answers in his and Dylan's discussions after the prisoners had been evacuated. In a surprisingly short time after the President had concluded his negotiations with the Canadian Prime Minister, two Sikorsky choppers had arrived to take away the Russians. Carter thought of them as vermin, and of their employers as the scum of the earth.

"Dylan, from past experience and from that leader's clues, even though he couldn't give us names, I have no doubt their employers are the Nabateans. Too bad Durand isn't still around to help us find them."

"I don't think he ever knew their exact location. You should probably delay your expedition until we can root them out."

"Unacceptable. It's more imperative than ever we find that city, and those nukes if they're still there, before these scumbags get their hands on them. You saw to what lengths they are prepared to go to achieve their goals. No, we must step up the launch of that expedition right now.

"I have one more question, and that is how did those rats get past your security measures? We can't go on expedition and leave our kids unprotected. We have to plug those holes."

"Carter, I can't answer that right this minute, but believe me, by the time the CIA and Sean gets through with said rats, we'll know. I suspect some very sophisticated detection and jamming equipment allowed them to see and bypass our electronics. The spooks will be ecstatic to get their hands on it."

"Before it disappears into their Black Ops division, make sure your engineers get to thoroughly examine it and come up with ways to beat it. I mean it, Dylan. If one hair on my kids' or wife's heads is harmed . . . ." He didn't have to finish the sentence. Dylan knew. He saw it in Carter's eyes that morning when he was about to execute the prisoners.

Dylan knew then that Carter was shaken to the core. He had a moment's white terror himself about what could have happened to the kids or Mackenzie or Liu. And Carter, of course, who was indispensable to national security.

## Chapter Sixty-Three

### THE PREPARATIONS

Bill Griffin had been busy locating just the right boat for the expedition. It had to be state-of-the-art, but not an obvious US Navy research vessel. And he knew just the boat.

*La Solitude* looked like exactly what it was — a luxury superyacht — designed and captained by Randall Branson, who was not only an old friend of Bill's, but a valued operative. Branson was, however, *not* exactly what he looked like. The billionaire had made his fortune in the communications industry, but before he was forty, he'd tired of the rat race. Leaving his business in the capable hands of a new CEO and his board, he'd "retired" — to the CIA.

Anyone who knew Branson knew he'd always wanted to captain his own yacht and sail the world. What most didn't know was he'd dreamed of being a high-tech spook ever since he'd watched his first James Bond movie as a young teen. His acquaintance with the director of the CIA through their college fraternity provided him with the opportunity to make that dream come true. He'd made Bill an offer he couldn't refuse — the use of the yacht for undercover work, provided he was part of the package — Captain of *La Solitude*.

*La Solitude* boasted modifications that made her perfect for the jobs she was assigned to. Accommodating fourteen guests in her seven staterooms, she was equipped for ocean travel with ultra-modern stabilization technology, advanced communications equipment, and every nod to comfort that Branson could dream up.

Three-quarters the length of a football field and thirty-seven feet wide, she provided a hot tub, sauna, Turkish bath, infinity pool, gym, gourmet galley, formal dining room, and several lounges. The latter housed sophisticated electronics gear and computer equipment that could be concealed when necessary – that is, when anyone was aboard who didn't need to know anything about the undercover work.

In addition to fourteen guests, *La Solitude* housed a crew of seventeen, including her captain. All superyacht crews were traditionally trained in several jobs for redundancy in case of illness or injury. *La Solitude's* crew took it one step further. They were trained also in weapons and hand-to-hand combat, deep sea diving, and the operation of the underwater survey equipment, including an ROV. Some were ex-SEALs.

She was perfect for the job. The only problem was she was already on assignment, checking out a suspected weapons dealer off the coast of Brazil. With no other asset that came close to having the specifications Carter and his team would need, Bill was ready to pull rank and reassign her, but first he sent Sean and Dylan to inspect and determine whether her existing equipment would be sufficient, and if not, decide what would need to be installed before the expedition.

Dylan returned to Freydís from his "Brazilian vacation"

raving about the yacht. He could hardly wait to show every inch of it to Liu, and Liu was just as excited for the voyage, even though potential danger lurked during its primary mission. A cruise on a luxury superyacht with the man of your dreams — what more could a girl ask for?

While Dylan was gone, Carter put Samantha in charge of obtaining the latest satellite imagery of the Alboran Sea and enhancing it to locate potential dive sites. He'd decided to include Mackenzie only after her impassioned arguments that she had the most rapport with the Dolphins, she'd been working with Liu and Sam on the Dolphin language, and that she'd never forgive him if he didn't. It was the last one that swayed him. As he said to Dylan when they discussed it later, "Happy wife, happy life."

Dylan was enthusiastic about taking Liu for many of the same reasons. Danger or no danger, it would be the adventure of a lifetime, and besides, he could protect her. Not only that, but she, along with most of the other adults living at the ranch, had been taking the same combat training Carter and Mackenzie had started. By this time, most of them were competent to protect themselves — as the Russian invaders learned two weeks earlier. Even Mackenzie's parents could if they had to.

As soon as the details of their research vessel were known, preparation for the logistics of the expedition began. Among the necessities was fully briefing Branson on the mission. Bill took care of that, and Branson was then equipped to plan for everything from fuel to food.

Carter had specified the need for an ROV, or remote-operated vehicle, to perform preliminary dives. The best satellite images were still too grainy to show the worst of any underwater obstacles and traps they might encounter. Branson wrote up a full report on his existing ROV, fully prepared to replace it if necessary. Looking it over, Carter was satisfied the ROV would fulfill all his requirements and then some, with the addition of one more instrument. Equipped with both a neutrally buoyant tether and a sturdier, load-carrying umbilical cable housing fiber optics and electrical conductors for power, data, and video signals, Branson's ROV also had custom additions. These gave it sonar capability in addition to its still and video cameras. It had a robot arm for picking up objects to be examined as well as instruments to measure everything from water clarity to sound velocity.

Carter's request was that it be retrofitted with a Geiger counter. Anyone swimming near the ancient nukes would also be equipped with dosimeters.

Planning for the expedition also included daily drills. Three SEALS arrived on Freydís to train with the three hand-picked EA men to make a seamless team. Most of the EA team were certified divers. Before the expedition launched, they'd all be experts. They practiced repelling boarders, taking turns being the good guys and the bad guys. Dylan, who directed the training as well as participated, told Carter it was almost as much fun as playing Cowboys and Indians as a kid. And they practiced underwater hand-to-hand combat. They all knew that if bad actors showed up, it would be their most important skill.

In the evenings, everyone gathered at the main house to be thoroughly briefed on the history of the undertaking. It was a lot to take in.

Back in D.C., James and Sean were having a battle over whether James would "get" to go. James insisted. Sean dug in his heels.

"Buddy, you're getting a little long in the tooth for this. Besides, A-Echelon needs you at the helm more than you need to go with us. We've got it under control. The President loaned us some SEALs, and my men are as good as they are. We'll protect Carter, Mackenzie, and the others. You'd just get in the way."

"Get your ass over here and say that to my face, *buddy*," James snarled over the scrambled line. "I'm still in top condition. I can take you any time, any place."

Sean laughed. "Yeah, right, grandpa. What does Irene say about it?"

"Doesn't matter what she says. I'm going. If I must, I'll appeal to the President."

Irene, standing in James's office and hearing only half of the conversation, could tell by his responses exactly what his younger friend on the other end of the line was saying.

"James, I agree with Sean. You need to stay here."

"*Et tu*, Irene?" he said. "Don't you start as well.

"I recruited Will Devereux when this snotnose was still in kindergarten. I recruited Carter and Mackenzie, and I've been on expeditions and missions with them all. I've been there to help rescue Mackenzie, Liu, and the children. Why would I not be going now? I should have been the first on the list of those who are going.

"So now you and Sean Walker get off my back. I'm going, and that's final."

Irene held out her hand for the phone receiver. James handed it over, still fuming.

"I have an idea, Sean. He promises this is his last mission, and we stop arguing with him."

"Will he do that?"

"I'll see to it."

"Okay, go for it."

Irene hung up. "Okay, James, you can go."

"Damn straight I can go and I don't need your permission."

"Maybe not, but you need your doctors' permission, and if you'll promise not to make this kind of a fuss next time, I'll see that you get it. You heard me. This is the last time."

Still grumbling under his breath, James gave a curt nod. It was settled. He was going, and he'd better make the most of it, because after this, he'd be put out to pasture.

Sean was going, of course. Dylan would be underwater with Carter much of the time, so a second leader was required for the fighting force.

## Chapter Sixty-Four

### SET SAIL FOR THE STRAIT OF GIBRALTAR

Even though Mackenzie had fought hard for her place on the expedition team, it was hard to leave the kids. Dylan assured her that the Nabatean-commissioned assault on Freydís wouldn't be repeated, or rather wouldn't stand a chance to get anywhere close to the children again. Carter added that if she didn't want to leave them, she was welcome to stay home. In fact, he preferred it. But the challenge only settled her mind to go.

"No, I'm Sunhead, leader of the land-humans, remember?" She laughed. "I'm your ambassador to the Alboran Sea Dolphins. We never have completely convinced the Chesapeake Bay pod that you are really the leader." She pointed to Carter. "You need me. I'll be all right."

Liam helped by sturdily announcing he'd be personally taking care of his sister Beth.

The whole family, including Ahote and Bly, Mackenzie's parents and brother, and everyone who'd found a temporary or permanent home on Freydís, was at the air strip to see them off as they headed to D.C.

From D.C., a military chopper took them with their personal gear to the waiting research vessel. It wasn't the most comfortable or luxurious ride they'd ever taken by air, but the ability to drop onto the vessel far out to sea outstripped the need for comfort. It was imperative the make-up of the expedition personnel remained a secret. Sean, who had flown in to vet the final preparations, was along for the ride, though.

For that reason, the flight began before dawn, and a few hours later the chopper would land at the naval base in Norfolk, Virginia, before refueling and taking off after nightfall to rendezvous with *La Solitude*. Of course, anyone who was sufficiently motivated could still track their movements, but this subterfuge made it a bit more difficult.

Mackenzie had been a little apprehensive about the night-drop onto the boat, but she needn't have been. Instead of what she'd visualized — each person dangling from a sling while the chopper hovered above — the chopper put down on a helipad on the boat's deck. Schematics of the boat hadn't prepared her for its size. After a guided tour of the ultra-luxurious boat by her Captain, Randall "Call me Randy" Branson, and seeing her and Carter's cabin, she was looking forward to the transatlantic crossing. This wasn't a tiny pleasure boat.

It had been decided that they couldn't brief the crew before *La Solitude* was out to sea. Every member of the crew was CIA and had been thoroughly vetted again when the yacht was given the assignment. But there was simply too much to get ready to brief them ahead of time. Like the evenings at the ranch, each shift's off-duty crew spent their waking hours in the company of the expedition team to learn why the urgency and secrecy.

Although that took only a few hours a day, it was necessary to limit the duration of the sessions so that Carter and those who were familiar with the history of his work could break it to them bit by bit. At times their "students" were just staring at them slack-jawed. There were times when some of them were quite vocal, especially Captain Randy, a self-made and independent man who didn't have the military training and discipline the others had.

So, it wasn't uncommon to hear him interject with phrases such as, "You must be kidding me! Ancient nukes? Intelligent humans from fifty thousand years ago! You sure you haven't been in the sun a bit too long, Carter?"

Those were the times when Randy would have the server bring out the scotch and soda and other drinks and hit it hard. It helped to numb the senses a bit, and it was almost as if it also helped them to be a bit more accommodating of the mindboggling information.

Carter would just smile most of the time. He had seen these kinds of reactions many times in the past.

Carter fed the information to them in chronological order, which meant they got to talking about the Dolphins last, and that was the proverbial straw that broke the camel's back.

"You stop right there, mister." Randy had his hand up. "I'm not risking damage to my brain by taking that in without some sort of anesthetic." He ordered the server to bring the drinks but told him to leave the full bottles, mixers, and buckets of ice on the table where they could get to it quick and easy.

Randy had downed the first double like a shot of schnapps, poured himself another stiff one, looked at Carter with drink in hand, and said, "You were saying something about dolphins?"

At some stage, Carter was worried they didn't have

enough alcohol and headache tablets on board to cure the Captain and his crew from information overload syndrome. But they got through it — the pictures, audio, and video recordings of Carter and the team talking to the Dolphins helped them understand and believe, along with the alcoholic beverages.

With little else to do but enjoy the sun and spray while the boat sped across the Atlantic, Carter's team thoroughly enjoyed the fourteen-day luxury cruise before the skipper informed them that the Pillars of Hercules would be coming into view within a few hours.

Except for the days when they'd be on the dive site itself, this was the most dangerous part of the voyage. They hadn't seen another ship in the open ocean, but there was always the risk of encountering pirates this close to the Spanish and Moroccan shorelines. However, any pirate trying to take *La Solitude* would find it a very costly mistake. Carter, Mackenzie, and the others all came out onto the open deck to watch for the first view of the Pillars of Hercules. None of them had ever seen it from the Atlantic, though Carter had seen it from the Mediterranean side before on a previous archaeological expedition.

Mackenzie was the first to shout with excitement when she spotted the Rock of Gibraltar from the port side. The others rushed to her as she pointed to the shadow in the mist far ahead. By this time, they were about forty nautical miles from the Strait of Gibraltar, the roiling passageway between Spain and Morocco, one of the busiest stretches of water in the world.

## Chapter Sixty-Five

### INTO THE ALBORAN SEA

A little under four hours later, they had entered the fray, making their way steadily through the strait without interference from the Spanish Coast Guard. They were expected. Because the US had a large military presence in Spain, diplomatic relations were cordial enough that all the authorities had to say was the boat was a private research vessel, headed for an unspecified location within the Mediterranean. No one felt it necessary to specify the Alboran Sea, connecting the Mediterranean with the Atlantic Ocean, or that the research was classified top secret-plus.

Following the vague references to their capital city that Liu and Carter had gleaned from the library of the giants, they studied what they had on the satellite maps and directed the skipper to a location due northwest from the City of Lights to the northernmost coordinate of the Alboran Sea, where a line would intersect the Spanish shore at the northeastern limit of the bathtub-shaped body of water. There they would begin their survey, using sensitive underwater depth-finders to map the sea floor in places of interest before sending the ROV down for a closer look.

Carter's team were relying on two things to help them find what they were looking for. First was the electronic data gathered from the satellite and other surveillance methods, and second was his hope to get help from the Alboran Sea Dolphins. Due to their hasty departure from the Chesapeake area when Rick was killed, he had no way of knowing the outcome of the ansible communications between Joanna and her Alboran Sea relatives, nor whether he and his expedition were even welcome in their territory.

He could only hope that the Dolphins of the Alboran Sea were as friendly and helpful as the American Dolphins were. He had to shrug off a fleeting thought that the land-humans from some of these countries bordering the Alboran Sea were not so friendly with infidel land-humans, particularly those from America. He could only hope that the water-humans of those parts were not of the same political and religious persuasion as their land counterparts.

A systematic, scientific grid search would be attracting all kinds of attention, at least two kinds of which they desperately didn't want to attract. There was no way to camouflage the boat from satellite observance, which would bring the Nabateans sooner or later. Nor would a slow, methodical patrolling from Spain to Morocco in a grid fail to attract pirates before too many days had passed. The area was simply too jam-packed with other vessels to expect privacy.

The references to the capital they had were so vague that unless they could pinpoint locations with their sophisticated equipment or the help of the Dolphins, the whole expedition would soon become a very expensive holiday paid for by the American tax payers.

## Chapter Sixty-Six

### CONTACT

They reached the first site on the afternoon of the second day after entering the Alboran Sea.

Carter didn't say it, but he was getting a little worried that they had not spotted any Dolphins yet. Not that he expected a welcoming committee and red carpet when they arrived, but still . . . he could not help but wonder about his earlier musings about political and religious persuasions.

Before they'd dive the site, they'd send the ROV down to have a quick look-see. He didn't expect much, as the depth meter showed it was only about twenty meters. The proximity to shore and the relatively shallow water made it inconceivable that the site hadn't been thoroughly explored previously.

"Carter, why are you bothering with this site?" Mackenzie asked.

"First, to be thorough. We can't afford to overlook anything. Maybe this site has been explored, and maybe not. You know I've on several occasions made ground-breaking discoveries on digs that have been "worked" for years. And second, because my refresher course in scuba diving was short, and this site is relatively shallow. I'll be glad of the practice. I'm rusty for record-level scuba diving, but this one's a piece of cake."

Put that way, it sounded like a great idea to Mackenzie. Carter had explained the limitations to her. The "official" world record — the Guinness — for a deep scuba dive was just over 332 meters (1,090 feet), and the diver who set it, a forty-one-year-old Egyptian diving instructor, had trained for it for four years. With no such training, she didn't want Carter anywhere near that depth.

The ROV was lowered from the launching bay and sent down to the site. For the next hour or so, the operator maneuvered it around under direction from Carter, stopping, hovering, turning back at times, focusing the cameras on certain features, taking still pictures and videos as it went along. While the operator returned, and docked the ROV, they all began studying the pictures and videos.

The next morning, Carter and Dylan had the honor of making the first dive of the expedition. Dylan, an ex-Navy SEAL, was an expert diver, so although he didn't have underwater archaeological experience, his skills and experience was comforting to Carter and Mackenzie.

Dylan stayed out of Carter's way as he swam among the ancient, drowned buildings, but was watching his back all the time. Carter was looking for anything that would give him a sense of the age of these buildings. Most useful would be pottery, coins, or other artifacts he could date almost on sight.

They'd been down on the first dive for about half an hour when a swiftly-moving gray shape brushed against

## The Alboran Codex

Dylan, causing him to cry out in alarm. Their linked helmet mics transmitted the cry to Carter and to the spectators watching the screens in the electronics room on deck. Mackenzie's and Liu's hands flew to their mouths at the same time. They both saw the "thing" moving past Dylan, but it was too quick to recognize. Their sigh of relief came in unison when they heard Carter's voice.

"Ms. Dolphin, I've been waiting for you. Where have you been all this time?" And then some muttering, following which Liu swore sounded something like, "I just hope you're not some religious nut job." She'd have to clarify that with Carter and Dylan when they were back on deck.

A weird, electric tingling went through Carter, and then he could hear a high-pitched sound transmitted through the water. He was certain the Dolphin was speaking to him, but without the translation device, he was helpless to understand or respond.

"Sam, you'll have to make a plan to connect the translation device to our helmets. We need to be able to talk to the Dolphins while we are underwater," Carter said right away.

"Onto it, boss," Sam replied enthusiastically.

"Dylan, what do you think? Should we cut the dive short and go see what this lady's saying? Or keep searching and hope she goes to talk to Mackie?"

"Up to you, buddy. She's probably just saying hi. Why don't you try waving at her?"

Carter lifted a hand and made a waving motion, feeling a bit silly. It was probably not a gesture they understood. To his surprise, the Dolphin "stood" on her tail and waved her pectoral fin in a reasonable facsimile of a human wave. Carter smiled broadly, and the Dolphin responded with the chittering he'd come to associate with Dolphin humor.

Seeing her understanding of his gestures, he pointed toward the boat above. The Dolphin seemed to bow a couple of times, almost like nodding, he thought. Then she swam upward toward the boat.

"I'll be damned," he muttered to himself in awe. "Mackie, be ready to welcome the guest we have been expecting for days now."

"That was something, all right," Dylan responded then flipped the switch on the mic so that only he and Carter could talk to each other. "These Dolphins, ah . . . water-humans, are just the most amazing creatures I've ever encountered. Please don't tell Mackenzie I said so, but they are even more remarkable than her wolves."

"I promise I won't tell her." Carter chuckled. "She might just decide to take out her unfulfilled revenge on you for the killing of JR by that Russian rat."

"My sentiments exactly." Dylan laughed and switched the mic back to all stations.

Turning to his task, Carter put the Dolphin encounter out of his mind and continued his meticulous search for an artifact. When Dylan's dive watch indicated it was time to return, he told Carter, who reluctantly concluded that this site had probably been picked clean years before and followed Dylan up.

On the boat, he found Mackenzie in a state of bliss. The friendly Dolphin had indeed understood his gesture and had come to visit. She and Mackenzie had been conversing comfortably, and the Dolphin was still in the area.

"Carter, she got a message from Joanna! It's true! They can communicate instantly, all the way around the world. It's like they're linked psychically. Joanna sent Merrybeth, that's this one, a picture of us!"

Dylan just shook his head and mumbled, "How the . . . ah, don't worry . . . just forget it. I'll never understand it."

In good-natured torment of Dylan, Carter took it in stride, as if this was an everyday occurrence for him. "I figured she would. And I don't think Dolphins know how to lie, so I believed her. It just took a little imagination to understand how it worked. So, what did she have to say?"

"Well, I'm sorry to inform you" —Mackenzie giggled— "but Merrybeth thinks I'm the leader. I guess Joanna didn't educate her on how we land-humans do things. We'll need to tell her and hope she doesn't get her nose out of joint!"

"Joanna didn't take it too badly. You and I just have to give her consistent information. Will you introduce me?"

"Oh, of course!" Mackenzie said with a big smile. Stepping to the rail hand-in-hand with her handsome husband, Mackenzie spoke into the mic. "Merrybeth, this is Carter, my mate."

The Dolphin rose vertically in the water and waved her flipper at Carter, then gave the characteristic Dolphin laugh, followed by a flood of other vocalizations.

"Greetings, Carter. You are very clever. I like this method of saying hello." She waved her flipper again.

Astonished, Mackenzie looked back and forth between the Dolphin and her husband. "Was that a wave?"

"I believe it was. I couldn't understand or talk to her when she introduced herself underwater, so I did what Dylan suggested to say hi. It looks like she understood me."

"Indeed, it does. Well, she's been asking me what we're looking for. I wonder if there's a way to get the idea across so she can tell us where to find the city without us having to do this onerous hit and miss searching?"

"I think we first talk to them about the giants," Carter

said. "See if they have any knowledge about the giants. If they know about the giants, then a very big part of our problem could be solved."

Mackenzie nodded. "I see where you're going. But it's late, and I see she's gone already. Let's get our ducks in a row tonight and ask the lady first thing in the morning."

## Chapter Sixty-Seven

### BRAINSTORMING

That night, after another dinner worthy of a five-star restaurant, Carter asked Captain Randy, Mackenzie, Liu, Sean, Dylan, James, and Sam to join him in the lounge area for drinks and a brainstorming session.

He laid out his plan to talk to Merrybeth about the giants and the prospect that she might know where they would find that city. His suggestion met with everyone's approval. What remained was to figure out how to get the message across to the Dolphin.

Sean sat back, closed his eyes for a while, deep in thought, and then very calmly said, "Pictures."

"Pictures?" Carter asked and then a big smile broke across his face. "Of course!" he exclaimed then started grinning. "So, your head does actually contain a brain. I could have sworn its only purpose was to keep your ears apart."

Sean slowly raised a middle finger in Carter's direction, and everyone exploded in laughter.

Captain Randy only shook his head — this was a tight knit group of very loyal friends who had obviously eaten a bag of salt together. He liked them and was excited to work with an outfit of this caliber.

When the bantering finally dwindled down, Sam laid out her plan of action. "Okay, tonight there's going to be no rest for the wicked. My sidekick already started work on setting up a link between the translator device to the diving communications devices.

"I will need all the help and brains we can muster to interpret those sonar images. So far, we were able to 'translate' what they have sent us, but we now have to figure out how we send sonar images back to them."

---

By the next morning, when the first rays of the sun announced the start of a beautiful day, they were ready. They'd had such an eventful night with getting everything ready, they didn't even realize they hadn't slept.

After breakfast, Mackenzie called out to Merrybeth. Within a few minutes, she appeared, accompanied by about ten other Dolphins. She introduced her pod, and then Mackenzie introduced everyone in her pod, as was required by Dolphin etiquette per Joanna's schooling back in America.

"How can we help you, Mackenzie?" Merrybeth asked once the introduction ceremony was over.

"My mate, Carter, wants to talk to you. He has lots of questions for you and pictures to show you. Is that okay with you?"

"Yes, Mackenzie. Joanna told me that you are afraid of sharks. We will be very glad to help you." It took a moment's thought before Carter and Mackenzie realized the Dolphins weren't talking about literal sharks, but the "land-humans" they wanted to steer clear of. A few moments of clarification on both sides set up the device to use context to decide whether to say "sharks" or "bad land-humans", the phrase Carter came up with to mean enemy.

"I am happy to speak with your mate, Mackenzie." Merrybeth followed her reply with a leap from the water, waving her fin as she fell back.

Carter laughed and waved back. Then he took the mic and began to explain that they were looking for a place where "big land-people" used to live, many generations ago. He was getting the hang of how the Dolphins understood time, but putting it in terms the translator could get across sometimes caused a few minutes' back and forth before he felt they were on the same page.

After explaining that this was a long time ago, Carter had to explain "big" and "little" and, as he remarked to Mackenzie much later, "just right", or the range of sizes of humans on the boat. At last, Merrybeth understood, or he thought she did, and supplied the whistles and beeps to the translator.

Finally, Carter and Dylan suited up and entered the water with images of the giants from the library. He couldn't imagine how Sam and her assistant had modified the laser printer to print on Captain Randy's linen tablecloths, but there the images were, almost as large as life. He and Dylan each held a side of the cloth while Merrybeth twisted back and forth to eye it first from the left, then from the right.

At last, she spoke, but with hesitations between her whistles, and a few consultations with her pod. "We think we know of a place like this," she said, after swimming around to see the back of the cloth. "It is bigger than this. Big land-people used to live here, but the place was once on land.

Now it is in water, and no land-people live there now. Carter, we are not sure. This 'picture' is like the edge between water and air. The caves where the big land-people lived are like your metal fish. You can go in and out."

She seemed to struggle with the concept she was trying to convey. Carter was equally puzzled, until Merrybeth swam around to look at the back of the cloth again. Then he flipped the switch so what he would say was only for Dylan's ears. "Oh! She doesn't understand the one-dimensional image. We forgot, so much of their 'vision' is actually enhanced by echolocation."

"Do we ask her to take us to the place, even if we aren't sure she understands the picture?"

"Yes, I think so. I'll discuss it a bit more with her." He flipped the switch again. "Merrybeth, when you talk to Dolphins in pods far away, can you see what they see?" Dylan tilted his head, and Carter made a thumbs-up gesture to assure him the question was leading somewhere.

"Yes, Carter. My friend, Joanna, showed me what you look like. I cannot explain to you if land-people don't do this."

"Well, some may, but most of us don't. Instead, we make images like this. Our brains supply the information that lets us see them as in and out. We call it three-dimensional." He held his breath during the pause while the translation device did what it could with his awkward explanation.

Merrybeth listened. Then Carter could have sworn she grinned. Her sharp little teeth were in full evidence before she spoke again. "I am sorry, my friend, that your vision is inferior to ours. But I will lead you to the old land caves, and you can go in and out. You understand, they are full of water now?"

"Yes, Merrybeth, we understand. We will follow you."

"We will swim for three suns and rest in the dark."

"I understand."

As she swam off, Carter and Dylan hastily made their way back into the boat to find that Captain Randy had been listening to the exchange with Mackenzie, Liu, and the rest and was ready to follow the Dolphins as soon as the men were aboard.

"That was quite a conversation," Mackenzie said.

"You know, they are so intelligent I forget while talking to them that there are so many things they can't experience. It's a struggle to think like an underwater creature with no houses, photos, and everything else we take for granted. And then, just when I'm thinking we're superior, I get my ass handed to me with a remark like she made about our vision being inferior. From her perspective, it is. We can't navigate by echolocation, and that freaky ansible thing is like science fiction come to life."

"I know, Carter," Mackenzie said. "It boggles the mind, doesn't it?"

As the yacht started to move, the party went forward to watch the Dolphin pod leaping in front of them while they followed at a speed to match the Dolphins', about eight knots.

Later, when the Dolphins stopped and began to circle the boat in the late afternoon, they had another conversation with Merrybeth. Carter again had to improvise as he described the destructive power of a nuclear weapon and asked Merrybeth what she knew of such a thing.

Somehow, her whistles and squeaks took on a haunting sound when she answered. "Yes, we know of these big noises. But it isn't just noise. They send powerful blows through the water. My mother taught me of such things that happened within her mother's lifetime. Many creatures besides us were killed or harmed. Some became unable to hear or see, and later many were sick and died even if they were far away from the blow. Some were thrown into the air and fell a long distance. Bad, bad, bad." The device translated those words with, "It was terrible."

In a low voice the mic wouldn't pick up, Carter said to the others, "I wonder if she's talking about the tests near Bikini Island in the last century?"

While the others talked softly among themselves about the remarkable "oral" history tradition among the Dolphins, Carter continued to question Merrybeth about even more ancient times. He asked if the "big land-people" had such weapons. Amazingly, a flood of whistles, clicks, and other vocalizations ensued. The translation device had trouble keeping up with it, but Carter signaled everyone to listen. What they heard astounded them.

"Oh, yes! In the time of the big land-people, there were also small people like yourselves. The small people learned of the weapons and made many. They threw them at each other, pod against pod, and some threw them at the big people. Everyone, including water-people, became sick, and almost all the small land-people died. Very few were left when the big land-people took away their weapons and stored them in the caves where we are taking you. Is this what you seek?"

Carter switched the mic off and hollered, "that's exactly what we seek!" It took a minute for him to calm down, before he flipped the switch on again and said, "yes Merrybeth, that's what we seek, but not to use them against our bad land-people. We want to be sure they don't find them and use them again, and we want to keep everyone safe from them."

"We will show you. Now I must rest. I will see you at next sun, Carter. Good sleep, Mackenzie."

Mackenzie spoke up then. "Good sleep, Merrybeth. Thank you for helping us."

"We like you. You are our land pod."

As soon as the translation device was off, excited talk broke out among everyone present.

They could hardly believe that conversation with another species would become so easy so quickly. Even more amazing, that the Dolphins would have knowledge of events happening millennia ago.

Carter reminded them there were several cultures where oral history was passed down from generation to generation because written language hadn't been developed among them. He cited several Native American tribes and some in other parts of the world that still didn't have a written form for their language, who practiced the oral history tradition even in modern times. But he had to remind them that oral history was also the source of a lot of myth.

After a while, Carter suggested they all turn in and rest while they could since everyone hadn't slept much the night before. Even though they had two days' more to follow the Dolphins, if he understood Merrybeth's prediction correctly, they still had a lot of work to do.

He'd prefer if everyone were alert since there were no guarantees the bad guys wouldn't show up at any minute.

## Chapter Sixty-Eight

### LAND-HUMAN CAVES

In the early afternoon of the third day, the Dolphins started circling the yacht, and Carter understood it to mean they'd arrived.

Merrybeth appeared off the port bow and danced for attention. Mackenzie got the speaker on in time for everyone to hear what she said. "Big land-human caves."

"Thank you, Merrybeth!"

In short order, they sent the ROV down for a look. A cheer went up from everyone in the electronics room when they saw what was below them. A large complex of ruins surrounded them in all directions. The architecture looked very similar to the City of Lights, with gigantic proportions. Carter was sure they'd found what they were looking for.

Despite quite a bit of damage, apparently from the frequent earthquakes in the area and tectonic plate shifting over the millennia, the city was magnificent. And vast.

From their satellite maps, they estimated the site could have a diameter of roughly twelve miles. It was far too big to thoroughly explore in one trip, but they hoped Merrybeth and her pod would be instrumental in helping them locate what they were looking for.

Carter asked Merrybeth if she and her pod would be willing to accompany him and Dylan when they made the first dive at the location where they were anchored. Merrybeth let out one of those giggling sounds and told him that she wouldn't have it any other way. According to her, when Mackenzie's pod members were in the water, they were her responsibility.

Carter and Sean, with Merrybeth and her pod in tow, went for an exploratory dive after the ROV had been retrieved and before an afternoon thunderstorm called them back to the surface due to poor light conditions. Their initial survey convinced them that the yacht was anchored over the most promising section of the city. Here, the buildings were enormous, sprawling edifices surely meant for public purposes, the CBD of the city. Farther out, though the buildings were still enormous, they were more compact, suggesting dwellings.

The two men measured the length and breadth of the municipal complex, as they decided to call it, and decided to make the most thorough search there, before exploring the rest of the city, if necessary. They hoped to find another library, with records of where the nukes might be stored, but they agreed that their priority was to find and retrieve any ancient nukes they could identify, even if they didn't find written records. If time permitted, the archaeologic value of the city merited a more thorough "dig", though the term was an oxymoron. Carter pointed out that they might indeed have to dig into the silt at the bottom to discover everything.

By the time, they returned to the yacht, the rain had started, and everyone scurried for cover and another gourmet dinner.

## Chapter Sixty-Nine

### TAKE OVER THAT DIG

The next morning, the skies having cleared, Carter and Dylan prepared for a series of dives. While the men got ready to disappear under the water, Mackenzie had an unshakeable eerie feeling something ominous was in the air, and she hailed Merrybeth.

"Merrybeth, I am worried about my mate and his friend," she said when the Dolphin raised her head above the water. "Will you and your pod please keep watch over them like you did yesterday? What they are doing can be dangerous for all land-people, and there are bad land-people who might want to harm them."

"Yes, of course, Mackenzie. We'll watch for them, as I told you before."

Carter, Dylan, and the dolphins had been gone for about twenty minutes when Mackenzie's ill-omened feeling appeared in the form of a boat, twice the size of *La Solitude*, about half a mile from their location. Her instinct was that the boat was there because of Carter's expedition, but for now they weren't making any hostile moves. They had lowered anchor and were just sitting there.

*What do those people want?*

She went to the small bridge to inform the captain and Sean about the company they had.

Sean and Randy grabbed binoculars and studied the boat.

"A Chinese flag," Captain Randy muttered.

"Why does that make me feel uneasy?" Sean asked. "I am going to put the men on standby and get some divers suited up and ready to go if required."

Captain Randy nodded.

Underneath, Carter and Dylan swam toward the center of the city complex he and Sean dived the day before. He pointed to the cluster of buildings, explaining to Merrybeth again what he was looking for in the most general sense.

The ruins stretched as far as they could see, and it appeared they were covered with lots of silt.

"That's strange," Dylan remarked. "I keep thinking the middle will be deeper, but I'd say the bottom is less than fifteen meters here. In fact," he said, checking his dive watch, "it's only twelve."

"Remember, this was once a land bridge, like we talked about yesterday. Some parts sank more slowly or were higher to begin with. You can't apply what you know about the oceans to this area."

"Gotcha. Let's get busy."

After about an hour of exploration, Carter became aware of Merrybeth and her pod swimming around them in rapid circles. They were not as close as before. It was as if they were forming a wall of protection around the two of them. Carter tongued his mic. "Dylan, look at the Dolphins. Do they seem upset to you?"

## The Alboran Codex

"Yeah, they do. Keep your eyes open for sharks."

"Sharks! In the Alboran?"

"There are about forty-six types of shark in the Mediterranean, not counting the human kind. Fifteen are potentially dangerous. Shark attacks are rare, but these Dolphins are agitated about something. It could be sharks, both kinds."

As Dylan spoke, Carter picked up movement from the murky waters behind. Soon there was no doubt. "Speaking of the human kind! Right behind you!"

Dylan turned quickly. Two strangers, close by, were hanging in the water, watching them.

"Where'd they come from? They're not ours," Carter said.

Dylan spoke through his teeth. "Don't know, don't care. I don't like it when uninvited guests turn up at my parties.

"Sean, did you copy that? We've got company down here — two of the human kind, but not from our pod. Could be of the land-shark kind. Any idea if they are friend or foe?"

He was surprised to hear Captain Randy replying instead of Sean, "A boat flying a Chinese flag anchored half a mile from us about an hour ago. We've been watching them. They must have been dispatching divers from an onboard launch chamber. That's why we didn't see them going into the water.

"Sean and six more are on their way down to you."

As soon as Sean heard Carter talking to Dylan about other divers, he had given the order to the divers, and they rolled out, fully geared up, in less than a minute.

Carter and Dylan had retreated into a building from a window in the top floor of the three-story building. The Dolphins suddenly appeared outside. Carter stuck his head out the window and looked around. As he watched, men began dropping all around them. He was relieved to see the familiar equipment of Navy Seals.

Before he could let Dylan know the cavalry was there, other men, with different equipment and insignia, appeared in the murk. A fast-moving projectile raced by him, close enough he could feel its wake. *"What the hell?* Dylan, we're under attack!"

Dylan spoke rapidly into the mic. As Carter began fighting off an attacker who'd found their location, he yelled, "Sean, bogeys. Get over here!" He was unaware Sean and his men were already engaged in battle outside the building.

Carter felt a blow in his arms, where his attacker gripped him with iron fists. The attacker flew forward from the whack a Dolphin had given him, still locked to Carter. It drove him into Carter hard enough to knock his helmet against a wall and give it a blow that made a microscopic crack.

Dylan had dived out the window as quickly as he could and engaged with the next attacker. Meanwhile, Carter's Dolphin spun in place and delivered a blow with his flukes that spun the man helplessly. Since he still had an iron grip on Carter's arms, the spin slammed Carter into the wall again, this time dislocating his shoulder. Carter knew he was in serious trouble with a right arm that suddenly quit working.

The Dolphin continued to batter his prey until the man let go of Carter, who was in severe pain and unable to make much forward progress with only one arm. At last, the attacker went limp and sank. The Dolphin swam to Carter and nudged him. Carter put his good arm over the Dolphin's back, and the Dolphin started for the window with him, but they wouldn't both fit through the opening. Carter heard the whistles of the Dolphin and felt the electric tingle again before his Dolphin pushed him out the window and toward another one that waited outside. The second one allowed him to put his arm around it, and they headed toward the surface.

In the dim underwater light, Carter could see SEALS and EA men engaged in an eerie, silent battle with more attackers, and everywhere he looked, a Dolphin was helping his team — ramming the intruders with their noses. As he was taken out of the fray, he worried about Dylan. Where was he?

Minutes later, as he was hauled aboard, he got his answer. Dylan sat on the deck, leaning against the superstructure having his cuts dressed by the medic. "What took you so long?" he drawled. Carter looked at him closely. His pupils were dilated.

"What did you give him?" Carter asked.

"A butt-load of morphine," the medic answered. "Had to. He was wild to get back down and help you, but the Dolphins kept nudging him up. He's got a sprained wrist and knife wounds that need attention."

"I guess we owe our lives to those Dolphins," Carter said, before emitting an *oof!* as Mackie tackled him. "Careful, Mackie. That shoulder's dislocated."

"We'll have that fixed in a jiffy," the medic said.

"What's the status below?" Carter asked, the pain of the relocation procedure causing him to speak in a strained voice.

"The Dolphins and our men have driven off the attackers. Two of them are dead, along with one of the SEALS and one of the EA men. We're trying to recover the bodies now."

"Dylan's going to be brutal when he wakes up," Carter said, beginning to feel the effects of the morphine himself. The last he remembered before waking up hours later was his Mackie, vowing terrible vengeance on the Chinese boat and its passengers.

As Carter drifted off, Sean spoke to Mackenzie and James.

"Those bastards killed Willy. He got engaged just before we deployed. What am I going to tell his girl? And the SEAL. That's going to be hard to explain to his widow, how her husband was killed on an archaeological research expedition.

"War is what those bastards want, war is what I'm going to give them."

Mackenzie felt the same; but somehow, she managed to say, "Look, James and I are going to report to Bill what happened. I'm as angry as you are, maybe even more so. But we answer to the President. It's his call. Let's get permission first."

"Better to ask forgiveness than permission. Oh, and one more thing. The men we fought down there were not Chinese. They were Caucasian. I'm willing to lay money they were sent by those fuckin' Nabateans. Chinese flag my ass," Sean hissed as he turned and walked away.

If the captain of the Chinese ship knew Sean Walker the way James knew him, and he overheard what Sean just said, he would have been a very wise man to immediately lift anchors and make sure he got distance between him and *La Solitude* posthaste.

But as it was, his orders were to stay put and wait for more boats and men to arrive to "take over" that dig.

## Chapter Seventy

### IN MEMORIA

Sean oversaw the recovery operation to bring their dead to the surface. For the rest of the day, after everyone else had been accounted for, the team was debriefed and their wounds treated. Carter grieved doubly — for the men who were killed and that he couldn't be involved in the recovery effort. A couple of hours after the bodies were brought up, a helicopter arrived from Naval Station Rota in Spain to retrieve them. From the base, they'd be sent home to their families.

While Sean was out of the way directing the recovery, James and Mackenzie reported to the President via secure satellite link. As soon as he heard there'd been an attack on US citizens in international waters, the President told them he'd get back to them. He summoned the Secretary of State to the Oval Office and then called them back.

"James, Mackenzie, I believe you've met the Secretary," he began. "I'd like you to repeat what you told me."

James was the spokesperson, and Mackenzie agreed he was best suited for it. The gravity of the occasion kept him from gloating that he'd been needed on this expedition after all. The only things on his mind as he repeated the events of the day were sorrow and a deep worry that this expedition would create an international incident, the last thing they needed when trying to keep a low profile.

The Secretary listened grimly and then asked a few questions — how far they were from any country bordering the Mediterranean, whether the report that the attackers were Caucasian, not Chinese, was credible, and if they were certain the flag on the nearby ship was Chinese.

"James, I'm sure you're itching to teach them a lesson, but I urge you to let us handle this. If action is required, I'll let you know."

"You damn well better let us know! What I'd *like* to do is blow the bastards out of the water. I've got just the team here burning to do it, too. Just give me the word."

Mackenzie laid her hand on James's arm and muttered, "James, your blood pressure."

He took a deep breath to calm himself. "Okay, I get it. We won't do that, unless ordered to. But keep us in the loop, dammit."

Fortunately for James, the President was used to his manner, so he didn't react to the tone of James's "request", though the Secretary bristled. "Simmer down, James. Of course, we'll keep you in the loop. We'll be in touch — you'll be the first to know what's happening."

When he ended the call, the President ordered the Secretary of State to get to the bottom of the unprovoked attack immediately. In response, the Secretary of State made a video call to his counterpart in China, the Minister of Foreign Affairs.

"Good morning, Minister. It seems we have an incident to iron out. What do you know about a ship flying your flag and harassing US citizens diving from their own boat in the Mediterranean?" His tone was firm, though not yet aggressive.

"I assure you, Mr. Secretary. I know nothing of this. What is the nature of the harassment, if I may ask? Your citizens tend to blow things out of proportion." The minister's face took on a slight sneer as he flicked his hand in dismissal.

"I wouldn't call two dead 'blowing things out of proportion', sir. I'd suggest you learn about it in a hurry. I don't know how long I can hold our Navy off." *Now* the Secretary's tone was aggressive.

The Chinese official sat up, squaring his shoulders. "Chances are, this is a commercial ship and has nothing to do with our navy or any military mission. However, if she is flying our flag, I assure you that any attack on her will be met with our severe disapproval. And our navy *will* come to her aid." He lifted his chin, staring to gauge the Secretary's response. He didn't have long to wait.

The Secretary's face turned red. He leaned forward over his desk, pointing at his computer screen and looking directly into the Minister's eyes.

"And I assure *you* that if you escalate this in any way, the 6th Fleet *will* respond. You have one hour to get back to me with information that the ship flying your flag is withdrawing from the area." He jabbed the button on his keyboard that would disconnect the call, then dialed the Chief of Staff.

"I need to see him right away."

The Chief of Staff replied, "He's waiting."

Twenty minutes later, the Secretary of State shook off his security detail as he entered the Oval Office.

"Sir, I regret to inform you that the Chinese don't

appear to be willing to cooperate. I gave them an hour. We've got just over half an hour to wait."

The President waved him to a chair. "Then we wait. I don't want to get into a shooting war with China over this."

"Agreed. However, our friend James Rhodes doesn't seem the patient type who would get permission first."

The President laughed. "If only you knew how true that is! However, I believe Mackenzie Devereux will sweet-talk him into waiting at least until he's heard back from us. Half an hour more won't make much difference."

The half-hour passed quickly, and with five minutes to spare, the Chinese Minister finally called back. "Mr. Secretary, we have been unable to determine who is aboard that vessel. It is not one of ours, and they have not responded to our requests that they withdraw from the area. Nevertheless, we will not take kindly to any attack on a vessel flying our flag, as I said before. I have nothing more to say to you." With that, he disconnected abruptly, no doubt in retaliation for the Secretary doing the same an hour before.

"Well, I guess that's their stance," the Secretary said. "How do you want to play this Mr. President? You know as well as I do that if the personnel on *La Solitude* take retaliatory action, it could get ugly."

The President folded his hands into a steeple and gazed at them before replying. "It's already ugly. I'll speak to the Chinese President." He signaled his Chief of Staff, who hurried out the door to arrange the call. "This snafu is getting out of hand. We can't leave James and the rest of them unprotected. Everyone on that boat is vital to national security in one way or another. On the other hand, if we scramble the 6th Fleet, we must tell our allies why. That's not a conversation I'm interested in having since we don't know how high in their governments

## The Alboran Codex

these Nabateans have infiltrated." Thinking of his former Vice President, he continued, "For that matter, we don't even know how high in *our* government they've infiltrated."

Moments later, the Chief of Staff entered the room again and signaled the President to activate his screen and camera.

"Good morning, Mr. President," he said. Unconsciously mimicking the Secretary of State, he continued, "It seems we have an incident and your Minister of Foreign Affairs has not been very cooperative."

The President of the People's Republic of China narrowed his eyes. "I am aware of this incident, as you call it. My Minister of Foreign Affairs has studied the situation. What part of 'these are not our people' did your Secretary of State not understand?"

The President took a breath and a moment to calm his sudden flare of temper. "Mr. President, need I remind you that although you maintain 'these are not our people' your Minister of Foreign Affairs was adamant that your government will protect the 'unknowns' just because they are sailing under a Chinese flag?

"This vessel is flying your flag, and you don't know to whom it belongs. Someone in your government isn't doing his job. To be frank, it is your government that has created the environment where this type of incident can occur. I demand that you determine who it was who attacked our citizens and killed two of them, or we will."

"Mr. President, I urge you to consider what you're implying. Any attempt to detain that ship will be met with the full force of our navy."

"Well, Mr. President, need I remind you that our 6th Fleet is right there in the Mediterranean? Are you going to force me to send them to the site, or are you going to get that boat with your flag on it to withdraw?"

"I will see what I can do about it," The Chinese President said in a soft, noncommittal voice, while refusing to look President Grant in the eye as he spoke or when he ended the video call.

President Grant's face and neck were as red as the Secretary's had been. "That bastard is not going to do anything. He is going to send one or more of his navy ships to the site."

"What do you intend to do, Sir?" The Chief of Staff was ready to do the President's bidding, whatever it was.

"I intend to calm down. Get the Secretary of Defense and the Chief of Naval Operations in here, and get James on the line. I'm going to make a preemptive move. We'll send one or more of our 6th Fleet ships to standby, kind of like my big brother used to stand there, not interfering, but making sure I didn't get my ass kicked in a school fight."

---

While he waited for the President to call back, James hadn't been idle. Sean had reported to him that Dylan was awake and ready to kick ass. Right after James found Dylan in his cabin and told him to sit tight and let the diplomatic process take its course, he went to consult with Randy regarding a memorial service for the teammates they'd lost.

Randy suggested the service be held on the deck, where there was room for all the scientific team, their security people, the remaining SEALs, and any of his own crew who weren't on duty. He volunteered to officiate, as the captain of the vessel.

James thanked him and went to speak with each man's commanding officer about a eulogy. He then enlisted Mackenzie and Liu to notify everyone to be on the deck within the hour for the service. The haste wasn't to his liking; however, he had a grave suspicion that things were about to get too hectic to wait.

For a quickly arranged service, it went well. SEALs and EA soldiers alike were stoic as their commanders praised their fallen teammates and remembered their good qualities. Mackenzie thought it was a nice touch that the teammates were given a chance to talk about their fallen comrades. She'd never been to a service where one minute people were holding back tears, and the next they were laughing at a fond memory the teammates shared. It made her wish she'd known them better.

At the end, James stood in front of the assembly and said, "Rest assured, your teammates will be avenged. If the scientific and security team as well as the SEALs will remain behind, we'll have a briefing on what's being done at the highest levels. Crew members, thank you for attending. You may be excused."

When none were left but those he'd asked to stay, James began the briefing. "Here's what we know so far. China is denying any military involvement, and they say they don't know who owns that ship or who's aboard. But, and can you believe this shit, just because its flying a Chinese flag, they have the protection of the Chinese navy."

Sean and Dylan vied to interrupt, and Dylan backed off to let Sean speak. "I say we blow the fuckers up, Chinese flag and all, and let the sharks know dinner's served. The sea sharks, that is."

"Hold on. They *are* saying they'll respond with military

force if there's an attack on her. I know, and I feel the same way, but I've been ordered by the President himself to stand down and let him handle it. We're also ordered not to make any more dives on this spot until the situation is resolved."

Carter listened to the exchange with dismay. He couldn't condone going against the President's orders, nor could he meekly sit back and do nothing. He glanced at Mackenzie, thinking they sometimes had telepathic abilities. *Like the Dolphins and their ansible.* He could almost guarantee she was thinking the same thing he was.

"What *can* we do, short of disobeying the President's orders?" he asked.

Liu, although born to Chinese parents, hated the Communist Chinese government and would do just about anything in her power to foil them or embarrass them. She timidly raised her hand. All this testosterone had her worried that something awful was about to happen.

"Yes, Liu. You don't have to raise your hand," James said.

She put it down self-consciously. "What I understood you to say is we can't dive here anymore. Did he say anything about sending down the ROV?"

"Hmm, now there is a good—" was as far as James got before Mackenzie interjected.

She shot to her feet. "The Dolphins! What if we enlisted their help?"

Everyone stared at Liu and Mackenzie and started grinning when they realized they had just been presented with a way around the restrictions imposed on them from Washington.

"At least the President can't forbid *them* to be in the water. Do it!" James exclaimed. "What can it hurt? If the Dolphins think it's safe and agree then I say we do it."

Carter said. "Mackie, can you explain to Merrybeth it could be dangerous for them?"

"Yes, of course. I'll tell them everything. But remember, they were there during the attack. They know already. Everyone should stop thinking of them as witless animals, and give them the credit their intelligence deserves. They may be innocents, but they aren't stupid."

Mackenzie's statement was proved true when she spoke to Merrybeth a few minutes later. For the first time, they saw an angry Dolphin.

"Who were those bad men?" she asked, swimming back and forth with tightly executed turns.

"We aren't sure, but we think they're the bad men who are trying to find the big people cave with the weapons before we do. If they do, it will be very bad. Would your pod be willing to help us with our search in a different way? You have been very helpful so far."

Merrybeth had something else on her mind before she answered the question. "I have called other pods. We will make the bad people stay away."

"Thank you, Merrybeth. We appreciate that."

"What different help would you like? We want to help you."

"Would you allow us to put equipment on your bodies? We will do it in a way that does not hurt you."

Merrybeth responded, "I will ask my pod."

The translation device emitted a rapid-fire series of whistles, clicks, and squeaks, then intoned, "Error." Mackenzie assumed it couldn't keep up with the various Dolphins speaking to each other. In a few minutes, Merrybeth was back. By then, Mackenzie had powered the device off and on to reset it.

"We will be happy to help in this way. They are excited."

Mackenzie clapped her hands in delight. "That's wonderful! Do you see the metal-fish over there?" She pointed, since Merrybeth was holding her head above the water. The Dolphin spun in place to look where Mackenzie pointed.

"Yes, I see it."

"That's where the bad people came from. We must conceal what we're doing from them. Will you have your pod, those who'd help with the work, come alongside our boat on the other side? I'll meet you over there to explain what we need from them."

As the engineers worked quickly at Carter's request to attach straps that would fit around the Dolphins to carry the comms equipment and underwater cameras, Mackenzie explained each device to the Dolphin that would receive it. Some of the others hung around to watch the proceedings and chitter among themselves, no doubt commenting on the odd land-people who couldn't send pictures to each other's minds like they could.

Liu, at Mackenzie's side, tried to count the dorsal fins that surrounded *La Solitude*, estimating there were now close to one hundred or more. Constant scanning of the waters below with their sonar equipment and confirmed by the Dolphins revealed no more divers from the Chinese boat. Liu couldn't blame them. If she'd been among them, experiencing the Dolphins' punishment on the previous day, she wouldn't enter the water again, either.

Soon they were back in business, seeing all they could from the safety of the deck while the ROV and the Dolphins explored the streets and hidden rooms of the sunken city. Overnight, they relocated to another site to continue, hoping to leave the boat with the Chinese flag behind. However, each time they relocated over the next couple of days, the Chinese boat followed. Irritating them to the nth degree.

## Chapter Seventy-One

### DIPLOMACY WITH A THUD

Sean and Dylan were becoming more and more enraged and less and less patient with the diplomatic process. Almost two days and nothing had changed. This diplomacy thing was not for them. They were usually called in after diplomacy failed and then they were required to move in, solve the problem, and move out.

Sitting around looking at what they knew the problem was, half a mile away and not being allowed to move a finger, was excruciating. So, they did what they knew best. They began to plot an operation to launch when the opportunity arose, one that couldn't be traced to them.

On the third day, early in the morning, the "researcher" Dolphins were working about seven miles from where *La Solitude* was anchored. As the images were transmitted to the viewer he watched, they showed something that looked very familiar to Carter.

"That almost looks like . . ." he mused.

"Like what?" Mackenzie asked, when he didn't finish his sentence.

## The Alboran Codex

"I don't want to say it out loud, yet. Can you get Sam to clean up these images? If this is what I think it is . . ." He trailed off again.

Knowing she wasn't going to get the rest of the story without Sam, Mackenzie rushed to the lounge where the core IT equipment was set up and the transmissions were recorded permanently on the server. "Can you enhance those last images ASAP? Carter's about to have a cow about what's down there."

Sam laughed. "Now that would be something to see. But yeah, I'll do it right now. Give me a few."

Twenty minutes later, a piercing whistle from inside the IT lounge alerted Mackenzie that Sam had something. "Carter, I think Sam wants you to look at what she's done," she said.

When Carter saw it, he gave a low whistle. "That's it! My God, look at them all!" Mackenzie and Sam peered at the screen.

"All of what?"

"Look. There. And there." He pointed at the screen. What looked like squares of some thin metal covered the sea floor, or rather the table of stone they were looking at. "Doesn't that look like the plates I found in the City of Lights? I think this is another library!"

Carter picked up the translation device and flipped the switch to speak directly to Ricky, one of the "research" Dolphins. "Ricky, can you go back to the entry of the cave where you were before? I need more pictures!"

"Yes, Carter. I go back."

Within minutes, Ricky was in the right location, and Carter started guiding him around. This time it was unmistakable. Rows and rows of what looked like shelves, each with stacks of the squares, appeared behind the table with the scattered plates. Carter's gut told him they'd made a major discovery.

And that posed a problem.

Hardly able to contain his excitement and sense of urgency, Carter called Sean and Dylan to meet him in the IT lounge.

"Look — there, there, and especially there." He jabbed his finger at the screen, saying "there" each time the image shifted. "If that isn't another library of the giants . . . We've *got* to go down there. The problem is, the ROV can't travel that far, so we can't use it to bring the plates to us. We can't move *La Solitude* to the spot, or we'll have those bastards over there under their Chinese flag all over us. What do we do?"

Sean and Dylan looked at each other with a gleam in their eyes. This was the opportunity they'd been planning for. And as they'd agreed in meetings to which they hadn't invited James or anyone else, better to ask forgiveness than permission.

"Come with us, Carter," Dylan whispered so that only Carter could hear. "It's our turn for show and tell."

In the privacy of their shared stateroom, Sean took over. "Okay, we're under orders not to blow that fucker out of the water. But they didn't say *specifically* that we couldn't cripple her, and for that we have a plan ready. We just have to make sure we have plausible deniability. In other words, we can't get caught."

"How're you going to pull that off?" Carter asked with skepticism.

"I'm glad you asked." Sean grinned. For the next few minutes, Sean outlined the plan with Dylan's occasional interjections.

It was simple in concept. Cripple the engines so the boat

couldn't move and take out their communications systems so they couldn't call for help afterwards. It would require four of them, Sean, Dylan, and two SEALs.

Carter immediately wanted in; but Dylan claimed his sprained wrist was nearly one hundred percent, while Carter's injured shoulder would make a long swim impractical. To Carter's disgust, he'd already conceded it when they sprang their intention to hitch rides with four Dolphins, lying along their backs and hugging close to confuse the Chinese sonar equipment.

"You son of a bitch! I wouldn't even have needed to swim very far." Dylan's grin told Carter he'd been had.

"I'll get you back, *buddy*," he promised.

Dylan just laughed.

Sean and Dylan had already briefed the two SEALs and Captain Randy, the only ones besides Carter allowed to know about the plan at that stage.

Captain Randy was brought into the plan only because they'd needed his help to secure some equipment they thought he might have, and in fact, he did. The final part of the plan required they bring Mackenzie in on it to request the Dolphins' help.

They waited until three a.m., and then slipped into the water on the blind side of *La Solitude*. The four volunteer Dolphins were in a playful mood as they sped toward the Chinese boat, each with a land-human holding onto their dorsal fins for dear life. They were surrounded by another twenty or so other Dolphins as part of the diversion strategy.

Before they got to the point where radio silence had to be maintained, Dylan spoke quietly into his mic. "What a rush! Beats a ride on those SDV's (SEAL Delivery Vehicles) we used back in our time any day of the week."

When they reached the boat, the pod split into two groups. The first group took the two SEALs to the back of the boat where they could secure the small C4 charges to the propeller shafts right where they came out of the boat. The Dolphins stayed close to them to cover them but never got in their way, while they shaped the charges to blow inward and rigged the detonators to a switch that would blow the C4 as soon as the props began to turn.

The Chinese boat's lonely and sleepy watchman saw on his sonar screen a pod of about twenty Dolphins arriving and hanging around their boat. *Probably setting themselves up to "sleep". Nothing to be worried about,* he thought.

Although he remembered reading somewhere that Dolphins must be conscious to breathe, which meant they couldn't go into a full, deep sleep, because then they would drown. Therefore, they had evolved in such a way that only one half of their brain would sleep at a time. A bit like a land-human mother with an infant.

The second group split into two and took Sean and Dylan to either side of the boat. They had the more delicate operation, even though their little gifts for the enemy wouldn't blow up. They had to secure a jamming mechanism to the hull like a limpet mine. This was the equipment they'd borrowed from Randy. They needed it to cling to the ship for approximately 12 hours and then drop off so it couldn't be traced. The Chinese, or whoever they were, would strongly suspect *La Solitude's* team, but they wouldn't be able to prove it.

The device had to be placed in just the right spot to cripple all comms in the ship, and it took some listening with sophisticated devices to find it. When they were finished with their task, Sean and Dylan with their Dolphin comrades joined the rest of the pod waiting for them and headed back home.

Back on deck on *La Solitude*, the co-conspirators congratulated each other. Carter, still a bit riled for being left out of all the fun, rained on their parade when he grumbled, "We still have to see if it works."

---

Early the next morning, *La Solitude* weighed anchor and moved off, at first setting course in a direction away from the underwater city, as if they had decided to give it up and leave the dig. Not five minutes later, a distant thud was the only thing they heard to indicate the C4 charges had exploded.

"I hope all evidence was destroyed," Randy remarked quietly to Sean, who stood next to him.

On behalf of all SEALs and ex-SEALs, Sean bristled. "Trust me, SEALs know what they're doing."

They watched for a while through binoculars at what looked like the entire crew of the boat scurried back and forth. A swarthy-skinned man in a snow-white uniform with bars on the shoulders was looking at them through a pair of binoculars and made obscene gestures in their direction.

Randy gave a big smile and wave in return saying, "And a good day to you, too, *sir*. Isn't that nice!" Randy said. "That other captain is telling us good morning." Randy and the others who knew what it was all about laughed and waved.

Once they were out of visual contact with the Chinese boat, Randy gave the coordinates for the new location, and they made their way there at Dolphin speed.

## Chapter Seventy-Two

### A FIRST TIME FOR EVERYTHING

In about an hour, they had arrived at the new location with no sign of the Chinese boat on their trail. No word had come from the White House, either, whether they could or couldn't dive the new location. James figured they were far enough away from the site of the attack that it was once again permissible to ask forgiveness rather than permission. However, standard procedure was to drop the ROV first, and so they did.

Carter literally hung over the shoulder of the ROV operator, eagerly looking at the screen not only to confirm his theory that the squares he could see were identical to those from the City of Lights, but also to make note of anything hazardous to divers. Seismic activity had made a mess of several of the buildings and had most likely been the cause of the plates scattering all over the rooms he was exploring. Were there any loose objects that could fall on a diver if another tremor happened while they were down? Were there places where ingress was through narrow openings that might close under the same circumstances?

Since his injured shoulder would prevent him from diving, he felt an increased obligation to make sure the remaining divers would have no problems.

Finally satisfied that a dive would be safe, he dispatched the ROV once more to pick up one of the plates and bring it to the surface for analysis. With Sam aboard, it would be short work to scan and translate the plate. He was ninety-five percent sure what they'd found was another library. He wanted to close that to one hundred percent before they risked the wrath of the President with an unauthorized dive, James's opinion notwithstanding.

With the first plate in hand, he had raised his certainty to ninety-eight percent. To his naked eye, the plates did in fact look identical to those from the City of Lights. He and everyone looking at it was very surprised at the pristine condition. Fifty thousand odd years under the sea water had done nothing to blemish the quality and readability. The plates must have been coated with some sort of non-stick agent.

"Almost like Spray N Cook," Mackenzie remarked to everyone's delight.

"One day we'll have to get metallurgists to analyze these plates and tell us what they are composed of," Carter said.

He had just handed it to Sam for the final analysis when the crewman set to watch the radar for unwanted visitors raised the alarm.

"Ship ahoy!" he shouted as he pointed at the radar screen. "It should be coming over the horizon on starboard soon."

Carter, Sean, Dylan, and James all raced to the bridge to join Captain Randy. Two pairs of binoculars made the rounds as each examined the horizon, and within five minutes they saw the superstructure on the approaching vessel breaking the skyline.

A minute later, James said, "That looks like . . ."

"A PLA Corvette," Sean finished.

"Chinese Navy," said Captain Randy, correcting Sean, who'd used the old term out of habit.

"No, shit!" exclaimed Carter. "Can we outrun her?"

"We're not abandoning this spot. This dig is ours. Let's see what happens. They can't seriously mean to attack us in broad daylight," James said, looking around for witnesses in other vessels. Unfortunately, there were none.

As the corvette continued to approach, Captain Randy grew nervous that the Chinese would attempt to board and confiscate his boat, or worse, blow it out of the water. He tapped James on the shoulder and mouthed, "Time to alert Bill."

The situation grew more and more tense while they reported the situation to Bill, carefully leaving out any mention of explosions aboard the Chinese boat they'd left behind.

"I doubt they intend anything but to intimidate you," Bill said. "If you've got any divers in the water, best to get them out. I am scrambling Hornets from Rota. Just give me a sec." The line went quiet for a minute or so.

When Bill came back on, James said, "Bill, may I just point out to you that no one thought anything of the other boat, either, until their unprovoked attack on our divers? How long?"

"We've been expecting that sort of antics from them and had the pilots on standby. They'll be in the air in less than five minutes."

Ending the call, the two men rejoined the others who were all but biting their nails as the corvette drew closer but then seemed to slow down when it was about three miles out.

They were still watching the ship, which had by now come to a stop about a mile away and had them speculating about its intensions, when they were interrupted by a thunderous roar passing them. Their heads spun to the left for the source of the sound, but they could see nothing. In unison, all heads spun to the right, just in time to see the twin exhausts and distinctive markings of two McDonnell Douglas F/A-18 Hornets at low level. While they watched, the Hornets climbed steeply in tight formation before making a wide turn to make another run.

On their way past *La Solitude* for the second time, the Hornets' course also took them over the Chinese corvette in a graceful air ballet. The loads of ordnance carried by the two Hornets were clearly visible.

By this time, almost every soul on *La Solitude* were on the deck. They were screaming, fist-pumping the air, and one or two jumped in jubilation. Based on the celebration on deck, the Hornets might have been giving a private air show for the entertainment of the *La Solitude* passengers, but definitely to the dismay of the corvette's.

Sean looked at James, his brows drawn together in a slight frown. "If my memory serves me correctly, the Chinese Navy carry SAMs on their corvettes, don't they?"

"Probably do, but they will be immensely stupid to try to use them. I wouldn't worry about it. Those Hornets can handle anything the Chinese throw at them. They don't want to start a shootout at the O.K. Corral with the 6th Fleet, believe me."

They all watched the show as the Hornets flew in wide circles above, occasionally making a thrilling low swoop over each boat just for emphasis. Within the hour, another two ships had joined the party — a renewed shout went up when the US Navy destroyers also arrived on the scene and parked themselves between the Chinese ship and *La Solitude*. The message was clear — *you want to get to* La Solitude, *you'll have to go through us first.*

Following Captain Randy's and James's call for reinforcements, President Grant was up early for a second call to the Chinese President. After a bit of saber-rattling on both sides, they agreed it was in no one's best interest to escalate the already tense situation.

In a display of brilliant diplomatic skill and leadership, President Grant gave the Chinese President, who was struggling to hide his frustrations because he was outwitted, an opportunity to save face. First, neither of them would order more vessels to the area. The Chinese President didn't trust himself to speak, so he just nodded his concurrence. Second, should anyone ask, the two countries had inadvertently scheduled a very small Naval exercise at the same time and place.

While they intended, and agreed to keep it out of the media at all cost, both would be prepared, in case of questions, to deny joint exercises. Certainly, China and the US would never schedule joint exercises!

The call ended on almost a cordial note — at least that's what it would have looked like to any observer.

The Chinese President was fuming when the screens went dead. His American counterpart was grinning when he remarked, "Thought I didn't have the balls to do it, did you?"

The way was now clear for Carter and his team to complete their mission.

Carter grinned. "My first dig under US Naval protection. There's always a first time for everything."

And the Chinese knew the American President would not hesitate to bring down that "full might" on them if they made one more move on that site.

They decided to let their corvette hang around for a few more days — just to make sure it didn't look like they had thrown in the towel — before they left.

But in the days and weeks to follow, heads were going to roll in the Chinese Politburo — no doubts about that.

## Chapter Seventy-Three

### EARNED A NICE SCOTCH AND A CIGAR

When Carter and Sean got the results of Sam's analysis of the plate, everyone breathed a sigh of relief. They were identical in physical composition, and the scanned language produced the same vocabulary that was already in the database — it was confirmed. This was another library of the giants, and it appeared from the ROV's underwater survey that it was huge. Enormous. At least twenty times the size of the library from the City of Lights.

"If there's nothing in this one about nukes, then they don't exist," Carter said to Mackenzie in a private moment. "But there will be, Mackie. We know from the Dolphins that the giants took fearsome weapons from the smaller humans of the time. I'd bet my life the information we need, and a lot more, is contained in this library."

"Just remember, your life isn't your own to bet anymore. I have a claim, and so do the children." Mackenzie smiled.

Carter had his hands up in surrender. "You know what I mean."

She just laughed, stood on her toes, threw her arms

around his neck, and kissed him. "Now, how are you planning to proceed?"

"Well, I had in mind that the two of us retreat to our—"

"Carter Devereux! You know what I mean!" she interjected with a faux-serious tone.

He shrugged and said, "Oh that. Well, that's a question for the group. Let's go and discuss it with them."

Once everyone was assembled, Carter made his announcement. "Okay, we now have confirmation that all those plates are like those we found in the City of Lights. I believe we'll find most if not all of the giants' secrets to their advanced civilization recorded and explained in them. The mission now is one of retrieval of every plate we can find.

"Two reasons. The first is we're looking for a record of where, if anywhere, they might have stored the ancient nukes they confiscated. If we can find them, we'd like to retrieve and neutralize them before someone like the Nabateans finds and uses them.

"Second, we may make great strides in practically every field where humans have an interest. Mackenzie has interrupted her own work for months, and if the library gives her the information she needs, that alone will be worth all the sacrifices we've made and the money we've spent.

"Yes, even the people we've lost.

"If respirocytes can be harnessed and utilized, it could cure many debilitating diseases and save far more people. Our country has fought wars for far less, and counted the sacrifice worth the result."

A cheer went up from the SEALs, who knew better than anyone what was worth their lives.

"Thank you for your support," Carter said, nodding to the SEALs. "All right. This is how we'll proceed. Sean will lead every man," he paused and looked at Mackenzie as he emphasized man, "who's a competent diver to retrieve the plates. I'll oversee control of the ROV from here to help. Even though we're privileged to have the US Navy to protect us on this mission, we want those plates here on the yacht as soon as possible. We'll go from there."

Dylan spoke up. "What about the nukes?"

"Just getting to that. Chances are you won't see them in the library," he quipped. "Sam and her assistant will scan and translate the plates as fast as their equipment allows, and we'll be on the lookout for mention of them."

"What do you want Liu and me to do?" Mackenzie asked.

"Let's have Liu working with Sam, and you with me," he answered as he winked at his wife. "Everyone clear on their assignments?"

James raised his hand. Laughing, Carter said, "Yes, James?"

"What's my role?"

"You've done pretty well so far, you and Captain Randy, to get the President involved right away and getting us all these powerful friends to protect us. I'd say the two of you have earned a nice Scotch and a cigar."

"My kind of assignment," James replied and winked. "Seeing that I've been told this is my last mission, I might as well get a bit of practice in what I'll be doing in retirement."

"If we're all clear, let's get started."

Carter hadn't remembered to include the Dolphins' assignments, so when Mackenzie asked him if he needed her to make any requests, he snapped his fingers. "Darn! Of course, they could look for the nukes, save us some time if they find them before we find any references to them in the plates."

"Could we show them pictures of modern ones? Can they be much different?" she asked.

"Let's see what we can find on it," he said, leading her to a computer to begin the search while everyone else got ready for the dive.

Looking at images of nuclear bombs, they realized a couple of design requirements would probably be the same in ancient times as in modern times. All images they could find showed a range of round or egg-shaped objects, or a tapered object that resembled a rocket.

"This makes sense," Carter said. "They'd have to be aerodynamic to stay on course for their targets if they were dropped from flying machines."

"Okay, I see what you mean," she answered. "I need to get the pictures across to Merrybeth."

# Chapter Seventy-Four

## THE BUNKER

Using the Dolphins to make the search for the nukes turned out to be more successful than Carter could have imagined. Once they understood, from the images, what Carter wanted, they swam into areas that the divers wouldn't have reached for several days at the very least. While the retrieval of the plates went on, the Dolphins searched every space they could get into and even organized a sort of grid.

Carter and Mackenzie made sure they mapped and tracked every part of the city that was being searched.

Mackenzie laughed quietly as Carter told her it was almost like he would have organized a land dig. Of course, the buildings were a bit jumbled, but there was no need to actually *dig*, except where the silt had built up on fallen walls. It wasn't exactly the same.

On the third day, a group of the Dolphins, two of them carrying harnesses with comms equipment on their backs, found a sturdy looking structure that stood in sharp contrast to the rest of its surroundings, which were all in a state of ruin. The structure was huge and reminded Carter of a military bunker.

He and Mackenzie guided the Dolphins around the structure looking for an entryway. They could find only one area where there could potentially be a door, a big one at that, but it was filled up with rubble and silt. The only way to know for sure was to get divers to investigate.

Set away from the central area of the city, where *La Solitude* was anchored while supporting the divers who were still retrieving plates, it would have been too long a swim for Dylan and a dive partner. Moving *La Solitude* wasn't an option. They reached a compromise. A small boat from one of the destroyers would take Dylan and one of the SEALS along with the ROV to the bunker. Carter was invited aboard to guide the excavation effort to avoid damage to the archaeological aspect of the site as much as possible.

Everyone was nervous, from Carter, Dylan, and the SEAL to the Captain of the Navy ship, who'd necessarily been informed of what Carter suspected — or hoped — was in that bunker. Not one of them had any idea how unstable a fifty thousand-year-old nuke could be. The very concept of a nuke that old was incredible, but Carter's certainty was enough to spook even the battle-hardened Navy skipper.

Dylan and the SEAL were sweating inside their wetsuits. After clearing the debris from the spot, they confirmed it was definitely a door — but with no way to open it. No obvious handle, hinge, or anything else but the outline that proved the break in the wall.

Carter said, "I've seen this before, and I know how to open that door. It's risky. The mausoleum at the City of Lights had just such a door, and we opened it with electromagnetic pulses from our ground-penetrating radar." He turned to the Navy Captain. "What do you have available that might be able to generate electromagnetic pulses?"

The ship's bosun was called in, and Carter explained what he required. The man nodded, "I've got just the thingamajig for your problem. Give me an hour, and it will be ready."

As promised, within the hour the bosun returned with a handheld device which two of his men had constructed using a few simple tools and materials, including a soldering iron, screwdrivers, enamel-coated wire, Scotch tape, and an old mobile phone. The device was packed in a see-through, waterproof bag, and he demonstrated to them how it worked.

Before they went in, Dylan suggested the ROV be sent in to open the door first. He had a healthy enough regard for his own skin that he didn't want to be right next to a nuke if it went off. Logically, he knew it would make little difference. A nuke going off inside the bunker would obliterate the bunker, him and his partner, and the destroyer as well. He still didn't want to be at ground zero if it happened.

Carter agreed for his own reasons. He wanted a look at whatever was inside before anyone else's impressions influenced him. He asked the ROV operator to proceed and then held his breath.

The makeshift EMP generator did its job as expected and had the door open in less than two minutes.

The ROV quickly revealed a cache of large, round objects made of an unknown metallic alloy, stacked on shelves. All expedition members present, in person, or by video experienced a mix of emotions that made some of them doubt their sanity.

They'd done it! But their emotions fluctuated from

elation that they'd probably found what they'd been seeking for so long, to a sudden anxiety attack on the part of Sam's assistant — it ran the gamut.

When Carter, Dylan, and the SEAL returned to *La Solitude*, before they did anything else, Captain Randy broke out a case of champagne he'd laid in for the occasion. The entire team celebrated appropriately, but Merrybeth was heard to ask Mackenzie why the land-humans were making such strange noises.

Carter himself developed a stomach-ache at the thought that anyone could have found them. If the artifacts were what he and most of the onlookers were almost certain they were, and they'd been found and somehow detonated, even inadvertently . . . It didn't bear thinking of. Countless lives, ancient cultural treasures — so much would be lost. But the horse had bolted.

"If we were at home, Carter, my mother would tell you not to worry about something that *could* happen. Instead, worry about making sure it *won't* happen," Mackenzie said.

"That's exactly what I've done my dear," he answered. "I've already spoken to Bill, and he's got a couple of nuclear scientists on the way to have a look at them. Meanwhile, we still have plenty of work to do. In fact, from what I've seen so far, there'll be work here for many years to come."

## Chapter Seventy-Five

### THE STRANGEST CARGO

Carter continued to direct the work below for the two days it took the scientists to arrive, while driving Mackenzie crazy as he constantly bemoaned the fact he was still not fit to dive. She understood his frustration. Carter was used to being hands-on. She comforted him by saying no one else would be as efficient as he was at directing the complex mission — she refused to call it a dig — because no one else had the eidetic memory to know who was where and doing what at any given point in time.

Within the next day and a half, the divers had cleared out the library. Thanks to the lightweight and virtually indestructible alloy the plates were made of, great armfuls of them could be stacked into makeshift containers and brought to the surface. One of the Navy ships was brought in right above the library to help with its onboard cranes in bringing up the containers.

Afterward, Carter set up a virtual grid and had them further explore and map the site so the permanent archaeological crew wouldn't have to do so when they got there.

It had taken two days for the scientists to arrive because it took a frantic search on the part of the NSA, with the President and the Director blowing down their necks, to locate two they could trust with the secret and who could be persuaded not to throw their toys out of their cots when they heard that the nukes they were going to see were over fifty thousand years old.

As it was, they still came as close to having that hissy fit as one can get and maintain dignity. One of them flat-out called it a lot of bovine droppings but quickly added he would, however, believe whatever the President of the United States told him to believe — until he could prove differently. It took several hours to convince each of them that it wasn't an elaborate prank being played on them. They finally agreed to go, but wanted their disbelief officially noted — in writing. They were not prepared to lose credibility amongst their colleagues as the two nut cases who went on a wild goose chase after fifty thousand-year-old nukes without written evidence of their protestations.

So, forty-eight hours after the suspected nukes were found, two very skeptical nuclear experts dropped in by helicopter to inspect them, first underwater through the lenses of the video cameras of the ROV.

There were, per their rough estimate, about five hundred devices of various shapes and sizes in that bunker. Compared to the over fifteen thousand modern nuclear weapons in existence, it was a drop in the bucket. On the other hand, no one could guess how powerful these ancient weapons were. Maybe five hundred could destroy the planet — who knew? And in the hands of the wrong people, just one of them could wreak havoc and unimaginable panic.

The two scientists had the same misgivings as the others about their chance of survival if any of those devices were, in fact, nuclear bombs and went off — not to mention if the whole lot of them went off at once. They remained incredulous about the whole thing. But they were also not prepared to take any chances and call it a hoax — not yet.

To validate it one way or the other, they had to get close enough to the devices to inspect them. Neither was a diver, and even if they were, neither would be expected to make a dive, and Sean was sure neither would volunteer.

By now, there were several destroyers and an aircraft carrier anchored nearby. So, they gave the order for everyone to clear the area and move out at least 10 miles minimum. No sense in wiping out half of the 6th Fleet in a nuclear explosion. Not with fifty thousand-year-old nukes. They kept only a skeleton staff on the ship with the two scientists on board, amongst them the captain.

The Chinese corvette had ungraciously tucked its tail between its legs and left the area days before.

Once it was only the one Navy ship left in the danger area, they sent down the ROV on its first of many missions fitted with different kinds of high-tech scanners, gauges, and measuring devices to determine just how "live" those "nukes" were. None of them were prepared to take a ride down in one of the mini-subs readied for them to have a closer look.

After two days of back and forth, the scientists agreed that it was probably safe to bring one of the "objects" — they still refused to call it a nuclear device – aboard for closer scrutiny.

Once the first "object" was secured on the deck and inspected, the nuclear scientists confirmed they certainly had been nuclear weapons, but they had been neutralized by some mysterious means. The scientists still appeared to be skeptical of the provenance of the weapons, but by now it was only because they hadn't had time to adjust to the surreal nature of it all. And Captain Randy, with his Scotch, was not on hand to help them assimilate everything as smoothly as he and his crew had the privilege of doing.

The core of fissionable materials seemed to be inert. But the half-life of the isotope that modern bombs used was over four billion years; longer even than the newly-expanded estimate of human history. Even if it had been a different isotope, none of them had a half-life that short. How could it be inert after fewer than one hundred millennia? That was a question they couldn't answer on the deck of a ship. They told Carter they'd need to take them back to their laboratories in the US for further study to even hope to understand it.

The other ships were called back, and carefully they started hoisting the ancient bombs out of the water with the help of a dozen or so divers. As each device was brought to the surface, they reassured it was neutralized, and then it was loaded onto one of the destroyers to transport to the USA.

That destroyer was certainly going to be the ship that carried the strangest cargo of any vessel ever to cross the Atlantic.

Two of the bombs were airlifted with the scientists and flown out to Rota in Spain, where a military jet was standing by to transport them to Los Alamos National Laboratories, the birthplace of the US nuclear weapons program. And although the facility's focus shifted at the end of the Cold War from developing new warheads to maintaining the safety, security, and reliability of the existing nuclear stockpile, they did continue research, design, and development of advanced technology concepts.

What remained to be seen was how well they were going

to cope with research on nuclear technology more than fifty-thousand-years older than what they had.

Not to mention finding out how those nukes were incapacitated.

## Chapter Seventy-Six

### PERMISSION TO STAND DOWN, SIR?

Carter conceded he'd be more comfortable with the bombs out of the site, and indeed out of the Mediterranean, even if they were crippled.

A few more days of mapping the site, and everyone aboard *La Solitude* agreed — they'd had a great time. They'd had a lot of fun, a lot of sadness, again commemorating the loss of their two friends, and a lot of adventure. But they also agreed it was time to head home.

Mackenzie asked Merrybeth to gather her pod where they could all hear the heartfelt thanks of the expedition members. Each of the land-people who'd had a personal encounter with a Dolphin thanked them by name and bid them farewell for now. No one could imagine not ever seeing or talking to their Dolphin friends again, so goodbye was not the right word. Most settled for "so long" and "see you later." Mackenzie was in tears when she and Carter thanked the whole pod and told Merrybeth they would see her and her "family" again soon.

So much depended on their potential involvement in the

dig. Would they see her soon? Mackenzie certainly believed so. On the other hand, she missed Loki and Keeva terribly, and her children even more. She'd be overjoyed to see them all again when she and Carter got home. Freydís was where her heart lived.

That afternoon when Captain Randy gave orders for *La Solitude* to set sail for home, Carter walked over to James and invited him to follow him to the lounge, where he ordered a double Scotch on the rocks for each of them. With drinks in hand, Carter turned to James and said, "Mission accomplished, Mr. Rhodes. You hired me to find you the ancient nukes. I found them, and they're on their way to America. Permission to stand down, sir?"

James choked up, and said, "You've done well, son. Your Grandpa Will would have been a very proud man today." He downed half of his drink and went out to the rails, where he stood alone and stared out over the waters of the Alboran Sea in the direction of Israel. After a while he raised his glass and whispered, "Ben Friedman, my old friend, you and your people can relax. We found them. All of them. I'll call you when I get back home."

## Epilogue

The 6th Fleet were tasked to keep a vessel on the site at all times to guard against anyone else from pegging a claim on that underwater city.

When the expedition team left the site, they were stunned to learn that their top-secret mission was now common knowledge among at least fifty known individuals, and who knew how many more unknown?

No one would ever know how, when, or by whom it was leaked, but leaders of every country surrounding the Mediterranean, plus the Chinese, the Russians, and privately, the Nabateans, had an opinion about the discovery. Carter noted that none of them mentioned the nukes, but he knew it was just a matter of time before that would be leaked as well.

Naturally, the Russians and Chinese were the least vocal in the media, where there was a frenzied buzz about an international conspiracy of an unknown nature. However, they were the most vocal through diplomatic channels.

The Russians wanted their citizens back, and the Canadians were under pressure to hand them over. That put them in the middle, since they'd allowed the US to take the ex-Spetsnaz operatives, so they were pressuring the US to hand them over. The operatives in question had applied for emergency asylum on humanitarian grounds, knowing that if their government got hold of them, they'd be lucky to wind up in Siberia rather than simply disappearing with no trace.

The Chinese still had their noses out of joint because of the explosions that crippled the boat that was flying their flag while remaining quaintly silent about their harassment of *La Solitude's* crew. Since no one could prove anything about the reason for the explosions, all traces of C4 having been washed away by the sea afterwards, they would get no satisfaction. This frustrated them enough to throw temper tantrums by means of the international media, which only served to make them look more foolish because they couldn't, and probably wouldn't want to if they could, provide information about the boat's true owners.

However, the Politburo did undergo what the Chinese media called a "minor" restructure, when the Minister of Foreign Affairs and the President both developed undisclosed health issues and announced their retirement.

The Mediterranean countries for the most part were simply grateful that the US had discovered an unspecified danger in the sea close to them and removed it.

No doubt some would have changed their tunes if they'd known the specifics. The only countries not taking this line were Egypt, Libya, and Syria. Egypt announced that Carter and Mackenzie were declared "undesirable aliens" and would be denied visas to their country in perpetuity. Carter would never see the City of Lights again —

well, at least until the Egyptians came to their senses, and that might take a long time.

All three countries made noises about claiming their share of the Mediterranean, but unfortunately for them, the "dig" site was off the coast of the Kingdom of Morocco, with whom the United States had good relations dating back to 1786. Morocco remained one of America's oldest and closest allies in North Africa. They had a zero-tolerance policy towards al-Qaeda, ISIS, and any of their affiliated groups. Morocco wanted nothing to do with the whole thing and granted the USA ten-years of exclusive rights to explore the site as they saw fit.

When he read the briefings supplied by Bill via James, Carter sighed. "So much for secrecy. It's only a matter of time before they figure it out, steal it, or a traitor sells it to them.

"And — I'm almost too scared to think of it — if we learn the technique used to neutralize those nukes, we're going to have another migraine to deal with."

Confused, Mackenzie had to ask. "Why do you say that? Wouldn't it be great if we could neutralize all nuclear weapons?"

"You'd think so, but look at it from an international, non-USA, perspective. We've got the library and the nukes. We'll eventually find it. I mean, not just us, but the United States. Then suddenly we'll be able to choose to neutralize everyone's nukes but our own. Where's the deterrent to use our nukes and balance of power then?"

"Carter, I see what you mean, but I'd rather have that capability in the hands of the USA than anyone else. Besides, we, the USA, is one of the few who would use it responsibly."

"Would we?" Carter retorted. "Remember a little

matter where the Vice President of the US was a Nabatean plant? Working with some Saudis to abduct our family and Liu so that we could help him and his cohorts develop technologies, including nuclear weapons, for the most fanatical Muslim group on earth, the Wahhabi sect, who is funding every crazy, fanatical Muslim terrorist out there? That man was *this* close to being President. Would you have wanted *him* to be in control of such an awe-inspiring power?"

"Well, if you look at it *that* way . . . No. Definitely not."

"Mackie, we have to look at it 'that' way," Carter said, making air quotes. "Just imagine for one second what would happen if the world's nuclear powers, including our NATO allies, wake up one morning and find out their nukes have been turned into very expensive but useless toys, and we were back in the era between 1945 to 1949, when the USA was the only nuclear power on the planet."

Mackenzie was nodding her head as the full impact of Carter's words sank in. She stared at Carter and started whispering, "We" —she pointed to him and herself— "should find a way to turn mutually assured destruction *by* the nukes, into mutually assured destruction of *all* the nukes."

# Next in the Carter Devereux Mystery Thriller Series

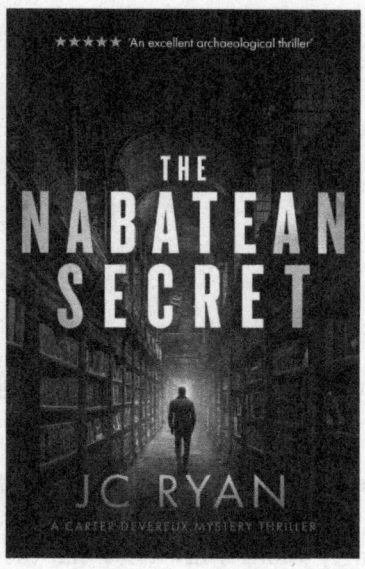

vinci-books.com/nabatean

**A hidden library. An ancient secret. A race against time to unravel the past to save the future.**

When archaeologist Carter Devereux discovers a concealed library that could rewrite history and expose the enigmatic Nabatean organization, A-Echelon must decipher its secrets while battling betrayal and deadly threats. As the Nabatean's sinister agenda looms, Devereux and his team are in a race against time to uncover the truth before it's too late.

Turn the page for a free preview…

# The Nabatean Secret: Chapter One

## US Army Garrison Patch Barracks, near Stuttgart, Germany, 2 a.m., January 11

Sentries at the Main Gate of Patch Barracks had turned away the last of the local Fasching revelers an hour or so before, laughingly joking with them that the Barracks were too quiet for their parties. A few soldiers, somewhat worse for wear after joining the locals for the opening night of Germany's "Fifth Season", straggled in around midnight. They were cheerfully waved through the gate by the envious guards, who had pulled duty that night and didn't get to celebrate.

Since then, the night had been still, only the night sounds typical of the region breaking the silence. The cell and radio tower behind the thick trees was lit by an eerie glow from the remains of the Fasching bonfire a few miles away. It would be six long hours until sunrise and their relief.

The peace of the night lulled them to silence.

Behind them, an eerie blue-white blinding flash bloomed.

No sooner had it lit the night sky than the first sentry opened his mouth to ask, "What was that?"

But the words never left his lips—before he'd even formed them, his lips, along with the rest of him, vanished. Had his mate not been meeting the same fate at the same time, he would have been shocked to see his comrade in arms evaporate into nihility.

Every living being, structure, and object within an 800-yard radius of the epicenter disappeared as if he, she, or it had never been there.

No one in the circumference of the blast zone survived to describe the beauty of the majestic, but fatal, blue-white flash. A few souls, lucky enough to be farther away, saw glimpses of it through the surrounding trees.

No one knew what it was.

The next person to arrive at the Main Gate of Patch Barracks found, much to his drunken confusion, nothing.

No gate, no trees, no cell tower. No barracks. No buildings. No guards.

Only emptiness.

Not finding the Main Gate where he was sure it must be, the soldier sat down on the ground. Alcohol and rationality have never been good stablemates.

His inebriated brain could not handle the duel, and mercifully, he passed out. He never heard the screams of pain and horror from the injured survivors far enough from the epicenter and fortunate enough to escape obliteration.

Later, first responders approached with caution, finding the drunk soldier passed out where the gate should have been and the void beyond, which had always been occupied by buildings.

They moved into the base to search for survivors. They found few, most of them critically injured and out of their minds with shock and confusion.

Everyone capable of speaking asked the rescuers the question the rescuers had wanted to ask the survivors: What happened?

## The Nabatean Secret: Chapter Two

### DAMN YOU, CARTER DEVEREUX!

### 18 Months Previously; 24 Hours After the Attack on Freydís

Graziella Marie Nabati paced the room, the very picture of an avenging angel. Most men would have quailed at her countenance, though she was coldly beautiful—like an iceberg. The man in the room with her was safe, however. Her son, Mathieu Nabati, was as angry as she, and in any case was only a hologram.

Graziella was in her mountain hideout high in the Andes in Peru, where she took up residence when the existence of the Council of the Covenant of Nabatea was discovered by the CIA. Her luxurious, high-tech lodging was close to the Incan citadel, Machu Picchu, where she felt as at home as she'd felt in her house above the ancient catacombs of Paris.

Mathieu, in contrast, was in his own hideout in a remote area of the Ural Mountains in the western part of Russia. His dwelling boasted the latest in quantum computing and communications equipment possible. Only his mother knew where he was and how to reach him.

"What is our situation?" Graziella managed to whisper instead of growl.

"Unfortunately, *maman*," he answered, "it was another miserable failure. Nine of the sixteen operatives are dead, and the rest have been captured, amongst them one wounded. They are in CIA custody and have been transferred to America.

"I have just learned they are trying to make a deal. No extradition to Russia in exchange for their cooperation. In other words, they are singing like the proverbial canaries, and they are beyond our reach. Only our care in putting several layers of go-betweens in place has kept us safe so far. But soon someone will peel away those layers.

"As you know, the leader of the task force is aware of who hired him. Once he gives up the Director, we are exposed. If he has not done so already."

"You know what to do," she stated. It never needed to be spelled out between them. As the primary guardians of the secrecy of the Council of the Covenant of Nabatea, they were of one mind. That secrecy was paramount. In its service, everyone except them was expendable.

"Of course. I'll see to it immediately."

Graziella nodded graciously. She trusted her son implicitly and with good reason. The last layer of go-between was one of the Council, but all councilors understood their position.

Peter Nikolaev, the Director of the Federal Security Service (FSB) of Russia, was about to suffer a fatal incident.

Nikolaev was a fit and vital man of fifty-seven years, as well as an important government official. His death would cause repercussions, no matter how it occurred. However, a violent death, even an auto accident, would raise more questions than a natural one. Mathieu set his mind to arrange the perfect assassination.

His first task was to locate Nikolaev.

After discreet inquiries, he learned that the Director had taken a holiday and was currently skiing the forty miles of groomed slopes located within the Rosa Khutar ski resort, site of the XXII Winter Olympics.

Mathieu, an expert skier, immediately recognized the opportunity to take care of the matter himself, which would avoid involving yet another person who would then have to be eliminated in an escalating series of incidents.

He notified his mother that he would be taking a small ski-holiday and that everything would be fine by the time he returned.

Twelve hours later, he inconspicuously followed Nikolaev as he made his way to one of the high-speed chairlifts and headed for the Ozernaya slope.

Once more, Nikolaev was making it easy for Mathieu.

Ozernaya was a perfect slope for speedy carving. Nikolaev exited the lift and prepared for his run. Mathieu was a few chairs behind him. When he got off the lift, rather than carving the slope like Nikolaev, he made his run in a straight line, easily overtaking his target. With no one to witness it and ignoring Nikolaev's indignant shout when they approached a line of trees at a speed of close to seventy miles an hour, Mathieu shouldered him ever so slightly—enough to steer Nikolaev straight into the trees lining the run. There was no time and no room for Nikolaev to counteract—the collision with one of the trees ended Nikolaev's life abruptly.

Travelling at thirty-three feet per second, Mathieu was almost ten yards away by the time Nikolaev met with the tree. He had no reason to check that Nikolaev was indeed dead. Even if he had survived the collision, he wouldn't survive for long in the extreme temperature. Other skiers would overrun his tracks and obscure the reason for Nikolaev's accident.

It was the perfect crime.

Mathieu was on his way back to his hideout by the time Nikolaev's body was discovered. When he arrived and contacted his mother, he found her watching news coverage of the "tragedy."

Tears streamed down her face for the loss of another noble Nabatean from their bloodline.

"Well done, my son." She sighed. "Our secret has been sealed again."

"Thank you, *maman*. I believe our immediate problem has been solved."

"True, but we have another, and it will not be so easily dismissed," Graziella said. "Our operatives were captured with the four devices we gave them to defeat the electronic defenses of that accursed Freydís. It won't be long before US security forces have reverse-engineered it, and then our advantage is gone."

"One problem at a time, *maman*. I agree, it is a setback, but there is little or nothing we can do about it. At least it can't expose the identities of the rest of the Councilors."

She nodded slowly. It was a relief.

Nevertheless, *Damn you, Carter Devereux!*

**Grab your copy...**
**vinci-books.com/nabatean**

## About the Author

JC Ryan is a bestselling author renowned for his intricate espionage, archaeological thrillers, and conspiracy mysteries. With over 30 acclaimed novels, including the popular Rex Dalton K9 Thrillers, Rossler Foundation Mysteries, and Carter Devereux Mystery Thrillers, Ryan has captivated readers around the globe.

Drawing from his diverse professional background—as a military officer, lawyer, and IT manager—Ryan creates compelling narratives that skillfully blend historical accuracy with thrilling adventure. He is celebrated as a master storyteller, known for crafting riveting plots, meticulous historical details, and engaging, multidimensional characters. Ryan's meticulous research lends authenticity and depth to each story, immersing readers in richly constructed worlds filled with intrigue, suspense, and adventure.

Fans of David Baldacci, Lee Child's Jack Reacher, Tom Clancy's Jack Ryan, Nelson DeMille's John Corey, Vince Flynn's Mitch Rapp, Mark Greaney's Gray Man, Gregg Hurwitz's Orphan X, Robert Ludlum's Jason Bourne, Daniel Silva's Gabriel Allon, Brad Taylor's Pike Logan, Brad Thor's Scot Harvath, James Rollins' Sigma Force, Steve Berry's Cotton Malone, and Dan Brown's Robert Langdon will find JC Ryan's novels equally compelling and unforgettable.

When not writing, Ryan enjoys spending time with his college sweetheart, whom he married in 1978. They are proud parents of two daughters, have two sons-in-law, and are grandparents to two grandchildren.